Prais

A MARINER'S TALE

"*A Mariner's Tale* is a stunning debut: a seafaring novel rich with lush imagery and colorful characters from an exciting new voice in Southern fiction. With deft narrative skill, the author takes the protagonist, a cynical middle-aged mariner, and his protege, a troubled young man, on a voyage of self-discovery that begins on an island in Florida and ends in an Irish fishing village. You don't want to miss this beautifully crafted page-turner!"

—CASSANDRA KING
Bestselling author of *Tell Me a Story: My Life with Pat Conroy*

"Hard edged and gripping. An intriguing mix of hope and fear. Fans of Pat Conroy's evocative novels are going to love this stirring debut."

—STEVE BERRY
New York Times bestselling author of *The Warsaw Protocol*

"Part nautical yarn, part romance, and part coming-of-age story, *A Mariner's Tale* is a page-turner, but Joe Palmer's beautiful prose slows the pace to a perfect rhythm, allowing the reader to participate in the wonders of nature and the resilience of the human heart . . ."

—SUSAN CUSHMAN
Author of *Friends of the Library* and *Cherry Bomb*, and editor of *Southern Writers on Writing*

"A beautifully drawn seafaring tale built around a marina of lovingly flawed characters who have, in different ways, been floundered by life; who in rescuing each other, manage to rescue themselves. Set in the lush beauty of the inlets, streams and maritime world of north Florida, *A Mariner's Tale* is told with great heart and uncommon compassion by an author who knows the life of tide and salt of the sea. I think fans of the hugely popular *Where The Crawdads Sing* would like this book, because the author describes nature so lovingly and accurately."

—JANIS OWENS
Author of *American Ghost, The Cracker Kitchen*

"A Mariner's Tale is a richly rendered story scented with sea spray and filled with salty characters seeking grace, mercy and second chances. Palmer writes with heart and authenticity, bringing life to an unforgettable crew worthy of the love and redemption we each hope to find in this life."

—NICOLE SEITZ
Author of *The Cage Maker*

"Beautifully written and riveting. As a horrendous storm threatens, an aging mariner and a troubled young man find new trust, and each their own path to renewed hope. The author's voice is reminiscent of many great Southern fiction writers and leaves one eagerly waiting for more."

—MONICA TIDWELL
Tristan Productions, NY theatre producer and award-winning filmmaker

A Mariner's Tale

By Joe Palmer

Published by

◤ köehlerbooks™

210 60th Street
Virginia Beach, VA 23451
800–435–4811
www.koehlerbooks.com

A MARINER'S TALE

JOE PALMER

A NOVEL

VIRGINIA BEACH
CAPE CHARLES

For Pam, my wife, my first mate and my best friend, the sun on my shoulders and the gentle breeze that fills my sails. You've been with me on this journey since the moment I set sail. You know every waypoint by heart. You are my true north, my beacon and my eternal love.

In memory of my brother, Michael C. Palmer, 1957–1992
Eternal Father, bless those who make their living upon the sea.
And shine the light so that they find their way home.
The sea is so big and their ships are so small.

CHAPTER 1

DUSK WAS ENCROACHING WHEN the sheriff of Ocean County's car edged into little North Florida boatyard and marina. On the other side of the yard, an older man with a sandy-gray ponytail stood on metal scaffolding running a power sander along one side of a sailboat. Slogging away at his work, he was oblivious to the sheriff's cruiser pulling into his marina, the tires crunching and scattering the crushed limestone.

The sky dimmed to the hues of a calico quilt as the sun continued its measured descent into the marshes beyond. A great blue heron squawked on a nearby mud flat while a lone, brown pelican dive-bombed the water nearby, hoping to fill its belly one last time before going off to roost on a tilted dock piling. The moon-faced sheriff opened the door and eased his bulk out of the car. He swatted sandflies while watching the other man work for a while, then put two fingers in his mouth and whistled. The other man, still unheedful of his presence, kept his back bent and went on working.

When his loud whistling failed to get the man's attention, the sheriff cupped his hands to his mouth and shouted, "Merkel! Yo! Jack Merkel! Damn it, man! Are you deaf? Merkel!"

At sixty-four, Jack Merkel still had a physical presence as sturdy as seasoned oak. Tall and roped with lean muscle, he had the hard-bitten look of an old salt. He'd been a career merchant seaman, then used part of his retirement pension to buy a trawler, spending the next ten years as a shrimper. His right arm was scarred from a shark bite he acquired late one summer afternoon while trying to untangle a fair-sized black tip from his trawl. He had wrapped his bleeding arm in his sweaty T-shirt, taped it snug and grudgingly surrendered the helm to his first mate. Diverting to a nearby port, he had refused the mate's entreaties to summon an ambulance and instead hailed a taxi for a ride to the emergency room, into which he strode, sunburned and cross. When he left the hospital, he had thumbed a ride back to his boat and went home. A week later, he severed the stitches with his pocketknife and plucked them out with a pair of needle-nosed pliers from his tackle box. Later, when the grotesque wound had begun to heal, he got drunk and had a shark tattooed above it. He still wore a gold hoop earring in his left ear that he got while yet a swaggering young sailor, drunk on cheap booze and on the prowl for whores one lust-drenched night in Singapore. A ship's anchor adorned his other arm and beneath it, the name *Stormy Coast*, the first merchantman on which he sailed.

The sheriff ran his hand through his thinning brown hair, leaned into his green and white county issue car and whooped the siren. Jack turned off the sander, set it down on a work bench jumbled with other tools, pawed the dust mask off his face and turned. He picked up a pack of cigarettes, tapped one out and lit it. The sheriff waved at him and cocked his thumb toward the rear door of his car. Jack acknowledged him with a curt nod and the sheriff opened the rear door and extracted a sullen looking boy who appeared to be in his late teens. The scrawny boy twisted and tried to pull away from his grasp. The cop snatched handcuffs from his belt, the polished steel catching the remaining light. With the agility of a man half his size and reflexes of one who'd played the confrontation game for years, he wrenched the boy's hands behind his back and snapped the cuffs onto his wrists. The ratcheting echoed across the yard, magnified by the stillness of gathering dusk.

"Fine, boy," the sheriff drawled. "If that's the way it's gonna be. Git on over there."

He shoved the boy toward Jack, who waited beside his work bench, patiently smoking and watching the cop prod his manacled charge across the yard. The kid shuffled dirty, sneaker-clad feet on the lime rock, kicking up little puffs of dust and cursing his uniformed captor. When the duo was a few paces from him, Jack raised one calloused hand in a halting gesture. He fixed his gray eyes on the boy for a moment and then shifted his attention to the lawman.

"Who's the kid, Hal?"

The sheriff shoved a stick of gum in his mouth.

"You tell me, Jack. He look like the burglar on your surveillance camera video?"

Jack pulled a bandana from the pocket of his stained khakis and wiped the fiberglass dust from his face. He studied the young man glowering back at him and then replied quietly, "Might be."

The kid sneered and spat at his feet. "Ain't done nothing, you old shit. Never even seen this place before."

Jack settled his eyes on the boy and took the cut of his jib from head to toe with a mariner's attention to detail, noting that the kid was nearly as tall as his own six-foot-three inches. He had dirty, straw-colored hair, a peach fuzz mustache he was trying to cultivate and pale blue eyes. They reminded him of the shark that'd nearly taken his arm—cold and without remorse. His arms were festooned with crude, homemade tattoos. He wore filthy jeans with a hole in one knee and a grubby yellow T-shirt. He repaid Jack's stare with a snarl.

"I'd like to kick your ass, you old sonofabitch."

"Reckon you would," Jack replied. "Bring him up to the office, Hal. Drag him if you want. It don't matter a tinker's damn to me."

He turned around and trudged toward a washed-out looking two-story building on the north end of the yard. A black Great Dane sitting on the covered porch stretched and trotted toward them, long tail wagging. He leapt up and licked his master's face. Then he dropped back down onto four colossal paws and sniffed at the kid. The boy halted mid-step and the dog snarled, revealing the tips of his teeth. The sheriff cackled.

"Good thing me and ol' Pogy wasn't here when you came calling," Jack said to the ashen-faced boy. "Don't believe he cottons much to you."

Smelling the boy's fear, the Dane bristled and growled louder. The kid's insolence turned to panic.

"Git him away from me," the kid pleaded.

The dog edged menacingly forward, tail flat. Then the kid broke. "C'mon, old man. Call him off."

Jack looked at the cop and smiled. "Well now," he said.

He made a barely audible cluck out of one side of his mouth. The dog came and stood beside him, his caramel eyes still glaring at the kid.

Jack looked at the cop again, nodded and started back toward the building. The dog trotted ahead and sat sentry-like on the porch, eyes never leaving the kid's face. Jack walked up the three steps to the porch and opened the door. The rambling building, weathered gray by the years, exuded the fragrance of cypress. A yellow, one-eared tomcat napped on a rocking chair near the door. The sun was sinking fast, a thin slice of orange settling deep into the bright green spartina marsh grass. A tugboat pushing a barge glided by on the Intracoastal Waterway. The skipper blasted the vessel's horn in greeting. Jack waved. The captain honked again and went on his way. A moment later, the red and green channel markers flashed to life just as the last fragment of sun vanished.

Jack held the screen door while the cop frog-marched his captive up the steps and shoved him through the door. He turned on a fluorescent overhead light, which buzzed like an insect trapped in a jar. The office was cluttered with papers, parts of boats, nautical charts, coils of rope and other accoutrements of the mariner's trade. An antique soft drink machine, the kind with the metal pull-down handle, stood in one corner and a plaque on the proprietor's desk declared "The captain is always right, even when he ain't."

Jack took the remote control from his cluttered desktop and aimed it at a monitor screen on the opposite wall. The screen blinked to life, gray and grainy at first, and then cleared. An image of a person climbing a chain link fence and cautiously picking his way across the moonlit boatyard appeared. The kid lowered his chin onto his thin chest.

"Ain't me."

The sheriff grinned and popped his gum. "Sho' is, kid. And wearing the same filthy-ass clothes you're wearing right now." He grabbed a hank of the boy's hair and yanked his head up.

The kid stared at his image easing through the boatyard, looking this way and that into the shadows, his attention settling on the building. Glancing around, the kid first tried the door and when it wouldn't give, he tried each of the windows. He picked up a small anchor and hefted it as if he meant to throw it at a window. After a moment's hesitation, he dropped the anchor and walked back down the steps, turning his head and looking toward the rear of the boatyard. He came to the work shed and found it padlocked. He peered around the yard and then headed toward a sailboat resting on metal jacks on a concrete pad near the water He walked over to the worktable beside it and picked up a hammer and a large screwdriver and returned to the shed. He jammed the tip of the screwdriver down onto the padlock and slammed the hammer down on it. When the lock didn't give; he repeated his effort, once more, then twice more and when it still wouldn't budge, he pounded furiously on it. Winded, he put his hands on his knees. Then he straightened, flung the screwdriver into the water and focused his attention on the sailboat.

Another camera captured his face in detail as he stared up at the deck of the vessel and began walking around it, glancing up and about as if looking for some way to climb onto it. Spying a wooden stepladder nearby, he went over to it. The boy propped the ladder against the boat and started to climb. The rotted ladder snapped soundlessly, spilling the boy onto his back. When he got up, he grabbed the hammer and charged the boat in a rage. Jack clenched his jaws and watched the intruder smash the sides of his beloved boat from one end to the other, inwardly berating himself for his rare act of carelessness. A fastidious man, he'd neglected to put a few of his tools away before he and the dog had climbed into his skiff and went off for a night of flounder gigging. The boy's final assault was on the rudder. Jack winced as he felt his boat's every wounded scream as steel shattered fiberglass.

Jack turned off the monitor and took a deep breath to settle the fluttering in his chest, avoiding eye contact with the boy for a few moments. The buzzing sound from the fluorescent light seemed to grow until it filled the room like the skirling of cicadas. He stepped closer to the manacled boy and stared into his eyes, searching for even a scrap of regret. What he got was hatred coiled tight as a rattlesnake.

"Don't eyeball me, you old bastard. Video don't mean nothing. Could be anybody."

The sheriff looked from the boy to Jack and nodded. "Could be, but ain't."

The cop reached into the front pocket of his trousers and pulled out a spherical-ended, slender tube made of silver for piping commands on a ship. He handed it to Jack. "Reckon this'd be yours," he said. "Got your initials engraved on it."

Jack regarded it for an interval as if it were a treasure. "My boatswain's call," he said at last. "Won it off an old bosun's mate in a poker game one night somewhere in the Indian Ocean. I whistle up Pogy with it sometimes. Where'd you find it?"

The sheriff cuffed the kid on his ear drawing a yowl and a string of curses.

"Sonny boy here had it in his knapsack when I collared him. Figured it was yours right away."

Jack stubbed out his cigarette in an ashtray fashioned from a big cockle shell and then went over to the drink box. He pulled the lever down and a bottle dropped into the chute with a muffled thump. He removed it, pulled the lever again and dropped another bottle into the chute. He popped the metal caps off both them and handed one to the sheriff. Then he walked over to the window and stared out at the moon while swigging the icy beverage. At length, he turned around, wiped his mouth with the back of his hand and looked the boy over again. His eyes shone with tears he refused to spill in front of the cop and the young hoodlum who'd trashed the sailboat he cherished. He saw the jailhouse in the kid's eyes, the insouciance of one who, although maybe not irredeemable just yet, tramped inexorably along the mean streets in that direction. But he also saw something else. Skirting the edges of the boy's fixed stare, he saw someone who'd lost his way, another throwaway in a world where everything was as disposable as the glass bottle wrapped in his fist. Despite his anger and sadness over his own loss, Jack looked into the boy's eyes and saw someone who'd never had a break. And even though he couldn't forgive the kid's trespasses, he couldn't bring himself to hate him for them, either.

"Why, boy?" he said. "Why couldn't you just steal and go on your way? Why'd you have to do that?"

The boy lifted his chin and narrowed his eyes. "Fuck you, old man."

Jack stood there for a few moments considering a reply, but knew that nothing he said would matter. He looked at the sheriff and shook his head.

"Get him outta here, Hal. Do what you gotta do."

The sheriff looked back at him and nodded gravely.

"Sorry, partner. I sure am sorry about this here mess."

He tossed off the remainder of his drink, set the bottle on the desk, turned around and shoved his prisoner through the door. The kid tumbled down the steps and landed belly down on the scrabble. When he wailed, the cop yanked him up by his arms and shoved him to the car.

Jack listened to the sheriff read the boy his rights; then the doors slammed and the car slewed around and went back along the causeway, its strobe lights pulsing across the marsh. When the car turned onto the highway and disappeared over the bridge, Jack whistled his dog in from the yard and closed the door. He picked up his cigarettes and lit one, then sat down and gazed at a framed photograph in the middle of the desk. When the cigarette had burned down almost to his fingers, he crushed it in the ashtray, put his hands over his face and leaned forward on his elbows. Pogy cocked his ears, whined, then padded over and nuzzled him. After a while, he knuckled his raw eyes, eased himself out of the chair and climbed the stairs to his home, the dog at his heels.

CHAPTER 2

POGY DANCED AROUND THE kitchen, woofing as Jack filled his food bowl. He set his dog's breakfast on the floor and watched him tear into it while pouring two cups of coffee.

"Slow down, Pogy," he said. "You'll get indigestion and fart all day."

The aroma of coffee filled the room. Jack picked up the mugs and walked downstairs to the office with them. The early morning sun washed the marina with a golden glow and a stillness of bath water. He knew that the late July weather would be stifling in a couple of hours. Weather forecasters were watching a growing system of storms forming off the west coast of Africa. Jack, a local whose family went back three generations, didn't fret much about the storms that sometimes menaced Florida during the June-through-November hurricane season. Mostly, they passed harmlessly offshore, riding the Gulf Stream and only causing a few days of high winds and surf. There hadn't been a direct hit on Morgan's Island in Ocean County in more than fifty years. The island and most of the county was tucked into a cleft on the extreme northeast coast of the peninsula and thus largely sheltered from tropical storms. A natural barrier island, it formed part of a chain of analogous sea islands from South Carolina to North Florida. The island, ten miles long and a mile at its widest, was separated from the mainland by the Intracoastal Waterway and only accessible by a drawbridge a couple of hundred yards from the boatyard.

Before he could step outside, Merkel heard heavy boots clunking on the porch, followed by his manager and dockmaster, Rafael Hernandez, who everyone just called Rafe, shouldering his squat, muscular frame through the door. As always, he was neatly groomed, his black, graying hair parted smartly on one side and his tanned face freshly shaven.

Jack handed him a cup of coffee. "Morning, Rafe."

The dockmaster grinned, revealing a gold tooth. Jack considered him to be one of those rare sorts who seemed to wear their cheerfulness like a second skin. In all the years Rafe had worked for him, Jack had only seen him sad once, when his brother died. Rafe took a couple of weeks off to return to Mexico bury his brother and grieve with his relatives. He returned from the trip with his sunny demeanor.

"Thanks, brother," he said. "So, what's on the agenda for today? I don't like the looks of that storm out there. It's a huge system and it's a Cape Verde storm. Could be bad news for Florida if it develops into a hurricane and heads this way."

"Let's hope not, Rafe. But maybe we should take a dock walk and inspect everything just in case. This place will fill up fast if the damn thing turns into a full blown 'cane and gets within five hundred miles."

"Good idea," Rafe said. "Let's get it done. I need to spread a load of lime rock on that bare area out back. We gotta paint Bo Riddle's

Hatteras next week if the weather holds and it's awful dusty back there. A good covering of fresh rock ought to fix that. I'll get some of the guys to help me. We ought to be able to knock it out before lunch."

"Well, come on, then," Jack said. "Oh, Hal Patterson dropped by yesterday evening with the fellow who messed up the place the other night. Just a kid. A real punk, but I kinda felt a little sorry for him."

Rafe's weathered face lit up and he laughed.

"Sometimes you're too damn nice for your own good. I'm sure Pogy would've sorted out that problem if he'd been loose in the yard and not out fishing with you."

Before Jack could reply, the phone rang. He caught it on the second ring and put it to his ear. He nodded and frowned.

"Okay, tell him I'll be there in ten."

He set the phone down. "Damn," he said. "Guess you'll have to do the inspection yourself. Judge Kicklighter has requested my presence for breakfast at Nell's."

"Better get running," Hernandez said. "What's up?"

"That kid's in court for formal charges this morning," Jack grumbled. "His Honor wants me there, but he wants to have breakfast first. I'd better take off."

Taking his cup with him, he climbed into an elderly Jeep Wagoneer, rolling down the windows so he could smell the marsh as he headed up the causeway to the road leading into town. Jack was spellbound by the spartina grass, the color of emeralds and worn like a monarch's cloak in the spring and summer, as well as the dull brown peasant's rags that clad it in the winter. He soaked up the marsh's fragrance, a bountiful distillation that reminded him of the smell of fresh oysters. Most evenings after work, he'd walk Pogy up the causeway along the edge of the marsh and watch the legions of fiddler crabs skittering wildly across the mud, brandishing their single big claws like cutlasses. He'd listen to the maniacal laughter of marsh hens in the deep grass. When the tide was in, he loved the popping sound of sea trout attacking small baitfish schooling near the surface, and he'd watch for signs of redfish hoisting their tails above the water as they foraged nose-down for crabs and other crustaceans on the bottom. Jack couldn't imagine living anywhere else.

Judge Kicklighter stood waiting for him outside the Harborside Café and Grille. It was next door to an antediluvian courthouse built of red bricks faded and smoothed by the years. The judge chugged contentedly on one of his legendary Dominican cigars. In private or with close friends, he indulged himself in the occasional and illicit Cuban cigar. He glanced at his watch as Merkel stepped out of his car, then grinned at his old fishing buddy as they shook hands.

"Two more minutes and I'd be assessing you a hundred bucks for next year's barbecue," he said, tossing the half-smoked cigar into a bucket of sand.

"And I'd be telling you to kiss my ass," Jack said. "Why are you bothering me today? I'm swamped."

"We have business this morning in my courtroom and I want you there. But while we have breakfast, I want to tell you about this new redfish lure I picked up."

Harborside Café and Grille was owned and managed by Nell Mason, a whip-thin woman of middling age with a raucous laugh and mercurial temperament. She either loved you or despised you, and she wasn't shy about displaying either sentiment. Locals just called the place Nell's. If you asked directions to the Harborside Café and Grille, you were marked as a tourist. The café was the official hangout for the courthouse crowd and all the attorneys and business owners downtown. The judge stepped to his favorite table in the back corner; it was as big around as a Conestoga wagon wheel and where Nell Mason's favorites and the town's gentry dined. There was a "reserved" sign in the middle of the oak table no matter how crowded Nell's was or how many people waited in line to be seated. No one but the chosen were allowed to sit there. It was rumored that more deals were made around that oak slab than at a meeting of Mafia bosses.

Nell rushed out of the kitchen when she saw them.

"What'll it be, fellas? The usual, Your Honor? Cheese grits for you, Jack?"

Both men nodded and made their way back to the table where mugs of coffee and a pitcher of orange juice were already being set out. The judge took off his hat, put it on the seat of the empty chair beside him and draped his coat over the back.

"Hal's bringing your young vandal in with the other arrestees today," the judge said. "The boy's bad news and I aim to go hard on him. Hal's already given me his version of events, but I'm going to want to hear from you on the record about your losses. That'll drive some of mine and the state attorney's office's decision-making. But first, we dine. No more business talk 'til court convenes."

Circuit Court Judge J. Harlan Kicklighter who Jack called "Harley," was a short, spare and austere jurist whose hair was more salt than pepper. The son of Jamaican immigrants, his skin was the color of roasted coffee beans. He was a dandy, given to sporting blue seersucker suits, bow ties, suspenders and Panama hats. A convivial man in his private life, he governed his courtroom with the ruthlessness of a warlord. Lawyers who crossed him were rebuked and whittled to nubbins. Defendants who riled him or failed to show him the deference he demanded were gutted like mullet. Nor were the innocent out of harm's way, for the judge, who everyone agreed was as blunt as the business end of a bullet, rarely missed the opportunity to point out in open court that a verdict of *not guilty* didn't necessarily mean *innocent* when he felt like a scoundrel had evaded justice.

Nor did his Honor suffer fool prosecutors or lying cops. A prosecutor with a sloppily prepared case could look forward to the career-chilling humiliation of hearing the court grant defense counsel's request for a judgment of acquittal. And any cop the judge believed to be either outright lying or exaggerating—gilding the lily, as he called it—earned swift reproach, dismissal as a witness, and admonition to jurors not to believe a word of it.

Judge Kicklighter allowed spirited defense of the accused. But when he leaned forward in his chair and began sliding his gold-rimmed glasses down his nose, the time for defense lawyers, as well as prosecutors, to sit and be silent was at hand. Courtroom regulars loved the spectacle of a showboating lawyer oblivious to hand signals from the judge indicating he'd had enough and was about to bite. Tardiness to proceedings on either side was also taboo. No excuses were acceptable. Latecomers were fined a hundred dollars, which Kicklighter directed the clerk of the court to deposit into a special fund tapped every Fourth of July to pay for a barbecue for members of the courthouse family and their families. The annual soirée was so popular that, as Independence Day grew near, lawyers would inquire of the clerk whether there were sufficient funds for the event. If it appeared that it might fall short, they took turns being late for appearance in order to fatten Kicklighter's kitty. The judge was keen to this harmless plot but pretended otherwise.

For a diminutive man, he had a tuba's voice that resonated through even a packed courtroom. It was authoritative, capable of causing breaths to be held.

He strode into the courtroom that morning, took his seat on the bench and immediately called the first case. "Time's a-wasting," he thundered.

For the next forty-five minutes, while Jack watched the proceedings, the bailiffs hauled one petty crook after another in front of the judge, who swiftly took pleas, set conditions of bail and appointed attorneys for the defendants who couldn't afford their own. In the interim, he listened, with the same jaded expression, to the same used-up excuses he heard every day. And, as always, he made the same reply. "Well, cry me a river."

"How much more of this torture are you going to impose upon

me this morning, Mr. Reynolds?" he asked the young prosecutor, after a particularly loquacious and frequently appearing troublemaker was marched back to the holding cell.

"One more, if it please the court," Reynolds announced.

"Well, get busy," the judge rumbled. "It would please the court to make his tee time today."

The antique ceiling fans clicked drowsily in the quiet and now nearly empty courtroom. During a recent renovation, the original heart pine floor planks had been sanded smooth and covered with several coats of varnish, its mellow aroma still perfuming the air. Motes of dust drifted among the rays of morning sun that slanted through the room's row of windows. The courthouse clock, high in its belfry, gonged ten a.m. The judge patiently clipped a new cigar while he waited for the bailiff to haul in the last defendant of the day.

In the small holding area outside the courtroom, there were muffled curses and scuffling. Moments later, the door opened and two big bailiffs shoved a handcuffed and foot-shackled sandy-haired youth into the courtroom. Jack immediately recognized the boy. About that time, the sheriff walked into the courtroom, nodded at Merkel and made his way to a seat up front.

"State versus Raymond Douglas Eleazer," the prosecutor said, hopping to his feet. "Charged with one count each of criminal trespass, criminal mischief, petty theft and resisting arrest with violence."

Clad in an orange jumpsuit, the kid glanced over at the sheriff and then at the judge. "That's bullshit! I didn't do any violence to that fat cop. I just pushed him a little."

Judge Kicklighter pushed his glasses down his nose and leaned forward on the bench and pinned the boy with a stare. "You're one step away from having your mouth taped shut. Wanna try me? And for the record, shoving a cop during an arrest is considered resisting with violence *and* battery on a law enforcement officer. One more peep out of you and I'll suggest that the state add that charge. Now, answer me politely. Can you afford a lawyer?"

"No sir," the boy said, hanging his head. "I don't have a red cent to my name or a place to stay."

"Well, now you do, thanks to the nice sheriff there who so kindly took you in," Kicklighter replied. "Three hots and a cot."

Then he looked over at a lawyer wearing a dark blue suit and sitting at the table across from the prosecutor's. "Mr. Bryce, I'm appointing the public defender's office to represent this boy. Any conflicts of interest?"

The rumpled middle-aged lawyer stood.

"None that I'm aware of, Your Honor. May I have a moment to confer privately with my client?"

"You may, but don't be all day about it."

While the attorney and his client talked quietly off to one side of the courtroom, the judge returned his attention to the prosecutor. "Mr. Reynolds, would you kindly hand me the sheriff's arrest report?"

The prosecutor pulled some papers from his folder and passed them to the judge, who took his time reading them. After a few minutes, the accused and his lawyer walked together and stood back in front of the bench. The boy hung his head and stared at his jail issue rubber sandals.

"We're ready to continue, Your Honor."

The judge nodded and looked to the rear of the courtroom. "Mr. Merkel, would you please step up here for a moment?"

Jack got up and walked to the front of the courtroom. The bailiff opened the heavy wooden gate for him so that he could stand right in front of the bench. Kicklighter removed his glasses, massaged the bridge of his nose between finger and thumb and then put the glasses back on.

"Can you put a dollar amount on your losses?"

"Four, maybe five hundred dollars for fiberglass resin and cloth, Your Honor. Another fifteen bucks for that brand-new screwdriver he tossed into the drink."

"What would you normally charge per hour to do the same work on someone else's boat, Mr. Merkel?"

"Standard rate's eighty an hour, Your Honor. I make it about forty hours of labor, taking into account the time it takes the glass to cure before it can be sanded. All total with the material losses, I reckon it comes to about four thousand dollars."

The judge nodded and looked at the prosecutor.

"Which brings this into the realm of felony criminal mischief instead of misdemeanor charges, Mr. Reynolds?"

The prosecutor popped back up beside his table.

"Yes, Your Honor. We'll amend the charges to three felonies—assaulting Sheriff Patterson and the extensive vandalism to Mr. Merkel's property. The state recommends bail set at fifty thousand dollars, that is, if he can make it and if he can find somewhere to stay and someone to be responsible for him while he's awaiting disposition of his case. Your Honor, Mr. Eleazer here is a repeat offender. Juvenile court and shelters don't appear to have taught him anything. The state's going to be asking for two years in the Florida Department of Corrections, followed by five years of probation and full restitution to Mr. Merkel upon his release."

"May it please the court?" the defense lawyer said, rising. "We're going to be entering a plea of not guilty today. It's obvious that my client can't make his bail, nor does he have anywhere to go even if he could. But I beseech the court that, given his young age, he just turned eighteen, that he be transferred to the halfway house while his case is being worked out."

Judge Kicklighter snorted loudly.

"Nice try, Counselor. Not a chance. Unless satisfactory bond arrangements can be made, he can cool his heels in the county jail until we're done with him. Anything else, gentlemen?"

The boy's face reddened. "This ain't right!" he shouted. "I'm entitled to a fair trial!"

The defense attorney cringed under Kicklighter's blistering glare.

"Oh, you'll get your fair trial and fairly soon, kiddo," the judge replied disdainfully. "And after a jury convicts you in fairly short order, I intend to hand you a fairly substantial visit to state prison. Is that fair enough for you?"

"But judge," the boy cried. "That cop shoved me down the steps at that marina last night. I like to've bit my tongue off!"

Kicklighter shrugged. "Well, cry me a river. Court's adjourned. Sheriff, take Master Eleazer here back to your posh resort. Mr. Merkel, I want to see you in my chambers."

The courtroom cleared and Jack followed the judge through the rear entrance of the and across the hall. They stepped into a small office occupied by a plump, gray-haired woman seated at an imposing looking desk covered with small framed photos of her grandchildren. She looked up and beamed at the two men.

"Martha, no calls or visits for a few minutes," Kicklighter said.

"Yes, Your Honor," she answered.

He opened the door to his chambers, the paneled walls crowded with law books, family photos and pictures of him holding trophy-sized fish, and went over to the windows. He looked out for a few moments as if studying something below on the street before turning around and looking at Jack, who stood waiting just inside the door.

"Jack, we've known each other a long, long time. And I know what's going through that hard head of yours, which is precisely the same thing that's going through that soft heart down beneath it. Take my advice on this: Don't even think about it. You can't fix every broken thing in this world, nor should you try, my friend. Understand?"

Jack stood silent, studying the dirt and grease under his fingernails and listening to the rhythmic clank of the brass lanyard on the flagpole outside. A group of people loudly laughed two floors below on the sidewalk and the clock gonged the half hour. he finally looked back at his old friend, who stood waiting for his reply. "I reckon so, Harley. I reckon so."

"Good. That's what I wanted to hear. Now go on. Get on back to work. And let's go fishing sometime before the week is over. I'm dying to try this lure on a big red."

Jack nodded, then walked out of the judge's chambers. Kicklighter, an astute man who prided himself on being able to decipher most people's thoughts and body language, shook his head sadly. "Yeah, sure," he muttered to himself. "Soft-hearted, pig-headed damn fool."

CHAPTER 3

AS THE LAST REMNANTS of the early morning mist burned off and the sky brightened to liquid aquamarine, Jack slowed his flats fishing boat and aimed it at the mouth of a narrow saltwater creek. At nearly idle speed, he babied it into the creek, barely disturbing the cordgrass on either side. Myriad creeks fed the Intracoastal Waterway like a sprawling network of arteries, some of them no more than a foot deep and half again as wide, where you could lose your way or become mired in the black pluff mud of the spartina jungle. The hard-bitten devotees who fished it called it the *skinny water*.

Around the first bend, he and the judge both spied a small white skiff. A fat man, shaped like a channel marker can, stood in the center of his boat holding a seven-foot monofilament cast net. Bucky Howard was the quarrelsome owner of one of the two bait and tackle stores in town. He lifted his chin in greeting and resumed studying the surface of the water ten feet from the bow of his boat where a slight dimpling on the surface marked the location of a school of finger mullet. As the mullet veered closer to his boat, Howard lifted the net chest high, placed one of the lead weights between his teeth and tossed it so effortlessly that it seemed nonchalant. The sun glinted on the monofilament strands and the net spread out into a perfect circle, shimmering like a silver dollar. The net made a swishing sound and barely disturbed the surface. Howard snapped his wrist, closed the net and hauled it in. It quivered with dozens of squirming finger mullet.

"You boys want a few of these?" he said, holding the net up.

Jack glanced at the judge and then back at the netter and nodded.

"Well, ease on over here and get you some, then," Howard said.

Jack edged toward the skiff until they were inches alongside one another. Howard handed him the net and Jack spilled a double handful of the gasping fingerlings into his live bait well and handed back the net, still brimming with fish.

"Say, judge," Howard said, spitting a stream of chewing tobacco juice into the water and pointing at Kicklighter's shirt pocket. "Can I git one of them commie cee-gars of your'n before I go?"

The judge took two Cohibas from his pocket. "Here, you damn pirate. Take two."

Howard stuck one under the edge of his grimy red ball cap, peeled the wrapper off the other one, bit off the end and shoved it in his nearly toothless mouth. "You boys better get to fishin," he said. "Them reds is already gathering up back yonder."

Howard leaned over, cranked his boat's ancient motor and angled toward the Intracoastal, the motor farting noxious clouds of bluish smoke.

"What a waste of a good Cuban," the judge fumed. "He didn't even spit his dang chew out."

Kicklighter's silvery lure landed with a soft plop and the water detonated like a satchel charge had been tossed into it. Kicklighter whooped in delight as his rod bent into a nearly complete semicircle. Before he could set the drag, the monster fish started spooling the reel.

"Mother Mary!" Jack said. "Tighten that drag right now, Harley, or that big sumbitch is gonna take every inch of line off your reel!"

The charging red fish, an old veteran at escaping the hook, darted headlong toward an oyster bed thirty yards away. Even if it couldn't throw the hook in its heart-pounding race to thwart its tormentor, the primitive, miniscule brain that guided its torpedo-like dash for freedom somehow knew that the fillet knife-sharp oysters would sever the line, leaving the hook to dislodge or corrode away in the salt water. Kicklighter thumbed more tension on the drag to slow the fish's momentum and began gently but firmly drawing back on the rod to set the hook bite deeper and hopefully turn the fish. At the last moment, just feet from the looming mound of jagged shells, the fish, finally starting to suffer from the hook in its jaw, suddenly jogged right and streaked toward a larger oyster bed nearby. The battle between man and fish turned into a long slog.

Gradually, the big red began to tire in the shallow water, where every move revealed its wide bronze back and the two quarter-sized black spots on each side of its tail. Desperate, it decided on another escape strategy. It reversed its course and hurtled right at its enemy, removing all the tension in the line so that it could breach and shake the hook loose. Feeling the sudden slack in his line, the judge began reeling frantically. And then the fish breached, exploding from the water, whipping its head from side to side, struggling to dislodge the hook. But Kicklighter's hook held firm and the fish crashed back into the water and continued to run straight at the boat.

By now, fisherman and fish were starting to wear down. The muscles in Kicklighter's arms began to tremble and he felt the beginnings of a severe cramp in his left wrist and hand that held tension on the rod.

"God a'mighty, Jack," Kicklighter said. "I don't know how much longer I can hang onto this booger. He's wearing me out."

"He's slowing some," Jack said. "Keep tension on the stick. Keep easing him back slow. Wily bastard's fought this battle before."

Sensing that its options were now limited, the fish turned again and aimed at the thick grass in shallower water, twenty yards athwart the starboard side of Jack's boat.

"Going for the grass," Jack said. "Game over if he makes it."

At that instant, the weakened but determined fish surged toward the spartina, churning brown billows of mud and trailing a foamy V-shaped wake. Jack shouted a final instruction to the judge who stood on the bow of the boat, arm and neck muscles quivering, back bowed.

"Now!" Jack said. "Turn him!"

Circuit Court Judge J. Harlan Kicklighter, who'd never lost control of the most contentious trial, feared that he was about to lose his first one in a sprawling, shin-deep backwater courtroom. But the fish miscalculated and as suddenly as the fight began, it ended. "You got him, Harley," Jack said, slapping his friend on the shoulder as he rose to assist him in landing the prize. "He's done. Reel him in."

When the judge finally drew the feebly struggling fish alongside the boat, both men gaped in childlike surprise.

"Jesus Christ, Jack," Kicklighter said. "He must be close to four feet long."

"He's a whopper, all right. Way over keeping size, but let's get him up here and measure him and take a picture of him before we turn him loose."

Jack reached over the side of the boat, placed one hand under the fish's belly and the other one under its tail, so as to avoid injuring it, and lifted it out of the water. Kicklighter held a measuring tape alongside it; just over thirty-nine inches, a full fourteen inches above legal possession size. The lure, barely embedded, fell from the fish's mouth and landed in the boat.

"You're damn lucky you landed this bad boy," Jack said. "Another moment and he'd be laughing. Okay, let's shoot your trophy and send him home."

Jack supported the fish properly while Kicklighter snapped three photos. Then he eased it back into the water alongside the boat. But instead of swimming away, it lay on its side gasping and flapping its tail weakly.

"On, no," Kicklighter groaned. "He's exhausted. We need to swim him a minute or two and get some oxygen through his gills or he's a goner."

Jack steered the boat around in slow circles while the judge leaned over the side holding the fish and moving it gently side to side in a swimming motion. After a minute or so, it began to struggle and then, with a wild shake of its tail, broke free and swam quickly away. Both men cheered.

"Wanna catch a couple of keepers on live bait for supper, Harley?"

The judge laughed and massaged his sore wrist and forearm. "Yeah, but nothing much over eighteen inches. I'm done fighting for the day."

Jack swung the boat and headed toward a deep drop-off they'd passed on the way in. A few minutes later, they both had their limit, both catches big enough to guarantee fine, meaty fillets.

Jack was placing the last fish in the ice cooler when his friend reached into the small cooler he'd brought along and pulled out two Jamaican Red Stripe beers and popped the caps.

"Here's to old fishermen and older friends," the judge said in his courtroom voice as he hoisted his brew.

"To liars, damn liars, pirates, poachers and scoundrels," Jack answered in their time-honored tradition.

The dark brown glass bottles clinked and the two men sipped their beers. The judge reached into his pocket, pulled out two more Cubans, snipped off the ends and handed one to his longtime fishing partner, confidante and friend. Jack lit it and inhaled cocoa-rich smoke, which bore the tropical and intrigue-filled redolence of a sultry Havana night. The beer settled tingling and cold into their bellies.

The voice sounded familiar but distant. Jack had been daydreaming and didn't know for how long, but that it was Judge Kicklighter's voice he heard rolling along in the sea mists of his reverie.

"Sorry, Harley," he said, blinking his eyes. His beer bottle was empty and he didn't remember anything after the first couple of swallows. "Woolgathering, I guess. What were you saying?"

Kicklighter stared intently at his friend and saw the pain and longing that occasionally revealed themselves in his gray eyes at moments such as these when his guard was down. Jack was a torn man, not one who complained, but carried himself with steady dignity, head erect, smiling when he could. But if you knew him intimately, as Kicklighter did, you could see the occasional limp in his demeanor. On his worst days, you couldn't make him smile or laugh no matter how hard you tried. Nor could you entice him to confide the depths of his troubles. Even his best friend, Kicklighter, who knew what the ache was and how it came to be there, wouldn't press him, reckoning that in time his friend would open up. He'd been waiting ten years for that day.

"I said you're a good man, Jack Merkel, maybe one of the best I've ever known. But you've got a head harder than Georgia granite and a heart softer than pluff mud. It's a bad combination."

"Well, hell, old buddy," Jack said. "What's got you fretting?"

"Don't play coy with me," Kicklighter said. "You know damn well what I mean. I'm talking about this cockamamie notion of yours you called me about last night wanting to play Father Flanagan to a no-good punk. Release him into your custody? Are you serious?"

Jack rolled his eyes and slowly shook his head.

"I guess that means the fishing trip's over."

"Damn it Jack. Don't change the subject," Kicklighter grumbled. "I know we're like brothers, but do you really think I'm going to release this joker to you? Have you lost your wits? He belongs in prison and will be if I have anything to do with it."

"You're the judge, Harley, not the jury and sure as hell not the executioner," Jack said. The judge threw one hand up like a traffic cop and cut him off. "Yes, I'm the judge, my friend, and I've been a judge since before we became friends, which is a long damn time ago if you'll recall. And I'm a damn fine judge of people, the way they think, what makes them tick, the things that make the weak ones cry and the things that can turn the mean ones into diamondbacks who'll lash out and bite your extended hand before you can snatch it back. And this kid is one of the latter, Jack. He's mean and, as you might've noticed, absolutely callous."

Jack held his composure. "Well, I think you might be wrong about this one, Harley. I got a sense of something when the sheriff hauled him up to my office. Yeah, he's a mean one, but sometimes dogs go mean when they're beaten down too many times and never given a chance."

The judge threw back his head and hooted so loudly that he scared a roseate spoonbill into flight.

"Well, skin my catfish. Jack Merkel, psychologist. How long you been in practice, son?"

Jack crossed his arms and scowled.

"That's enough, Harley. Disagree and tell me hell no, but don't sit here in my boat and mock me. It's not very becoming of you and it sure as hell ain't a fair way to fight."

Both of them sat glaring at each other as time spooled out like the fishing line during the first crazed run of the judge's trophy red fish. It was the judge who gave first.

"Well, hell. I guess I did sorta screw the pooch, didn't I?"

"Well and truly, Your Honor. And with extreme prejudice."

And then the judge laughed. "I guess this is where the captain of the ship makes his contrary first mate walk the plank. I'll save you the trouble and take my cigars and my beer and just slip over the side and swim on back. I ought to be there by tomorrow if I don't drown or get eaten by a bull shark in the river."

Jack leaned over and placed his hand on his friend's cooler. "Uh-uh. You can have the cigars. The beer stays here."

"Oh, hell, I don't have court today," Kicklighter said. "Let's drink the rest of the damn things and catch ourselves a beer buzz and then I'll share some final thoughts with you and give you my verdict. Fair enough?"

Jack shrugged. "I guess I don't have much choice."

The two men drank the remaining four beers, swapped dirty jokes, laughed, bragged and lied about fish they'd caught, and enjoyed the company of one another like brothers.

"Okay," Kicklighter said, finishing the last of his beer. "Here's my take on it. That Eleazer kid is like that red fish I caught back there. He's wild, strong willed, hard and doesn't think about anyone else's survival but his own. He's also a wiry, strong-looking bastard and I'm guessing he could bull-rush you and knock you on your ass if he took a mind to. But here's the difference, Jack. I don't think you can tame or tire this fish. You'll wear one another down so bad that one of you'll drop dead—and it won't be him. Then he's off the hook and on to the races. He's run eleven times already. Homes, halfway houses, juvenile shelters, you name it. He's calculating and vigilant and I don't think you can contain him if I turn him over to you."

Jack smiled broadly. "If? Ah, now there's a ray of hope. He ain't running anywhere, Harley. Pogy'll see to that. Rafe'll poleax his ass at the first hint of nastiness, and he damn sure ain't getting out through the marsh or across the river. Give him to me for a few days and lemme have my pound of flesh from him. I promise you; I can handle him. I need to do this."

Kicklighter swatted away a thumbnail-size horsefly.

"I know you need to do it, buddy. But for who? If I turn this snake over to you and he gets away—"

"Put an ankle monitor on him then," Jack cut in. "One of those new GPS trackers. He can't get away from a bunch of satellites."

Kicklighter chugged on his cigar and flashed Jack a wide grin. "Sonofabitch. You have been scheming. All right, let's head on back."

When they entered the no-wake zone heading into the marina a few minutes later, Jack throttled down and let the boat drift ahead on its own momentum. They parked it in Jack's personal space on the floating dock nearest the office and washed it down.

Afterward, they divided the fillets, shook hands and congratulated one another on a great day on the water. Judge Kicklighter had taken the first step back to the parking lot and his car when he paused and looked over his shoulder. Jack looked back at him with eyebrows arched. "Forget something, Harley?"

"No, I just want to hear this one more time. Why are you doing this for this punk?"

Jack's smile just touched the edges of his mouth. The look on his face was a serene as a monk.

"Because he can't repay me any other way. And even after he serves a sentence, he'll be a criminal still because he can't pay me. It's what this kid needs. Because I don't think anyone's ever really given him a good turn. Because I gotta."

"About what I figured you'd say." Kicklighter replied. "You'll be hearing from me."

CHAPTER 4

FOR THE SECOND TIME in three days, Jack stood before the majestic oak bench of Circuit Court Judge J. Harlan Kicklighter. But this time he appeared as a common petitioner before the honorable court, praying for a ruling that he no longer felt confident he'd get. The telephone call from the judge that had interrupted his previous evening's supper of fried fish, grits and hushpuppies had been terse and businesslike.

"Be in my courtroom first thing in the morning and I'll give you my decision," he'd said and then hung up.

Jack had set the remainder of his dinner on the floor and whistled. Pogy trotted in from the deck where he'd been snoring so loud that Jack had to step away from the door while he took his telephone call. The dog walked over to the food and dove in.

Jack poured himself a cup of coffee and wandered out onto the wide upstairs deck. He walked over to the rail, set his cup on it and fished his cigarettes out of his shirt pocket. The sudden flare of his lighter momentarily robbed him of the cat-like night vision he'd always had. He drew in the first draught of smoke and by the time he exhaled his visual acuity had returned. The full moon cast its light upon the marina, the surrounding marshes and the wide, meandering river, painting it all the ethereal hues of a tintype photograph. He smoked and pondered the circumstances, breathing the seductive fragrance of jasmine growing on the trellis below. He crushed out his smoke, tossed the cold remains of his coffee into the yard and went inside to bed.

Dozing fitfully that night, he finally got up, showered, dressed and went downstairs, Pogy dogging his heels. He stopped at his desk, wrote a note to Rafe that he had to go to court again that morning and tacked it on the bulletin board with the daily checklist. He let the dog out to perform his constitutional, put him back inside and then walked back out to his car.

He stepped into Nell's just after sunup and headed toward the big, round table where he ate a light breakfast, sipped coffee, chatted with his usual waiter for a few minutes and then went for a walk along the waterfront until it was time for court. When he arrived, the courtroom was empty but for an old bailiff with the air and manners of a butler.

"Mornin' Henry," he said to the officer as he stepped inside the courtroom.

"Good morning, Mr. Merkel," the bailiff replied formally. "You're a bit early."

The two men shook hands.

The bailiff turned his head toward the judge's entrance behind the bench and checked to see if the door was closed. "Cranky this morning," he said, cupping his hand to his mouth and whispering like a conspirator. "Step lightly today. Don't know what's come over him, do you?"

"I reckon I do," Jack said as he made his way to the front of the courtroom and sat down.

A few minutes later, the public defender entered the courtroom and paused beside Jack.

"Mr. Merkel, I'm Mason Bryce, Mr. Eleazer's lawyer."

Jack pushed himself to his feet and the two men shook hands. "A pleasure. I'm glad the boy has a lawyer who seems to care."

The lawyer's eyes crinkled with a short-lived smile.

"Mr. Merkel, I can't tell you how much I appreciate what you're trying to do for my client. But I don't think Judge Kicklighter will agree to it and I can assure you that Brad Reynolds will sling as much mud as he can to prevent it. I walked by the judge's chambers on the way here. He and the sheriff are having a rather spirited conversation about it. My best guess is that Sheriff Patterson and Reynolds will team up against you. And my client really pissed off the judge the other day, as you'll recall. I guess we'll just have to hold our breaths and hope for a miracle."

The lawyer walked through the heavy, spring-loaded swinging gate and went to his appointed table. A few moments later, the cocky young prosecutor strode into the courtroom and almost passed Jack before he noticed him sitting there. He abruptly stopped, turned his head sideways and leered through a pair of oversized and ugly black-framed glasses that made his pointy face look like a raccoon. "You gotta be kidding me," he sneered, as he turned to walk away. "There's no way in hell Judge Kicklighter's going to release this punk to you. What a joke."

Jack stood. "My daddy always told me that the measure of a man is whether or not he can stand his ground and say what's on his mind to another man's face," he said without raising his voice. "You toss words over your shoulder while walking away. Not much of a man, I'd say." The prosecutor stiffened and the back of his neck flamed crimson. "Go ahead, son," Jack said mildly. "Spit it out or swallow it and be damned."

Judge Kicklighter paused in the narrow passageway behind his bench listening to the exchange and then strode into his courtroom. A petite young court reporter with chestnut colored hair and dark eyes followed him out and took her seat just below the bench, where the judge made himself comfortable in his big chair. The elderly bailiff stepped up to call the court to order but the judge lifted his hand and stopped him and glowered at the prosecutor who began randomly shuffling papers around on his desk "Well, Mr. Reynolds. Seems to me you've just been hauled out to the woodshed and whipped in fine style. Now, if y'all will kindly stop waving your manhoods at one another—pardon me, Ms. Mobley, don't record that—I'd like to get on with business. Since Mr. Merkel is the petitioner, I'll allow him to go first. You should use your time to prepare for your argument lest you continue to make a damn fool of yourself when it's your turn. Mr. Merkel, please approach the bench and proceed. Deputy Higginbotham, please administer the oath."

Sheriff Patterson ambled into the courtroom, his Sam Browne belt squeaking with every ponderous step. The judge looked up at him and beckoned him to approach the bench. "Do you have your prisoner here, sheriff?" he asked.

The lawman nodded. "I do, Yo' Honor. He's back yonder in the holding cell."

"Excellent. Let's leave him in there to stew until some of the juice is cooked out of him. Then you can haul him out to hear my decision. Please continue, Mr. Merkel."

Jack walked over to the witness podium and cleared his throat. The court reporter began to type.

"Your Honor, young Mr. Eleazer broke into my boatyard and damaged a sailboat I've been building with my own hands for the past ten years. Actually, she's been sitting in the barn gathering dust and pigeon droppings for most of that time and I only recently hauled her out to resume my work on her."

The prosecutor sprang out of his seat and lifted his hands in a beseeching gesture toward the judge. "Your Honor, could we please skip the history lesson and get to the issue here?"

Kicklighter shoved his glasses down on his nose and glared.

"Let me tell you something, Mr. Reynolds. And this is the only warning you'll get from me. If you have some pearls of wisdom you wish to scatter before this court, you'll do so with the politesse and the decorum I require of all within this sanctum of justice. And you'll wait your turn to do so unless I solicit commentary from you. If you don't, then I will take supreme pleasure in having the good bailiff here escort you out of my courtroom, from whence I'll bar you from further attendance to this matter and demand a more studious and deferential assistant state attorney from your office. Are we clear?"

"Yes, Your Honor," the prosecutor said. "I apologize to the court, learned counsel and to Mr. Merkel as well."

The public defender managed to keep a poker face though he wanted to stand up and cheer. The judge glanced over at him, reading him like a court brief and signaled for Jack to go on.

"As I was saying, Your Honor, this young man inflicted some mighty grievous wounds on a cherished possession of mine. If he's found guilty either by plea or jury verdict, part of the sentence you'll likely impose upon him will be complete compensation for those damages. Am I correct?"

Kicklighter leaned back and his chair and nodded. "Absolutely. Not only does he owe a debt to the state for his transgressions, but monetary damages to you, the victim. So, yes, I will hold him accountable for those damages whether I take a plea and sentence him to probation or prison or whether he's convicted and sent to prison. Upon completion of his sentence, he'll serve a probationary period that will require restitution. Otherwise, I'll return him to prison to serve out the remainder of his sentence."

"Your honor, this boy ain't ever going to be in any position to repay me once he's released from prison or even if you only sentence him to probation," Jack said. "He has no employment and will probably never be gainfully employed after his release, which means that he'll just get caught up in the grind and he'll never be able to repay his debt to anyone, including me."

The judge rolled his eyes and frowned. "Well, cry me a river. So, let's hear your proposal on the record and then I'll take argument from the state and the sheriff and then I'll hear from counsel."

"Release him into my custody, your honor," Jack plowed ahead, going for broke. "I'll assume full responsibility for him while his case proceeds. Let the sheriff put an ankle monitor on him in case he gets the urge to run, which I assure you would be not only pointless but dangerous, and I'll make him work his tail off in the hot sun every day. The sheriff can take him back to the jail every night and return him to me each morning for as long as things work out. While I have him, and if he's willing, I'll teach him some lessons that'll serve him well in the future. Otherwise, this kid, and that's all he is, will end up just another con."

He paused while the paddle wheeled ceiling fan clicked away the moments like a loud stopwatch and the court reporter tapped away rhythmically on her machine. Just when everyone thought Jack was finished speaking, he picked up where he'd left off.

"I know he's a hard case. I know he's run like a deer from every place he's ever been sent. But let me have my pound of flesh and the debt he owes me while y'all decide what's best. If it don't work out, I'll hand deliver him back to you and you can do what you will. But, by God, give me a chance to try."

Judge Kicklighter leaned forward on his elbows and steepled his fingers under his chin, his big Masonic ring telegraphing its golden worth. He leaned back in his chair and stared at the ceiling for several long moments. Having collected his thoughts, he leaned forward again.

"Why should I use the power of the court to sanction a mission that's likely doomed from the outset, Mr. Merkel? I'll give you one more chance to try and convince me."

Jack drew himself up as straight as he could. "Because it's the right thing to do. Because I'm the victim. And because, if you can't see your way to doing this, then I reckon the state'll find me an unwilling victim and an uncooperative witness as well. That's all I have to say, Your Honor."

Judge Kicklighter watched him trudge back to his seat.

"Mr. Reynolds," he said to the chastened prosecutor. "Let's hear from the state. And no theatrics this time."

The prosecutor stood beside his table and spoke.

"May it please the court, honorable counsel and the High Sheriff. The state is strongly opposed to this proposal. No doubt that Mr. Merkel has sincere intentions. In fact, the state applauds his conciliatory attitude toward the defendant. However, this isn't a social experiment but a criminal case involving a perpetrator who gives the word recidivism a whole new meaning. You've read his lengthy criminal record, Your Honor, so I won't belabor the issue. This young man's life has been on a collision course with the penitentiary since he was fourteen. All efforts to correct that course have been abject failures. He is clever and patient and he will run again at the first opportunity."

He paused and turned around to look at Jack and then returned his attention to the judge.

"Your Honor," he said, "I see an honorable man with a forgiving nature. If this was a high school kid from the community who did something stupid while feeling his oats after drinking too much beer with his buddies, I'd be inclined to agree that sweat labor meted out by the person he'd wronged might be a valuable lesson. But Raymond Douglas Eleazer is no longer a kid who did something stupid. Despite his relatively young age, he's well on his way to being a hardened criminal. He's a risk to the community as well as to himself. The state opposes this offer and prays the court to proceed with the disposition of this case either by trial or a plea of guilty. It's time for Mr. Eleazer to pay the fiddler his fee, Your Honor."

"Thank you, Mr. Reynolds. Sheriff Patterson, do you have anything to add?"

The sheriff stood and shook his head. "No, Judge. You already know my position. No use in repeating myself."

The sheriff sat back down and Judge Kicklighter directed his attention to the public defender. "Counselor Bryce? How says the defense?"

The lawyer stood, rail thin and somber as an undertaker.

"Your Honor, I don't think I could say anything more eloquently than what Mr. Merkel has proffered to the court. I concur and, should you grant our motion, I will endeavor to make sure that my client fully understands the ramifications of all of this. I would like to go on the record to disagree with the state that Mr. Eleazer is irredeemable. I've heard His Honor say many a time that not everything that's broken can be fixed."

"And you'll hear me say it a thousand more times if you hang around my courtroom long enough, but please excuse my interruption and continue," Kicklighter said.

"Yes, Your Honor. I agree with you that there are indeed some things broken beyond repair. But sometimes, that which seems irreparable can be restored in the hands of the right craftsman. When I was a child, I was playing one day with my papa's gold railroad watch, which my daddy inherited. I'd been told dozens of times not to, but I couldn't help myself. I dropped it and it bounced all the way to the bottom of the wooden stairs in our home. It shattered of course, but even worse, it shattered my daddy. He was inconsolable, so much so that he didn't even whip me for it. But Mama picked it up and while Daddy was at work the next day, she took it to an old watch repairman who had a little shop in our town. He looked at the busted watch and told my mama not to worry. A week later, he brought it to our house and it was as good as new. It even kept better time. And you know what, Your Honor? He wouldn't accept a cent for his work.

He said fixing something so broken that no one believed it could be fixed was a blessing to him. That's all, Your Honor."

The silence in the courtroom was palpable.

"Very well, gentlemen," the judge said. "Let's take a short recess while I go back to my chambers and make my decision. Don't leave the courtroom. This shouldn't take long. Sheriff Patterson, please come with me."

"All rise," the old bailiff cried ceremoniously. "This honorable court is now in recess."

Judge J. Harlan Kicklighter rose from his bench and swept out of his courtroom with the sheriff in tow.

Five minutes later, the bailiff again cried, "All rise! This honorable court is now in session, the Honorable J. Harlan Kicklighter presiding."

The judge sat and leaned forward on his elbows. "I'm going to cut straight to the chase here, folks. In all my years on the bench, I've never been asked to rule on a motion like this. It goes without saying that it's a rare thing. And gentlemen, rare things seldom happen in real courtrooms. It makes for good television drama. But in the real world? Well—"

He stared at the ceiling again and sighed loudly. Jack felt his hopes waning and couldn't understand how his old friend could so cavalierly dismiss him after seeming so agreeable about it the morning before. He uttered a silent prayer that he'd be able to forgive his friend for what he seemed determined to do.

Kicklighter picked up his glass and took a sip of water. "Every now and then, despite the traditional wisdom that has it otherwise, the wheel needs to be reinvented."

Sheriff Patterson shifted slightly in his seat, turned his head toward Merkel and after taking precautions to make sure that none but he would notice, tipped him a wink worthy of a cheesy vaudeville actor.

"So, here's my decision, gentlemen, and I'll consider no challenge to it, Mr. Reynolds. Sheriff, will you please fetch the defendant?"

The sheriff walked back to the holding cell. The prosecutor sagged in his seat and the court reporter ceased typing, looked up at the judge and smiled. For the first time that day, the judge allowed himself one too. Jack looked over to where the public defender was sitting and noticed that he was the only one in the room who still appeared to be holding his breath and reckoned that it was habit forged by years in the crucible of the courtroom where the melting of all hope was a reality as hard as prison bars.

The door opened and the sheriff led his prisoner into the room and over to his lawyer's table. The lawyer stood, took his client by the elbow and led him to the podium in front of the judge. The boy looked around the room, blinking and it was only then that Jack realized the boy had no idea why he was there. Then it dawned on him that this was all part of the judge's plan, part of his grand scheme to humble him. The lawyer whispered something in his ear. The boy straightened and looked up at the judge, who was already bearing down on his face.

"Well, Master Eleazer. It would appear that a Good Samaritan has appeared on this storm-tossed road to perdition and offered to bind up your wounds and offer you sanctuary in his humble abode."

The boy looked at him quizzically and then at his attorney and shrugged.

"What I'm saying in my own playful way, young gun, is this," the judge continued. "The gentleman behind you there, I believe you've met, is Mr. Jackson Merkel, owner of a small but widely regarded local marina you recently burgled. There you committed a dastardly and cowardly atrocity on a boat that Mr. Merkel has been building with his own hands, an object as innocent as you are guilty, but which you deemed, in some sort of deranged fugue, to be a fitting target of your depravity. Are you following me, young fella, or should I use smaller words?"

The kid lifted his head and peered at him. "I'm gettin' the gist of it, judge," he said without affect.

"Good, then let's move along. Mr. Merkel here has offered, and I have accepted, a deal that'll allow you to pay him for the damage you did while, at the same time, giving you some daily respite from the jailhouse. But here are the caveats. They're few, but consider each one to be as loaded as the good sheriff's sidearm. If you run, you're toast. If you disrespect the good Mr. Merkel in words or actions, you're burnt toast. If you refuse to do as he requires, if you dig in your heels and continue to behave like the hopeless punk I personally believe you to be and crap on this deal, I'll grind your burnt toast young tail under my heel and bury your hopes of freedom for as long as the statutes permit. Blow this and you'll either plead straight up guilty or go to trial. I will not accept a plea bargain. And whether you plead or get convicted by a jury, I intend to take you out like the trash. Is that clear?"

The boy glanced at the lawyer, who leaned over and whispered in his ear again.

"Yes sir," he said. "I, uh, I thank you, judge."

Kicklighter snorted derisively. "Don't thank me, hotshot. Personally, I don't like the idea, but Mr. Merkel here drives a hard bargain. And I believe, I sincerely hope, that'll you'll find out that he's not only a forgiving man, but a hard taskmaster. Before this is all said and done, you might wish you'd stayed in the hoosegow. One other thing. At the close of each business day, Sheriff Patterson himself will take you back to the jail for the night. And if you behave yourself, he'll return you to Mr. Merkel's care each day. Play or pay, mister. The choice is yours."

The judge paused for a moment to let his words sink in, and then waved dismissively to the sheriff hovering silently beside the bench. "Get him out of here, sheriff. I'm done with him . . ."

He looked at the young hoodlum and fixed him with a malevolent smile. ". . . for now."

CHAPTER 5

JACK AND RAFE WERE pulling the shaft from a boat with a shattered propeller when Sheriff Patterson drove into the boatyard two mornings after the boy's hearing. Rafe stopped what he was doing, tapped his boss on the shoulder and pointed a stubby, grease-stained finger toward the police car coming down the causeway toward the marina. Jack glanced over his shoulder and saw the sheriff's car approaching, then climbed down from the scaffolding where they'd been working.

"Come on, Rafe, I think you should join the welcoming committee."

Both men wiped the grease off their hands as the sheriff opened the car's rear door and allowed his prisoner to step out. He was still wearing his orange jumpsuit, rubber shoes and handcuffs. Jack noted the boxy black monitor strapped to one ankle.

"Mornin' fellas," the sheriff said, leading the young man toward them.

The boy kept his head down as the men exchanged handshakes. The day was already stifling. Jack cocked his thumb over his shoulder in the direction of the sprawling front porch.

"Let's get out of the sun and do our business, Hal. We're gonna be out in this heat all day."

Pogy bristled and growled as they approached. The boy lifted his head, saw the dog and looked sideways at Jack. "Hush, Pogy. Behave," he admonished.

The dog whined and sat obediently but kept his eyes on the boy as the sheriff walked him up the steps.

"Get you a Coke or something, Hal?"

"Fine idea," Sheriff Patterson said.

'How 'bout you, son?" Merkel asked.

The sullen youth looked down at his feet again. A long moment stretched out, punctuated by the rumble of a forklift moving a boat.

"Suit yourself," Jack said, walking into his office.

He returned a few moments later with three bottles and handed one each to the sheriff and to Rafe.

"Obliged," the sheriff said, tilting his bottle up and draining half its contents in a couple of hard gulps, followed by a loud belch.

"Thought you were bringing him by yesterday morning,' Hal," Jack said quietly. "Rafe and me waited around all day."

The sheriff pointed at the black box strapped to the boy's ankle.

"Our agreement was a GPS monitor, not one of the regular ones, and I didn't have any. I had to special order this one. It came in special delivery just this morning. Sorry, I shoulda called you yesterday and told you. Jack, this little toy is expensive. And I want you to know if kiddo here happens to somehow get shed of it or break it, you gotta pay for it to be fixed or replaced. Fair enough?"

"Fair enough," Jack replied.

"Rafe," Patterson said to the other man. "Would you babysit junior here while I have a private word with Jack?"

"Sure, Hal."

"Boy, if you get a notion to break and run, lemme assure you, if Rafe don't get you, Pogy will."

But the kid continued to stare downward and said nothing. The sheriff motioned Jack to the opposite end of the porch.

"I reckon you wondered what convinced Judge Kicklighter to do this. Well, I did. I wasn't sure he was going to do it, not even for you, although I could tell it grieved him bad."

"So, what happened, Hal?"

The lawman set his bottle on the porch rail, pulled a blue bandana from his trousers pocket and mopped his face.

"Oh, he wanted to do it. He trusts and respects you about as much as any man I know. But you know he's a stickler about the law and precedent and he was getting hung up on that. Look, buddy. This boy is messed up somethin' bad. I didn't know how bad he was messed up 'til I found a psychologist's report in all the other stuff I got from the last place he was before he hightailed it. It's a pitiful thing, a hurtful thing and I agree with you. Jail ain't gonna fix it. Whether you can get through to him or not, hell, I don't know. I'm just a country cop."

Jack looked up the long causeway toward the main road and watched a procession of log trucks roar past on their way to the paper mill. A small boat filled with laughing and yelling teenage boys and their squealing girlfriends whizzed past on the Intracoastal. Jack watched them and listened until the boat's engine noise faded in the distance.

"Anyway, I held the doctor's report back and used it as my hole card when I wasn't sure things were gonna break your way. I think this is somethin' you both could use, Jack. But if you don't succeed, it's gonna break your heart and I think you oughta know it. And another thing, you helped a fat old redneck like me get voted into office with the snobs on the island so I figured I owe you big time. If you can get through to this boy, it'd be a plumb miracle. If you cain't, well, I think his life is pretty much done. Just so you know."

The two men stood looking at each other for a long time and the sheriff's words settled into Jack's gut, cold and heavy as wet sand.

"That bad, huh? Just what in hell has this boy done, Hal?"

The sheriff shook his head sadly. "Survived, Jack. Survived. Listen, I gotta git on back to my office. Here's the handcuff key. I'll let you take them off. Maybe that'd be a good start, maybe mean somethin' to him. I'll leave it here with you. If you gotta, put them back on him, holler and I'll come pick him right up."

The sheriff handed him the silver key. Jack allowed himself a smile. Both men grasped one another's hands and held on for a moment.

"Thank you, Hal. Listen, can I see that report?"

"Naw, I can't do that, Jack. It's confidential stuff. Only way you can see it is if the judge releases it to you. I ain't got that authority and besides, I don't think it'd be the right thing to do right now anyway. You're a perceptive man, my friend. You got more horse sense than any man I know. You crack this kid's crust and you'll figure it out yourself. If you cain't, hell, it won't matter no how. And one other thing. I don't wanna hear about it if he tries to skedaddle and you catch him, you hear me? I won't have no choice but to come take him away. You catch him, you corral him, ain't none of my affair if I don't know about it."

The sheriff started to walk away and stopped again. "I'll give you one hint about that report. This boy ain't no dummy. No siree, he ain't."

And then he clomped back to the other end of the porch, stopping to shake Rafe's hand.

"Listen to me, young gun," he said to the kid. "And you listen good. I ain't never done nothing like this for a prisoner before. You mess this up and I'll turn your young ass into a project. Count on it." He scratched Pogy's ears, walked down the steps, got into his car and left.

Jack watched the car head back up the causeway to the main road and turn toward town. When the car was out of sight, he looked down at the shiny little key in his hand and pondered the irony of it. It was so light as to be nearly weightless, so miniscule that it got lost in the wide grip of his hand and he'd momentarily forgotten he was holding it. A tiny thing, yet it sparkled with the light of freedom and the strength to break the steel bonds of imprisonment.

After some moments had passed, he went and stood in front of the kid, who kept his eyes focused on the porch boards beneath him. "Hold out your hands, son," he said, keeping his voice low.

The kid didn't move or give the slightest clue that he'd either heard Jack or seen him standing inches away from him. His breathing was nearly imperceptible.

"Hold out your hands to me, son. I'll turn you loose if you will."

The kid still made no acknowledgment. Jack watched him for a moment to see if there'd be any other and when there wasn't, he simply nodded, took in a deep breath and let it out slowly.

"Okay. It's up to you. But I wouldn't want to walk around a marina handcuffed all day long."

As he put the key into his pocket, the kid lifted his head slightly and muttered something under his breath. Jack looked at Rafe who raised his bushy black eyebrows.

"What's that?" Jack said. "You're gonna have to speak up a little, son. You might've noticed it's a little noisy 'round here."

The kid looked up at Jack with hooded, suspicious eyes. "No you won't," he said bitterly. "Ain't nobody ever turned me loose."

"Well, then, I'll be the first. Give me your hands, son. I'll take those cuffs off you and they can stay off 'til you decide they go back on. But that'll be your decision, not mine."

The kid didn't budge for a moment, but then slowly lifted his hands. Jack noticed the tremor, which reminded him of a dog that's been beaten so many times that, no matter how badly it wants a treat being offered, it can only sidle and cower, its aching hunger overshadowed by the remembrance of beatings past and the raw fear that surely the other hand conceals the dreaded stick.

"That's it. Lift 'em right up here. Ain't nobody gonna hurt you."

Jack reached out with one hand and placed it gently on the kid's forearm, his eyes drawn to the trail of round red scars. The muscles in the lean arm beneath his hand knotted and recoiled at his touch and Jack knew in that moment that no one had touched the young man in a long time except to hurt him in some way. He kept one hand on the kid's tremulous wrist and inserted the key into the handcuff lock with his other. The manacles clicked open. Jack stuck the handcuffs and key in his pants pocket and gave the boy's wrist a gentle shake.

"There. It's done. Better?"

The kid didn't reply, nor did he look up and meet Jack's eyes. He managed only a slight nod.

Jack looked at Rafe who smiled and winked.

"Come on," Jack said. "Let's me and you and Rafe go back around to the workshop and find you something to wear. Cain't have you running around my damn boatyard in jailhouse clothes and flip-flops."

The kid stood there for a moment and Jack thought that he meant not to move. He avoided reaching out and touching him but waited patiently for a response. Keeping his head low, the kid took two shuffling steps toward him and then stopped and shook his head.

"What's the matter, son?" Jack asked.

"Can I have that Co-Cola now?" the kid said, never raising his eyes.

"Sure," Jack. "Many of 'em as you want."

Rafe fetched a bottle and handed it to the kid who tilted his head back and drained it in four hard gulps. When he belched, some of the brownish foam came out of his nose. He stood there for a long moment and held the empty bottle and then handed it to Jack.

"Want another one?" Merkel asked.

The kid shook his head and belched again.

Jack wished that the kid might at least mumble some acknowledgement of the favor. And yet at the same time, he had already resigned himself to knowing that obstinate silence was about the best he could expect, at least for a while.

"All right, then. Let's go see about some work clothes."

This time the kid fell in behind him. They walked around to the back of the building and into a small, dimly lit and dusty shop. A workbench crammed with tools and boat parts lined one wall, a row of red metal lockers lined another. An overhead fan moved the hot air around the room. Two other men were getting a drink of water from a cooler. Both stopped and greeted their bosses. One was short with an unkempt reddish beard; the other was a muscular baldheaded young black man. The nametag on his blue shirt identified him as Eddie. He flashed the boy a wide smile. The other man cocked his head at the newcomer.

"This is a new hire, Jack?"

"Yep. Need to get him some work clothes and hard shoes, Neal. Anything in the locker?"

"Think so," the man said. "Lemme look."

Eddie walked over to the kid and stuck out his hand.

"Hey, I'm Eddie Kraft. What's your name?"

The kid didn't move or make eye contact with him, nor did he reply. Eddie looked at Jack, tilted his head to one side and narrowed his eyes.

"This is Raymond Eleazer," Jack said. "He's a little shy but he's gonna be working for us for a few days till we see how things go."

"Oh, okay," Eddie said. "Well, nice to meet you, Ray. I gotta get on back to the forklift. Got a boat to move."

He tossed his paper cup into the trash can and walked out of the shed. About that time, Neal returned, holding a faded, pale blue shirt with the marina name above the left pocket, a worn pair of khaki trousers and a beat-up pair of low-cut, steel-toed boots.

"Here you go, bub," he said. The kid didn't move or even acknowledge the man offering them.

Neal looked at Jack and Rafe puzzled and then gave the boy a sour glare. "Cat got your tongue, kid? I ain't got all day."

He dropped the clothes on the dirty concrete floor and strode out of the shop, muttering darkly as he headed toward a nearby aluminum building full of boats. Rafe excused himself and followed. Jack waited until the two men were out of sight before speaking to the kid.

"Look, son. This ain't gonna work unless you make it. Pick up your clothes, go on over to the bathroom and get changed and then come on back out."

The kid stood there for a little while as if he hadn't heard Jack and then scooped up the clothes and shoes and trudged over to the bathroom, closing the door. A few minutes later, he came back out wearing the clothes and boots and holding his jail issue clothing and rubber shoes in one hand. Jack took them and put them in an empty locker. The kid watched with a blank expression.

"This is where your stuff goes from now on. Come on outside. I want to talk to you a bit and show you around the yard. You need to know where everything is and what it's for."

There was a bright red golf cart parked just outside. Jack walked out to it, climbed behind the wheel and patted the black vinyl seat beside him. "Come on," he said. "Let's go."

Jack put it in gear and together they drove across the yard toward the sailboat the kid had damaged. The sun beat down on them and both were sweating by the time they reached the boat. It was evident Jack had been working on it. There was fresh fiberglass that still needed sanding and ragged gouges and holes in the places he'd not yet begun to repair. Jack pulled alongside the boat on the shaded side and got out, crooking a finger for the kid to follow him. They stood in the shade for a few moments, side by side.

"It's bad, but I've seen worse," Jack finally said, reaching out and running one hand along a freshly sanded area. "I ain't gonna dwell on it, but I want you to know that this boat is very special to me. You're gonna have to help me fix the damage you done. No grudges here, but you owe it to me to help make this right. And while you do, I'll teach you how to do better things with your hands. Deal?"

The kid dropped his chin to his chest and shrugged.

"Good. Now let's ride around the rest of the marina for a bit and then there's one other thing I need to show you."

They spent the next ten minutes lumbering around the boatyard in the golf cart. Jack pointed out the big yellow forklift and explained what it was used for and how it was operated. They drove over to a massive rolling travel lift on four huge wheels nearly as big as a passenger jet's tires and he told Ray how the big lift lowered its heavy straps into the water and could lift boats as long as fifty feet. Jack turned the golf cart around and they went over to the aluminum boat barn, where they watched Eddie and Neal use the forklift to put a boat onto a storage cradle.

Jack turned the cart around and maneuvered it out of the building and into the furious stare of the midmorning sun. They trundled toward the long, narrow limestone causeway toward the main road with Pogy trotting behind them. They'd gone about halfway when Jack came to a halt and got out. This time, the kid followed, keeping a cautious distance as he looked out into the marsh. The tide was coming in, but the oyster beds everywhere were still visible. Jack stood there studying his beloved marsh, its filling waters, the scurrying fiddler crabs, and basked in the rich fragrance of it. He let his gaze trail across the marsh and spoke to the boy in a low voice.

"Prettiest place on earth, to my notion. Can't imagine living anywhere else. It's so wild and wonderful. But it can also be deadly. It can take your life right quick. I want you to listen and I want you to listen good because if you don't, you won't get a second chance."

He pulled his cigarettes from his shirt pocket, tapped one from the pack and lit it. There was a southeasterly breeze freshening across the marsh. A sudden rush of coolness filled the air as a large gray cloud cast its shadow over. The tinny smell of rain drifted across the marsh on the wind. Jack glanced at the darkening sky and reckoned they might get some although he doubted it would last for more than a few minutes. He smoked quietly for a minute or so while the kid gazed across the marsh with the same flat stare he'd worn since his arrival.

"There ain't but one other way out of my marina unless you go by boat, Raymond," Jack said, looking at the side of the boy's head and noticing his dirty ears and grimy neck. "This road is it and it's a long haul to the highway, nearly half a mile. Intracoastal on two sides of the property and the marsh here on the other two sides. If you run, Pogy will get you. If you think you can outrun him, you never saw a Great Dane run. You'll drown or get eaten by a bull shark if you try to swim the river. Nobody can swim across that current."

He looked back over the marsh and smoked a bit more and gave his words a chance to settle in.

"But it's the marsh you really gotta worry about. It's beautiful but it'll kill you in a New York minute. Looks like it'd be easy, don't it? Wait 'til low tide and just walk over. But that'd be a bad mistake. Those oysters? They're scattered all throughout this marsh. Can't get around them. They'll fillet your feet and legs like a flounder. Slice right through the leather in your shoes. Bleed to death in no time. But the worst thing's the pluff mud. It's thick and it's deep. You'll sink to your waist real fast. The harder you struggle to get free, the deeper you'll get sucked in. And when the tide comes back in, you'll drown. The crabs'll pick your bones clean in a day's time. Not a soul will ever know what became of you."

He let his words hang, finishing the last of his smoke and pinching it out before sticking the butt in his shirt pocket.

"But you ain't gonna run, are you? Come on. Let's get on back. We got work to do."

As they started back toward the yard, Jack tried to start a conversation. He asked Raymond where he'd come from, about his folks, what kind of things he liked to do, if he had a girl. Jack talked on and on to his unresponsive passenger, asking questions, making a joke, trying to get a response, until the kid turned to him and gave him the same cold, hateful look he'd given him the evening the sheriff dragged him into his office.

"Judge says I gotta work for you. Ain't gotta be your goddamn friend. Stop talking at me."

Jack faced straight ahead, giving himself time to consider before responding. "Okay," he said. "No more talk then, Raymond."

The boy spun back around and flared at him, biting off words like bullets firing. "Name's not Raymond, goddamnit!"

"Sorry, son. What do you go by?"

The kid didn't even bother to look at him. Nor would he answer the question. The impassable marsh of silence lay between them once again and Jack inwardly cursed himself for his clumsiness. He drove the rest of the way back to the yard in silence.

When the sheriff stopped by that evening, he got out of his car and watched from the distance as Jack and the kid worked on the old boat together. Jack stood on the scaffolding running his sander on the fiberglass while the kid followed along behind him wiping off the sanding dust with a cloth and running a bare hand over the glass, checking for smoothness. All the other workers had gone for the day. The sheriff noticed that neither of them spoke. But they worked steadily and in unison and both appeared engrossed in their labors. After a while, the sheriff walked across the yard toward them. The boy saw him coming first and stopped working. Jack set his sander down on the scaffolding and climbed down, the boy behind him. The boy stepped back as the sheriff approached and resumed his head down posture.

"Evening, Jack. How'd it go today?"

"Fine, Hal. Got me a dependable worker here. Does what he's told. Pays attention to details. Don't talk much though, but we're working on that, ain't we, son?"

The boy glowered at him but said nothing.

The sheriff nodded and took another pair of handcuffs from his belt.

Jack frowned. "I wish you wouldn't, Hal."

The sheriff thought about it for a moment and then put the handcuffs back on his belt.

"All right. I reckon I won't. Kid eat today? He don't seem to approve of my table fare."

"Who would?" Jack laughed. "Yeah, he ate. Rafe went out and got sandwiches for everybody."

"Well, then I guess we better get on to the house," the sheriff said. "Come on boy, go on to the car."

The kid started toward the car, then paused, and looked down at his unshackled wrists. He turned slightly, as if to look back. Jack studied him, hoping for some small hint of acknowledgement. But the kid only looked back down at the ground, fell in beside the sheriff and walked back to the car.

CHAPTER 6

JACK MERKEL'S MARINA AND Boatyard was a riot of activity. The forklift snarled around the sunbaked yard. Rafe and one of his helpers took turns pounding with a hammer and chisel on a set of big, rust-frozen bolts. An old gasoline-powered generator that ran an air compressor roared so deafeningly that the boat painter operating it had to wear earplugs while sweeping one arm back and forth as he laid down another coat of pungent epoxy paint on the hull of the Hatteras yacht. On the other side of the yard, Jack and the boy sanded fiberglass on the damaged sailboat. Periodically, the noise would become too much for Pogy who would tilt back his block head and bay.

The kid had been working for almost a week and Jack still didn't know what to call him. He'd made it plain that it wasn't Raymond. So, when Jack talked to him or told him to do things, he made a point

not to use any form name. He'd slipped once and called the kid "son."
The kid stopped and gave him a look as bitter as vinegar.

"I ain't your son, old man!"

"No, you ain't," Jack said quietly and with practiced patience. "But I still don't know what to call you and you won't tell me."

The boy stared insolently for a moment then picked up his sander and went back to work as if the exchange between the two of them had never happened.

The noise in the boatyard sometimes got so loud that even Rafe's loud, shrill whistles to get someone's attention couldn't overcome the racket. Two summers past, a dock worker got his hand smashed between a concrete piling and a large boat when he didn't hear a shouted warning. Jack had driven him to the emergency room and, after taking the man home with his hand bandaged, he went out and bought air horns. That same afternoon, he assembled all his employees, gave them each an air horn to carry on their work belt and impressed upon them not to hesitate to blast their horn if they saw a dangerous situation unfolding. Better that everyone should be startled and stop all activity than for someone else to be injured or worse.

The weather disturbance that forecasters had been watching in the Eastern Atlantic had mushroomed into a large tropical storm. Predictions were that it would continue to grow in intensity and size and become the season's second hurricane. The first one, named Abel, died an early death in the Gulf of Mexico two weeks earlier, less than twenty-four hours after its name day. It also failed to live up to breathless expectations that the gods of wind and sea would resuscitate it and send it plowing toward Mexico's Yucatan Peninsula. But Rafe, who was born and raised on the hurricane-ravaged Yucatan, was increasingly fretful about this one. Over the cups of coffee the two men shared on the front porch each morning, he told Jack that his gut was telling him not to ignore Tropical Storm Brenda.

"Have you seen the size of her, *jefe*?" he said for the second time that morning. "Everything's lining up just right—barometric pressure, water temperature, atmospheric conditions, steering currents. I think we gotta plan ahead for this one. I really do. The course she's on is aiming her right at us."

Jack lit a cigarette and contemplated for a moment. "Well, it's still a week out. Dontcha think we have at least another day or so to bide our time and just monitor the thing before we start worrying too much?"

"No," Rafe said. "We don't. This thing's coming. I feel it in my bones. Gonna be one big bitch kitty of a storm by the time it crosses the ocean. We're gonna start feeling its claws long before it gets close to here."

Jack knew that his foreman's history with hurricanes made him jumpy. If it had been anyone else, he would've dismissed the warning as premature. But the Hernandez family had been uprooted and dispossessed three times when Rafe was a boy. The last time, they gave up and moved inland. It was hard to ignore his concerns when he was so adamant.

Part of the reason Rafe had such a deep friendship with his employer was because neither one of them tended much toward superfluous talk. They bantered a bit among themselves and their employees, but for the most part, both men tended toward circumspection. As a result, both had learned over the years, as well as had those who knew the two old salts, that when one of them eventually did edge his way around to making pronouncements, the other one usually got onboard.

Jack recollected a certain tropical storm that had kissed the island on the lips as it had passed through a few summers back. Nearly everyone, including smiling, airbrushed local television weather forecasters, had dismissed it and said the little tropical storm would pass comfortably seaward if it survived long enough to reach them. Even the robotic recorded voice of the National Weather Service radio alert had downplayed it. But Rafe had insisted that the storm would hit them and probably on the high tide. Jack yielded to his warnings and had ordered his employees to prepare the marina for a storm.

And strike it did. Fortunately, it was a glancing blow instead of a head-on wallop. Even then, there had been severe flooding, leaving the island without power for two days off and on. Boats in the much bigger and wide-open city marina downtown had been damaged enough that the owners had to file insurance claims. But Merkel's Marina rode it out without anything more threatening than seawater cresting the tops of the seawall and a bunch of debris that had taken the better part of a day to pile up. The only thing that had altered the dire outcome Rafe had predicted was that the storm arrived on the low tide.

Now Jack yielded to his friend's concerns about Brenda. "So what's your game plan, buddy? Spit it out. You got my attention."

"I knew you'd come around," Rafe teased. "Okay, first things first. We gotta finish painting Bo Riddle's Hatteras today. That painter is fast. Already got one good coat on. He gets the next one on today, the paint'll be cured out enough that Bo can come pick her up day after tomorrow. That'll free up a bunch of space we'll need back there to start tie downs. Meanwhile, we've got two or three other projects we can knock out today if we hustle. I've got enough help to do that and you and that asshole kid can finish sanding that fiberglass patch on your boat. I'm glad you never got around to putting the mast on it."

Jack considered this last and nodded. "Yeah, me too, *amigo*. I'll want to make sure she's strapped down and secure and it'll be all that much easier to do if we don't have a forty-five-foot mast poking up to get knocked cattywampus by high winds and tearing a big hole in the boat if she gets dismasted. Okay. Summon the troops and let's give them their battle plan. Overtime today for anyone who wants it if we can't get it all done before quittin' time."

It was 102 degrees in the marina by lunchtime. Rafe blew his horn and stopped all work and told everyone to head into the shop, cool off, grab a bite to eat and get back to it. It was loud and hectic. By mid-afternoon tempers and patience were frazzled. Jack was just about to call for a fifteen-minute break when an air horn blasted. He spun around just in time to see the kid walk into the path of the forklift. He was in the blind spot; Eddie, the driver, couldn't see him. The air horn blast startled the driver enough that he shifted into neutral, but his foot didn't make it to the brake in time. Shuffling along in his customary head-down posture while heading off to the shed for more sandpaper, the oblivious kid didn't see the forklift or look up when Rafe screamed, "Hey kid!"

The left fork knocked him to the ground and the panicky driver managed to lock the brakes just before a massive tire could crush the kid, sprawled face-down just inches away.

For the first time that anyone could recall, Jack lost all semblance of his legendary self-control as he ran roaring across the yard.

"Goddammit! Eddie, back off now! Hey, kid, are you okay? Talk to me, damn it!"

The huge forks cleared the boy who was sprawled on the lime rock, and Jack rushed to his side and pulled him to his feet. Blood poured from a cut on the kid's chin, but he seemed otherwise unhurt. Jack took him by his arms. Eddie leaned over and vomited when he saw how close he'd come to crushing his coworker. Rafe helped Eddie down from the lift and led him, frightened and shaking, into the shop. Everyone else stood there, no one knowing what to do next. The ensuing hush stretched out seemingly without end, crawling by in the grim cadence of a funeral procession, in which it had nearly resulted.

The kid wrenched himself loose from Jack's grip and bolted toward a nearby outbuilding where there was a restroom. Before Jack took the first step to run after him, he realized that he needed some time to regain his own composure. He looked up and saw all his employees still standing motionless, all eyes upon him. He took a few deep breaths, lifted his hand and summoned them to gather around. The last to join the group were Rafe and Eddie, who sipped on a soft drink.

"You okay, buddy?" Jack asked a still trembling Eddie Kraft.

"Y-Yeah. A little sk-skeered, that's all."

"We're all a little scared right now, Eddie," he said, smiling weakly. "Anyone here not a little scared right now?" He studied the faces of his crew. "It's okay. Every one of y'all did exactly what you were supposed to do."

There was angry murmuring toward the rear of the group. Jack looked around to see where it was coming from.

"Neal, you got something you want to say?"

The man scratched his scruffy red beard and spat, his face flushed with irritation. He had a gruff, loud voice and it always sounded like he was yelling when he spoke.

"That asshole kid's gonna have to learn how to pay attention and communicate, boss. This is bullshit. He cain't just walk around this place with his chin on his chest and his brain gone off to East Jesus somewhere. What if poor Eddie there had run him over? Huh? How'd you like to live with that?"

Neal Basemore was as ill-tempered as the old tomcat that stalked the premises. Not an ambitious man, he never aspired to foreman duties, but he was good at his job, detail oriented and the go-to guy when Rafe or Jack weren't available. His weakness was that once you got on his bad side, it was hard to get paroled. Rafe joked that Neal's good side occurred about as often as a solar eclipse.

"Well, Eddie didn't run over him, Neal," Jack finally said. "Who blew the air horn, by the way?"

Neal jabbed a dirty thumb into his own chest. "I did, by God and just in the nick of time. If Eddie—"

Jack raised his palm and silenced him. "You done good, Neal. Now let it go. It's over. This was a good lesson for all of us about keeping our heads on swivels, me included. Everybody take fifteen and then back at it, okay?"

The group started breaking up, but Eddie hung back. Jack had a soft spot in his heart for Eddie Kraft, the shy, prematurely bald young man who sometimes stuttered when he was excited. Eddie was the youngest of seven children and had been a stud linebacker in high school. By the time he was a junior, coaches and college scouts from all over the country were jostling each other at games for a look at Eddie's moves. To everyone's shock, he signed with Appalachian State because he'd fallen in love with the mountains on a Boy Scout camping trip when he was younger. Eddie put his little college on the map his freshman year. A sweet-natured lad off the field, he was a swift footed assassin on it and broke college records for quarterback sacks as a starter. The NFL had its eye on him by his second season. And then in a tight game against Georgia Southern, Eddie suffered a concussion so severe he was never able to play again. Suddenly, he was just another poor black kid from a small North Florida town, and the sport he loved, as well as the college he loved more, went on without him. But Eddie also loved boats and he loved offshore fishing. He'd been working for Jack since he left college, saving his money up for a fishing boat of his own and studying for his captain's license. He'd bragged to Jack earlier that week he would be taking his test in three months and if he passed, his oldest brother, a dentist in Atlanta, was going to help him buy his first boat and set him up in his own charter fishing business.

Eddie waited until all the other men had gone off to the shop on their break before approaching Jack.

"That k-kid gonna be okay, J-Jack?" he asked earnestly. "Looked like his chin was cut b-b-bad."

Jack put his arm around Eddie's shoulder and turned him toward the outbuilding where the boy was still holed up.

"It's not a bad cut, just bled a lot," he said. "Come on, let's you and me go check on him."

The two of them walked across the yard and onto the wood planks of the covered porch of the little pastel blue building that was a bathroom on one side and a place for boaters to wash clothes on the other side. Jack put his hand on the bathroom door and pushed, but it didn't budge. When he tried to turn the brass doorknob, he realized the door was locked from the inside. And then he heard the muffled sobs. Backing away from the door as quietly as he could, he glanced at Eddie, hoping that he'd not heard the boy crying. Eddie's wide-eyed gaze and open mouth gave him away. Jack put his finger to his lips and pointed to the yard. The two of them stopped when they were far enough away from the building that Jack reckoned they could talk without being overheard.

"That b-boy's crying in there, ain't he?" Eddie said. "He's had a b-bad life. He t-tries to act hard but he ain't. He's skeered, just like I was when they said I c-couldn't play b-ball anymore. Didn't know what I'd do. I was a-sh-shamed. He is, too."

Jack was moved by the empathy Eddie had for a stranger who'd been nothing but rude to him. He put his arm around his shoulder again and pulled him close. The mid-afternoon sun scowled hotly down on them and Eddie's head glistened with sweat. The two of them stood silent for a moment, feeling the sun's intensity and the frigid aftershocks of a tragedy narrowly averted. Jack wished there were more Eddie Krafts in the world.

"You still helping young boys out in your neighborhood who think they might want to play football?"

He removed his arm from the man's shoulders and reached for his cigarettes.

Eddie smiled, bent over, picked up a chunk of lime rock and sailed it out over the water. A seagull chased after it thinking it was something to eat and reeled away screaming in frustration just before it hit with a wet plunk.

"Yeah," he said, "Couple of them g-got talent. Most of 'em just n-need a big b-brother."

A klaxon horn suddenly began its strident, repetitious yonking. Jack and Eddie turned and looked back toward the highway and saw the dark span of the drawbridge rising. On the other side of the bridge, a sailboat backed water and waited clearance to pass. About that time, the handheld marine radio on Jack's waist crackled. He pulled it from his belt and turned up the volume.

"Merkel's Marina, Merkel's Marina," a woman's clear voice hailed them. "This is sailing vessel *Starshine* requesting docking permission. Over."

"Sailing vessel *Starshine*," he answered. "This is Merkel's Marina. Go to channel nineteen for docking instructions, Captain."

"Roger," the sailboat captain said.

Jack glanced up and saw his crew hustling out of the shack toward the docks. Each of them wore their own handheld radio and heard the captain's hailing.

"*Starshine*, this is Merkel's Marina," Merkel said into his radio. "What's your vessel's length and draft, Captain?"

"Merkel's Marina, this is *Starshine*," a breezy voice replied. "Length overall forty feet, draft five feet. Are we a go?"

He pressed the talk button and smiled, waving his crew toward a dock farther down.

"That's a go, Captain. Come into the channel, bear to starboard and make your way to G Dock. Crew will be waiting there for you."

A moment later, all forty feet of the custom-made luxury sailboat glided into view. The long, sleek hull shimmered in the sun, as white as a new tooth. The weather decks were a sand color to keep down the glare in the cockpit.

"Holy shit, that's a house!" Jack heard one of his men exclaim as they sprinted by on their way to the dock to await the boat's arrival.

"That ain't no house, boys," Rafe said. "That's a damn *hacienda*."

Jack's binoculars were around his neck. He raised the lenses to his eyes and swept the deck of the big cruiser from stem to stern noting and admiring the precise tautness of the lifelines, the meticulously maintained, glittering stainless steel standing rigging, and the fact that there didn't appear to be a single dirty spot on the entire vessel. When his eyes came to the cockpit, he saw the woman who had the helm. He could see two boys aboard, one in the cockpit talking with the captain and the other one checking lines to port. Then he realized the kid still hadn't come back from the bathroom and he started to worry.

"Rafe, ya'll go ahead and get *Starshine* all tucked in," he said into his radio. "I'll join y'all in a minute to greet the captain, but I need to go check on the kid first. He's still in the head."

Rafe keyed the microphone twice in acknowledgment. Jack started back for the bathroom building, returning his radio to his belt as he walked. The bathroom door was still locked but he didn't hear any sounds from inside. He rapped lightly on the door with his knuckles. "Hey! You fall in and get stuck?"

He waited a moment for a reply, and when none was forthcoming, he knocked on the door again, more insistent this time. "Hey, in there. You're scaring us out here! You okay?"

He was just about to call out again when the kid answered. His voice was thick. The antagonism was still there but lacking its knife edge. "I'm fine, old man. Just give me another minute, will ya?"

Jack sucked in a deep breath and let it out slowly, relieved. He had started to worry that the kid had locked the door, climbed out the rear window and run, even though he shouldn't have been able to get by without someone seeing him. Plus, Pogy usually barked and chased after anything running.

"Okay, take your time. Come on down to the end of G Dock when you're done. There's a boat just come in you'll really want to see. We'll be down there helping the skipper get her secure."

Jack went out to meet his newest guest. By the time he got there, his crew had the yacht secured, dock lines neatly coiled and shore power and water connected. The boat's big diesel engine thrummed evenly. The captain cut the power just as Jack arrived. An attractive woman with the sun-burnished look of a seasoned sailor stepped lightly off the boat. He reckoned her to be in her mid-forties. She had green eyes, auburn hair cut short, and a wide, sensuous mouth.

She wore khaki shorts and a cotton white blouse over her athletic figure, a Baltimore Orioles baseball cap and faded blue canvas deck shoes. She strode confidently over to Jack and extended her hand, flashing a bright smile.

"Mr. Merkel. Margie Waller. It's so good to meet you. I started checking with other boaters about marinas in the area and you come highly recommended. I believe I've got a wonky rudder here that needs attention."

"She's beautiful, Captain," he said, admiring the boat. "I've got you kind of squeezed in here. We don't often get yachts this size. I can make arrangements if you'd rather be downtown. It's much more in your class. This is pretty much just a working guy's marina, as you can tell."

The woman threw back her head and laughed, an audacious one that turned all the other men's eyes toward her.

"Oh, I'm quite done with the snooty-yachty types, Mr. Merkel. My ex-husband was one of those. This is my divorce present from him. The boys and I just brought her up from Freeport. We're off for Baltimore as soon as you get her fixed up. I really don't think it's anything serious. I've a hunch we might've snagged a crab pot somewhere along the way."

He leaned over the dock and examined the stern of the beamy vessel.

"I can put you in the slings and have a look. If that's all it is, I can probably have you on your way later today if you didn't damage anything badly. If you need any gear I don't carry while you're here, me or one of my guys can run you into town. There's a good marine supply store there."

The woman thanked him and turned around to confer with two teen-age boys standing in the cockpit. The oldest boy, a cheery looking lad, was tall and had his mother's auburn hair and green eyes. The younger one was shorter, with black hair, dark brown eyes and a pale complexion. The expression on his face suggested moneyed arrogance.

Jack had gone about halfway down the length of the dock on his way back to the shop when his radio crackled. He started to key the mike in acknowledgment just as Eddie's anxious voice broke in.

"Th-th-that boy's running!"

Then he heard Pogy's insistent barking and looked up just in time to see the kid sprinting headlong up the causeway toward the road. Pumping his fists furiously and with his head thrown back, he raced along the causeway with the determination and intensity of an Olympic runner.

"Damn it!" Jack said, feeling a hard knot form in his guts as he realized that the kid might make it to the road after all. "Damn it! Pogy, go!" he shouted at the dog. "Go get him!"

Barking fiercely, the dog darted across the yard behind the kid with the explosive quickness and agility of a deer.

Jack knew the dog wouldn't hurt the kid, but the kid didn't know that. Pogy would catch up with him and head him off with an aggressive display of ferocious barking, growling and posturing. The kid was afraid of the big Dane anyway, so Jack was confident he'd stop running once the dog caught him. About that time his radio sounded again. This time it was Rafe.

"Need a hand, Jack?"

"No thanks, Rafe. I can take care of this by myself. A show of force'll just make it worse. Ya'll take care of Captain Waller."

"Okay. Yell if you need me. I'll keep my eye on you and come running if he gets nasty."

Jack dashed up the gangway to the yard and jumped into the golf cart, wheeled it around and sped along the causeway. Heart pounding, he watched Pogy run the boy down and spin around to confront him. He lunged at the boy snarling and snapping as if he meant to maul him. Panting and out of breath, the kid leaned over and put his hands on his knees, looking wild-eyed from side to side for another avenue of escape.

"Don't run, boy!" Jack bellowed, as a sudden fear settled into him that Pogy might actually attack the boy. "Please, don't do it. He'll get you this time. Off, Pogy! Leave it!" he shouted at the dog, which immediately ceased its attack, its job done.

The kid sat down in the middle of the road, leaned over, put his hands over his face and began screaming, a long, loud wail that carried out over the silent marsh like a wounded and cornered wild animal. Jack slammed on the brakes and ran to the kid, who continued to howl as Jack stooped down beside him. The kid's face and hands were covered with blood and the front of his shirt was red stained as well. Jack grabbed his hands and tried to pull them away from his face. The kid tried to wrench away and swung his head from side to side, slinging blood and saliva all over Merkel.

"Stop it," Jack said firmly, grabbing his shoulders and giving him a shake. "Stop it right now. You hear me? Just stop it."

The kid stopped screaming and began babbling incoherently. Jack relaxed his grip on his shoulders and looked at his face. Blood still poured from the cut on his chin, which was bigger than Jack had first thought. He clearly needed medical attention. Stricken with sudden pity, Jack tried to pull the kid closer.

"Lemme go! Lemme go! Lemme go!" the kid screamed in his face, flailing and spitting at him. "Lemme go, goddamnit, you old sonofabitch! Lemme go!"

Jack refused, continuing to hold onto him, speaking quietly as he urged him to calm down. After a few minutes, the storm blew itself out. Panting with exhaustion and spent fury, the kid went limp and Jack slowly released him. He reached under the kid's chin and lifted it, took note of the welling cut, pulled his bandana out of his hip pocket, pressed it to the wound and drew the boy to his feet.

"Hold it there and get in the cart. We need to get you back up to the shop and get this cleaned up."

"Is it bad?" the kid said, sounding now like a frightened child.

"Won't know 'til we clean it up some," Jack said, wheeling the cart around and heading back toward the marina. "No, don't let the pressure off it or it'll just keep bleeding."

They rode in silence back to the shop with Pogy bounding along beside them, barking playfully and occasionally running around them. By the time they got back, the work of the day was continuing under Rafe's supervision. He keyed his microphone three times in succession, their code for "Is everything okay?" Jack keyed his once in return for yes. The kid sat at the long table where the crew ate their lunch and stared blankly out the open door. Jack went and got a small first aid kit and set it on the table, then went to the sink and wet a clean rag with warm water. Blood and snot had dried all over the kid's face. When Jack started to wipe the boy's face, he reached up and tried to take the cloth from him. Jack pushed his hand away.

"Leave it alone and keep pressure on that chin 'til I get this mess cleaned up so I can see how bad it is."

The kid looked everywhere but at Jack. When he'd finished cleaning the kid's face, Jack opened a sterile gauze pad and poured hydrogen peroxide on it.

"Okay. Move your hand now. This might sting a bit, but I need to get a look at that cut. Looks like the bleeding's about stopped."

The kid eased his hand away from the wound and Jack cleaned around the edges of it. The boy winced and grunted when Jack got too close to one edge. After he was done inspecting and cleaning the injury, he put a fresh cotton gauze pad on it and taped it down. Then he went to the uniform locker and got a fresh shirt and returned to the table.

"That one's soaked with blood. Take it off and put this one on. I'll be right back."

He disappeared into his office and left the boy. Alone, the kid stood and slowly removed the soiled and blood-soaked shirt and put on the new one. He thought about making another run for it but noticed Pogy sitting and watching. "I hate you, you fuckin' mutt," he cursed, going to the sink and washing off the caked blood on his hands and forearms. When Jack came back, he had a Coca-Cola in one hand and his car keys in the other.

"Come on," he said, abruptly. "Go get in the car."

Jack walked out to his Jeep and got in. The boy followed but stopped beside the car and stood looking at him. He handed the boy the bottle. "Come on. Get in. Let's go."

The kid just turned his face to the window and stared out at the marsh.

"You taking me back to jail?" the kid mumbled.

Jack let the question hang like a low storm cloud for a moment.

"What do you think? You ran. I guaranteed them you wouldn't. You heard the judge."

"I don't wanna go back to jail. I won't do it again."

Jack looked over at the boy and shook his head slowly.

"No, I ain't takin' you to jail, kid. Going to the emergency room. That cut needs stitches."

They were pulling into the hospital parking lot when the boy spoke again.

"It's Doug," he said, still looking out the window.

Jack eased the Jeep into a parking space, turned off the engine and looked over at him. "What?"

The kid shifted around in the seat, looked at Jack as if seeing him for the first time and deciding to give him a chance.

"Doug," he repeated, calmly. "My name's Doug. That's what I prefer to be called."

CHAPTER 7

JACK DIDN'T KNOW WHICH was worse the next morning, the thunder rumbling in the distance, the pelting rain, or what they'd discovered when Rafe hoisted Margie Waller's sailboat from the water.

The vessel's captain had been correct when speculating that she'd snagged a crab pot line, but she couldn't have been more wrong in her assessment that the results were probably nothing serious. She waited with her sons at the rear of the boat and silently watched Jack examine the stricken rudder. Staring at a deep gouge in it, he wiped his face as seawater gushed out and splattered on the ground. Margie Waller clenched her jaw and winced.

"I'm sorry, Captain," Jack said. "This ain't good. That's why her steering felt sluggish. Rudder's full of water and I suspect the tang's damaged. Rudder's ruined. I can't fix this. We're gonna have to get with the factory and order a new one."

"Order a new one?" she said, her voice rising. She stepped closer to him, stiffening, narrowing her eyes and jutting out her chin. "Everyone I talked with on the way in said you can fix anything. What, just because I'm a woman and not some good-old-boy—"

He put both of his hands up and cut her off. "That's got nothing to do with it, Miz Waller."

She stepped even closer, almost touching him. Jack flinched.

"Don't patronize me, goddamnit. I'm forty-five, not four or five."

Jack eased back and took a deep breath. "I'm sorry if it came across that way. It wasn't intended. And I'm not trying to take advantage of a woman. Besides, I'm guessing you know enough about sailboats not to be so easily fooled anyway. Now, can we please start over?"

Margie's oldest son put his hand on her shoulder and spoke quietly to her. "Mom, please let him finish. I don't believe he's trying to pull anything on you." The youngest boy laughed.

"Fine," the woman said. "But don't play any games with me, okay? And let's cut the Miz and Mister crap. It sounds phony. I'd prefer we all be on a first-name basis if we're going to do business."

"Suits me," Jack said, knowing that Eddie Kraft would struggle with calling a female customer by her first name. "Now, can we please just start all over?"

The woman took her son's hand off her shoulder and stepped back a bit. "Well, okay. But please, no razzle-dazzle, okay? Just stick to the facts."

"Okay, see this?" He handed her a nearly two-foot-long piece of black rope crusted with barnacles. "Heavy nylon line with a metal core. Some crabbers use it because it keeps the traps down better. But they're bad news when they get fouled in a rudder or prop."

She turned the rope in her hands and examined it, and then handed it to her oldest son.

"This line snared your rudder and you dragged the whole rig along, trap and all, until the weight of all that drag caused the line to gnaw into your rudder. Good thing the line's old and the metal finally gave or it might've sawed through your whole rudder. It's a miracle it didn't get your prop, too."

While they were talking, Sheriff Patterson drove up, got out of his car and let his prisoner out of the back seat. Doug Eleazer wore his marina uniform instead of the orange jailhouse jumpsuit. Jack was relieved for the boy's sake. He smiled and gave the sheriff a friendly nod. "Morning, Hal . . . Doug," he said. "Come on over here and have a look at this."

The sheriff shook his head. "Sorry, folks. I got a passel of work to do today and this weather ain't making it any easier. See you at quittin' time, kid."

Doug watched the sheriff waddle back to his car, then looked at Jack and rolled his eyes. Jack laughed.

"I think the sheriff's taking a shine to you, Doug. That's the nicest thing he's called you yet. Come on over here. You remember Margie Waller from yesterday? This is Doug, skipper. He just started working for me this week. The sheriff gives him a ride to work every morning."

Her anger abating, the woman gave Doug a wide, toothy smile, looked him in the eyes and stuck out her hand, gave a firm shake, and looked closely at the bandage on his face. "How's your chin today? Your boss says you took quite the spill."

She pointed to a thin, pink scar on her wrist. "See this? Sliced it wide open cutting up a pineapple. Hurt like stink, too."

She smiled at him again. "We've all got scars of one kind or another," she said. "*Character references* I call them."

"Yes ma'am," he said, looking away. "I reckon my face'll look a wreck."

She touched him lightly on the arm. "Your face is just fine. You'll just look more rugged. Like Mr. Merkel here." Then, to her sons, "These are my boys. Seth here is about your age, I'm guessing. John's fifteen. Boys, where are your manners?"

The older boy stepped forward, smiled and shook Doug's hand. "Hey, Doug," he said, brightly. "Sorry about your accident, man. Ouch!"

The younger boy sneered and muttered under his breath. Margie's face reddened as she glowered at her younger son. "Excuse me a moment, gents," she said through her clenched, perfectly white teeth as she seized the boy by his arm and hauled him a short distance away.

Eddie walked up and tossed Doug a yellow rain slicker. He caught it, shrugged into it and nodded at his co-worker.

"Pardon the interruption," Margie said, returning to the group and leaving her son to stew alone. "I'm sorry. John's being an ass." She looked at Doug and cocked her thumb over her shoulder. "Don't take it personally. I'll sort this out later."

She looked at her watch and then at Jack. "Okay, so, please explain why you can't fix this instead of ordering a new one?"

He put his hand on the rudder with its ragged gash. "Here, let me show you something."

He stuck two fingers into the hole, from which the flow of water was finally starting to slow, and pulled out a sodden, whitish blob between his thumb and forefinger."

She took it from him, rolled it between her slender fingers for a few moments and then wrinkled her nose.

"Ugh! It feels and looks like soggy styrofoam."

"You're pretty close," he said. "It's the foam core of your rudder. Put your fingers in there and poke around. That's it. The outer part that you see is fiberglass. But the inside is a type of foam. Sandwiched inside the foam is a metal framework, the tang. The foam soaked up water like a sponge. It's deep damage. I can actually feel the tang and I suspect it's compromised."

Doug looked at his boss and cocked his head to the side. "Waterlogged, like an old surfboard?"

It was the first time that the troubled teen had shown a smidgen of interest in anything. It was a milestone and Jack inwardly prayed that it wouldn't be the last.

"Exactly," Jack said. "And what usually happens after that?"

"Eventually it delaminates," Doug replied. "Fiberglass separates from the foam. Can't fix that."

Seth broke into a wide grin and gave him an admiring look. "Cool! You a surfer, dude? I'd love to learn to surf."

"Naw," Doug said timidly, looking to Jack for approval. "Ain't ever been on a surfboard, but I worked a few weeks last summer for an old dude that made 'em and fixed 'em, and he showed me. The foam gets rotten. A good whack and it snaps."

Jack smiled and held out his hand, palm up. Doug slapped palms with him and smiled back at him.

"Doug's right. If it was a little water and I wasn't worried about the tang, I'd risk draining it, let it dry out real good and then repairing it. But your rudder's waterlogged. I'm real sorry, Margie, but I'm just not gonna be responsible for a gimmick job like that."

He suspected she was a competent skipper who knew enough about boats and sailing that she didn't fear crossing the ocean with two kids as her only crew. He also surmised that, like most boat owners, Margie didn't know everything about her boat. He'd seen it many times. One skipper might be able to recite the bible of rigging from back to front but might struggle with chart plotting. Another skipper might be able to work a chart like Magellan but not understand something as critical as the electrical wiring. Some were woefully ignorant about foam and fiberglass. Some of them were a hard sell, and that often meant scaring them with the facts. He suspected that Margie Waller was such a captain. She'd been with a prideful, wealthy yacht owner long enough that even though she admittedly didn't care to live that life anymore, some of the egotism had rubbed off on her. He braced for her continued skepticism.

"So, what's the worst that could happen if you just did a quickie fix and sent me on my way to Baltimore?" she said. "It isn't that far."

"You could run into heavy seas off Cape Hatteras strong enough to stress it so bad that you might experience catastrophic rudder failure, lose steering, flounder, take on water and sink," he said. "I'm not going to take that chance. Sorry."

"But how do you know for sure the tang's damaged?" she said.

"The only way to be certain is to take the rudder apart, and then we'd have to replace it, anyway. Look, call the company, ask for technical support. See what they tell you. I'm pretty sure I know but you need to hear it from them. I'll be in the office in the meantime. Eddie, Doug, come with me. Rafe, stay here in case Margie needs something. Leave the boat in the slings for now."

Rafe watched Jack and the others stride off across the yard toward the main building. Margie glared at them as they walked away and then directed her irritation at Rafe. "Well, don't just stand there, Mr. Fernandez. Get me that number."

"It's *Hernandez*, ma'am, not Fernandez," he said mildly. "But that's okay. It's easy to make the mistake. And please, call me Rafe. Do you have the paperwork and owner's manual for the boat?"

She gaped at him with obstinacy. "Well, of course I do. It's in a big envelope in the stateroom. Why?"

"The owner's manual will have the toll-free number for the company. The problem right now is, your boat's up there and we're down here. I can't send you up there to get it because we'd be all kinds of liable if you fell and got hurt. But, if you can tell me exactly where it is, I'll go get it myself. Are you okay with that?"

She exchanged a glance with her eldest son, who calmly took charge from his exasperated mother.

"It's okay, mom. I've got this." And then to Rafe, "In the stateroom there's a built-in safe above the settee on the starboard side. The combination is—"

"Seth!"

"Mom, calm down. The combination is three right, nine left and four right. It's a red packet with a flap. The owner's manual is in it."

Rafe smiled at the boy and politely addressed the woman, who was looking off to the side. "Tell you what," he said. "I'll punch the number into my cell phone and when I come back you can call them on my phone. I'll stand off to the side and give you some privacy."

Then Rafe excused himself and climbed a ladder aboard. Back moments later, he handed the waiting captain his phone. He waited in silence with the rain driving down so hard on his hooded slicker he could hardly hear while the woman had a brief telephone conversation. He only heard the last part of it.

"I see," she said, curtly. "Thank you very much."

She handed Rafe his phone.

"It seems as if I need a new rudder," she said without preamble and then gnawed her bottom lip for a moment. "I also have apologies to make. I've been a bit of a bitch, I'm afraid. Now, if you'll excuse me, I need to go attend some urgent business with Mr. Personality."

The rain hung on with tenacity until early afternoon. The sun's tardy appearance brought no relief. When it finally seared away the last of the soggy wet clouds and turned its scorching wrath on the yard, steam rose in thin white wisps from the wet lime rock and shallow puddles. Within minutes, the heat and humidity combined felt intense enough to steam clams.

All work had ceased in the yard for most of the morning due to a band of violent thunderstorms rumbling their way through. Lightning strikes came so close that they cracked like limbs snapping, leaving the acrid smell of scorched ozone in the air.

Margie stood on the marina office's porch watching the primal display of nature in extremis and fretting about her yacht being singled out by an errant bolt. When he noticed her standing outside with a worried expression, Jack went out to investigate.

"I know that sailboats are generally pretty safe from lightning strikes on the water because they're grounded through the mast and hull," she said, flinching at a sudden window-rattling burst. "But it's sitting up here high and dry on that steel cradle you put it on after you took it off the lift and it's a sitting duck. This lightning's scary."

"I make sure we ground any boats we put on the yard. It's rare for anyone's boat to get hit here. Hasn't happened in ages and we get these storms all the time."

When the storm cleared, Jack ordered his employees back to work. He chose Rafe, Neal and Doug to help remove the stricken rudder. Within a few minutes, their work clothes were drenched in the pitiless heat and humidity. Margie had changed into a pair of faded denim shorts and a paint-stained T-shirt and insisted on helping. Jack argued against it because of liability concerns, but she marched off to his office, handwrote a liability waiver on a sheet of printer paper, signed it and then brought it back for him to sign and Rafe to witness.

The job proved to be a little more difficult than Jack thought. After some degree of laboring and cussing in the skull-popping heat, they had the rudder safely off. Margie mopped the sweat off her face with a shop rag.

"So, what's next?" she said, impatiently. "How long before I get a new rudder on here?"

Jack cleaned his hands with mineral spirits and wiped them on his trousers and then lit a cigarette.

"The factory guy said they can fabricate one. I'm sure they have the dimensions for it stored in a database for this boat, but I think we should ship them this particular rudder just to be on the safe side. One degree of design variation could make a difference."

Margie ran a grimy hand through her hair, smearing it with dirt and sweat. "How long will that take? I was hoping to be in Baltimore before the week's out. I have to take care of my aunt's estate and get Seth ready for college in Virginia."

Jack looked at Rafe and then at Doug, who'd suddenly discovered his feet again. "Turnaround time and installation could be nearly two weeks. But there could be another problem that keeps you here awhile."

"What now?"

"Tropical Storm Brenda, which is expected to become a hurricane."

"And a really big one," Rafe added. "And I think we're gonna get a piece of it, if not all of it."

Margie exhaled loudly, then turned and stared for a long time at the surrounding marsh, which shone in the afternoon sunshine as green as an exquisitely cut emerald. A long flock of brown pelicans flew over low and slow in a perfect V formation. A small group of fishermen, who'd braved the morning's belligerent weather laughed, drank their beers and jostled one another over some shared hilarity while they dressed a mess of fish at the cleaning station. The local tugboat captain sounded the horn of his fire-engine-red boat as he swung back toward his yard shoving an empty barge. As was his custom, Jack lifted his arm and waved. A pair of ospreys keened loudly as they wheeled overhead. Margie took it all in and finally turned back to Jack and smiled.

"A body could fall in love with this place," she said.

He smiled back. "Some of us already have. If it was a gal, I'd marry her."

She studied him with eyes that penetrated his carefully tended poker-faced mask. It dawned on her that there was something about the reticent marina owner that intrigued her. He wasn't wealthy— or if he was, he hadn't noticed. He didn't dress like a count or take women waltzing at formal balls. He was rough cut, with the calloused and weather-worn hands of a seafaring man, a man who lived as comfortably within his skin as a wild creature. But she sensed there was also something profoundly wholesome and principled about him, a quality she could almost reach out and touch.

"I'll bet you would, too," she said and deftly shifted her attention to Rafe. "So, tell me about this huffy broad named Brenda that's got you twisted in knots, Mr. Man. Kind of early for such dire prognostications, isn't it?"

"I know hurricanes, *Senora*." he said. "My life, it has been shaped by them."

And then he told her his story, about his family's desperate life on the Yucatan Peninsula, the wrath of hurricanes so terrible that they wiped little towns as clean as newly minted coins, and how his family and others whose husbands, fathers, sons and brothers made their living upon the cobalt-blue back of the Gulf of Mexico struggled to beat the odds in a game they were too poor and too unlucky to play.

She listened in gaping amazement. When he was done, her gaze returned to the marsh and the river. The tide was out and the air was infused with the fecund aroma of pluff mud. A passing cloud momentarily hid the sun's scalding stare and the faintest stirring of breeze ruffled her auburn hair. Out of the corner of one eye, she saw Jack watching her. When she turned and looked full on at him, he gave her a crinkly smile. She took secret delight in noticing the dimples that gave his face a boyish quality despite his years.

"I've learned not to argue with Rafe when he's like this," Jack quipped. "He's part philosopher, part mystic and he's almost always right."

The three of them laughed together, Jack in his low chuckle, Rafe with a hearty guffaw that made him wheeze. And when Margie heard her own laughter, high and bright as the sun on polished brass, she realized that it'd been a long time since she'd allowed herself that simple comfort. She returned Jack's smile and was stricken by a tiptoeing awareness that she felt an attraction to him.

"So, no chance of me heading out for home for the time being, huh?" she said, quickly changing the subject.

"Not until that storm gets on out of the way," Jack said. "About the time we get that rudder back from the company it might well be on us. And even if it misses us, it might still be near enough that it'll be too unsafe to venture offshore."

She turned and pointed at the river.

"But if I went up the Intracoastal?"

"It'll be a zoo," Rafe said. "Every marina along the way's gonna be full up. You'd be hard pressed to find a sheltered place with good dockage for a boat this size."

"And if it does come here? What'll we do?"

"What everybody does when a hurricane comes," Jack said reaching for another cigarette. "Skedaddle or hunker down and pray. In the meantime, you can live aboard your boat here in the yard if you don't want to stay in a hotel. The steel cradle your boat's in is safe and sturdy. We'll put the stairs alongside her so you and your boys can get in and out easily."

When they resumed working on his boat, Jack stopped what he was doing and nudged Doug. "So, you've got a little experience with fiberglass work, huh? I didn't notice that on your résumé."

Doug put down his sander, removed his dust mask and looked expressionlessly at him for a moment. Then slowly, as measured as a wary fish approaching a baited hook, the faintest of smiles emerged. Jack held his breath, praying that what he thought was a smile really was and not just some hopeful contrivance of his imagination.

"You didn't leave enough space on the form, Pop," he said. "I mean, my résumé being so long and all."

Jack laughed at their shared joke, then tilted his head to one side and studied the boy's face. "Pop, is it?' he said. "That what you're gonna tag me with?"

Doug wiped dust off his face as his smile blossomed into a grin. "Reckon so. Nobody else calls you 'Mister Merkel' around here and it ain't easy for me to call an old person by his first name. And I know 'old man' ain't gonna cut it anymore."

Jack scratched the side of his face and swatted away a mosquito. "Pop," he said, a grin spreading across his worn features. "I like it. Pop it is, then."

When the sheriff came by to pick him up that evening and return him to the jail, Doug had already changed back into his jailhouse clothing. Jack handed the sheriff a clean uniform and the boots.

"I appreciate you letting the kid come dressed for work," he said. Just before he climbed into the back of the sheriff's car, Doug looked back at Jack and waved goodbye.

After they left, Jack put the tools away and was walking across the yard back toward the building when Margie stepped out of one of the shower cabanas wearing khaki shorts, a peach-colored blouse, sandals, and toweling her hair dry.

"Hey, Jack. Wait up a minute."

He gazed at her a little harder than he'd intended to and fumbled with his cigarettes while she came striding up. "Hey, what's up, Margie?"

She didn't stop until they were almost touching. He took a half-step back and looked across her shoulder at the river. It was slack tide. The sun was just beginning to set and its golden light was reflected on the lethargically moving water. She peered up at him and captured his eyes with hers. "Listen, I'm really sorry about being bitchy about my boat again this morning," she said, seizing both his knobby wrists in her petite hands. "Forgive me?"

Jack blinked at her sudden touch and glanced away shyly. "Well, if you were, I didn't notice so don't worry about it," he said, laughing suddenly and hoping that she hadn't noticed his discomfort.

"Thanks," she said, letting go of his wrists. "I want to stay on your good side."

The scent of her shampoo was exotic, almost feral. Again, she held his eyes as he stood there taking in the fragrance of her hair.

"Well, good night, Jack. Sweet dreams."

"Good night, Margie. Sleep well."

When he turned and walked toward the building that was home and office, she put one hand in her pants pockets and toyed with her hair with the other one, letting her eyes trail him across the yard. She didn't realize that she'd been watching him until he disappeared inside.

Later that evening, Jack sat outside on his deck admiring the stars and listening to the sounds of boys' laughter from the dry-docked boat while he sipped a beer and smoked. Again and again he revisited Doug's smile, now etched in his mind like scrimshaw. The conversation he'd had with Judge Kicklighter the day of their fishing trip came to mind, his reminder that one cannot fix every broken thing.

"Tell me I can't catch this fish, you ornery old bastard," he said, getting up and stretching the kinks out of his back before going inside. "Tell me I can't."

CHAPTER 8

JUDGE KICKLIGHTER TOOK A long swig of orange juice while the waiter poured Jack another cup of coffee. The door to the kitchen swung open as their waiter came along and set a steaming platter of fried eggs and bacon down on the next table. Nell left her place by the cash register and hustled to the kitchen and yelled at the cook staff to work faster.

"Hal Patterson says he believes our little project is working," the judge said, jumping right to the point. "Just two weeks into it, too. I think both you and Hal are getting your hopes too high too soon, but that's me. Tell me about it."

"Lemme finish my coffee first," Jack said. "But let's get out of here before we talk about it. Too damn noisy in here this morning."

The judge downed the rest of his orange juice. "Works for me. We can take a little walk and I'll have myself a cigar."

They stopped at the cash register and paid their tabs.

"You're putting on weight, Your Honor," Nell said, taking their money. "You need to lay off my biscuits awhile. Jack, honey, you need to eat more of them. You're as skinny as a snake these days."

The two men stepped out onto the sidewalk. It was shaping up to be another scorcher. Tropical Storm Brenda had mushroomed into a Category 3 hurricane, packing winds of 125 miles and tracking toward the vulnerable Windward Islands of the West Indies. The news was grim. The massive and fast-moving storm system was expected to gain strength, veer toward Haiti and the Dominican Republic and then turn northwest, toward the Florida coastline. They still had a few more days, hoping the storm would weaken as it crossed the mountains of the Dominican Republic.

"Could be some real shitty weather on the way from what I'm hearing," the judge said, lighting a cigar. "That's one big storm system, too. Looks like it'll swallow the whole damn Caribbean."

Jack tapped a cigarette out of its package and lit it.

"Yep, it's got Rafe sweating seawater and now he's got me started. Plus, I have a new tenant with an expensive yacht in the yard who's scared to death, and that ain't making things any easier."

They waited for the light to change and walked toward the harbor. Two shrimp boats were just shoving off from the docks, seagulls shrieking and wheeling about them, hoping for a handout. The captain of one of the boats, a longtime friend of Jack's who'd taught him the business after he'd gotten out of the Merchant Marine, saw him and the judge approaching the old wooden docks and hollered at them from the wheelhouse of his boat. Both men waved back at him. The darkly tanned, silver-haired old shrimper grinned, tooted his horn and swung the bow of his trawler around into the current. The nets swung from their outriggers, and strikers on both boats bustled about checking gear and lines.

"Old Harvey's made enough money to retire a hundred times over," the judge said as they watched the trawlers move off downriver.

"But I heard he made a bit of it catching square grouper and not shrimp. Ever heard that rumor?"

Jack shook his head in exasperation. "You've asked me that a dozen times, Harley. Answer's still no. Nell just likes juicy gossip."

"Uh-huh," Kicklighter said. "So Rafe's babysitting the boy this morning? I sure hope he minds his Ps and Qs while you're away."

"He will. Don't expect any trouble at all out of Doug. He's a good kid."

"Doug, huh? So that's what he goes by. What's he call you? I hope not some of the words I've heard coming from his mouth. That'd really piss me off."

Jack grinned. "*Pop*. He calls me Pop."

"And you're okay with that?"

"Suits me fine. Neal's called me worse a bunch of times."

"Hal tells me the boy tripped and nearly got run over by your forklift operator," the judge said. "Says he gashed his chin open so bad you had to take him to get stitches. And you paid for it out of your own pocket, too. Submit a bill to the court and I'll see to it that the clerk reimburses you. Fair's fair."

Jack spat on his fingers, pinched off the burning end of his cigarette and put the butt in his shirt pocket to dispose of later. "No. This is on me. I think my taking care of him like I did might've been what finally cracked the ice. It was on the way to the emergency room that he suddenly spoke up and said to call him Doug."

"Hasn't tried to run, has he?"

"Nope."

"Liar. Oh well, at least he didn't succeed. Hal says the kid really seems to like the arrangements. I can't believe you sweet-talked Hal into letting the boy put on a uniform before he leaves the jail every morning. But I have to admit, I think that was a smooth move on your part."

Jack gave him a sly smile.

"Kinda like the way you enticed that big ol' red fish. It's all a matter of bait and presentation."

"Don't go getting ahead of yourself, my friend. You might have a hook in him, but you haven't caught him yet. There's still a lot of water between you and him. You keep that in mind, you hear?'

"I reckon you won't let me forget it anytime soon. Doug's coming along, better than I thought he would at first. Works hard, pays attention, asks questions about things. He's good with his hands. He actually seems to be pretty smart."

The judge chugged on his cigar, blowing out a stream of spicy smelling smoke. He didn't say anything right away, and Jack could tell he was deep in thought, tugging back and forth between questions, answers and decisions. The judge watched a large motor yacht churning a wake in its path that drew the attention of a marine patrol officer in a small boat nearby. The water cop wheeled his boat around and dashed after the cruiser, his blue strobe lights flashing.

"Yeah, he's a pretty smart kid," the judge finally said. "That's what all the reports on him say at least."

The comment reminded Jack of something Sheriff Patterson had told him the day he dropped off the boy to go to work. He debated whether to bring it up, deciding there wasn't any downside. The judge would either talk about it or he wouldn't.

"Hal says there's a psychologist's report on Doug that's pretty heartbreaking."

"He did, did he? Sonofabitch. He knows better than that."

Jack chose his words carefully to avoid riling his friend. "He just told me he read it and it was a sad thing. If I'm going to try to be a mentor to this young man it might be helpful if I knew his story."

The judge considered his comments for a few moments. "Might be. I don't know. Let me think about it. It's sensitive and privileged information. It's also pretty goddamn graphic. You've had the boy barely two weeks. I don't know if it's time yet."

"Come on, Harley. What could it hurt?"

The old judge bristled and gave him a sharp look. "Don't push me, now. When and if I decide it's appropriate for you to see the file on this kid, I'll allow it. I could throttle Hal for even mentioning it." He glanced at his watch. "I need to go back to the courthouse. I've got a hearing in two hours and the lawyers for both parties are pompous assholes. I have to prepare myself for two hours of torture."

The two men headed back in the direction they'd come from. They stopped across the street from Nell's where Jack had parked his car and shook hands.

"Sorry I snapped at you back there, old buddy," the judge said. "Let me give the report some thought. Maybe you do need to see it. I'll get back to you about it, okay?"

"Sure. Take your time. You know where to find me."

Jack spent the remainder of the morning running errands, and the marina was in high gear when he returned around noon. Rafe and his crew had just put the big, newly painted Hatteras back in the water. Two sailboat owners were unable to come move their boats, which meant removing them from their slips and placing them in heavy steel cradles.

Jack was pleased to see Doug enthusiastically assisting the perpetually grouchy Neal guide a yacht being lowered into the water off the cradle slings. Doug stood in front of the boat with a firm grip on the bowline while Neal worked the stern line. Jack walked up just in time to notice that the Doug had wrapped the end of the line around his hand to get a better grip on it, a dangerous practice. Before he could warn him, the boat shifted to one side and the sudden tension on the boat yanked the boy off the dock. He fell into the water and came up sputtering and cursing. Neal doubled over laughing.

"You're supposed to be working, not swimming, pissant. That'll learn you not to get a line wrapped around your hand next time. You really think you can arm wrestle a big-ass boat like this and win?"

Jack trotted down the ramp and pulled Doug out of the water. His face reddened. He quickly looked away and fidgeted with his wet clothes while Neal continued hooting.

"Shut up, Neal," Jack said. "You fell into the drink three times your first two weeks here or had you forgotten?"

Jack reached into a nearby dock box and removed a large towel and handed it to the boy. "You okay?"

Doug stared at the ground and shuffled, saying nothing. When he looked back up, he wore a grin.

"Just drowned my pride. And I'm a sight cooler than I was a minute ago."

"Nothing to be ashamed of," Jack said. "Ain't a soul here who hasn't fallen off a dock at least once. I fell in last winter and nearly froze my ass off before I could get out. Now run up to the shop and get some dry clothes on. We'll wait for you."

While he was gone, Margie stuck her head out of the shop and yelled. "Lunch is on me when you hooligans are ready to eat. I ordered pizza." Pogy trotted up and tried to scoot past her into the building and she grabbed his collar. "Better hurry, guys," she yelled again. "Pogy says he's hungry."

Margie had laid out the pizzas on the large wooden table inside the shop. It was hot, so she'd turned on all three ceiling fans. The oddball combination of the aroma of pizza and workshop smells filled the air. Seth, her oldest son, wearing baggy shorts a Grateful Dead T-shirt, ear buds, and flip-flops set paper plates on the scarred table, bobbing his head to his music. The youngest boy, John, preppy in new khaki shorts, a blue and red striped polo shirt and deck shoes came into the shop with two large bottles of Coke and blue plastic cups. Doug came out of the bathroom wearing dry clothes and the two nearly collided. The two stood face to face staring down one another. Jack and Rafe came in from the yard and stopped in mid-step, glancing at the two youngsters locked into their truculent stare-down. Margie watched nervously from the other side of the room. Seth stopped what he was doing and shot his brother a warning look.

"Don't be an asshole, John," he said.

Doug's frown turned to a smile and he extended his hand. The younger boy, disregarding Doug's proffered handshake for the second time since he, his mother and brother arrived at the marina, stepped around him and went to look at the pizza.

Margie looked at her son, then at Doug and shook her head. Pogy sidled over to the table and sniffed at the hot pizza boxes.

"Well," Margie said. "Now that the formalities are out of the way, let's eat this damn pizza before it gets cold or this monster of a dog beats us to it.

After everyone had their fill, Doug eyed the last piece

"Go ahead," Rafe said, sliding the box toward him. "Eat it up."

When he took the slice from the box and set it on his plate, Pogy came and sat next to him, whined and put one big paw on his leg, then whined again while staring intently at him with his big liquid eyes. Doug raised an eyebrow and looked across the table at Jack.

"What's with Pogy?"

Jack, Rafe and the other marina employees exploded in laughter.

"We always give Pogy what's left over when we're all done eating together," Eddie said, wiping a smear of pizza sauce off his chin. "He thinks you're stealing his food."

At that, the big Dane scooted as close to Doug as he could get and laid his huge head on the boy's lap, drooling on his trousers. He whined again loudly and began thumping his long tail on the floor. Everyone's eyes were on the boy as he broke off half the slice and held it out for the dog. Despite his massive size and his eagerness for the treat, Pogy picked the morsel out of Doug's fingers as gently as a youngster kissing his first date. Then he lifted his big head and began licking the boy's face.

"Well I'll be damned," Jack said. "I think Pogy has a new best friend."

"Don't let the big galoot fool ya, pissant," Neal said, tossing a wadded-up napkin at Doug. "He's just in it for the damn pizza."

That evening while Jack was straightening up his desk, he found a large manila envelope addressed to him in Judge Kicklighter's looping, back-slanted cursive handwriting. When he opened the envelope, there was a thick packet of papers inside of it along with a brief note from the judge on his official court letterhead.

Y'all were busy when I stopped by so I decided to just leave this here for you. Upon further consideration, I'm of the opinion that it's time for you to see this. I don't, however, believe this is something to discuss with young Master Eleazer right now. Keep it to yourself. You'll know when it's time. Sorry I was so brusque this morning. I know what this means to you and my heart, although sometimes not my judicial temperament, is with you all the way. Your friend always
– Harley.

Jack went over and got a Coca-Cola, lit a cigarette, sat at his desk and began reading. From time to time, he found it necessary to stop and get up and walk around before he could continue. The windows were open and the window fan whirred quietly. The scent of jasmine, evocative of a love long ago, filled the room with its nighttime perfume. When he'd finally read the last page, he put his elbows on his desk and his face in the palms of his hands and wept. When he stopped, he picked up the framed photograph from his desk and gazed longingly at the faces of a smiling, golden-haired woman with one arm around a tall, tow-headed teenage boy sporting a mischievous grin. He ran his fingers gently over the forever-young images frozen there and wept yet again. This time the sobs were fierce and hurt his ribs, putting a deep ache in his chest.

He put the papers back in their envelope, locked them in his safe and went upstairs and sat with Pogy on his deck as was his custom every night the weather permitted. He was lost in thought when he heard someone calling softly to him from below. He leaned forward in his chair and saw Margie standing at the bottom of the long wooden staircase smiling, a bottle of wine in one hand and two glasses in the other.

"Permission to come aboard?" she asked playfully.

Jack managed a wan smile, considered her request for a moment and then nodded.

"Permission granted," he said with a trace of grief still thickening his voice. "Come on up, Captain. Watch that first step."

CHAPTER 9

WHEN SHE'D FINALLY DECIDED to chance strolling over to see if Jack was up for company, Margie had put on a pair of soft white cotton shorts that accentuated her trim and tanned, shapely legs, a salmon-colored boat-neck shirt and her faded blue canvas deck shoes. Her sons were in their stateroom listening to music. She had stopped in the galley and took a bottle of her favorite wine from the refrigerator and two wine glasses.

Her pulse had quickened when she glanced up while crossing the yard and saw him sitting alone on the second-floor deck, smoking a cigarette and apparently woolgathering. He was leaning back in a lounge chair staring up into the night sky, heedless of her footsteps as she drew near. Reluctant to walk upstairs unannounced, she called out. He got up from his chair and met her at the top of the steps.

"I'm not intruding, I hope," she said, handing him the wine and the two glasses. "I hate to drink expensive wine alone and was thinking you might like to help me. Got a corkscrew, Captain?"

He looked at the label on the wine bottle, handed it back to her, set the glasses on a small teak table beside his lounge chair and smiled listlessly.

"Yeah, I'll go get it," he said. "Be right back."

He wore faded khaki shorts, an old Hawaiian print shirt and was barefooted. When he excused himself to go inside, she caught the clean scent of Irish Spring soap and smiled at the carefree masculine smell. He left the door open and she heard him rummaging around in the kitchen. He returned a few minutes later, held up the corkscrew and smiled again, a little brighter this time. Pogy slipped out behind him, came over and sniffed at her and then licked her hand before going to a corner of the deck, where he sprawled out and began gnawing a large bone.

"Haven't used one of these in a while," he said, when she handed him the bottle again. "Don't be surprised if I botch it. Ah, here it goes." The cork slid from the bottle with a light pop and he filled both their glasses half full.

"Cheers!" she said, holding up her glass and smiling. He tapped his glass against hers and smiled back at her. "Cheers!"

He set his glass on the table, pulled another lounge chair up and pointed at it. She moved her chair to face him better and sat. She ran her other hand through her hair and looked into the constellation filled sky.

"What a view," she said after a few moments of stargazing.

He took a sip of his wine and glanced up. "I get so caught up in it," he said. "It has a language all its own."

She took a sip of wine, set her glass down and tilted her head to one side and looked at him.

"Let's just sit and listen a bit. I'd love to hear it."

They sat in rapt silence beneath the great onyx bowl of the night sky and gazed at the diamond brilliance of the stars. Moonlight leached away the colors in the marina below, turning it into a black and white photograph. Jack's silent contentment didn't seem to her a sign that he was shutting her out, but rather, allowing her to share a place he so clearly held sacred.

"Penny for your thoughts?" she said.

He took another sip of wine and stared out into the yard, avoiding eye contact.

"One penny was never enough," he said.

Before she could inquire further, he glanced up and pointed.

"See that bright speck of light crossing the sky way up yonder? It's the International Space Station. Right on time. I always watch for it when I'm out here at night."

She chuckled and set her glass on the table, which he'd moved between them.

"You're the master of deflection," she said. "So tell me. What's the story about you and young Doug? I'm thinking something more than the usual employer-employee relationship." She stopped abruptly and covered her mouth with one hand. "I'm sorry. I didn't mean to insinuate there's anything inappropriate. Ugh!' she said and frowned, tapping her knuckles on her forehead. "Now I've embarrassed the shit out of myself."

He waved his hand dismissively and lit a citronella candle on the table to deter mosquitoes. "No offense taken. He's had some difficulties and a really hard life. I'm just trying to help him out. He's been giving me a hand with my boat in addition to working here during the day."

"I wasn't asking you about the boat, as if you didn't know. I was asking you about Doug. What's the story?" she said, smiling.

Something in the marsh disturbed a bird from its sleep. Its signature call, like loud mocking laughter, startled Margie. She jumped from her chair and looked out toward the spartina jungle.

"Good God, what's that racket?"

He smiled and she thought that his face looked even more rugged awash in moonlight. When he laughed, it caught her off guard. "A marsh hen," he said. "Sounds like a crazy person cackling, don't it?"

He got up and walked over to the edge of the deck and looked at the marsh. She waited a moment and then went over and stood beside him, following his gaze. A breeze stirred the palm fronds in the trees that grew beside the deck and they made a sound like the shuffling of cards. The occasional sound of her sons' voices rolled across the yard from her boat. The scent of late blooming jasmine permeated the air where it mingled with another aroma, a woman's smell, one standing near enough to reach out and touch, maybe even wanting to be touched. It was a smell of soap and clean hair and a subtle, barely perceptible floral scent tinged with the sweet bouquet of expensive wine. She edged closer and fixed him with her green eyes and smiled at him, shining its intensity in his face. It had the effect she desired, and he smiled back at her.

"Sorry if I seem a little awkward," he said. "I haven't had female company in, well, a long time." And then added after a gentle laugh, "And never one who brought expensive wine."

She edged closer. Her fragrance filled his nose. He gripped the deck railing in two big fists and breathed deeply, drawing it in. She reached out and touched him on the forearm and felt the muscles twitch.

"I'm sorry," she said, pulling away her hand, embarrassed. "I'm a toucher. I forget myself sometimes."

"It's okay. Not every day that I get pawed by a pretty woman."

She laughed again, that bright, explosive laugh that made him want to laugh with her.

"Okay," she said. "One more question and I'll let it drop. Why does the sheriff bring Doug here every morning and come back for him in the evenings? What's with this kid, Jack? He has such pained eyes."

He let the question settle before answering. "Come on. Let's go sit back down."

He eased into his chair and waited for her to sit. She sensed that something was on his mind and waited politely while he gathered his thoughts.

"Have you ever seen a dog that's been beaten and abused?" he said. "The way it growls and bares its teeth, but at the same time, keeps its tail tucked between its legs? The way it looks away from you and won't make eye contact?"

She set her glass down and nodded. "Yes. The man next door to us when I was a kid had an old hound like that. Everyone said he was vicious. But he just had trust issues. It took me a long time to make friends with him. I tossed him pieces of cheese every day trying to coax him to me. He'd eat the cheese, growling the whole time. It took me a month before he'd eat from my hand. One day his owner just up and moved away and abandoned him. My father let me keep him. He lived to a ripe old age."

She stole a glance at Pogy and knew that the happy-go-lucky dog had never suffered more than a mild rebuke from Merkel.

"So, he never was a bad dog at all, was he, Margie?"

"No, just afraid and lonely. It left scars. Even when he was old and had been with me for years, he still cringed if someone nearby picked up a broom or anything else that looked like a stick that his asshole owner beat him with."

Jack let a long moment slide by before replying. "Well, there you are."

"Jack Merkel, that has to be the most roundabout way of answering a question I've ever heard in my life."

He took a drink of wine, set the glass down, leaned back in his chair.

"Your turn," he said. "What's Margie Waller's story?"

She shook her head. "No fair. You've hardly told me a thing about yourself."

"Not much to tell," he said. "What you see is pretty much all there is to know."

"I doubt that," she said. "But okay. I met Howard one night when I was a rookie trauma nurse in a hospital emergency room in Baltimore. He'd sliced off the end of his left pinky when he got it caught between a winch and a line during a regatta. I was young and impressionable, and he was charming and rich. We started seeing each other. Six months later, we got married on some Saudi sultan's yacht in New York Harbor."

She set her glass down and then surprised him. "Hey, can I mooch a smoke? Jesus, I never smoked much but sometimes I want one."

He reached for his pack, shook one out, handed it to her and then leaned across to light it for her. She held his wrist while he lit her cigarette and stared brazenly at him.

She blew a thin stream of smoke to one side.

"You have the saddest eyes I've ever seen. Mmm, God that's good. I haven't had a smoke in ages."

"Talk about me changing the subject," he said. "You haven't skipped any lessons either."

She took another drag on her cigarette, coughed, exhaled and fanned the smoke away.

"Howard was a trust-fund baby. Stinking rich. We spent the next five years sailing around the world. I got pregnant with Seth and we decided to settle in the Bahamas. We spent most of the twenty-three years of our marriage in the islands, except for trips back and forth between Baltimore, which is my home and *Bahhhston*, which is Howard's. He's a goddamn Boston Brahmin. Have you ever been around Brahmins?"

Her voice took on a hard edge before he could reply.

"They think they're fucking royalty. Plus, he was a cheat from the get-go, as I belatedly learned."

Pogy got up from his spot on the deck, walked over to his water bowl and noisily slurped, then sidled over and slobbered all over Margie's face when he licked her.

Jack groaned and scolded the big Dane, who just looked at him and wagged his tail.

Margie wiped the drool off her face with the palm of her hand and leaned over and hugged the dog and he rewarded her with another soggy smooch.

"I haven't been kissed like that in years, big boy. I didn't get that much tongue from Howard during our entire marriage. Brahmins are as cold as cods. The old joke is that a proper Brahmin woman makes plans for high tea while she's making love. You can only tell if she's had an orgasm if she drops her day timer."

Jack laughed hard.

"Anyway, Howard turned out to be a shallow, arrogant asshole, a mile wide and an inch deep. Totally self-absorbed. Clubby, preppy and, ultimately, boring as hell. But by the time I realized I didn't love him anymore, probably never really did if you want to know the truth, I was pregnant with John. I endured his patrician ass-holiness and his tail chasing for as long as I could stand it and then filed for divorce. It took a long time to sink into my thick skull that money really can't buy happiness."

A squadron of helicopters on a night mission from the navy base in nearby Jacksonville approached from the south. The muffled *thup-thup-thup* of their rotors flogged the air as they reached a roaring crescendo passing overhead.

"How'd he take it?" Jack said when it was quiet again.

"I don't think it even made it to his radar screen. We'd not been, umm, intimate for a long time. I suspected he was keeping a mistress. Most men like him do. By then, I didn't care one way or the other. I just wanted out. John's fifteen. Seth's eighteen. I left Howard when John was thirteen. I waited a year to give the boys time to process it all before I finally filed for the divorce last year."

"And you got the yacht in the bargain," Jack said.

She laughed again. "Oh, that's the little boat. You should see the big one. He kept that one. I can't complain. He left me financially secure."

"The boys?"

"Seth detests him. He never wanted the spoiled rich kid life. Howard drove him bat shit about going to Harvard like he did, but Seth's wanted to go to the University of Virginia since he was a sophomore in high school. It irked Howard, and his constant snobby putdowns of his son's college choice destroyed their relationship. John? That's another story. He's my son and I love him, but he's a lot like his father. He'll stay with me a little longer, but he's already made it clear he's going back to Howard."

Neither of them said anything else for a while. They listened to the buzz saw trilling of mole crickets and the occasional heron squawking in the darkness. The wind shifted and brought the aroma of the marsh to them. The evening passed in its unceasing crawl and both of them realized that several minutes had slipped past unnoticed. Margie glanced at her watch.

"God, it's getting late. Did we drift off to sleep or what?"

Jack sighed contentedly and stretched.

"Daydreaming comes easy around here on a night like this. I've enjoyed the visit, Margie."

"Same here. You get to pick the spirits the next time, though. Whoo! I'm a little toasted."

She got up and swayed. Jack stood up quickly and caught her. When he did, she started to lean into him and then checked herself. Startled, he drew away from her blundered embrace.

"Damn!" she said. "I guess I'm a little tighter than I thought."

"It's okay," Jack said. "I'm a little buzzed too, and the wine's making me sleepy. Lots to do tomorrow."

She picked up the glasses and he walked her to the stairs and then down.

"Thank you for the nice evening," she said. "I haven't had a real conversation with another adult in I don't know how long. Might I ask a personal question before I go?"

"Okay, but I won't guarantee I'll answer."

"Fair enough. When I went into your office looking for some paper to write that release of liability so that you'd let me help you work on my boat, I couldn't help but notice the photo on your desk of that nice-looking young man and pretty woman together. Is that—"

"My son and my wife."

"Are you divorced, too?"

"No. Goodnight, Margie. Thanks again for the wine and the company."

She stopped a short distance away and watched him walk back up the stairs with the dog at his heels. She was still standing there looking up at his house when the lights went off inside.

CHAPTER 10

IN THE EARLY MORNING hours of July 25, Hurricane Brenda swelled into a Category 4 storm packing winds of 145 mph. She ravaged the Virgin Islands, upended Puerto Rico and left Haiti and the Dominican Republic drowning in her massive wake before turning her malevolent eye on the Southeastern coast of the United States. A hurricane watch went into effect from the Florida Keys to the Lowcountry of South Carolina. Most meteorologists and hurricane experts predicted that Brenda would grow.

Jack, Rafe and Margie stood in the office watching the latest tropical weather updates. The day was sunny and warm, the sky a flawless blue. Even the stultifying humidity of the past few days had dissipated some. Margie watched, horror-stricken, as news camera footage showed the devastation and human suffering left by the storm as it plowed through the islands.

"My God! The poor islanders," she said. "Most have nothing to begin with and now this."

"In all your years living in the Bahamas, you never got hit by a hurricane?" Jack said.

"Nothing serious. Oh, we got slapped around by a tropical storm here and there, and a few baby hurricanes, but never one like this."

"I gotta tell you guys, if the mountains of the Dominican Republic didn't even slow this thing down, it's gonna get much bigger and more dangerous by the time it hits the Gulf Stream," Rafe said. "A Category 4 hurricane is already a killer. A 5? That's a monster. Now we're talking Hugo, Andrew and Katrina."

Jack set his coffee cup on his desk and looked outside. "As pretty as it is today, it's hard to comprehend that in three or four days this thing could be chewing us to pieces," he said. "Storm that size would swamp Morgan's Island. Except for a big dune on the south end, the highest point on this ten-mile-long, one-mile-wide sand spit is the fifty-two-foot hill where the lighthouse is. Even a smaller storm could wreck this place, depending on the tide, moon phase and strike angle."

Margie pulled a chair from the corner and sat, eyes fixed on the nonstop scenes of destruction flashing on the television screen. Jack looked at Rafe, jerked his head to the left and stepped to the other side of the office out of her hearing.

"We gotta get her and those kids outta here while the gettin's good, Rafe. You weren't here for Dora in '64. She was just a Cat 1, and she kicked this island's ass with ninety-mile-an-hour winds, kicked it hard, and it wasn't even a direct hit. That was down around St. Augustine. A whole row of beach houses here got swept into the ocean. Water was knee-deep downtown. Christ, we've got ocean on the front porch and the Intracoastal on the back porch."

"We ain't getting off that easy this time, *hermano*," Rafe whispered. "Unless something gives or she swings more north, this little island is gonna get whacked hard. You think Margie'll leave?"

"I think she will. No mother would intentionally put her kids in that kind of jeopardy."

She muted the television and ambled over to them.

"Did I hear my name whispered in secret? Honestly, if the secrets of the world depended on the inability of men to whisper, what a mess we'd be in. So clue me in, gentlemen."

The two men looked at each other and shrugged. Jack motioned her over and pointed out the window.

"Pretty summer day, not a cloud in the sky. But in about three or four days, if things don't drastically change, those same television cameras might be here showing the wreckage of this little island. Margie, you need to take the kids and go home to Baltimore."

She stared out the window, running her hands through her hair and thinking.

"I suppose you're right. I hate to abandon *Starshine,* but I'm scared. I can't take this kind of chance with my boys. I can stay in Aunt Lucy's condo and start attending whatever unfinished business she left when she died. We can return once the storm passes."

She looked from Jack to Rafe.

"How soon should I leave? I mean, things do change with the weather, especially storm forecasting. My God, they're hardly ever all that accurate 'til the last minute."

"I think you've safely got another couple of days to get your boys ready and things together," Rafe said. "We'll help you unload and store any valuables on the boat you can't take with you. The airlines will continue northbound and westbound flights 'til the last possible minute. South or east? No way. But yeah, I think you'll be okay here a day or two more."

Margie shook her head. "Fly? No way, gentleman. I'd as soon ride out that hurricane. Flying scares the shit out of me. No, I'll rent a car and drive. There is a place to rent a car here, isn't there?"

"Sure, there's a Hertz right up the road and an Enterprise at the municipal airport," Jack said. "We should make the reservation right now, though. You can always cancel it if things change. But if the storm really looks like it'll come here and they even mention the word *evacuation*, you'd better hightail it. It could end up being like Hurricane Floyd in 1999 where the entire state tried to flee north all at the same time. There were jammed roads, full hotels and people sleeping in their cars in the parking lots of shopping centers and motels."

Doug clomped into the room and stopped abruptly, his eyes darting from one person to another.

"Mornin', Pop. Mornin', Miz Margie. Mornin' Mr. Hernandez. Did I interrupt something? I can go back outside if y'all want."

Jack smiled and went over and put his hand affectionately on the boy's shoulder. "No, we were just talking about the storm coming. You want some coffee?"

"Yes, sir. That'd be nice."

"Well, help yourself. Wanna do the dock walk today? Think you're up to it?"

The boy perked up and grinned broadly, showing a mouthful of straight white teeth. The morning dock walk to check the condition of the boats and docks in the marina was considered one of the plum early morning jobs. It was a job that meant responsibility and trust. It meant checking every boat, electrical connection, fitting and cleat on every dock, the condition of every dock, and then signing your name to the report. Jack grinned back at him and cocked his thumb at the clipboard with its attached pen hanging on the wall behind the desk.

"Get to it, then," he said. "Oh, and there was a mama manatee and her baby down near C Dock just after sunup this morning. Grab the camera off my desk and snap a photo of them if they're still hanging around. Old Kate's been around here a long time. She'll let you get pretty close to her. Get a good one and I'll send it to the newspaper to print and tell Larry to put your name on it as the photographer."

Doug grabbed the clipboard and pen off the wall, snatched the camera off the desk and bolted to the door. Margie halted him in mid step just before he put his hand on the brass knob.

"Hey, Doug. Speaking of storms. There's gonna be a doozy right here next time you call me Miz Margie. It's just Margie. Got it, kiddo?"

"Same here," Rafe said. "Mr. Hernandez was my father. I'm just Rafe."

"Yes, ma'am, yes, sir," he said, opening the door and trotting across the porch and down the steps.

Rafe shook his head and laughed, muttering something to himself in Spanish as he headed over to the counter for another cup of coffee. Margie gave Jack a level gaze and smiled approvingly.

"You've got a friend in the boy already. What a nice touch. You're great with kids."

He turned quickly away. "Think I'll have another cup of coffee and step outside for a smoke."

When he closed it behind him, she raised her eyebrows at Rafe.

"Rafe, what in God's name? Did I say something wrong?"

"No. Gotta get to work. The crew's already here. See you later, Margie."

She waited until he was gone and then went over to the desk and looked at the photo of the woman and the boy. She studied it for a moment, finished her coffee and walked outside. Jack was standing by the rail, smoking and looking out at the marsh. She edged closer to him, following his gaze to the spartina and hooked her thumbs in her shorts pockets.

"That's got to be the prettiest color green I've ever seen in my life," she said. "When Howard and I were newlyweds, we went to Cartagena to visit an old Colombian gentleman he knew. Later, he said he wanted to show me something. He took me to a store down the street, an emerald merchant's shop. There were so many of them, a few near as big as hen's eggs, and they were so exquisitely green that the whole store seemed to glow with the color of the stones. When I look out at the marsh, that's what I think about—emeralds."

"I didn't know you were a poet and a ship's captain both," Jack said, cutting his eyes toward her and smiling. "I wish I had your gift for words. That's exactly the way I would've described the spartina grass if I had the words for it."

A breeze shifted across the spartina and it seemed to flow like green water, slow and languid, moving with feline grace. Margie inhaled its briny perfume, holding it inside as long as she could before releasing it and wishing that she could've held it forever. She studied Jack in profile out of the corner of her eye. She saw the marsh and the sea in him and the tides, the waves upon the ocean, raw and gray. He was coils of tough hemp rope and as hard as a marlin spike, but the part he kept concealed, she speculated, was as soft and vulnerable as the meat of a clam when exposed. He spoke most fluently in his long silences. He was so near at times that she only need reach out and touch him. Other times he was leagues away.

She didn't notice that he also studied her from the corner of his eye. He thought her beauty surpassed that of his beloved marsh, a tall order in his book. The green of her eyes reminded him of the spartina. He admired her grit and the way she jutted her chin defiantly when challenged. He saw the poise of a ballerina and the boldness of an explorer, the confidence to set sail across the sea on a boat crewed only by teenage boys, unperturbed by the treachery that lurked just beneath the placid aquamarine waters of the Gulf Stream. Her smile came as quick as a summer thunderstorm, with the intense brightness of its sharpest lightning. And her laughter reminded him of the wind chimes another woman had once crafted from seashells.

She tossed her head and her auburn hair caught the sunlight and shone like burnished copper.

"You don't have the words, you say. You don't need words, Jack. You say more without words than most people who are considered eloquent say with them."

He leaned on the railing and laughed softly. She stared him right in the eye and put her hands on her hips, sticking out her chin. "Did I say something funny?"

"No. I always figured most people found me boring. I don't have loads of friends, you know."

"No, I suppose not," she said. "But it's not because you're not interesting. Men like you are choosey who their friends are and so they don't have many—just folks they can be themselves around."

"Ah, you're a psychologist now?"

"Nope," she said. "Just a woman who was married to a very superficial man. Friends galore and not a sincere one among them. And then, along comes his polar opposite."

He looked at her for a long moment and then smiled.

"You have a nice smile, too," she said, flushing.

He gestured toward the steps. "Come on, I need to have a meeting with the crew. We've got a lot of work and preparation to do and we need to get started on it soon. Might be I could use your help, too."

Jack stood at the head of the table sipping a Coke in the hot, dusty shop. Rafe stood beside him holding a clipboard. Neal, Eddie and Doug sat in folding metal chairs on both sides of the table. Margie and Seth took chairs at the opposite end. John didn't join them. The paint contractor, a short, fat man of about twenty-five and wearing a paint-splattered uniform wandered in from the job and leaned against one of the metal lockers. An oscillating fan hummed and blew loose papers off a nearby table.

"First of all, I don't want panic or crazy rumors to take hold here," Jack began, when he had their attention. "All of us know what a hurricane is and how bad they can be, especially one of Brenda's size. And we all know that the most horrible predictions here usually turn out to be false alarms. But we haven't had a threat like this in a long time and so for now, we're going to prepare for the worst and hope for the best."

The room was a maritime stew of smells; the bitterness of thick old hemp rope, coiled in a dark corner like a python, the fruity aroma of raw teak and cotton rags saturated with teak oil, the subtle flavor of varnish, the pungent urgency of curing fiberglass resin and the faint reek of diesel. Jack looked at Rafe and nodded.

"We've got eight sailboats, including Margie's," Rafe announced. "By lunchtime, we want them augured down and strapped, fore, aft and amidships. Sink the augurs six feet.

Use the steel reinforced straps on *Starshine*. She's too big for the regular ones."

He pointed at Neal.

"Pick a couple of our part-timers and jump right on that as soon as we're done here.

"Eddie, I want you and Doug to start at one end of the marina and work your way to the other end picking up anything that could become airborne—plastic cones, wood pallets, tires, paint cans and anything else that weighs less than a small car—and stow it in the barn. Doug, everything on the docks up to snuff this morning?"

Doug glanced at his own clipboard. "There's a cleat on Dock Four down toward the end on the right—"

"Starboard side, pissant," Neal said.

Doug shot him a dark look. "'S'cuse me, *starboard* side, that looks wobbly. I think the bolts under it are probably corroded. The hose bib on A Dock needs replacing, too. Everything else looks tight."

He broke into a grin and held up his camera. "I got four good closeups of the mama manatee and her baby. She was nursing him!"

Everyone cheered except Neal, who just rolled his eyes.

"Okay, gang, anything else or any other ideas, see me or Jack," Rafe said. "Questions?"

Neal cleared his throat. "I hate to sound morbid, but what happens if worse comes to worst and the marina is destroyed?"

Jack tapped a cigarette out of its pack. "Don't think that ain't crossed my mind, too. The short answer is we rebuild it."

"So, we'll still have jobs?" Neal said.

"Yeah, and I might even pay you. Anybody else?"

Eddie put up his hand and Jack pointed at him, "Eddie?"

"Jack, you think you can advance us any pay if we have to evacuate? Staying in a hotel and eating out can get expensive."

"Don't worry, Eddie. I'm going to advance every one of you a week's pay. In cash. Even if ya'll ain't working, you'll still get paid while you're out. Anybody find they can't make ends meet, suck up your pride and call me. We're all in this together." He swept his gaze around the room.

"Go do your jobs and don't get in too big of a hurry and get hurt. We've still got three days or so before the storm comes, if it comes. Anything else?"

Seth raised his hand and cleared his throat. "Mr. Merkel. What's going to happen to *Starshine*? Mom says we have to go to Aunt Lucy's condo in Baltimore and leave 'er here."

"Don't worry, son," Jack said. "I'm gonna take real good care of *Starshine*. I'll stand out there and hold her down myself if I need to. Me and Pogy." At the sound of his name, the dog lifted his muzzle, looked up at Merkel and barked.

The boy wiped his hands on the sweaty gray T-shirt he wore and blinked. "But won't you be evacuating, too?"

Jack shrugged. "I don't know. Maybe, maybe not. We'll see."

Margie shot him a wide-eyed look that he ignored.

"Okay. Meeting's over. Tacos for lunch today. On me. Now get outta here."

Margie waited until they were all gone and then strode over to him. "You said I might be able to help you today. What did you have in mind?"

He pointed toward the office. "I've got a list inside of customers with boats here. I want to call each of them and give them the opportunity to come and get them if they can, especially the small ones and the few that are in the barn. You can help me with that."

She stepped closer to him, drew back her shoulders and scowled. "And what the hell do you mean, you don't know if you're going to evacuate? You're not planning to ride out the storm in this marina, are you?"

He looked beyond her, his gaze straying out the door and settling on his marina. "It's all I've got, Margie. All I have left. I can't just walk away from it."

She reddened, put her hands on his chest and shoved him. His coffee sloshed over the sides of his cup. "You could die, goddamn it! Don't be a fool!"

He drained off the last of the cold coffee and took a long draw on his cigarette. "I was on a freighter in the North Atlantic in a big storm once. Worst damn storm at sea I ever experienced. Huge waves, one after another. I was scared we'd all die. And then suddenly I wasn't. Hell, I even went up to the bridge and did what I could to keep the old man calm."

Margie shook her head, her forehead creased. "I'm not following you."

He walked over to the door, watched his crew work for a few moments and turned around to face her again.

"I quit being afraid of the sea and the wind a long time ago in a winter storm far away. I'm a mariner through and through, Margie. This is my ship, my home, the only one I have."

Tears welled in her eyes and she blinked them back. "And you'll go down with it," she said, her voice cracking.

He answered her question with a silent stare. She spun around and stormed off toward the office, spitting back over her shoulder. "I should've known it. Damn you, Jack Merkel! Just damn you!"

After the door slammed, Jack waited a moment and then started to follow her. and try to explain to her that he knew how to take care of himself. He was about to open the door and decided to leave her alone and let her cool off, and walked out to the boatyard to check on his men.

CHAPTER 11

ON JULY 27, HURRICANE Brenda hovered seaward of Florida for the next twenty-four hours, momentum stalled. Predictably, as is nearly always the case in hurricane forecasting, when one of the big storms has a change in attitude, all the weather models meteorologists rely upon go as skittishly wild as a moth in a lampshade. Some of them had the storm turning north and aiming at Bermuda or veering far north by northeast and hitting the Canadian Maritimes. The most optimistic predicted that wind shear would lop off her big head and kill her.

The last prediction got traction when the storm was downgraded to a Cat 3 with winds of 126 mph. By the end of that day, her maximum sustained winds leveled off at 111 mph. Becoming bolder, forecasters predicted continued weakening. She was still a big storm, her rain bands reaching out hundreds of miles in all directions, clutching at the peninsula from afar and drenching it with rain. But Rafe, who had been obsessively monitoring every change in forecasts, found no consolation in any notion that Brenda might soon be finished. He remembered the last big hurricane that finally drove his family inland when he was a boy. It broke his father's heart. It, too, had been predicted to weaken and die. His father got old almost overnight. He'd been a fisherman since he was a boy and the sea was his love. He never got over it and chafed at having to be a poor farmer.

Jack sat in the living room of his home above the marina office and listened to the staccato patter of rain on the deck. It was dark outside and the only light in the room came from the television screen, where a garrulous meteorologist held forth in front of a map of Florida that showed a weakened, but still huge, Brenda lurking offshore like a serpent coiled to strike. But the airbrushed newscaster with the plastic grin predicted that Brenda would soon be history. The camera panned back to the station's news desk where a perfectly coiffed young woman chatted idly with a likewise perfectly coiffed young man. Jack snorted and glanced over at Pogy, who sat on the leather sofa beside him, seemingly intent on watching the news.

"Good Lord. They look like department store mannequins and sound like jabbering zoo monkeys."

He reached over and ruffled Pogy's fur. "The dickens are you waiting for, a dog food commercial? C'mon, big guy. Let's get us some breakfast. I've got me an appetite this morning and a feeling today's gonna be nasty all day."

He lined the big cast-iron skillet that had once belonged to his grandmother with slices of thick-rind bacon and set it on the gas burner. While it sizzled and popped and filled the kitchen with its country-smoked fragrance, he cracked eggs into a bowl. He started out with two, then changed his mind and added two more, thought for a moment, and tossed in a fifth one for good measure. By the time the bacon was browning on one side, he had beaten and salted the eggs and then he flipped the bacon and sent it crackling and sizzling anew. He took a plastic bag out of the freezer and emptied four frozen biscuits onto a cookie sheet and put them in the hot oven. Within moments, their crusty, homespun aroma joined the smells of coffee and bacon. Before the bacon was done, someone knocked at the door.

Pogy barked loudly and trotted to the door. Jack wiped his hands on a dishtowel and went to see who it was. He opened it and saw Margie standing there draped in a big yellow rubber raincoat. A northeast wind whipped the rain slantwise and the palm tree fronds clattered like dry bones. She wiped water off her face with the back of her hand and shivered. It was still dark outside.

"Come on in out of the rain," he said, moving aside for her. "Here, give me your rain slicker before you drown in it."

"Jesus," she grumbled, shrugging it off as the water puddled on the heart pine planks. "It's like a monsoon out there. Shit!" she yelped. "I'm ruining your floor!"

He took the raincoat from her and took it to the laundry room to dry. When he returned, she was on her knees mopping up the water with a big wad of paper towels she found on the kitchen counter. She wore tight, faded jeans and a black T-shirt and had slipped off her wet canvas shoes and set them by the door on a towel. Her jeans hugged and accentuated her shapely hips. He caught himself gawking and quickly looked away, embarrassed.

She hopped nimbly up and wadded the sodden paper towels.

"Sorry about the water on the floor. And I'm sorry about yesterday. Truly I am. Can you forgive me for being such a bitch? God, it smells delicious in here."

The way she flitted from one subject to another amused him. He caught himself smiling.

"So, you came over here in the pouring-down rain before daylight to apologize to me for something yesterday that I'd already forgotten about 'til you brought it up just now?"

"Yes," she said, sticking her hands in her pockets and glancing down at her bare feet. "It bothered me all night. I wanted to catch you alone before everyone else gets here and things get hectic, which I suppose they will, what with this goddamn messy weather we're having. I was completely out of line."

She looked back up, held out her hand the way she had the first time they met, and gave him a lopsided smile. He accepted the handshake. "It's already forgotten," he said.

He took the wet paper towels and threw them in the trash.

"Besides, I didn't take it personally. Everyone's a little nervous right now, including me."

She looked at the television set and the newscasters chatting amiably, and scowled. "Assholes. They're so annoying. I listened to the National Weather Service on the marine radio while I was getting dressed. This storm is a viper. It might be a wounded viper but it still has fangs and venom."

Jack took the bacon from the skillet and set it on paper towels folded on a plate, poured food in Pogy's bowl and dumped the grease into it. Margie watched him and laughed.

"Aren't you afraid all that grease will upset his stomach? God, I'd hate to clean up after this big boy."

He sniggered as he set the skillet back on the burner, poured the beaten eggs into it and began scrambling them.

"He'll eat anything, and it doesn't seem to faze him."

He glanced at the television and then Margie. "Have you made your evacuation plans?"

"Yeah, for tomorrow. I'm gonna wait and see what this thing's gonna do before we bug out, though. I dread getting on I-95 and driving in the best conditions. What does Rafe think about the latest?"

Jack picked up the skillet, scooped the scrambled eggs onto a platter, forked the bacon on top of them, took the biscuits out of the oven, set them beside the pile of eggs and turned off the gas.

"I don't know. Fretting, most likely. He'll be along directly. Want some breakfast? There's plenty."

She eyed the food hungrily and pushed a stool to the bar. "I thought you'd never ask."

He poured two cups of coffee and pulled up a stool across from her on the other side of the bar.

She picked up a biscuit, took a bite and moaned. "*Mmmmm,* damn good for canned biscuits."

"Who said anything about them being canned?"

She paused with a forkful of eggs halfway to her mouth. "Nuh-uh. You didn't really make these. I mean, holy shit! Did you really make these?"

Jack picked up a piece of bacon and took a bite. "Yeah. From scratch. My mee-maw taught me how to cook. I'm the only one in the family that got her biscuit recipe before she passed. I make a batch every week and freeze them. Take a few out every morning and pop them into the oven for breakfast."

Margie put the half-eaten biscuit down, put her chin in her palms and propped on her elbows. "You build boats; you repair engines; you run a marina. You take in strays and you make the best goddamn biscuits I've ever eaten. Any other skills?"

She pinned him with her eyes and smiled impishly.

"I'm told I play a mean fiddle. But it's been awhile since I rosined up a bow."

"Interesting. I'm not half bad with a guitar." She paused before adding: "Maybe we can play together sometime."

She studied his face to see if he'd caught her meaning and rolled her eyes when she realized he hadn't.

"What's the matter?" he asked.

"Never mind," she said. "Mmm. Biscuit's soooo good! So, your grandmother taught you to make biscuits. Did your mother teach you any other kitchen skills? Are you parents still alive?'

A gust of wind blew the rain against the windows making a noise like someone threw a handful of rice at them. Pogy noisily lapped his water in the kitchen. Jack took another biscuit off the platter and drenched it with gallberry honey. Margie finished the rest of her breakfast, then reached for another biscuit with one hand and the honey with the other, wondering if he would answer her question.

"No, they were killed in a car accident," he said. "Same as—" He stopped abruptly and began cutting up the biscuit with his fork.

She leaned forward again.

"Same as?"

"Forget it," he said. "Let's just enjoy the biscuits and honey for now. Gotta feeling we ain't gonna get much pleasure out of the next day or two."

The day gradually dawned, pale gray. The rain stopped, but the sun didn't even try to put in an appearance. Without a word, Jack got up and began clearing the table. She followed him to the kitchen.

"Penny for your thoughts?"

When he looked at her, she saw the agony in his face writ large in trembling lips and unshed tears.

"Please don't say that again," he said, so quietly she barely heard him.

"Huh? Penny for—?"

"Don't," he repeated. "Please."

He began washing the dishes. She picked up a towel and dried them. They worked side by side in silence. The sky turned a darker shade of grief and began to weep again.

The phone on Jack's desk rang and interrupted the conversation he was having with Margie and Rafe about the storm. Rafe didn't believe the big hurricane was going to die. It was only taking a breather, getting ready for the next round. Jack wanted to hear the rest of his thoughts on it but excused himself to take the call. Sheriff Patterson was on the other end. He sounded like he'd been up all night.

"Morning, Jack. I'm with His Honor. He wants us in court first thing."

"What's wrong, Hal?" Jack said, his voice going up an octave. "Is it Doug? Is he okay?"

The sheriff heaved a sigh and cleared his throat. "Yeah, it's about the kid, but don't get yourself all perturbed. He's okay. But we've gotta little problem to deal with and I've got a tight time frame. Get on down here quick as you can. Don't go to the courtroom. We're in Judge Kicklighter's chambers."

The line went dead before he could reply. Jack exhaled noisily and tightened his jaw.

"What's wrong, *hermano*?" Rafe asked. "You get some bad news? Where's the boy this morning, anyway?"

Jack pulled his raincoat and a broad-brimmed canvas hat from a rack in the corner, put them on and started for the door without a word. Margie started to follow Jack to the door.

"Jack?" she said.

He paused just long enough to reply. "I gotta run down to the courthouse for a bit. I'll be back directly. Listen, Margie, keep trying to reach the people on the list you couldn't get hold of yesterday. Rafe?"

"Yeah, man. Whatcha need?"

"Get the front-end loader and a crew of the guys and start moving lime rock off the big pile out back and dump it down where that creek runs up alongside the property on the west side. Push up some dirt and pile that and the rock together and make a berm. It won't keep the water from spilling in if it floods, but at least it won't come rushing in all at once."

"Got it. Anything else?"

"Yeah, round up all the tools, especially the power tools, and put them in the utility trailer in case we need to get everything off the property to higher ground. Won't do us a damn bit of good trying to straighten up around here if all the tools are lost or ruined. Oh, and make sure all three portable generators are gassed up and in running condition. And top off the gasoline storage tanks in case we lose power to the pumps. That'll do 'til I get back."

He turned and walked out into the rain, letting the door close behind him.

Margie moved closer to Rafe with a puzzled expression "What's going on here?"

Rafe shrugged. "You were standing right there, Margie. You know as much as I do."

She put her hands on her hips and glared at him. "Don't patronize me. I'm not some naïve little girl. It's about Doug, isn't it? Why doesn't someone just tell me what the story is with that boy?"

Rafe did a slow ten count, inhaled deeply and let it out slowly to quell his annoyance at being interrogated. "You're gonna have to talk with Jack about that. It ain't my place."

"Is the boy in trouble of some kind? It must be something like that or else this wouldn't be such a big deal."

"Listen," he said. "And this is all I'm gonna say, even though I maybe shouldn't. Doug's had some hard knocks. I don't even know the full extent of it. All I know is Jack's kinda taking up for him and helping him out. He's like that."

"Yes," she said, and then smiled. "I can see that."

Jack slogged along through the sluggish traffic. He parked in a space in front of the courthouse and trotted up the courthouse steps, pushing his way through one of the two massive oak doors. A gaunt old deputy with saggy jowls and bags under his eyes sat in a tilted-back chair reading a fishing magazine. He looked up and saw Jack coming and grinned.

"Better hustle your ass. Kicklighter'll hold you in contempt if you keep him waiting."

In chambers, the judge and sheriff were drinking coffee and

joking. The room smelled of good cigars. Both men stood and all three shook hands. Courtesies done, the judge gestured everyone to sit, not wasting a moment.

"Let's put our heads together for a moment before counsel and the prosecutor arrive, gentlemen."

"Where's Doug, Harley?" Jack asked.

"He's in my library with Miz Martha, eating breakfast. She insisted on feeding him. God help him if he tries to slip away from her. Hound Dog's on security today."

Kicklighter then cocked his thumb toward the sheriff sitting across from him. "Hal says things are working out quite nicely. I'm impressed, Jack. I really am. I'm gonna let him take over from here. Sheriff?"

Hal set his cup on the end table beside him and leaned forward. "I gotta move my prisoners, Jack. God only knows what that storm's gonna do, but I can't wait 'til the last minute to get sixty-five prisoners to higher ground. Every jailhouse between here and Atlanta will be full up with Florida prisoners."

The sheriff was starting to perspire under his armpits. Jack examined his face, looking for a clue as to what might be on his mind. He tamped down the irritation he felt rising. "And you're going to take Doug with you. That could be a real setback for him, you know."

Before the sheriff could answer, Jack turned on the judge. "I don't like this at all. I think we've got this kid turned around. He's a good boy. He's just never—"

Kicklighter raised his palm and cut him off. "Oh, for Pete's sake. Don't go getting melodramatic on me. It ain't your style. Let Hal finish."

The judge watched Jack fidgeting in his chair and reaching for his shirt pocket. "Go on. Have a smoke. Hal, open that window over there but not all the way. I don't want water on these fine refinished floors."

The judge got up and turned on the ceiling fan and a tall floor fan on the other side of the room. In his inner sanctum, J. Harlan

Kicklighter had exempted himself from the no-smoking rule and no one argued with him except his longtime secretary, Martha Banes, who hectored him mercilessly about being a scofflaw and setting a bad example for others. Each time he had to endure another session of her scolding and finger-wagging, he swore he'd never do it again and then promptly broke his promise. Jack suspected that the two of them loved their little ballet. The stern, blue-haired septuagenarian was fiercely devoted to her boss. She'd worked for him ever since he'd been on the bench, before his own hair began to turn white. An armed bodyguard wouldn't have been more protective of him than the sharp-tongued Miz Martha, as she was known about town.

Jack fished out his smokes and lit one. The judge handed him an ashtray. "Go ahead, Hal," the judge said to the sheriff.

"I'm in a bind here, Jack. Our arrangement's working out great. This little work release program we put together is about the best I've seen. But here's the rub. Doug's still a detainee in the Ocean County Corrections Center, which ain't a problem while the jail's here. But technically, it's fixing to get moved to Valdosta. Our agreement is that Doug works for you in the daytime but goes back to jail in the evenings. How the hell do I manage that now? Drive him back and forth from Valdosta every day? See what I mean?"

He tossed down the rest of his coffee and pulled a stick of gum from his shirt pocket. "The only way in hell this thing would work," he said, peeling off the paper wrapper, "is if this boy was actually out of jail on bond, which he ain't. I don't know what the hell to do now." He pivoted in his chair and looked at Kicklighter. "Judge, help me out here. I ain't got time to fiddle-fart around with this thing. What am I gonna do?"

The judge stared out the window as if collecting his thoughts and then cleared his throat. "I think it's time for a bond hearing," he said, looking at first one man and then the other. "I'll entertain a motion by counsel to release the boy on bond if a responsible party will stand good for it. Of course, you know I usually set a high bond whenever

I can justify it. On the other hand, I have occasionally allowed a defendant released on recognizance as long as a responsible third party is willing to assume responsibility for him."

The door opened and Miz Martha let in the young assistant state attorney and the public defender. The prosecutor was red-faced with exasperation. The other lawyer wore a calculating smile.

"You're late, gentlemen. I'm fining both of you a hundred bucks. You know what to do."

"We've been waiting in your courtroom fifteen minutes, Your Honor," the prosecutor sputtered. "The bailiff just told us y'all were in chambers."

Kicklighter thumbed his glasses down his nose, looked over the top of them and gave him a cold stare. "Well, cry me a river, Mr. Reynolds. Okay, let's take this to the courtroom."

Reynolds drew himself up to all six feet of his heron-like frame and pushed his luck too far. "Now wait just a minute here, judge. Has the State been back-benched? Is that the way of it?"

The public defender winced and suddenly remembered there was something of utmost importance in his file he needed to review. The sheriff screwed his eyes closed. Jack, intimately acquainted with the range of emotions conveyed by his friend's face, sucked in a deep breath and held it as he saw the thunderhead building. The look the judge gave Reynolds would've taken ten layers of varnish off. His voice, just above a whisper, cut like a saw blade. "What did you just say to me, you officious little snot? Did you just accuse me of judicial misconduct?"

The prosecutor quailed. His eyes bulged like a bullfrog's behind his thick glasses. "No, Your Honor. I . . . I—"

Kicklighter twisted the knife and mocked him derisively. "Aye aye? What? Are you a sailor now, Mr. Reynolds? Speak up."

The prosecutor's face had gone from apple red to as white as bleached bone.

"No, Your Honor. I'm sorry, Your Honor. I didn't mean to suggest—"

Kicklighter cut him off and pressed the attack. "Let me tell you something. You are perilously close to a citation for contempt, a one-night stay in Sheriff Patterson's stately manse and a Florida Bar ethics complaint by a sitting judge in good standing. Now, I'm going to give you five minutes to compose yourself and then we'll meet in my courtroom and carry out the business of the day. But if I so much as get a whiff of anything less than good ol' Southern charm and courtesy about your high-handed young ass, I'll let the good sheriff here school you on your manners. Got it, mister?"

The terror-stricken prosecutor did an about-face and fled the judge's chambers. A loud bumping sound and a muttered curse followed, and then Miz Martha came into the room smiling.

"Mr. Reynolds forgot to open the door before he tried to go through it, Your Honor. I believe he busted his nose. Bless his heart. Can I get y'all more coffee?"

"No ma'am," Kicklighter said. "Thanks, Miz Martha." The woman closed the door and returned to her desk.

When court convened five minutes later, Reynolds sat at his table dabbing at his nose with a white linen handkerchief. The bailiff called court to order. The court reporter looked up at the judge and nodded, then Kicklighter asked the public defender the nature of the business he desired to take up with the court. Patterson looked over at Jack and winked, and Jack suddenly realized what a display of stagecraft he was witnessing. When Bryce stood up and walked to the podium, he glanced at Jack and smiled. If the prosecutor noticed it, he didn't let on.

"Your Honor, my client called me this morning to inform me he's to be moved to another jail this very day. That's why I called you to ask for this hearing. I would humbly ask the court to further inquire of the State why this is necessary, as it will impact the agreement we've made with regard to Mr. Eleazer and Mr. Merkel. Surely there must be some way to resolve this, short of sending my client to another jail far away." The attorney sat back down.

"Mr. Reynolds," the judge said to the prosecutor. "Let's hear from the State on this."

The lawyer put his handkerchief in a pocket, got up and spoke quietly. "Thank you, Your Honor. Sheriff Patterson called me early this morning and told me he has to move his detainees to a correctional facility in Valdosta, Georgia as a precautionary measure because of this hurricane. I'd like to call him to the stand to testify, Your Honor."

"Well, go ahead, then," Kicklighter said, playing his part like a pro.

The sheriff got up, ambled to the witness stand and the bailiff swore him in.

"Good morning, Sheriff Patterson," the prosecutor said. "Is it true that you called me this morning to advise me that your concerns for the safety of your inmates has led you to decide to remove them to a safer location in the event Hurricane Brenda strikes this area or close enough to cause concern?"

Patterson wore his game face and nodded gravely. "Yes, that's true. Sheriff Dink Lokey called me yesterday and said he'd save me some space in his jail for my inmates in the event I want to evacuate them. But he said I needed to make a decision real quick because he's already getting calls from other Florida sheriffs."

Reynolds warmed to his game without realizing it'd already been played in his absence. "Thank you, sheriff. And when do you expect the transfer of prisoners to occur?"

"Late this afternoon, sir. I've already advised my inmates to contact their next of kin and their attorneys to let them know they're going to be moved to another facility for a few days."

The prosecutor smiled and stepped back from the podium. The courthouse clock gonged the half-hour. A sudden gust of wind rattled the windows.

"Thank you, sheriff. Anything else?"

The sheriff looked up at the judge and then over at the table where the defense attorney sat, and then back to the prosecutor. An artfully contrived expression of concern clouded his face. "Yes, sir. There is."

Reynolds frowned. "What would that be, sheriff?"

Patterson hesitated for a long moment before replying. It'd started to rain hard again and it pelted the windows like buckshot. The light in the courtroom grew so dim that the bailiff got up and turned on the lights. The old courthouse transmitted sound like a telephone. Footsteps fell upon the stairs outside the courtroom. The ceiling fans clicked somnolently and the sound of car tires on the wet pavement below sounded to Jack like the hissing sound made when a wave retreats across a sandy beach on its way back into the ocean. After what seemed like minutes had lapsed, the sheriff went on with his testimony.

"Well, as Mr. Reynolds here has said, this does have an unpleasant impact on the arrangement we've made with Mr. Merkel over there about my detainee. I'm reluctant to do that, if you want to know the truth of it. It's been successful. Real successful and I hate throwing a monkey wrench into the works, which I'd be doing if I had to haul the boy off to Valdosta with my other detainees. I think it might even amount to a big stumbling block for Mr. Eleazer."

The judge sat upright in his chair, removed his glasses, massaged his eyes, put his glasses back on and sat for a while without saying anything. Finally, he sighed overdramatically and leaned back in his big chair.

"Good Lord, gentleman. Isn't this a pickle? Where do we go from here?"

Mason Bryce stood and recited his lines with practiced conviction. "Your Honor, I'm going to ask that the court set bond for my client. We've heard the sheriff's assessment of how this could affect my client. I agree."

"Thank you, Counselor," Kicklighter said. "You may be seated. Mr. Reynolds? What says the State?"

Chastened and reluctant to invite further ire from the judge, Reynolds played his cards conservatively. "While I agree that transferring Mr. Eleazer to another jail unfortunately mitigates against the work release agreement, which I also agree is a little perturbing to all parties, the State included, I have the same trepidations I did the first time, Your Honor. Mr. Eleazer is a proven flight risk. That being said, into whose custody could he be released with a guarantee that we'd ever see him again?"

Jack stood, realizing that was his cue, the idea having been adroitly placed in his head without anyone having directly said so.

"I'll do it, Your Honor. I'll go his bond and stand good for his compliance with the court. I ain't had a moment's trouble out of him. He works hard, does what he's told to do and even takes the initiative to do tasks on his own."

Kicklighter smiled at his old friend and nodded. "Thank you, Mr. Merkel. You may sit down."

After Merkel took his seat, Kicklighter looked at the two lawyers and the sheriff. "I don't know, gentlemen. It's a tough call to make. I'm still apprehensive. But, let's have ourselves a bond hearing, shall we? Sheriff, go fetch Mr. Eleazer and bring him in."

When the sheriff returned with his prisoner, the boy's eyes went straight to Jack's. The two smiled broadly at one another. Patterson led his prisoner in front of the bench and stood beside him.

"Good morning, Master Eleazer. I'd like to ask you a question," the judge said. "Have you ever played Monopoly?"

"Good morning, Your Honor," he said quietly, raising his eyes to look at the man who presided over his life like a god. "Yes sir, I've played Monopoly. Me and my sister and my mama used to play it all the time."

Kicklighter gazed back at him and the faintest hint of a smile touched the corners of his mouth.

"Well, then. I reckon you know what a get out of jail free card is."

CHAPTER 12

JACK AND DOUG SAT side by side in the cramped, stuffy holding cell behind the courtroom and chatted while Sheriff Patterson stooped, then unlocked and removed the satellite tracking device from the boy's ankle. Grunting with the effort, the sheriff rose and put the tracker back in its box. "Slick, Jack. That was some slick work."

Jack elbowed his old friend and laughed. "I guess I learned a little bit about playing cards when I was in the merchants. I figured the only strong objection would come from Reynolds and he was already so skittish about the ass chewing he got earlier that I gambled he wouldn't protest too much for fear of getting another one."

Patterson adjusted his heavy belt and crammed a stick of gum in his mouth.

"Well, if kiddo here decides to go bye-bye, I'm gonna look like a damn fool for going along with it." He eyeballed the boy and jabbed a hefty finger at him. "Don't you even get the notion. You run off and make me look bad and I'll personally sic the dogs on you when we hunt you down. You hear me?"

Doug surprised both men by standing up and extending his hand to the sheriff, who stared at it in disbelief and then shook it.

"I won't run. I promise. It wouldn't just make you look bad; it'd make Pop here look bad, too. I ain't running again. That's a promise."

Patterson gripped the boy's hand tightly and looked him in the eye. He was a strict, by-the-book cop. But he didn't hesitate to play rough, as Doug had learned to his great misery the evening the sheriff frog-marched him out of Jack's office and shoved him down the steps.

Patterson let go of the boy's hand and draped a big arm around his shoulder, speaking quietly. "I know it's been bad for you, son. I surely do. But listen here. You got yourself a chance to break that streak of goddamn bad luck and have yourself a life."

Then he gave him a squeeze and released him.

They shook hands again. "Here's my card with my personal cell phone number on it. Trouble comes looking for you, don't you give in. Gimme me a holler. I'll be there."

Patterson reached out and tapped a knuckle under Jack's chin. "Close your mouth, Jack. You're lettin' all that hot air out."

He turned and walked to the door, paused and glanced back at them. "Don't fiddle-fart around with this here storm, Jack. You got responsibilities now."

"Yeah, I reckon I do, Hal. Some big ones. And thanks again."

"Don't thank me," the sheriff said, opening the door. "But I got a feeling you're gonna owe a certain circuit court judge another backcountry fishin' trip when this here bad weather passes."

And then he was gone.

When his lumbering footsteps were finally swallowed by the courthouse, Doug gave Jack a questioning look. Relief mixed with a smattering of bewilderment spread across his face. He looked back into Doug's eyes and also thought he saw just a lingering hint of trepidation, the wariness of the wild animal that, when set loose from the trap, hesitates at first to flee back into the woods and to safety.

"That's it? I'm free? I can just go back to work with you now?"

Jack realized that Doug hadn't yet considered the broader implications of his release and the deeper meaning of his freedom.

"Not just back to work, son. Home. You're going home with me, to your home and mine. And it'll stay that way for as long as you want. This is a new chance. For both of us."

"What do you mean?"

Jack considered the boy's question for a moment. "I'll tell you a story one day, but not now. Can you wait?"

"I guess I don't have anything but time."

"Not so, Doug. You've also got a friend to count on from now on. Understand?"

And then, before Jack saw it coming and could react, the once angry, troubled hoodlum who'd broken into his boatyard and broken his heart stepped quickly forward and wrapped his arms around him.

"Thank you, Pop. Thank you."

Jack stood there rigid and awkward for a moment before finally relaxing and returning the boy's embrace. "You're welcome, son. And thank you."

When Jack and his crew broke for lunch at noon that day, they scrambled to the dryness of the shop, all of them sweaty beneath their rain gear. The sky split wide open like a gray, gaping wound and the steady rain bled upon them in a deluge as band after band of Brenda's wet fury turned the boatyard into a sodden mess. It hammered the tin roof of the shop so forcefully and so relentlessly that it was necessary to shout to be heard above the din. Margie and both her sons, exhausted and nerve wracked by the rain's pounding intensity and the incessant clanging of halyards upon the metal mast of their big sailboat, fled the vessel and bolted to the shop to join everyone else, not even bothering to put on raincoats before abandoning ship. They were drenched to the skin by the time they made the short dash to the big building. Jack immediately noticed that Margie's clothing was plastered to her body like cellophane, leaving nothing to the imagination. He put his hand on her back, grabbed a big towel from a locker and quickly maneuvered her to the back of the shop. She eyed him perplexed as she took the towel from him.

"What's the matter?"

He positioned himself between her and his crew, handed her a light jacket off a nearby hook and glanced away to give her some privacy to cover herself.

"Well, let's just say you put on a bit of a wet T-shirt contest for the guys."

She glanced down and gasped, then snatched the jacket from his hand and shrugged into it, a crimson stain spreading from her neck to her face.

"Oh, shit! I didn't bother to put a bra on this morning. Jesus, this is so embarrassing." Then she laughed. "Damn it. I might as well have come skipping in here buck naked."

"Well, that probably would've ended the workday," Jack quipped to cover his own awkwardness. "Go on inside the office. I'll meet you there in a jiff. I just need to talk with the guys for a few minutes."

She zipped the windbreaker and wrapped the towel around her waist.

"Thanks for the save, buddy. I owe you."

Jack joined her there a few minutes later. She'd toweled her short hair mostly dry and was sitting at his desk, feet propped up and reading a boating magazine when he walked in.

"Come in here to gape, big boy?" she teased, hoping to see him blush again.

"No, just came to get you some dry things to wear. No point running in the rain back to your boat. Wait here a minute."

He walked quickly across the room and up the stairs. Pogy trotted into the office, came and licked her hand and then shook the water off his drenched fur, spattering her with it.

She petted the dog and talked to him and he looked at her with his big eyes as if he understood every word she said. The rain had slackened but she knew it wouldn't last. It'd been one rain band after another since right after daybreak. The sun hadn't appeared once. A cacophonous noise, coming in ascending and descending waves like some mad orchestral arrangement and sounding like hundreds of inflated balloons being rubbed simultaneously, came from an area near one side of the building overgrown with cattails.

Jack came back down the stairs and saw her looking toward the cattails. She pointed out the window.

"What in the dickens is that ungodly racket?'

He stepped over to the window carrying a pair of threadbare jeans and a faded red cotton short-sleeve shirt and handed them to her.

"Southern leopard frogs. Bad weather really gets them going. You should hear 'em at night, though."

She held the pants and shirt away from herself and examined them. "How the hell do you sleep through that racket?

"They're not so screechy and harsh-sounding at night. It's more of a steady, mellow sound. Lulls me to sleep every time."

She looked into his eyes and smiled.

"You really are in love with this place, aren't you?" she said.

He looked out the window again and nodded. "Sometimes I wish I could part the scenery like a curtain and just disappear into it."

She started to ask him why and then thought better of it.

"Well, I'm going to pop into the bathroom over there and slip into these," she said, then walked away. She closed the door behind herself, looked in the mirror, fussed with her hair, made a face and smiled at her reflection.

To her astonishment, the clothes were a perfect fit. She switched off the light and opened the door and was about to ask him whose clothes they were when she realized that she already knew the answer.

The rain still hadn't let up that evening when Jack drove the boy and himself into town. There was a tumbledown seafood shack balanced precariously on wobbly-looking, barnacle-encrusted pilings far down on one end of the docks. The proprietor, Jackie O'Brien, a cantankerous old New Englander with a brogue as thick as clam chowder and a temper as sharp as a well-honed fillet knife, was frying shrimp, clams and fish in a stainless-steel vat full of boiling grease. The aroma of the battered seafood, its crust cooked the color of amber and as crunchy as the fries he served with them, greeted Jack and Doug in the little parking lot beside the joint.

Hurrying inside, Jack glanced around and saw only two tables were taken. At one of them sat a couple of local crabbers—dirty, ragged looking men wearing rust-colored canvas coveralls and white rubber boots. They were sipping beer and waiting for their orders. Both looked up and waved at Jack when he and the boy came in. The water puddled around them on the rough-hewn planks. A young couple, dressed in a manner that marked them as tourists, stood at the counter waiting for the owner to take their order. Both wore matching gaudy T-shirts and ball caps from a local store that made most of its money selling such items to out-of-towners, especially those from up north. O'Brien, a large man with a beer belly and a bad leg, stopped what he was doing and hobbled over to wait on them, though without much warmth. The man asked for two fried clam platters and some white wine to drink while they waited for their food. Jack saw the indignation flare across the owner's broad face, glanced sideways at Doug and whispered, "Uh-oh. This is gonna be ugly."

O'Brien leaned across the counter and stared at the unsuspecting couple as if they were wayward schoolchildren who needed rebuking.

He pointed a stubby finger at a sign on the wall that read *Beer only. No wine. Don't ask... The Management.*

"Whassamatter?" he taunted. "You illiterate?"

"Sorry," the man said, clutching his wife's hand and backing away as if he expected the scowling O'Brien to vault over and attack him. "We'll just have Cokes." They retreated to an empty table far away from the counter and began whispering to each other and stealing nervous glances at their tormenter.

Jackie O'Brien had heard the screen door bang shut when Merkel and the boy entered. "Jaysus, Mary and Joey! Don't stand there drippin' water all over the deck. What the hell can I getcha tonight, Merkel, ya old pirate?"

Jack and Doug stepped up to the counter and O'Brien limped over to them. His face was red. Wild, white hair stuck out from around his chef's hat and he wore a grease-spattered white apron over his sweat-soaked white T-shirt that proclaimed in bold letters, *I'm a Masshole—What about it?* Doug's eyes were drawn to the apron.

"Who are you eyeballing, boyo?" the man snapped."

Doug edged away from the counter and put his hands up in a submissive gesture. "I was just wondering what a *Masshole* is. That's all."

The man looked over at the two crabbers who watched with amusement. The young couple at the other table looked terrified and seemed to be trying to decide whether to leave before their order was done.

"Hey, fellas. Tell boyo here what a *Masshole* is. And say it loud, damn ya."

On cue, one of them stood up, pointed his finger at the proprietor and roared drunkenly, doubling over laughing. "An asshole from Massachusetts!"

When Jack laughed along with them, Doug laughed, too, checking first to make sure the man was in on the joke.

"You shanty Irish bastard," Jack chuckled. "Fix us both up with a seafood platter all the way."

The man nodded and mopped his sweaty face with a rag. "You want chips with it?"

"Yeah, Jackie. chips with mine. Doug?"

The boy studied the menu. "I'll have fries with mine," he said, drawing another glare from the owner.

"Chips *are* fries, ya eejit. Hey where'd you find this mongrel, Jack?"

Jack reached over and put his hand on the boy's shoulder. "Jackie, this is Doug. He's working for me and staying out at the yard. Doug, this is Jackie O'Brien, proprietor of Jackie's Seafood Shak and shanty Irish bully from Boston."

"Southie, ya bastihd," the man said. "Southie."

Moments later, he returned with a beer for Jack and a big frosted mug of Coke for Doug. Jack waited for him to go back to the kitchen.

"He's really not a bad sort. He was a career Marine and boot camp drill instructor. He got his leg shot up in Vietnam. Had to retire before he got his time. A little ill-tempered at times but really a nice guy. He likes to mess with his customers. Don't take it personal. Personal is when he ignores you."

While they were sipping their drinks, the door opened and Rafe ducked in from the rain. He looked over and saw them and started to walk over to them when O'Brien shot him a defiant stare and pointed at the umbrella stand. He mumbled an apology and hung up his umbrella to dry before joining Jack and Doug.

"No feckin' tacos tonight, ya beaner," O'Brien yelled.

The tourist couple at the other table stopped eating and looked at each other with horrified expressions. Doug glanced from Jack to Rafe to O'Brien and shrank down into his chair. Rafe waggled his bushy eyebrows at the boy and then rounded on O'Brien, who stared fiercely at him, playing along.

"Oh, well, how about the Irish seven-course special?"

O'Brien scratched at his head and grinned. "Awright, smartass, let's hear it. What's that?"

"Six pints of beer and an overdone potato, you Beantown Masshole."
The proprietor roared and shuffled back to the kitchen.

"Yeh, yeh. Seafood platter all the way. Got it, Rafe."

"Hear the latest about the storm?" Rafe said, pulling up a chair.

"No. What about it? More rain?"

O'Brien brought Rafe a mug of beer and returned to the kitchen.
Rafe took a long swig. "She's moving again. Started about an hour or
so ago. *Madre de Dios!* This damn storm is really worrying me, Jack."

"Moving this way?"

"No, she's turning southwest. National Weather Service says she
might go between Miami and the Keys and head out to the Gulf,
maybe toward Mexico. But the steering currents are unstable, so
they don't really know for sure."

Jack sipped his beer and considered it for a moment. "Well,
maybe that's good for us, at least. She still weak?"

"For now, but that one guy who calls them right almost all the
time? He says she's gonna strengthen and dial it up again. He's the
only one making that prediction."

"So, where's he say she's gonna go?"

"Miami, maybe the Glades, maybe push on through to the other
side of the Peninsula and head north. Maybe, maybe, maybe. Who
really knows? This storm sort of reminds me of Inez back in 1966.
I was twelve. She hit the little fishing town of Progreso, where we
lived. Everyone had to leave. All of my father's and uncles' boats
were destroyed. That did it for Papa. We never returned. We were
too poor to start over again. They called her *la loca*, the crazy one,
because she was so unpredictable and dangerous. They even retired
the name after that one."

"You're right, old buddy. Who really knows what the damn
thing'll do?" Jack said. "I stopped by the store today to pick up a
few groceries and there was a mob of people in there. Bottled water
completely gone and cranky customers demanding more. I felt sorry
for the kid who works that aisle."

Doug had been sitting quietly and listening to the two men talk, taking it all in. "That sounds like a lot of coin tossing and guesswork to me," he finally said.

Both men looked at him.

"Know a bit about hurricanes?" Rafe said. "Tell us about it. I like to hear what other people say about the damn things. My Papa died young and broken on account of them."

Doug swirled the ice in his drink and took a sip, then answered, sadness creeping into his voice.

"One killed my grandpa and grandma. Hurricane Hugo. It knocked down a big tree that fell on their house in a little town near Charlotte. The power lines came down with it and the house burned up before they could get out. Mama was just twelve and was staying with her aunt and uncle in Asheville when it happened. They raised her after that." He paused. "Mama says—used to say—I favor grandpa a lot."

Sudden thunder rattled the old building. The rain drummed a staccato beat on its rusty tin roof. A jagged burst of lightning made the lights go dim for a moment. A draft blew napkins off a table. Rafe shook his head and gave the boy a sympathetic look. "That's awful, my friend. Where's your mama now?"

Jack shot Rafe a tardy look. The boy pushed his chair away from the table and got up. "I need to use the bathroom. Where is it?"

Jack pointed to a short hallway. Doug excused himself and left.

"Damn. Did I say something I wasn't supposed to say? *Mierda.* I'm sorry, buddy. What's the deal?"

Jack took a drink of his beer and breathed a long sigh. "It's a long story, *compadre.* A long and sad story. Do you mind if we not get into it right now? I'll share it with you later."

"Any time, *'mano.* Any time. Thanks for the heads-up before I pushed it. I hope I didn't upset him too much."

"He'll be okay. Don't worry about it."

Doug returned and continued. "Anyway, nobody in the foothills of North Carolina ever thought they'd see a hurricane, Mama said. I'm with Rafe, here. I wouldn't bet on anything."

A few moments later, O'Brien brought out their food and set it on the table. Doug picked up a fork and attacked his food, oblivious to the two men at the table with him. He completely abandoned all pretenses of table manners as he wolfed down his supper, eating French fries with one hand while stabbing shrimp and clams with the other and cramming them into his mouth. Before he could ask for more, O'Brien appeared with a plate containing half of a Key lime pie and set it in front of him.

"I make the best Key lime pie on this island," he bragged. "Wicked good. You take what you want. If you don't like it, I'll take it back to the kitchen and getcha something else."

Doug looked at the pie and then up at O'Brien. "I never had Key lime pie before."

"No? You're in for a treat, kid. Tell you what. You eat what's left of this pie and your meal's on Jackie."

"But you two bastihds—" He wagged a blunt finger at Jack and Rafe. "No freebies from this Masshole. G'wan kid. Eat it up."

They finished their meal and when Jack and Rafe went to the counter to pay, Doug stacked up the plates, silverware and empty mugs and carried them to the other end of the counter and set them down.

"Well, wouldja look at that?" the restaurant owner said. "Hey, kid. Bused a few tables, have ya? Wanna job?"

"Thanks, Mr. Masshole, but no thanks," he said. "I've already got one. A good one."

O'Brien leaned over the counter laughing so hard he wheezed. They could hear him all the way to the nearly flooded parking lot.

CHAPTER 13

THEY CALLED HER A vagabond wind. She'd defied all predictions, confounded the experts and walloped Miami, packing winds of 120 mph after she ballooned into a Cat 3 storm, then tore through Biscayne National Park and took aim at the Keys. The Conch Republic had hunkered down and awaited its beating. Instead, the increasingly nomadic Brenda ripped through the Everglades, exiting at Cape Sable and into the Gulf of Mexico. And then she stalled, as if hesitating while she decided where to go next. Weakened by her trek across land, she was downgraded to minimal Cat 2 status. Eager to be rid of the storm that held millions in thrall as it roamed gypsy-like, weather experts timidly conjectured that would probably be her demise. But the next day, she roared back to life and veered northwest toward New Orleans. Then she bobbled and stalled yet again. At that point, the experts broke down into warring tribes of differing prognostications and admitted among themselves, but not with the storm-weary and nervous public, that they had no idea what the capricious storm would do next. It was around that time that a weather forecaster dubbed Brenda a "vagabond wind." But by then, northeast Florida and Morgan's Island seemed to be out of danger.

Rafe crouched on his haunches in the shop examining the new rudder for *Starshine* that'd arrived from the factory that morning, swearing at the latest radio weather update. "Vagabond wind. Damn weather people. Why do they always feel like they have to get cutesy with everything? Nothing cute about a hurricane, especially one that can't seem to make up its mind who it wants to clobber next."

Jack and Margie stooped beside him and watched as he set the rudder aside and reached inside the shipping container. Margie leaned closer. "What's wrong, Rafe? You seem a little cranky today."

He rummaged around in the shipping crate and retrieved a small plastic bag with a long stainless steel bolt in it and set it aside. "Well, there goes getting this damn rudder on today after all. Looks like the factory sent the wrong bolt and we don't have one that'll work. We're gonna have to call them and have them ship us one."

He looked up at Margie. "Sorry. I just don't think it's wise to take Brenda so lightly. She's still out there and she's still a hurricane."

"And on her way to party in the French Quarter," Margie said.

"We don't know that for sure," Rafe said. "The forecasters ain't been right so far. Why start now? I still don't think we're in the clear."

But the afternoon weather argued otherwise. The skies were blue again and the temperature was in the low nineties, though the days of rain had seemingly emptied the air of all its humidity. Margie canceled her rental car reservation. Her sons had gotten up early that morning, borrowed a skiff from Jack and gone fishing. They'd returned with a mess of flounder that even Jack found impressive. The younger, John, had a bloody homemade bandage on his right index finger. Margie gasped when she and Merkel met them at the cleaning table to admire their catch. "What the hell did you do to your finger?"

He stared at her and ignored her question.

"Tell Mom and Mr. Merkel what a dumb thing you did," his brother teased.

The boy reddened. "Shut up, Seth!"

"He stuck his finger in the flounder's mouth trying to get the hook out," Seth said, struggling to contain his laughter. "The flounder latched onto it and wouldn't turn loose. I had to pry its jaws open with my pocketknife."

The younger boy picked up a handful of fish entrails and flung them at his big brother. "Yeah, well I caught the biggest flounder, asshole," he yelled.

Margie stepped between her sons, pushing them away from each other. "Okay, that's enough. Seth, get your fish cleaned. John," she said, seizing him by an elbow, "come with me and let me clean that up and put a decent bandage on it before it gets infected and falls off." She stuck her jaw out and shook her finger at Jack, who was chuckling at the boys' antics. "Can it, Merkel! Don't egg 'em on!"

He lowered his gaze and smiled sheepishly. The older boy turned away so his mother wouldn't see him grinning and went on cleaning fish. Jack watched Margie drag the still fuming John across the boatyard.

"You sure you want to have a relationship with my mom?" Seth said, after checking to make sure she was out of earshot. "She's a firecracker."

Caught off guard by the question, Jack picked up a fillet knife off the cleaning table and began absentmindedly honing its blade. The boy studied the expression for a moment, picked up another fish and began filleting. "Don't tell me you haven't thought about it."

"Might be I'm not looking for a relationship right now," Jack said quietly, hefting a large flounder.

Seth placed his fillet knife down for a moment and studied Jack's face. "We'll see about that. Listen, don't get me wrong. Mom's not a swooning belle desperately seeking a man. I mean, c'mon. She's rich.

She's pretty; but she's independent and tough as hell. Anyone who goes up against her will find out really quick that she's a force you don't want to mess with. Men? Ha! In the islands, I watched them trailing around after her like hounds. All kinds of them. One was a damn senator. She put 'em all on skates. But she's obviously drawn to you. And that speaks volumes to me, Jack. Volumes."

For the first time, Jack caught himself musing about what it'd be like to have a female companion back in his life. And then his thoughts went down that sad road to a little cemetery where his one and only love lay buried, realizing he still wasn't ready to let her go.

While frying the flounder fillets to crisp, golden excellence, Jack regaled everyone with tales about his sailing days in the Merchant Marine.

He painted vivid portraits of ports and adventures in faraway places like Singapore, Hamburg and Amsterdam, with its famed Red-Light District. But he saved his favorite place for last. For it was Dublin, on the River Liffey, that captured his heart.

"I'd always wanted an authentic Irish tweed coat." He smiled as his thoughts returned to the little shop in Nassau Street where a handmade Donegal Tweed of a rich brown and subtle gold herringbone weave caught his eye. It'd cost him almost a half a month's wages, but he craved it. He remembered the suppleness of the virgin wool and the trace aroma of lanolin that still imbued it when the diminutive old woman with merry blue eyes who owned the store held it for him as he'd slipped his arms into the sleeves, and the way she'd cooed in admiration when she turned him around to check the fit.

"But the music," Jack went on, returning to the present. "It was everywhere. Buskers on every corner, playing fiddles and pipes, guitars, tin whistles and harps. The whole city seemed to be singing." He looked away for a moment with a dreamy expression. "I fell in love with Dublin and sometimes dreamed of returning there to live out the rest of my days." He stopped again and then went on. "I think I would've made a fine Irishman."

"Why didn't you?" Doug asked.

Jack took a sip of the beer he'd been nursing and walked over to the large window overlooking the deck and his marina below. He stared out at the darkness of the river glowing silver in the moonlight and the slumbering marshes beyond.

"Ah, Doug. There's just so much that holds me here. Some things you just can't leave behind and walk away from. At some point in a man's life, he comes to know that he's set his anchor someplace that holds him where he is, no matter how much he longs to roam. Once he's comfortable with that, a dream of going someplace else is just a foolish notion."

The two of them locked eyes and took the measure of one another until Margie broke the spell as she began setting the table. "Well, aren't you the philosopher this evening, Jack Merkel? A Renaissance man for all seasons. I'm impressed."

In that moment, she thought she wanted nothing more than to touch him, to lay her head against his chest, listening to his heartbeat, feeling his warmth and inhaling his fragrance. He laughed softly as he moved to help her. Doug picked up a pitcher of iced tea off the bar and began filling everyone's glasses. Margie set the platter of fish on the table.

"Come on everybody," Jack said. "Let's eat this supper while it's hot."

After supper, they all pitched in washing the dishes, putting them away and tidying up the kitchen. Afterward, they gathered outside on the deck. Jack sipped a beer while Margie nursed a glass of white wine, complimenting him again on his cooking and raving about his hushpuppy recipe. Seth and Doug occupied a far corner of the deck and amused themselves in quiet conversation with the occasional boisterous laughter. After a few minutes, the younger boy came out of the house and sat with them. A moment later, he got up and stalked downstairs, sniggering contemptuously. Seth jumped up and flung a plastic cup full of ice at him. John flipped him the bird.

"What the hell was that all about?" Margie said, putting her wineglass down and storming over to them. "What's going on here, Seth? Why did you just throw that cup of ice at your brother?"

The boy whirled around to face his mother, his jaw muscles knotted in fury.

"I'll be so glad when you send him back to the old man! He's such an asshole. He's just like the old man. He ruins everything." Angry tears welled in Seth's eyes. "I hate him!"

She took him by the shoulders, guided him back to his chair and stood behind him. Doug watched silently, expressionlessly, as Margie massaged her son's shoulders. He was normally mild mannered, a peacemaker who kept a level head when everyone else quarreled. But she also knew that her firstborn kept tamped down a fire of antipathy toward his father and, of late, she'd noticed, toward his brother as well. The kettle was bound to boil over at some point, and she reckoned with sorrow that the moment had come at last.

"No, you don't hate him, Seth," she said calmly. "He's your brother."

"No, he's not!" he said, through clenched teeth. "He's just the old man's little doppelganger." He laughed bitterly. "He's even beginning to look like him. He's not like us, Mom, you and me."

She grabbed a nearby chair and sat close beside him.

"Will you tell me what happened?"

Before Seth could answer, Jack came and stood beside her, his eyes searching hers for a clue as to what had so quickly gone wrong. She stole a quick sideways glance at Doug, then looked back up at Jack who took the hint and put his hand on Doug's shoulder. "C'mon over here with me a minute, okay? Come on, now."

Slowly, the boy got up and Jack put his arm around his shoulder and led him away. Margie waited until they were a safe distance away before addressing her son. "Spill it, goddamnit. Right now."

The boy put his head in his hands and took a deep breath. When he finally looked at Margie, there were fresh tears. "We were just shooting the breeze." He wiped his nose with the back of his hand. "Having a good time and then all of a sudden, John called Doug white trash. Just like that. No provocation at all. Just said out of the blue, 'Damn, where'd you get all those white trash tattoos?' The same kind of crap the old man does, just pulls an insult out of thin air and cuts you with it before you can even see it coming."

She patted his hand and got up and walked over to the other side of the deck where Jack stood with his arm around Doug, speaking in a low voice. She stepped quickly to Doug, put both her arms around him and hugged him. He stood rigidly for a moment, not acknowledging the gesture, and then he put his head down and buried his face in her shoulder and began to cry quietly. Jack stepped aside as Margie swayed gently back and forth with the boy.

"It's okay, sugar. It's okay. That's it. Let it all out. It's okay now."

And then he wrapped his arms around her and clung to her and wept bitterly. "Mama," he whimpered. "Elizabeth."

She gave Jack a look over Doug's shoulder and cut her eyes over to where Seth stood staring into the darkness. He nodded and then walked woodenly away.

"C'mon, kiddo," she said to Doug. "Let's go inside a moment, okay?"

She walked him into the kitchen, wet a dishcloth with cold water and began wiping his face with it, speaking gently and reassuring him as she did. When he had settled down, she steered him into the living room and sat him down on the sofa.

"I need a beer," she said. "Can I get you something while I'm in the kitchen?"

He didn't respond for a moment and she feared that she'd lost him again.

"No. I'm all right now."

She sat beside him, drank a couple of swallows of the icy brew and then held the bottle toward him. "Here you go, pal. Have yourself a swig or two and clear your throat."

He gazed at her in surprise. "Oh, I couldn't do that. I don't think Pop would like it."

"C'mon, have some." She grinned and gave him a conspiratorial wink. "It'll be our little secret. Besides, I don't think Jack Merkel is going to kick you out of the house if I give you a couple of sips of beer because my son is a total asshole and said something really shitty to you. And don't tell me you've never had any before. Here, drink up."

He took the beer from her, tipped the bottle up and gulped. Then he handed it back to her, put his hand over his mouth and belched politely.

"Better?"

"Yes, ma'am."

"Oh, stop it with the ma'am stuff."

She laughed then tilted the bottle to her lips again, drained most of the remaining beer in two big gulps, then opened her mouth wide and let loose with a long, rude belch. Doug gaped at her for a moment and then leaned over, laughing.

"That's the ticket. That's the Doug I want to see. Now listen, I know what my jackass kid said to you. No, no. Don't say anything. Listen to me. I'll deal with him for that, bet your ass. But don't ever let some punk kid knock you down like that again with nothing more than a smart mouth. Got it? You're better than that, tougher than that, too."

She got up from the sofa, took him by the hands and pulled him up. "Oh. Who's Elizabeth?"

"My sister," he said, quietly. "I haven't seen . . . never mind."

She squeezed his hand. "It's okay. Now, I'm going to run back over to the boat, kick Johnny's trash-talking little ass and come back with my guitar. I'm in the mood for a jam session. Think you can convince that big galoot Merkel to drag out that fiddle of his before I get back?"

The look of delight that spread across his face reminded her of a sunrise she'd seen one morning as she'd sat alone in the cockpit sailing over from the Bahamas. Tentative at first, it had brightened until its fulsomeness filled the early morning sky with its glow.

"Wow," he said, boyishly. "I'd sure like that a lot. I bet he will, don't you?"

She smiled at him and patted him on his cheek. "How can he say no?"

When Margie got to her boat, her son was sitting in the salon playing his video game as if nothing had happened. She snatched the game from his hands, dropped it on the deck and stomped on it. Then she leaned over and slapped his face, leaving a red palm print. He stood up, glared defiantly and she slapped him again.

"Wipe that goddamn look off your face or I will with the back of my hand. If I ever, I mean *ever* find out that you've done anything like that again while you're still in my custody, I won't send you back to your father. I'll stick your ass in a juvenile facility and let him worry about getting you out. Come tomorrow, you *will* take your snobby ass over there and make a sincere apology to that young man in front of your brother, Merkel and me, as witnesses. Now pick up this goddamn mess and go to bed."

She was walking across the yard with her guitar case in hand when she heard the sound of a fiddle playing. She laughed and walked faster, anxious to get there. She found Jack sitting on a three-legged stool sawing his fiddle. He made a silly face and waggled his eyebrows. He took a break to rosin his bow while she tuned her guitar, then tucked the old fiddle under his chin and began to play. She finished tuning just in time to join him on the song. Within moments, Doug and Seth were stomping their feet and singing along.

Jack, who had closed his eyes when he began drawing his bow across the strings, opened them again, looked across his fiddle at Margie and joined her in harmony for the tune's ending. They clung to the last note like it was a treasure and smiled at each other. Margie sent him a slow wink. He caught himself a breath away from returning it and smiled shyly instead.

"Do we make beautiful music together or what?" she said.

"I think maybe we do," he said, softly. "All of us."

That night, while Morgan's Island slept, Hurricane Brenda reawakened in the Gulf of Mexico, whirled eastward and charged with a murderous fury at little Punta Gorda, Florida, and its 16,000 unsuspecting, vulnerable residents.

CHAPTER 14

CAUGHT OFF GUARD BY the storm's unpredicted and sudden right
hand turn, the hurricane center sprang into action, sending out a flood
of information, predictions and alerts. But none of it came soon enough
to save Punta Gorda. Law enforcement and the county's emergency
management services didn't have enough time to adequately warn the
sleeping citizens of the little town that they were in the gun sights of
a Category 4 hurricane with winds of 155 miles an hour. Many of the
evacuees who heard the disturbing predawn warnings and fled their
homes were caught on the congested and frenzied roads. Thousands
more woke to a monster beating down their doors. At just after five
a.m. on July thirtieth, Brenda roared ashore at twenty miles an hour.
It wasn't there long, but in the brief time it took to rampage through
the boating and fishing paradise, with its sixty miles of canals and
seventy percent of its population living on the water, nearly every

building in the little town was either destroyed or badly damaged. Thousands, many of them retirees in mobile home parks, were left homeless. Worse, Brenda killed a dozen people, some of whom were trapped on the roads trying to escape. Punta Gorda in ruins, she set her sights once again on the state's east coast and plundered on. This time, meteorologists were confident in their prediction—New Smyrna Beach lay directly in Brenda's path as she cut through the heart of the state.

Pogy woke Jack just before five a.m., wanting to go outside. When Jack turned on the deck lights and opened the door to let the dog out, he noticed the light rain that had just begun to fall. There was a little wind but nothing to get excited about. Waiting for the dog to smell and anoint every post, plant and shrub in the yard, he went to the kitchen and started the coffee, idly turned on the marine radio and switched it to the National Weather Service, hoping that the rain was just temporary. When he heard the tinny, robotic National Weather Service automated announcement, he whistled and walked quickly to the living room and switched on the television. A meteorologist was reporting on what had happened during the night and the devastation in Punta Gorda. The announcer halted in mid-sentence as the station cued to video from the beleaguered town. The video, most of it rain-blurred, showed water surging into neighborhoods, debris flying and people running frantically to cars and to the houses of neighbors. A palm tree, uprooted and turned into a flying battering ram, slammed into a mobile home and destroyed it.

Moments later, Pogy came trotting back inside, followed quickly by Margie, who shook the water off her umbrella and hung it on a rack by the back door.

"Holy shit!" she said. "Can you believe it? I got up to pee and couldn't go back to sleep. I went to the salon and switched on the tube and this is the first thing I saw. I thought they'd said that storm was wandering north and fizzling out."

"They did. Apparently, they didn't see this coming at all until it was damn near on top of Port Charlotte and Punta Gorda. They weren't able to get the word out 'til it was too late."

They both stood silent, glued to the images of the devastation that were unfolding on the screen. After a few minutes had passed, Jack turned down the volume and went to the kitchen.

"Well, while you're here, would you care for some coffee? I'd fix breakfast for everyone, but I don't think the kids would appreciate getting woke up so early."

"Sure, might as well. While you're at it, how about some more of your biscuits and honey?"

He gave her a bashful smile and went to the refrigerator and took out a package of his frozen biscuits and spread them on a baking sheet. Margie helped herself to a cup of coffee while he slid the biscuits into the oven. The two of them sat at the dining room, neither saying anything for a few moments.

"So, what now, Jack? I mean, with this storm?"

"I'm not sure. They say she's gonna barrel across the middle of the state right past Orlando, and head out into the Atlantic. Maybe crossing that much land will knock the steam out of her. She's moving fast, about twenty miles an hour, which is a good thing because it limits the time she has to hang around and do more damage. For the time being, I don't think we have too much to be concerned about. It's not even raining as much as it was a few days ago. Maybe we'll be okay after all."

"I guess we'll have to wait and see what our resident hurricane expert has to say about it," she said. "No doubt Rafe will have his own predictions. Poor guy. I can't imagine the heartache his family went through, surviving storm after storm in Mexico. He told me the other day about what his father and uncles went through trying to hang in against the odds as struggling fishermen in the Gulf. One of his uncles drowned when his skiff capsized during a squall. Rafe said that he'd never seen his father cry before, but that he did for days after losing his youngest brother. It broke him. It wasn't long after that that a hurricane took everything they had and they left and never fished again. That's why he's so tense about this one. He's afraid, though he'd never admit it. By the way, is he married? He seems like such a sweetie but I've never heard him say anything about a wife or family."

Jack stirred his coffee for a moment, trying to decide how or even if to answer. Rafe Hernandez had been with him a long time and there was a strong bond between them. Over the years, their relationship had deepened until the gentle yard superintendent had become like a brother. He didn't want to say anything that would violate the relationship but he'd come to trust Margie's discretion, as well as her compassion for others, especially those who'd been unlucky and damaged in some way. She'd joshed in Spanish with Rafe one afternoon, going so far as to call him *viejo,* the Spanish word for *old* but which also had a deeper meaning than simply aged. It's also a sign of respect for a person's elder status, and Jack could tell that his longtime friend had been secretly pleased by not only the application itself, but by the mere fact that she'd made the effort to converse with him in his native tongue. After thinking about Margie's question a little longer, he decided it was safe to reply. He got up and went to the oven and checked on the biscuits.

"Years ago he was married," he said, sitting back down. "His wife was a bit younger than him. He's had a hard life and it left its mark on him at a fairly young age. When he began to look older than his years, she dumped him for a younger man. He woke up one morning and she was gone."

"What a shitty thing to do to such a nice guy."

"Don't ever say anything bad about her in his presence," Jack said. "After all that betrayal, he still loves her. He told me one time that if she came back to him, he'd forgive her and go on loving her. She was his first love and his last."

"So, he never remarried?"

"No. He's very Catholic in his beliefs. Marriage is until death. He doesn't even have a girlfriend, hasn't since his wife left him."

"That's so sad. So I guess there were no kids, either, huh?"

"She had a miscarriage and there were no more pregnancies. Rafe said she blamed it on him."

He cut off the conversation to fetch the biscuits along with plates and forks and a brand new jar of tupelo honey. Margie picked up the jar and studied it.

"This honey looks different from the stuff we put on our biscuits before. Such a beautiful golden color with just a hint of green." She took the lid off the jar and sniffed it. "Sweet Jesus! I thought the other honey had a nice bouquet, but this is positively dreamy. I guess all honeys aren't created equal, huh?"

"Oh, no. Tupelo honey's the gold standard of honeys. First of all, it's not easy to get most of the time. It comes from the white tupelo tree, which only grows in a few river swamps in the southeast. The Apalachicola River Valley's where the best comes from. Honeybees can't resist them, but the blossoms come and go in two weeks. A lot of what passes for tupelo honey is actually either fake or blended. This is the real deal."

She eyed the bottle again. "Where'd you get it?"

"A friend of mine over in Gulf County. He literally picks up all his hives and trucks them over to the Apalachicola River swamps for the blooming season. The trees grow in the water or right beside it, so it's hard to get to them. He gives me honey in exchange for fresh fish."

She set a biscuit on her plate and poured the honey on it, sparingly. Jack laughed.

"Be generous. I've got plenty more where that came from."

She poured more honey on the biscuit, forked off a bite and tasted it. Jack watched as she closed her eyes and chewed blissfully.

"My God. They should refine this into sugar. It'd put the cane and sugar beet producers out of business."

He took the jar from her and poured a generous helping onto

his own biscuit. "Ah, but it doesn't crystallize like other honey. You could leave this jar in the pantry a hundred years and it still would be the same buttery, slow moving-stuff it is right now. Did you know it's the only honey that diabetics can eat?"

She scooped up another bite. "Really? Why's that?"

"It has a really high fructose level and metabolizes quickly in your body. That's also what keeps it from crystallizing. My doctor recommended it several years ago when my blood sugar got a bit elevated. I'm lucky to have a reliable source. It's pretty rare, the real stuff, that is."

She looked across the table at him and studied his face for a long time, her smile growing wider and her eyes sparkling green, then nudged him with her foot under the table.

"Kind of like you."

"Huh?"

She put her fork down and smiled impishly. He shifted in his seat.

"Rare, like you. Sweet, slow-moving—the gold standard against which all men ought to be judged. Every day you wow me with something I never knew. You have such a passion and a love for everything you experience. It flows through your veins like this honey."

Jack glanced down at his plate, folding and refolding his napkin.

"Oh, I don't know about all that. I don't think that way at all."

She glanced across the adjoining living room, with its sturdy ceiling beams and warm smelling tongue and groove cypress walls, to the hallway leading to the home's bedrooms and lowered her voice. "Listen," she said, again settling her eyes on him and clasping her hands on the bar. "I'm really sorry about John's behavior last night. No, I'm not just sorry; I'm mortified about what he said to Doug. It's all I can do to look at him right now. His hostility's inexcusable and embarrassing."

Fine lines appeared and etched her forehead. She gave him an imploring look that seemed to him almost a cry of silent desperation.

Then she lowered her eyes and released a long, bitter sigh. It spoke to him of a vulnerability that she'd never revealed before, a betrayal of the gritty persona that he'd assumed went bone deep. And it dawned on Jack that, like him, she bore her own wounds behind a stoic mask. In that moment, his heart went out to her as an inner voice whispered to him that she was a kindred spirit, one who'd lost the child that she'd nurtured as tragically as he'd lost his own, just in a different way. Tentatively, and with a tenderness he'd long believed that his years of hard grief had left behind like bleached bones, he reached across the table and laid one rough palm upon her folded, trembling smooth hands. The pain she felt transmitted to him like an electric current.

"I don't know what to do," she whispered. "I'm afraid I'm losing my baby."

Jack was still searching for something he could say to comfort her when Doug shuffled into the room, rubbing his eyes sleepily, his hair still tousled from sleep and wearing the faded, albeit clean threadbare jeans with a hole in one knee, and the yellow T-shirt he wore the night Sheriff Patterson had dragged him into the marina. "I thought I heard someone in here," he said. "Mmmm, coffee. I think I'll fix myself a cup, if it's okay."

Jack looked at him and grinned. If the boy took note of the faraway look on Margie's face, he didn't let on.

"Doug, you live here now," he said, shifting around to greet him. "You don't need my permission to pour yourself a cup of coffee or fix yourself something to eat."

"Wow! Biscuits and honey," he said, perching on a stool beside Jack. "Oh, yeah. I think I will."

He set a biscuit on a plate and, without bothering to read the label on the honey jar, poured some on it. He stuck his fork into a chunk of biscuit, dripping honey, and put it in his mouth and smiled.

"Mmmm. Tupelo honey, too."

"So you're familiar with it?" Jack said.

The boy stared off beyond Jack's shoulder for a moment as if contemplating something.

"Yeah, my mama sometimes got it from a beekeeper up in South Georgia where we lived for a little while. It was our favorite. I ain't had any in ages. *Mmm*. Good stuff. This beekeeper really knows his honey."

Neal bent beneath the engine cowling on the forklift, cursing aloud. By noon, the drizzle had let up and the sun had come back out and the humidity in the yard was oppressive. "Goddamnit!"

Eddie Kraft looked over his shoulder, saw Margie standing nearby talking with Rafe, and turned back around with a horrified expression. His prematurely bald head and his face were shiny with sweat and he pulled a bandana from his hip pocket and mopped his face and head. "N-Neal. M-maybe you ought to cut out the c-cussing. M-Miz Waller is right over there."

Neal, who doubled as the official mechanic, looked up, his face smeared with black grease, and glared at the young forklift operator.

"So what? She cusses like a goddamn stevedore, herself. Don't tell me you ain't heard her."

He wiped the grease off his hands with a dirty rag.

"This thing's fucked, Eddie. Fucked! There's a bad ring or something in there and I can't get to it to see what the hell's going on. How long did you let the sonofabitch blow oil before you came and got me?"

A look of indignation flashed across the face of the otherwise good-natured man. This time, he didn't stutter when he spoke.

"I didn't let it blow oil at all, Neal. I came and got you soon as I noticed it."

"Well, you should've c-c-c-come and got me s-s-sooner."

Eddie balled up his fists and took a quick step toward him. Jack approached and calmly stepped in between the two men.

"C'mon guys. I know. It's hot and miserable and everyone's nerves are frayed but I can't have y'all beating each other up like a couple of hooligans. What's the problem here?"

The two men continued to glower at one another.

"Damn forklift's spraying oil, boss man," Neal said. "I don't know how long. Eddie says he just noticed it. But something's busted in there and I can't get to it to see what it is."

"So, what do we do, Neal?" Jack said.

"We gotta tear the damn thing down and hope it's something as simple as replacing a ring in the engine."

"How much time do you need for that?"

"I can have her completely torn down in two hours if you'll free up Eddie to help me. I've got extra rings in the shed. If that's all that it is, I can prob'ly have her up and running again sometime this afternoon."

Jack nodded and clapped both men on the shoulder.

"Good. Get busy, then. And no more fighting. Got it? "

Jack walked over and joined Rafe and Margie on the front porch.

"I guess you've been keeping up with the hurricane announcements today," Rafe said. "Punta Gorda pretty much got wiped out."

"Yeah," Jack said. "And now central Florida's taking a beating. I heard they recorded wind at nearly a hundred miles an hour in the suburbs just north of Orlando. Looks like New Smyrna Beach or Daytona is gonna get walloped in the next few hours. Funny, the weather's been drizzly off and on here today but nothing bad, especially with a storm like that in the vicinity."

He glanced at the sky and shrugged. "Fast-moving, tight storm's the reason why. From what I hear, even fifty miles away from the eye it ain't generating much bad wind or nasty weather at all. She's weakened some in the last hour, down to Category 2 status again."

Margie pulled off her sunglasses and glanced from one man to the other. "So, what do you think the storm will do once it goes back over the ocean, Rafe?"

He considered the question for a moment as if calculating figures in his head. "One of the top specialists in the hurricane center is saying he's pretty confident that Brenda's finally running out of gas and that her last run across the state's likely to finally take the wind out of her sail, pun intended."

Margie wiped a speck off her sunglasses and put them back on. "But what do you think, Rafe?" she asked. "You've been right so far."

He considered it for a moment and smiled. "I'm thinking they might have it right this time. This thing can't last much longer. It's already hung around way longer than most storms. I mean, it could even drift by here as minor tropical storm or tropical depression. We'll get some wet, windy weather but I don't think we're gonna see Hurricane Brenda."

"Good, that means we don't have to worry about bugging out after all," Jack said. "We've had our share of tropical storms over the years. I worry about flooding a little bit, but we can deal with that."

New Smyrna Beach got lucky. Hurricane Brenda was just barely a minimal hurricane by the time she hit the little beach town just before midday on July thirtieth. Early that evening she was downgraded to a tropical storm. By the time she stalled again off St. Augustine early that same evening, she was barely tropical storm status with maximum sustained winds a paltry fifty miles an hour. That night, Jack and Margie sat in his living room watching the weather coverage and noting the celebratory atmosphere in the newsroom. The local meteorologist again hammered it up for the camera. Brenda had finally gone off to hurricane heaven, he quipped.

When Jack saw Margie out just after ten that evening, it'd begun drizzling so she put up her umbrella and looked back at him from the edge of the deck.

"The next time I come over to watch television with you, I'm bringing popcorn and we're gonna watch a chick flick together. No more Weather Channel. Okay?"

He laughed and waved goodbye.

"We'll see. Sleep tight, captain."

"You, too, skipper," she said and then hurried away in the rain.

He went inside, undressed and got into bed. He lay awake for a long time thinking about the sassy yacht owner who'd sailed into his marina and seemed eager to take charge of him. But this time, instead of chasing his thoughts about her away, he let his mind mull over them and when he did, they meandered to her face, with its full-lipped smile and perfect white teeth, to the sparkling green eyes that always seemed to be searching his, to her bawdy laughter that made him want to laugh with her, and how deftly she found opportunities to be near him. He allowed himself to cling to those thoughts as he drifted off into profound sleep and had dreams that didn't haunt him for the first time in years. In his dreams, the sailboat building had been completed and he and Doug, who'd become his son, were sailing together.

Margie lay awake in *Starshine*'s expansive master stateroom listening to the soft patter of raindrops on the boat's deck and the wind strumming the rigging. Her mind went again and again to the sensation of Jack's hand on hers. Just before she slept, it came to her that she wasn't just physically attracted to him, but that she might be falling in love with him.

Tropical Storm Brenda snored, sleepwalking north.

CHAPTER 15

RAFE HAD TURNED OFF the television at eleven p.m. and went to bed. For the first time in days, he didn't toss and turn and fret. Brenda had wobbled and stalled just off St. Augustine. The old city was getting lots of rain, high surf and beach erosion but that was about it. He woke up at four a.m. with a gnawing sensation that something wasn't quite right, a little mouse nibbling persistently away at the edge of his sleep. He went downstairs to the fridge for a drink of water and turned the television to the Weather Channel. No significant changes had been noted. A small tropical wave that lay eastward of what was left of Brenda had been picked up on radar, but it was one of many waves from the Eastern Caribbean westward, fairly common and nothing to give anyone pause. He watched the news for a few minutes and convinced himself that his renewed apprehension was the result of his childhood experience. He turned off the television, prayed a decade of the rosary for the repose of his father's soul, and went back to bed. He woke up at six-thirty a.m., his usual time, and looked out the sliding glass doors of the old beach house he'd renovated on the north end of Morgan's Island. Something felt wrong. The wind was blowing harder than it ought to have been, and it seemed a little too dark outside for that time of the day, which was the time he always showered, shaved and got dressed before heading down to the marina for his usual morning coffee with Jack. It was also raining harder than had been predicted on the news he'd watched before going back to bed just after four. But it was the appearance of the ocean that he found most disconcerting. He'd been up for nearly an hour and the waves seemed to have gotten bigger even though the tide was halfway out. The ugly grey waves capped with seafoam tossed and heaved. The ocean seemed to be roaring. He slid open one of the doors and stepped onto his balcony overlooking the ocean. The raindrops stung when they hit his face and the wind blew his hat off. Going back inside, he got a towel out of the bathroom, dried his face and head and went downstairs to the living room, and again turned on his television. The remnants of Tropical Storm Brenda had edged offshore of St. Augustine during the night but had stalled and was expected to continue to weaken further. He turned off the set and fished his car keys from his pocket.

He was almost to the door when he stopped and turned around and went back upstairs, remembering that he'd not closed the storm shutters. Looking out at the ocean, he was amazed at how big the waves were getting.

He found Jack in a mood befitting the storm. The weather didn't seem nearly as bad at the marina located on the backside of the island, but Rafe sensed its mounting intensity.

"Help yourself to some coffee," Jack said, scowling out a window at his sodden boatyard. "It's supposed to pour down rain all damn day. National Weather Service says Brenda will probably stall in the vicinity today and not give us much trouble but we'll get pissed on all day."

"Well, at least we got all the pressing work done that we needed to take care of," Rafe said. "Why don't we call the guys, give 'em the day off and just drink beer and play cards? I buttoned up my place before I left. If it's okay with you, I'll just crash here this evening rather than deal with the mess at the beach. Maybe get Margie and the boys over this evening and watch old movies or something."

"You know what, old buddy? That sounds like a plan. If you'll run over and get Margie and the boys, I'll fix breakfast."

Just as he was leaving, Doug wandered into the room, hair still wet from his shower. He made a beeline to the coffee pot.

"Did I hear somebody say breakfast? Need some help getting it ready?"

Jack put an arm around the boy's shoulder. "Sure, why don't you go ahead and start cracking eggs and beating them while I get the bacon and biscuits going. There's also another coffee pot under the counter over there. Get that going, too. One pot ain't going to be enough for everybody. There's orange juice in the fridge."

When the boy reached under the counter to get the coffee pot, he found an apron and put it on. Jack looked at him and grinned. Doug grinned back.

"When Mama taught me and Sis how to cook, she always made us wear aprons."

"It sounds like she was a wise and wonderful mama," Jack said, placing strips of bacon in the skillet.

Doug's smile faded.

"She was. I miss her a lot. Sis, too." His voice cracked and tears welled. "Mama's dead and I'll probably never see Elizabeth again. It hurts so bad." He took a deep breath, let it out and smiled weakly." Listen, Pop, I just wanna say thank you—"

"You don't need to thank me for anything. I'm just glad to see you out of the mess you were in."

The boy cracked eggs into a metal bowl and shook his head. "No. I do need to thank you, for me, more than anyone else. It's been a long time since I had a home, a place where I feel like I belong. I feel like—" He blushed and turned his head.

Jack moved closer. "Feel like what? Go on."

"Naw, not right now, okay?"

The two of them worked in silence for a few moments, the only sounds the gurgling of the coffee maker, the sizzling of bacon, the clink of the metal whisk as the boy beat the eggs, the patter of rain and Pogy's snoring on the living room rug.

"There's an old picture of you and a lady and kid about my age on the back of the dresser in my bedroom," Doug said. "Is there some connection between that photo and the clothes I've been wearing and the ones you gave Margie after she got soaked the other day?"

Jack sucked in a sharp breath. He fumbled for a nearby fork and began absentmindedly flipping the pieces of bacon in the skillet. Then he bent over and opened the oven and checked the biscuits. He burned a finger, uttered a soft curse and when he jumped up and turned on the cold water to soothe the pain in his finger, Doug put a hand on his forearm.

"Jesus," the boy whispered, reading the pain in Merkel's eyes and suddenly understanding its source. "Are they—?"

Jack watched the water spiral down the drain, thinking about how, for the past ten years, his life had been doing more or less the same thing. He turned off the tap, dried his hand on a dish towel and then nodded, avoiding eye contact with Doug.

"Dead," he answered, numbness washing over him like cold waves. "Ten years now."

And then his voice failed him altogether. Doug's reply was a barely audible. "Pop. I'm so sorry."

About that time, Rafe came bursting through the door. Margie and both sons followed, crowded under one big umbrella.

"God, it's shitty out there," she said. "It's hard to believe that this storm isn't going to be a big deal, but the weather people are saying no. Funny, I've been checking the news off and on since I got up at daylight."

"Me, too," Jack said. "Guess we can all breathe easy now."

After breakfast, the adults cleaned up the kitchen and the boys retired to the living room to play cards. They took a short bathroom break and Margie happened to glance over and see Doug and John in a corner talking quietly. After a few moments, John extended his hand. Doug took it and the two boys shook hands. Margie watched and took in a deep breath and let it out slowly, saying a silent prayer of thanks. Jack also took note and reckoned that at least one storm had passed.

Around noon, they were all in the middle of a raucous game of draw poker when the alert weather forecast alarm sounded on the marine radio. They listened in stunned silence as the robotic voice announced that Tropical Storm Brenda had unexpectedly merged with a tropical wave offshore St. Augustine and was now Hurricane Brenda, and was strengthening rapidly and that it would likely make landfall in Vilano Beach, a little more than an hour away, and then skirt the coastline northward. Worse, her eye had widened again and the barometric pressure within the storm was falling precipitously. Moments later, the local storm center predicted a hit on Morgan's Island at three p.m. and if she continued to strengthen at the current rapid rate, possibly as a Category Three storm.

Margie put a hand to her mouth and gasped. "Oh, God! What are we going to do?"

"The only thing we can do," Jack said, getting up and immediately assuming a calm control. "We gotta bug out. Rafe has his car and I've got mine. Run to your boat and grab anything that's near and dear to you and I'll do the same here. Let's get back together here within thirty minutes, okay? Everybody stay calm. We can do this. We have time yet."

"You thinking what I'm thinking?" Rafe said.

"Yep, the judge's hunting cabin up near Macon. If we don't waste any time, we can get out of here before the shit hits the fan and be up there before sundown."

Just then Jack's cellphone rang. "Jack?" It was the judge. "Y'all get your asses out of there as soon as you can. Hal Patterson just called and said there's about to be a mandatory evacuation of Morgan's Island ordered. They're gonna close down the bridge to incoming traffic in a few minutes so they can use both lanes to clear the island quicker. How about I meet y'all up at that big truck stop just off I-95 at the Brunswick exit in, say, two hours? We'll all go up to my cabin together. We should be safe there."

"Thanks, Harley. We're just making preparations. We should be on the road in the next forty-five minutes. Thank God Rafe's here. Between his Suburban and my old Wagoneer, we can get everyone out of here, Pogy included. It'll be crowded with our stuff but we can do it."

"Good," the judge said. "Listen, don't mess around. Hal says the emergency management folks are saying we're definitely going to get hit, and probably hard. They're getting all patients except the critical ones that can't be moved out of the hospital and will keep the emergency room open as long as they can. Both of the elementary schools, the middle school and high school, as well as the National Guard center, will be open for anyone who can't get out, God willing that doesn't happen. After they fill up, Lord only knows where any stragglers will go. Y'all pack up and hustle, hear me?"

Dale Burdette's old tractor-trailer rig was on its last legs. It'd been jury-rigged together with little more than hope, rusty wire and promises for the past year while he saved up for another truck to haul logs to the paper mill on Morgan's Island. But big rigs cost money and Burdette, who'd suffered a heart attack and was out of work for six months, didn't have it to spare. He was queued up with five other logging trucks when the weigh station operator came out of his building and walked rapidly from truck to truck, stopping momentarily to holler up at each driver.

"Mill's shutting down, Dale," the exasperated weigh station attendant shouted above the din. "Hurricane evacuation. You gotta turn this thing around and skedaddle."

"But my load!" Burdette complained. "What am I supposed to do with it?"

The attendant looked up at him, made a face and yelled back at him, "Take it home with you for all I care. Now go on, Dale. Get out of here. You're holding up the show."

Cursing loudly, Burdette swung his rig around and began creeping back in the direction he'd come from, grinding through the gears as he tried to gain speed. By then, the word had gotten out and there was a line of cars ahead of him, all moving toward the bridge to get off the island. Nearing the center of the drawbridge, Burdette braked hard and veered to the left to avoid rear-ending a small car that suddenly broke down in front of him. The truck jackknifed and flipped on its side, spilling dozens of pine tree trunks everywhere. One lane remained partially open and panicky drivers began jockeying to get into it. It worked until a speeding pickup truck driver tried to jump ahead of the merging traffic and skidded into Burdette's truck. Both of them burst into flames. The only avenue of escape from the island was shut down. Now all the roads were packed with stalled cars full of terrified residents trying to figure out what to do next.

Rafe was helping Margie load her family's important papers, clothes and personal things in his big SUV when they heard the collision a few hundred yards away. They glanced over toward the bridge as a pall of oily black smoke billowed from the wreckage. Margie shrieked.

"What the hell's going on, Rafe? What just happened?"

"Looks like a bad accident on the bridge. I'll run up where I can get a better look. I need you to get back inside the house right now, okay? Get Jack to the side so you don't scare the kids and let him know. I'll be right back."

Without a word, she turned and ran. Minutes later, Rafe returned soaking wet and motioned both of them to the other side of the room. Doug and Seth exchanged worried looks. The younger boy looked questioningly at his mother. After a moment of whispered conversation, she walked over to them.

"Okay guys," she said. "There's been a little change of plans. Rafe and Jack and I are going to go downstairs to the office and discuss it. Y'all sit tight for a few, okay?"

"Don't worry, Margie. Y'all go take care of business. We're cool," Doug said.

Downstairs in the office, Jack spoke first.

"Looks like we're already on the leading edge of this storm. Margie, the bridge is done for. It'd take hours to clear and that's if they could get a fire crew up here to extinguish the blaze, which they can't."

"Why not? They can't just let it burn."

"Yeah, they can and they will," he said. "Rafe said one of the deputies up at the road told him they're gonna use ambulances, fire trucks, city vehicles and school buses to ferry the people off the road and the bridge. But it'll take a while. Everything's a mess and getting worse on the roads. This island has seven thousand residents and most of them didn't get out of here in time."

Margie wiped away a tear with the back of her hand. "Including us," she said.

Jack put his hand on her shoulder and squeezed lightly. "Including us."

"So, what do we do?"

"We're going to do what good sailors do, Captain. We're going to secure the decks, batten down the hatches and ride out the storm," he said. "We just need to come up with a quick float plan. At least we're on dry land and not out there on the ocean somewhere."

"Dry for now, anyway. But for how long?"

Jack held his arms out. "Look around. This place is made of solid stuff—pure cypress. The beams and supports are sturdy; the walls are sound. Sure, it'll likely get wet downstairs but we should be high and dry upstairs. While we've still got water, we're gonna lug five-gallon buckets from the shop up here and fill them with fresh water in the shower."

"Those old sails we've got in the sail locker we've been meaning to throw away?" Rafe asked. "Glad we didn't. We can cut those up and nail them over the windows in case the glass gets blown out. Ain't storm shutters but it'll help."

By the time they'd finished planning, the wind howled so hard they could barely hear one another. A driving sideways rain sounded like a waterfall against the side of the building. Pebbles of loose limestone began pelting the building like a hail of bullets. The sky turned the color of plums. An explosion sounded as a transformer nearby blew out, taking the power with it. Moments later, the marina's emergency gasoline powered generator started.

Margie feigned a smile. "Well, at least we have electricity."

"For now," Jack said. "But it might not last long so let's round up all the flashlights, batteries, lanterns and candles we've got around here and get ready. At least we have gas to cook with if we need it. It'll be the last thing to go if things get really bad."

Brenda's eyewall lost little intensity as it moved into the area on the incoming tide as a solid Cat Three storm with 125 mile an hour winds. The storm's surge drove fifteen-foot waves into beachfront homes, toppling and smashing all but the sturdiest and most elevated. The Intracoastal Waterway overflowed, and the river poured into the downtown areas and the homes and businesses along the river, cresting the island's creeks and marshes. Poorly constructed homes began to come apart in gusts that occasionally topped 130 miles an hour. Power lines toppled, sparking fires that added to the destruction. Brenda had been on Morgan's Island less than five minutes when she claimed her first lives: a terrified young couple was crushed when the massive oak tree in their yard fell on their bungalow. One of the island's oldest churches, built in 1897, was severely damaged and would take months to repair. Flying debris struck everywhere like artillery fire. The sky turned from dark purple to a sickly green pallor. Brenda's howls were deafening and terrifying as the horror-stricken islanders dug in and prayed to be spared.

Jack, Rafe, Margie and the boys rode it out in the living room. Despite the battering the building took, the roof and walls held, although the sound of shattering glass occasionally could be heard above the wrathful howling of the wind as flying debris began breaking the windows in the building. The heavy pieces of sail that Jack and Rafe put over the windows contained the shards of glass, but they didn't stop the driving rain that poured in when the glass broke. Everyone busied themselves with mops and towels to keep the inside of the house from flooding. The rock and earthen berm that Rafe and his crew had built to keep swollen creek water from rushing in failed within minutes and the floodwater surged through it. The constant sloshing of storm-tossed water as it overflowed the basin of the marina vexed Jack, who knew that his marina would be in a state of disarray, if not all but lost.

For the next two hours, Hurricane Brenda pounded steadily. The sturdy cypress house shuddered and groaned like an overmatched prizefighter being pummeled in the ring. The sound of flying debris crashing into the building was deafening, and every time some heavy object slammed into it, the building reeled and swayed. The creaking, groaning timbers reminded Jack of that terrible night during the storm in the North Sea so long ago, when his freighter shuddered, pitched, yawed and complained with every wave that lifted it high and dropped it again, with no respite for hours. When no one was watching him, Jack's eyes searched the cypress beams and timbers again and again, praying silently that they would hold. But like the outgunned, overmatched freighter, his building held on tenaciously and refused to yield, just as he had assured everyone it would. Suddenly, the din began to abate and an eerie silence replaced it.

Margie, who'd been huddled on the sofa with Doug and her boys, went over to Jack. "Is it over?" she asked, hopefully.

He took a deep breath and shook his head. "Only round one. We're in the eye. It'll be calm for a little while and then it'll hit us again. Look, I hope not, and don't want to scare you, but the back side of it could be worse. I have a hunch it will be and we have to be ready. Let's do a quick damage assessment while we have time."

The three of them went downstairs and peered outside. Jack whistled loudly. "I'll be damned. Would you look at that?"

Margie and Rafe crowded out around him. The boatyard was filled with debris. The only part of the yard not underwater was a small area in front of the office, although it was surrounded by water on three sides. Two sailboats were visibly damaged, but neither Jack's nor Margie's was one of them. Another sailboat was missing, a large powerboat was capsized with a hole ripped in the bottom, and a partially destroyed motor yacht lay on its side nearby. Neither Jack nor Rafe had ever seen the boat before. The Intracoastal Waterway was filled with debris from destroyed and adrift boats and houses. The roof of the boat barn had been mostly ripped off and had disappeared.

The wind was light and the sun shone down through the big circular opening. All around the opening, mountains of ugly gray and black clouds swirled.

"Reckon it's safe to let the boys out for a few minutes?" Margie asked.

"No," Jack and Rafe said at once.

"It won't last but a few minutes, and then it'll get just as nasty again," Jack said. "Go get them and bring them downstairs and we'll let them look outside, but they can't go outdoors. We can't take that chance."

They all stood huddled together on the front porch for a few moments marveling at the chaos.

"The other side will come now," Rafe told the boys. "But we know how to do it now, don't we? Anyone scared?"

Margie studied the faces of all three boys and stepped forward, grinning. "No fraidy cats here."

"Good," Jack said. "Let's get back inside and hunker down."

The wind was just beginning to pick up when Jack looked around the room. "Anybody seen Pogy lately?"

He called for the dog, but he didn't come running as usual.

"Shit," Margie said. "You don't suppose he slipped by us while we were looking outside, do you?"

"Oh, no," Jack said as the wind began whistling and screeching around the building. "Oh, Pogy."

Doug jumped up and bolted for the door. Jack yelled, "Don't go out there!"

He was gone before anyone could stop him.

Jack turned and yelled "Rafe! I gotta go get him!"

He took the stairs two at a time, ran through the office and was halfway across the unflooded part of the yard when he realized that John was right behind him. He had to crouch low, too, because the wind picked up.

"John! Get back in the house! Now!"

The boy squinted against the battering of rain, sand and pebbles being flung by the wind. He shook his head and pointed. "There he is! He's got Pogy!"

Doug came running low across the yard, leading the big dog by its collar, shouting at it. "Run, Pogy, run!" Pogy clenched a drowned marsh rabbit in his jaws like a trophy and seemed to think it was all a game.

Out of the corner of his eye, Jack caught just a glimpse of something flying by, followed by the sound of impact and a loud cry. The piece of wood had glanced off Doug's head and flew away.

The boy pitched facedown onto the ground, blood gushing from a ragged wound. Pogy dropped his prize and began whining and licking Doug's face. When Jack and John got to him, Doug wasn't moving. Each of them grabbed him under an arm and dragged him back to the building with Pogy following. When Jack opened the screen door to the office, the wind flung it away.

They managed to get Doug into the office and the big door shut and dead-bolted. Jack dropped to his knees beside the boy, cradled his bloody head in his arms and moaned, saying his name over and over as the tears ran down his face. John ran yelling up the stairs.

"Mom! Come quick! Doug's hurt really bad! Help!"

CHAPTER 16

DOUG WAS SEMI-CONSCIOUS and whimpering in pain when Jack and Rafe got him upstairs and into the dining room. He opened his eyes, but he quickly lapsed into unconsciousness without uttering a word. Margie's long-dormant training as an emergency room trauma nurse awakened. With military precision, she delegated responsibilities to Jack and Rafe, as well as to her sons.

"Rafe, clear off the dining room table and push it to the center of the room and let's get Doug on it," she said with a calmness that surprised even her. "It'll be our treatment table. Jack, we need sheets and blankets. We have to get some under him and cover him to keep him warm. He's going into shock. We're also going to need lights in case the power fails—flashlights, lanterns, candles, whatever you can scrounge up. Tell the boys where to find them while you get blankets and sheets for me. I don't want to be fumbling around in the dark."

Jack and Rafe placed Doug on the table. When Jack hurried away to get sheets and blankets, Margie turned her attention to Rafe who stood there staring. The ragged gash started just beneath Doug's hairline above his left eyebrow and extended back above his left ear. Blood poured from the wound and pooled on the table. Margie put her hand over it and applied pressure. "Rafe, I saw a big, metal footlocker with a red cross on it in the office. I take it that's the first aid box. Is it well stocked?"

"It's got all kinds of stuff in it," he said. "One of our boat owners is an emergency room doctor and a friend of Jack's. He helped us get all the supplies and put it together. We've never had to use that one before, only the little one in the shop."

"We're going to now," Margie said, opening Doug's eyes with her fingertips and examining his pupils. "John," she said, calling to her youngest son who came into the room carrying a propane lantern, "run downstairs with Rafe and help him lug the first aid box up here."

"Okay, mom," the boy said, giving the table a wide berth while looking at Doug stretched out on it.

Before they left, Margie reached out, took Rafe by the elbow, pulled him close to her and lowered her voice. "I'm gonna to need an assistant, Rafe. Can you handle that? It's going to be messy and I can't do this alone if we're to save Doug."

He glanced down at Doug and then back at Margie. A tear slipped down one cheek and he knuckled it away. "I think so," he whispered. "But what about Jack? He—"

"No, Jack's too emotionally involved. It'll be too much for him. I need a steady hand and a clear head, *viejo*. I'll lead the way. We can do this together."

He looked down at the boy's pale face, stroked one side of it tenderly with the palm of his hand and nodded. "*Si, mi amiga.* I will help you." A thin smile spread across his worry-lined face. "I like it when you speak to me *en espanol. Gracias.* Your Spanish is good."

She smiled back at him and touched his hand.

"We'll talk in Spanish if we need to," she said. "I'm going to have Jack concentrating on talking to Doug and encouraging him in case he can hear what we're saying. Now, go get me that first aid box."

Lacking a blood pressure cuff and stethoscope, Margie was unable to determine Doug's blood pressure, but his heartbeat was rapid, which she knew was likely from blood loss and shock. His breathing was so shallow that she thought he'd stopped a couple of times. He'd had a healthy tan but now his skin was pallid and clammy, another indication of shock. Without intravenous fluids and drugs, there was nothing she could do but keep his legs and feet elevated to keep as much blood as possible circulating in his upper body. Checking his pupils again, she prayed that there was no leakage of blood in his brain, but feared that there probably was, and that he also had at least a minor skull fracture. The piece of wood that had struck him left dirt and debris in the wound, which would need thorough cleaning. She prayed there'd be sterile water and saline solution in the first aid chest. The dirty wound needed cleaning, but for the time being, a potential wound infection was the least of Doug's problems.

Jack returned carrying a stack of sheets and blankets. Seth followed behind him with a box full of flashlights, spare batteries and candles, and set them on the bar. Margie looked up. "I want to start piling them on Doug. We'll use them as we need them. Seth, hand me a flashlight. Then go in the kitchen and fill a big pot or something with hot water and bring me a stack of clean washcloths."

Seth came to the table and gave her a flashlight. When he saw Doug's face, he stopped abruptly and hurried off to get washcloths and hot water. Margie kept pressure on the wound with one hand while stroking Doug's cheek with the other one and whispering to him, "It's going to be okay, baby. You're going to be fine. You'll be chasing Pogy around the yard before you know it."

At the sound of his name, the dog came into the room and walked over the table. He whined, sniffed Doug's face and began licking it. Margie was about to shoo him away when she noticed a slight fluttering of Doug's eyelashes. She sucked in a deep breath and let it out slowly.

"Good boy, Pogy," she said, reaching over to stroke the dog's muzzle. "Your buddy knows you're here. Keep up the good work."

Rafe and John lugged the big first aid box into the room and set it on the floor beside the table. Frowning, Jack reached for Pogy's collar but Margie stopped him. "Don't be upset with him. It's okay. When Pogy licked his face, his eyelids reacted. He's unconscious but maybe not that deep yet. Let's get a blanket under him and a couple over him. Then we're going to get real busy."

Seth returned from the kitchen with a plastic dishpan full of hot water and a stack of washcloths tucked under one arm, set everything on the table and then retreated to the other side of the room. John went to him, leaned into him and wailed. "I'm sorry, Doug! I'm sorry I was so mean to you. Please don't die!"

Jack went over to the boy and wrapped his arms around him. "He's not going to die, John. He's going to be okay. And you helped save his life. Hold onto that."

The wind came up again and grew increasingly louder until it became a sustained scream as Hurricane Brenda drove her fists into Merkel's sturdily built home for round two.

The first aid box was well stocked. Margie allowed herself a smile behind her surgical mask when she thought about how meticulous Jack had been in making sure that it was as near perfect as could be, right down to the disposable masks and surgical gloves that she and Rafe wore. There was even an external cardiac defibrillator. She instructed Jack to plug it in and prayed that it wouldn't be needed. Rafe was proving himself to be a calm and capable assistant. She'd quickly shaved the hair from around Doug's scalp wound with a sterile razor from the first aid box so she could clean it and get it bandaged. While she worked, Rafe, standing across from her, kept pressure on the bleeding wound by pressing his fingertips and a sterile pressure dressing over the wound as Margie deftly worked around him.

"You okay over there, nurse?" she asked, never lifting her eyes.

"Hanging in there, doc," Rafe answered. "How's our patient doing?"

"He's hanging in there, too," she said, handing him the bloody cloth she'd been using and taking a clean one he gave her with his free hand. She glanced over her shoulder at Jack, who'd pulled a chair close to the table where he sat holding Doug's hand. She couldn't help but smile about the story he was telling the boy about the fishing trip with Judge Kicklighter.

"Atta boy," she said. "Keep talking to him. Unconscious and comatose people often have an acute sense of hearing. You're doing great. Give him something to laugh about inside if he can hear you."

Moments later, the house shuddered as a piece of steel pipe drove through the kitchen ceiling. Water began pouring in. Almost immediately afterward, the power failed.

"Boys," Jack said calmly. "There are a couple of plastic five-gallon buckets in the laundry room closet. Go get them and start catching that water and pouring it down the kitchen sink." Seth started to the laundry room but John stood frozen in fear and stared at Merkel. "John," Merkel said to the boy. "This ain't a big deal. Just a little water. Now go help your brother. Both of you are gonna be busy catching and getting rid of that water and soaking up the rainwater still coming in the windows. You can do this. Don't panic."

The brothers formed a two-man bucket brigade and it wasn't long before they were teasing each other. "I hope we're getting union wages for this, Captain Merkel," Seth said, pouring a bucket of water down the sink.

"You'll get better than that if you can keep this room from filling with water," he said. "Y'all are doing a great job. Keep it up."

Margie smiled behind her mask and began cleaning Doug's

wound with brown antiseptic solution Rafe poured on a large piece of gauze for her.

"Okay, Rafe," she said when she was done. "Let's get his head bandaged and this bleeding stopped." She put a clean piece of thick gauze on the wound and held out her hand for the long roll of cotton gauze Rafe held. "Okay, here's what I need you to do for me. I want you to stand right here where I am and hold this dressing in place while I start wrapping his head. That's it. Keep the pressure on it. You won't hurt him."

She began swaddling Doug's head, moving Rafe's fingers one at a time until she got the stricken boy's entire head wrapped. Blood immediately began seeping through the bandages. Rafe breathed heavily. "Shh. It's okay. Don't worry about it."

"Do we take the dressings off and start over?"

"Nope. Here's the thing about a scalp wound. It'll bleed like crazy but if you keep piling on the dressings, it'll generally clot and then all that cloth will bind to the wound and seal it. I know it looks horrible but that's the easy part. Hand me three more rolls of that gauze and hold them down while I wrap his head some more."

Blood continued to seep through the second application of gauze, though not as much. Margie saw Rafe wince and reached over and patted his hand. "It's okay. You did well. It'll seep for a while and if it doesn't stop, we'll just keep piling on the gauze, but I think this'll do. Let's give it five minutes."

She checked her watch.

"How are you holding up, sweetie?" she asked Jack.

His face was haggard. "Okay. I'm worried about his breathing. It's so shallow and slow."

"I know. But at least he's not breathing rapidly and irregularly. That'd concern me more. As long as it remains the same, I won't worry too much."

In the kitchen, John called out to his mother. "He's not going to die, is he?"

"Not if super nurse Margie Waller has anything to say about it," she said. "I worked in the emergency room of a tough city, kiddo. I've seen 'em lots worse than this make it. Doug's young and strong and he's a fighter."

Jack took one of Doug's hands and began stroking it. "That he is. So, what do we do now, super nurse Margie Waller?"

"We wait. And we pray."

Minutes seemed to drag into hours. As Jack had predicted, the back side of Brenda was worse. The sturdy house shuddered nonstop. The debris slamming into it was deafening. Margie remained focused on her tasks, but in the back of her mind, a sinister voice whispered that the building wouldn't hold much longer. She pushed the thought away and repeated her checks of Doug's vital signs and, after a while, noticed that the bleeding seemed to have stopped. She used the opportunity to get her patient cleaned up a little. She soaked a washcloth in warm water and tenderly wiped away all the blood. "That's it, baby," she whispered as she worked. "You hang it there for Merkel. He needs you. We all need you."

Rafe thought about how gentle and sweet Margie was under her tough, take-no-prisoners exterior. She'd not had him fooled; Margie reminded him of his long dead sister.

"That table can't be too comfortable," he told Margie. "Maybe we should move him over to the sofa, make him a bed there."

She got up and took him by the elbow and led him aside, speaking quietly. "As tempting as it is, I don't think it's a good idea to move him if we don't absolutely have to. He could have a neck injury and if he does, moving him could make things worse."

"Is there any way to tell? I mean, could he be paralyzed?"

"I don't think so, but it's possible. My gut tells me he didn't sustain a neck or spinal cord injury because it looks like the wound was a glancing blow to the side of his head. But there's no way to be sure without medical intervention and evaluation. Don't mention this to Jack, okay? He's worried enough as it is."

"No problem."

She stood on her tiptoes and kissed his cheek.

"You're such a big sweetie, Rafe."

Brenda finally took her leave of Morgan's Island. The house's constant trembling and groaning abated as the roaring of the wind died. By five that evening, it was over. Even the water had stopped pouring in through the roof. Jack walked over to the deck and opened the doors. There were still bands of showers moving through but it had stopped raining for the moment as the sun broke through the clouds. Rafe stepped over to the door and stood beside his longtime friend and looked out, soon joined by Margie and her sons.

"Let's go outside and see what it looks like," Jack said. "I'm getting cabin fever."

There was a light breeze blowing from the southeast and it rippled the surface of the water that filled the marina and the entire boatyard. The house itself had been spared the worst of the flooding, the water just touching the walls. Nearly all the windows were cracked or broken. The railings on one side of the deck had been torn away. Most of the roofing tiles were gone. Jack's insurance would cover the damage, but he feared that it'd be a while before everything could be fixed. He thought about cranky Neal and smiled. The man was a jack-of-all-trades and could fix just about anything, even roofs. Because he and Rafe and his crew had managed to pull the remaining few boats from their slips, none were adrift. Jack took a quick look around and saw that most of the bigger power boats and the sailboats that had been anchored into the ground a few days before the storm hit had been mostly spared all but minor damage but for the capsized boat with the hole in the bottom. The mast on another sailboat had broken but it held in check by the stays and shrouds that supported it. Jack looked out over the surrounding area and saw that the river, when it flooded and overflowed its boundaries, had filled the marshes. Not even the tips of the spartina were visible. The Intracoastal looked like a floating junkyard. The air was laden with the briny fragrance of the sea. As he stood looking out over all the water surrounding them, an osprey circling high above swooped and plunged, instantly pulling back up with a large fish clutched in its talons. Watching in quiet admiration, Jack was reminded of the Biblical story of the flood and the rainbow, and took it as a sign that normalcy had returned to their world.

Rafe, Margie and her sons stood alongside him, all of them gazing in wonder at all the water and taking in the blessed silence.

A trio of otters swam by, oblivious to the strangers watching them and the fat, elderly pelican that spent its days lazing in the sun on a dock piling, preened itself and then spread its wings and flew away in search of food, gliding low across the surface of the water. From somewhere nearby, the regal great blue heron that Jack had named George squawked harshly as it flew in and landed on one of the floating docks that miraculously hadn't been lifted high enough to come off the pilings that held it in place. Glancing around, Jack noted that all the other docks remained safely on their moorings.

Margie's younger son stepped forward and pointed at the yard below them. "Wow. Look at all that water."

It started to rain again so they all went back inside. Jack went downstairs with Rafe to check on the office and shop and came back with good news. There was water on the floor of each but nothing damaging. It was then that Jack's thoughts returned to Doug. He went over the boy and gazed at him. Margie came and stood beside him and took Jack's hand in hers, giving it a reassuring squeeze before releasing in and bending over the boy. She opened each eye and directed the intense beam of a small flashlight into them. Both pupils immediately contracted, a reaction that relieved her greatly. She took his wrist in her hands, glanced at her watch and counted his heartbeats, noting that his pulse had returned to close to normal. His breathing was still shallow but hadn't weakened further. Jack watched her closely, searching her face for any signs of alarm. Seeing none, he let out the breath he'd been holding.

"What do you think?" he said. "Is he going to make it?"

"He's made it this far. He's young, strong and a fighter. And he doesn't appear to be any worse, so that's good. But he does need more attention than we can give him here, so why don't we go to the living room and sit down and see what our options are for getting him to the hospital."

Now Jack took charge. "I think the first thing I need to do is get in touch with Hal Patterson. It might be that he can help us out here."

"We still got that little dinghy and outboard engine out there in the storeroom at the back of the shop?" Rafe asked.

"Last time I looked it was still there, Rafe. What've you got in mind?"

"I can gas her up and motor up the causeway to the main road and see how deep the water is and how far. If it's deep enough for Hal to get one of his guys in here with one of their patrol boats, we might be able to get Doug close enough to the hospital that they can meet us with a rescue crew or something. We're only talking a little more than a mile."

"That's a thought," Merkel said. "I hope the hospital's still in one piece. Go ahead and give that a try while I talk with Hal. Take a radio with you."

Margie's sons had gone to the kitchen to dry spilled water off the floor. Jack called out "Why don't you guys go help Rafe get the dinghy and motor ready and in the water. Maybe one of you can ride along with him in case he needs a hand with something. What do you think, Rafe?"

"Great idea. We'll go as far as we can in the dinghy and check the water depth along the way. It'll help Hal decide what kind of resources he needs, so why don't you hold off on calling him 'til I get back to you?"

"Margie, you okay with me taking one of the guys along to help me out?"

Before she could answer, John spoke up. "I'll go, Mom. I'll be okay."

She ran her fingers through her hair. "Well, sure. But you do exactly as Rafe tells you, understand?"

A few minutes later, they heard the sputter of the dinghy's little outboard engine as it sparked to life. Seth came tromping back up the stairs.

"They're on their way," he said. "Little motor fired right up."

Jack went over to Doug, stood beside the table and took one of the boy's hands in his.

"Hear that, Doug? We're gonna get you out of here and to the hospital soon. Hang in there, son."

Margie came over and checked Doug's pulse and pupils again. A little later, the radio crackled and Jack grabbed it. "Go ahead, Rafe. What's it look like out there?"

"Better than I thought. There's enough water depth to get a larger boat within three blocks of the hospital. After that, it gets shallow fast. If they have one of the big rescue wagons standing by at the emergency room, they can drive in the shallow water close enough to transfer Doug from a boat to the ambulance. Go ahead and call Hal. We'll head on back."

Jack signed off and put in a call to the sheriff. He got Patterson's voice mail but before he could put his phone down, the sheriff was calling him back.

"You guys okay out there, Jack? I was just about to call you."

Jack quickly told him what had happened and their plan.

"Might be we can pull that off," the sheriff said. "Marine patrol has their hands full right now, but one of my guys has an eighteen-foot boat with a real shallow draft. Lemme talk with him and get back to you."

They heard the dinghy returning moments later. Seth jumped up and ran downstairs to greet them and lend them a hand. The phone rang again.

"Charlie Shackleford's on the way," the sheriff said. He's also bringing two paramedics along who've been standing by out here. Give him about twenty-five minutes."

Twenty minutes later, they heard the deputy's boat arriving and went downstairs. The boat got as close to the building as it could. Two paramedics got out of it and waded toward the building carrying a long, wide piece of wood with straps on it.

"Good, they brought a back board and a neck brace with them," Margie said. "Now they can move him out of here without worrying about his neck."

The paramedics examined Doug, started an IV and determined that it was safe to move him. They carried him downstairs and waded out to the boat with him. Jack followed and climbed in with them. When he looked around, Margie was right behind him.

"Got room for one more passenger, skipper?"

"Sure, I think we can handle that," the deputy said.

Jack looked over at Margie but she spoke up before he could say anything.

"The boys will be fine. Rafe says he'll look after them since he's gonna be there a while anyway. I'm not about to let you and this child out of my sight."

One of the paramedics checked the bag of intravenous fluid while the other one took Doug's vital signs and called the information in to the emergency room; a medical team was standing by. The deputy slowed the boat when they saw an ambulance about a hundred yards ahead, its lights flashing and its crew waiting in the road.

"I can get y'all about another fifty yards and then it'll be too shallow, so you'll have to wade the rest of the way," the deputy said.

A few minutes later, the rescue crew put the injured boy in the ambulance and told Jack and Margie to go up front and ride with the driver.

"I'd feel more comfortable back there with him," Jack said.

"No, sir," the young paramedic replied. "It's gonna be a little busy back here and there's not much room. We'll be at the emergency room in about two minutes."

Jack leaned into the back of the ambulance and took the boy's hand, giving it a squeeze. "Hang in there, son. Everything's gonna be okay now."

Then he walked around to the front of the ambulance and climbed into the front seat with the driver and Margie.

Jack and Margie sat on a fake leather sofa in the emergency room waiting area. The walls were painted a soft pastel blue. There were cheery lamps and plastic flowers on tables in both corners. The gray linoleum was tracked with mud. One of the windows in the room was cracked where something had struck it. A nurse came into the room and whispered something to a young couple holding hands and praying across the room. They got up and followed the nurse from the room, the girl beginning to sob, leaving Jack and Margie alone.

"They can't let him die," Jack said, leaning over with his face in his hands. "Please God, don't let him die. I can't do this again. I can't."

Margie wrapped him in her arms and held him tight. After a moment, he surrendered to his pain and pressed his face to her shoulder. She stroked his head and consoled him and waited for his anguish to pass. She held him a little longer until he pulled away, looking embarrassed.

"I'm sorry. I didn't mean to—"

She reached over and gently put her hand on his mouth.

"Hush. There's nothing to be ashamed of. You love the kid and he loves you. That's pretty obvious."

She stood and massaged his shoulders. He finally relaxed and leaned back, yielding to her fingertips.

"Better?

"Yeah. I guess so."

"How about a Coke?"

He nodded, his eyes red and raw. "That'd be good."

The blinds were open and the moonlight shone into the room. After Jack finished his drink, he leaned back on the sofa and closed his eyes. Margie set her drink down and scooted over until they were touching side to side. She put her arm around his shoulder and hugged him. They sat there in silence for a moment, the only sound the soft squeaking of the rubber soles on nurses' shoes as they passed the waiting room.

"How long have your wife and son been dead?"

He didn't answer for a moment. "How'd you know?" he finally said.

"I'm a woman and a mother, and it's written all over your face. I've seen the photos. The boy looks like you."

Jack blew his nose into a tissue.

"Teddy got a lot of his mom's looks. He favored Penny a lot more than me, thank God."

Margie let the name sink in a minute, remembering their conversation in the kitchen when he'd asked her not to say *a penny for your thoughts* again.

"Penny and Teddy. What happened?"

"Teddy and his buddies went surfing. He slipped and fell, and his board hit him in the head and knocked him out. He was drowning before his buddies could pull him out of the water. Penny called me and then took off for the emergency room. A log truck plowed into her when she ran a red light in her rush to get there."

He turned away toward the window and looked at the moon.

"I had to choose," he said, his voice strained. "Penny was barely alive when I got there and I went to her first. She died about five minutes later. Teddy died before I could get to him. I never got to tell him goodbye. He was just eighteen, same as Doug. I can't lose someone else like this. I can't, Margie."

He composed himself after. And then he began to cry again.

"It was almost ten years to the day that Doug broke into the boatyard and vandalized the sailboat. Penny, Teddy and me built it ourselves and had been working on it when they died. After they died, I couldn't bear to look at it but I couldn't bring myself to get rid of it, either. So I put it in the barn and abandoned it. Coming up on the tenth anniversary, I decided I needed to finish it—for them and for me. And then Doug came along."

A gray-haired nurse in pink scrubs came into the room with a young doctor who shook Jack's hand.

"Mr. Merkel, I'm Doctor Patel. We've got all the tests done and his scalp sewed up. Your son has a minor skull fracture that'll take a little while to heal, a nasty concussion and a small hematoma on his brain where the blow caused it to bleed. That's what caused him to be nearly comatose."

Jack quickly caught the meaning and brightened. "So he's not comatose now?"

"No. He's unconscious off and on and will be until we can get that hematoma taken care of, and the bleeding on his brain. We're going to have to send him down to one of the big medical centers in Jacksonville for that."

He smiled at Margie and shook her hand.

"Doug's a lucky boy," he said. "He likely would've died from shock if you hadn't been there to respond so quickly."

"Can we see him?" Jack asked.

"I don't see why not," the doctor answered. "You can wait with him until the helicopter gets here to transport him. Don't be surprised if he seems a little confused, or if he drifts off while you're talking to him. The nurse will see you back. Send for me if you have any other questions."

When he was gone, the nurse smiled brightly at Jack and Margie. "Ready?"

They followed her to the room. Doug lay propped up in bed. He wore a pale green print hospital gown. A white sheet and blanket were pulled up to his chest. There was a fresh bandage on his head. A cardiac monitor beeped and another machine kept track of his breathing. An IV bag dripped a clear solution into his arm. He slowly turned his head to the side when he heard them approach his bed.

"Pop," he whispered. "What happened?"

CHAPTER 17

THE INTENSIVE CARE UNIT cubicle near the nurse's station was brightly lit and smelled of air freshener. Jack watched the boy's chest rise and fall. Each time he inhaled and exhaled, Jack did the same. From time to time, he glanced up at the heart monitor. The only sounds in the room were the soft hiss of oxygen mask and the sparrow-like chirp of the heart monitor.

Doug had not awakened since being brought back to the intensive care unit room after the two-hour operation to remove the blood clot from his brain and stop the leak that caused it. The neurosurgeon, a tall, silver-haired man with a soft Alabama drawl, told them afterward that Doug was lucky to be alive, that the blow would've likely killed him instantly had the flying piece of wood stuck him directly. He told them he was confident that Doug would quickly recover from his wounds and that he would most likely sleep until all the effects of the anesthesia had worn off, which might be several hours. The surgeon had also advised them that Doug might seem disoriented upon awakening but that the confusion wouldn't linger. After the doctor left them, Jack began his bedside vigil.

"C'mon, you need a break," Margie said, tugging his arm. "It's been a long, grueling day. Let's go downstairs for just a little while. You can even slip outside for a smoke."

"No. He might wake up while we're gone and be scared. I want to be here when he wakes up."

She sat beside him on the sofa and slid her arm around his shoulders.

"I don't know what I would've done without you," he said. "or what Doug would've done without you. He might've . . . might've died. Christ, why didn't I get us out of there?"

She saw his eyes fill with tears and took his hand, edging closer so that their shoulders touched.

"But he didn't die. Don't beat up on yourself for not leaving. The goddamn storm bushwhacked us. You and Doug are gonna finish building that boat and go sailing off in the wind one day like a couple of carefree gypsies. Like two vagabonds."

He turned his head away and knuckled his raw eyes.

"All the way here, I thought about Teddy. I was nearly forty when me and Penny got married, kinda old to be starting a family. She was younger than me and she wanted kids, at least one. But she had problems all during her pregnancy. Teddy was almost two months premature. The doctor said no more pregnancies."

He seemed on the verge of saying something else but he turned away quickly, gaze going out the window, retreating again to the quiet, safe harbor where he went when he needed to escape his hurt, an uncharted place where she couldn't follow. She thought about her own sons safe in Rafe's care, and knew that it would break her if something happened to either of them. She got up and walked over to the bed and stroked the sleeping boy's head, bent and kissed him on the cheek, then went to the door. Just before she went outside, she looked back at Jack and smiled.

"You stay here and look after Doug. I'll run downstairs and get coffee and sandwiches and bring them back, okay?"

"Thank you. That'd be good. I could use something to eat and a little hot coffee right now."

After she left, he got up and went over and sat in the stiff-backed plastic chair that had borne the weight of pain and grief of so many others. He took Doug's limp hand in his, held it for a moment and touched his lips to it.

"Sleep, son. Get your rest. You're gonna be fine. I'm right here."

Then he surrendered to his marrow-deep weariness and finally into sleep. Penny came to him for the first time in years. Smiling radiantly, she reached out and took his big rough hands in her own, which were as small and soft as a child's, held them to her face and kissed them. She was barefoot and wearing a yellow sun dress of gauzy cotton, and she smelled of jasmine blossoms. She looked exactly as she had the day they'd met when he'd seen her picking wildflowers along the sandy road beside the ancient graveyard called *Bellisma Foresta,* Italian for *Beautiful Forest.* He was cleaning the graves of his parents when he noticed her. She'd woven some of the flowers into her long, flaxen hair and she looked like a humble peasant girl in her simple, yet elegant beauty. He was so smitten that all he could do was stand there and gawk at her like an awkward teenager. She studied his face for a moment and then giggled like a child. Her laughter reminded him of little bells ringing, a sound he still heard whenever he thought of her. She teased him with a puckish smile and blew him a kiss. "Penny for your thoughts?" she said in the same playful way she'd say to him so many times again, during their years together.

When he tried to speak, his mouth wouldn't form the words, and she reached out and placed one delicate finger upon his lips. "Shhhh, hush, my darling," she whispered in his ear, letting her fingers trace the weather-beaten lines of his face, closing her eyes as she did, as if committing his face to memory. "It's okay now."

"Don't go, Penny," he said. "Please. I need you."

He tried to reach for her but his arms had turned to stone and she began to fade before him.

"Penny. Don't go."

Then he was standing before their graves, hers and Teddy's. He closed his eyes and tried to summon her but the only sound he heard was the sifting of the late afternoon breeze through the ragged gray beards of Spanish moss in the ancient regal oaks and fragrant red cedars that surrounded him. The perfume of wildflowers and jasmine lingered as he clung to its fading music, which sounded like whispers. But he could not hold onto the gossamer flimsiness and it evaporated like a wisp of ground fog at sunrise. He was about to call out to her again when another sound startled him.

Doug coughed and then coughed again, and then called out in a hoarse voice shot through with pain and confusion. His mouth and throat were as dry as the cicada husks clinging to the bark of the oaks in the cemetery, and his bloodshot eyes were unfocused and afraid.

"Mama? Mama? Where are you, Mama?"

Jack leaned and took the boy's hand in one of his own and with the other, stroked his forehead just below the bulky white bandage.

"Doug . . . son," he said, putting his face to the boy's. "You're back. Thank God, you're back."

The boy stared at him for a moment, bewilderment in his eyes and then slowly, as slowly as the green returning to the spartina in late spring, recognition and memory began to dawn in them. He squeezed Jack's hand. "I was just talking to Mama. Did you see her?"

Jack smiled and told the harmless but necessary lie. "Yes. And just before she left, she said to tell you that she loves you."

Doug closed his eyes and smiled, contented as a suckling child who's just been fed, then licked his parched lips. "Thirsty. So thirsty."

The nurse had told them that when he woke up he'd probably want water and that he could only be given small sips of it through a straw, and only if he seemed alert enough, and only after she had examined him to be certain there was no danger of him inhaling it and choking. Jack pulled the chain beside the bed. Moments later, a nurse pushing a cart with a laptop computer on it glided into the room. She smiled brightly at them and went directly to the boy's bed.

"Well, hey baby," she said cheerily, resting one hand on his. "Nice nap? Want a little sip of water now? Think you can hold it down?"

"Yes, ma'am."

She looked over at Jack and winked. "And such good manners your young man has, papa. Okay, sweetie. Let's play a game first. Tell me your name, first and last."

"Doug Eleazer," he croaked.

The nurse beamed and made an entry in the computer.

"Excellent! How old are you?"

"Eighteen."

"Okay, now tell me what month this is."

"July. And this is Jack Merkel. He has a big black Great Dane named Pogy. Can I have that water now, please?"

The nurse laughed, closed the laptop and filled a plastic cup with water.

"I'll do it," Jack said, reaching for it.

The nursed handed him the cup.

"Baby sips. Call me if you need anything."

She turned around and left the room. When she was gone, Jack elevated the head of the bed a few degrees. He put the straw between the boy's lips and held it steady with his fingertips and watched him suck greedily at it. Water dribbled down his chin and Jack picked up a napkin off the table and gently blotted. Then he wet it with a little more water and bathed the boy's face, wiping the yellow crust from the corners of his eyes, the dried saliva from his chin and the brownish antiseptic solution that had trickled down both sides of his neck and dried there. Doug lay still with his eyes closed while Jack tended to him. When he was done, he slipped the straw back into Doug's mouth. Unnoticed by either of them, Margie stood in the doorway and watched. After a few moments, she stepped back into the hallway and cleared her throat noisily before striding into the room.

"Well, hey, kiddo," she said, leaning over and kissing the boy's cheek. "Welcome back from your trip. Bring back any souvenirs?"

"Only a bad headache," he said and then a troubled look clouded his face. "Pogy. Did Pogy—"

Margie put a finger on his lips. "Pogy's fine. That was a brave and foolish thing you did, but you probably saved his life. It nearly cost you yours, though. You had us scared to death."

Margie handed Jack the bag with the sandwiches and coffee in it and then turned him around and steered him to the sofa.

"Sit yourself down and eat and have some coffee. Nurse Waller is taking over for a while."

She gave Doug more water and then rearranged his pillow and sheets and lowered the head of his bed. She held his hands and hummed softly. Within a few minutes, he was asleep again.

"Is everything all right?" Jack said.

"He's fine. He'll sleep a little while and wake back up again. That'll go on for a few hours 'til the anesthesia wears off."

She went over to him and took the cup out of his hands and made him lie back on the sofa. She pulled off his boots and set them on the floor. He'd not realized how exhausted he was and felt sleepy right away. She perched on the edge of the sofa beside him.

"I called Rafe and the boys. Everyone's okay. Rafe says the damage is bad but not as bad as he expected it'd be. He thinks the marina can be up and running again in a few days. He's already talked to Neal about the roof. He'll go ahead and grab some tiles before they're all gone. His brother and Eddie said they'd help. Rafe's rounding up some guys to help clean up the mess and has already found someone to fix the boat barn. Oh, that missing sailboat? Rafe notified the Coast Guard and warned them a big sailboat was adrift somewhere. Marine Patrol found it. It's toast. The sheriff called, and the judge. I told them Doug's fine and will go home in a few days."

Jack's only reply was a soft snoring sound. She looked at him and saw that he'd already fallen asleep. She got up and went to a nearby locker and got a light cotton blanket and covered him with it. Then she eased a small pillow under his head. She stood back up and turned to walk away and then stopped and returned to him and kissed him lightly on his forehead.

CHAPTER 18

MARGIE SAT WITH HER sons and Doug in lounge chairs a short
distance from *Starshine* sipping iced tea as Jack and Rafe installed the
new rudder. When she saw Jack step away from her boat, grinning
and thrusting both fists above his head, she uncrossed her fingers,
hooted and stood up dancing. Taking their cue from her, all three
boys did likewise. When Margie saw that Doug had joined the
celebration, she whirled around, jabbed her finger at him and yelled,
"Sit your ass back down, and put your hat back on, baldy. It's too
damn hot and humid out here for you to be jumping around cutting
the fool. You've only been out of the hospital a week. Remember what
the doctor said when he discharged you?"

The boy stole a glance at Margie's grinning sons, rolled his eyes
and sighed theatrically. "Yes, ma'am," he said. "'Take it easy for a

few days. Don't do anything strenuous and don't go out in the sun without lots of sun block and a big hat on your noggin.'"

Margie had driven Doug to the hospital in Jacksonville to have his wound checked and his dressing changed, as well as another MRI to make sure no blood was leaking inside his brain. Doug studied his reflection in the mirror while the nurse put a light bandage on his head. He rubbed his hand over his scalp and grimaced.

"I might as well just shave off the rest of it," he had complained, putting his hat back on his nearly bald head.

"You'll do no such thing," Margie had said. "Do that and you'll have to coat your entire head with sunscreen when you go outdoors."

He looked and her and frowned. "Well, what else can I do? I'll look like a clown 'til the bald side catches up to the side with hair."

She gave him a playful poke. "You have beautiful hair. We'll just shorten up the other side and you can wear a big red bandana on your head like Eddie Kraft does, until the bald side grows back out, which won't take long."

She paused, squinted and looked at one of his ears. "Ah! Your left ear is pierced. Big gold earring there and you'll make a fine pirate instead of a clown."

"I always wanted to be a pirate," he said.

"Hell, who hasn't?" she said and then hugged him.

Jack and Rafe approached, wiping sweat and grease from their faces and hands. The hurricane had bulldozed a thick, long wrack of brown and decaying spartina grass into the boatyard. It looked like hundreds of yards of carpet made from dirty brown straw. In time, the sun would cure it until the long tobacco-brown strands were hollow tubes as dry as tinder and with a pleasing fragrance like hay cured in molasses. Meanwhile, the rotting clutter reeked. Jack decided to just leave it alone until it was dry enough to pile and burn at the rear of the yard. A few things got broken and needed repairing or replacing, including Rafe's boat which was damaged, though not too badly, by falling debris when the storm blew off the top of the boat barn, but, all in all, he reckoned he'd dodged a big bullet. Miraculously, Rafe's house hadn't been destroyed by the surge of seawater during the storm. Part of the deck had been torn away and the bottom floor got flooded. But Rafe's insurance would cover the cost of the damage.

Neal and his crew had put a new roof on the building a few days earlier and after a few days the marina had mostly been restored to order. Among the spoils washed onto the marina grounds was a massive insulated cooler. Eddie quickly claimed it, boasting that it'd make a grand addition to his charter fishing boat when he got started in the business, which he was confident would be soon. After getting off work, he spent an hour cleaning it up, and when he finished it looked brand new.

Jack announced an early lunch break and a cold beer for each of the adults for a job well done.

"Anybody seen Pogy lately?" he said, looking around the yard.

Seth raised his hand. "I keep seeing him sniffing around back there. I called him but he won't come to me."

"Probably something got drowned back there and died during the storm," Jack said.

"Hey, Doug. Feel like riding the golf cart back there and checking on what Pogy's up to? See if you can coax him into coming back with you. He loves to ride in the cart. Last thing I want is that big galoot rolling around on a rotting carcass."

Doug mopped sweat and laughed. "Sure, but I'm gonna take a piece of rope with me. If he's been rolling in something stinky, I'll tie him to the cart and he can walk behind me."

Everyone laughed and Jack pointed toward the rear of the shop. "If that's the case, haul him to the outside cleanup station and give him a good wash down. There's a big jug of dishwashing soap and a scrub brush."

Doug started walking to the golf cart and turned around. "He won't put up a fuss or try to bite me, will he?

"Pogy? Naw. He loves baths but step away fast when you finish before he shakes or you'll get a shower. Have fun."

Doug climbed into the golf cart, slipped his hat off and laid it and the coil of rope on the seat and headed off in the direction of the old plywood shed that had managed to survive the storm. He'd never been on that part of the property so he dawdled and took in the scenery. The flood waters had submerged the area and when the water receded into the marsh, it left behind drowned spartina and other marsh grass baking in the sun. Doug closed his eyes and paused a moment, inhaling the odor, which had a mucky, feral smell tinged with brine that he found oddly pleasant. Thousands of fiddler crabs skittered around and feasted upon the dead fish that'd been stranded when the flood waters receded. George, the great blue heron, came swooping down in a rattle of feathers and long legs and charged headlong, hissing at a smaller interloper hoping to capitalize on the easy pickings. But the bigger heron's bullying and bluffing convinced the younger bird that another eatery might prove more to his liking, as well as his safety.

The vanquished heron flapped away, defeated, while a trio of turkey vultures, looking like cartoon undertakers in rumpled black suits, glanced up from what might've once been a possum to bear witness to his frustrated exit from the diner. Doug smiled at Jack's custom of bestowing names on all the animals that took up residence in the marina and wondered what names he'd give the three vultures. The skies were blue again and the ospreys glided, shrieked and swooped in a feeding frenzy. The breeze blew across the spartina turning it into a kaleidoscope of varying shades of green. The sun beat down on Doug's sore head and he covered it again with the oversized straw hat Margie had given him. She told him that she had a surprise for him but that he'd have to wait another day or two. He wondered what it might be as he put on his sunglasses to keep the glare from his eyes as he was still prone to the occasional nagging headache. He leaned back in the seat, put both hands behind his head and drank it all in—the bright blue sky studded with marshmallow puffs of clouds, ospreys wheeling and keening overhead, the breeze that felt silky on his skin and cooled him, and the dry clattering of palm fronds that sounded like muffled applause. The single sustained bass note of the horn that the familiar tugboat captain sounded in greeting to his old friend every time he pushed one of the long steel barges along the river past the marina gladdened him and he drank in the big-hearted, arms-wide-open all of it like wine until it made him drunk and nearly delirious with joy.

"God, I love this place," he said aloud. "I wish I could stay here forever."

Doug rumbled off toward where the property and the marsh met searching for the Great Dane. Sure enough, there were a couple of dead raccoons, a dead possum and a cluster of dead fish, all stinking to high heaven in the hot sun. He called to Pogy but the dog ignored him and began wallowing on the dead possum. Doug wrinkled his nose in disgust and tied his bandana around his face. "Pogy, come here, damn it!" he shouted at the dog.

The dog wagged his tail and ignored him.

"Come on, Pogy. It's hot as hell out here and it stinks. Come on, boy."

But Pogy continued to ignore him and went about his mission. Cursing, Doug throttled forward until he was few feet from the shed. Nearly gagging, he got off the cart, tied the rope to Pogy's collar and dragged him away to the shop to bathe him. Predictably, after the wash down, the big Dane shook himself from head to tail and drenched Doug, who just laughed and hugged the dog before leading him back to where everyone else was still waiting.

Jack and Margie sat side by side in reclining chairs on the deck, sipping bottles of icy beer and staring up into a flawless nighttime sky that was ripe with all the sparkling fruits of the universe. Jack took a sip and pointed at a meteor trailing a fiery scratch across the heavens. They watched in silence until the meteor winked out and vanished. Margie took a swig of beer and shifted around in her seat. "Did you make a wish?"

Jack reached into his pocket for his cigarettes. "Mine already came true."

"Will you tell me what it is?"

"I don't need to. You can see for yourself. It's safe and sound asleep in one of the spare bedrooms."

She didn't say anything for a few moments and then raised her bottle to him in a salute.

"That was sweet and beautiful. And I'll bet you another beer that he's dreaming about his wish come true, too."

Jack uncapped two more beers, handed one to Margie, lit a cigarette, leaned back in his chair and pointed up at the sky.

"Can you believe that something so peaceful looking just tried to kill us?"

"There goes my Jack, deftly changing the subject again. Hey, I haven't seen you smoke more than maybe ten cigarettes in the past two days. What's going on? You've practically had one glued to your lip since I first met you. Trying to quit, I hope?"

He blew a succession of perfect smoke rings.

"Trying to quit. Last night I woke up four times craving one."

She eyed him slantwise, took a drink of beer and put her hand over her mouth and burped. "'Maybe you've got your reasons you want to quit now that are a little more nuanced than just trying to kick the old habit."

He rolled his beer bottle between his palms and stared out over the marsh, taking his time, gathering his thoughts. "Maybe I do."

She got up and pushed her chair closer to his. She sat back down and reached out, laying a hand on his forearm. She felt the muscle twitch but then it relaxed; he made no move to pull away. "Tell me about Doug. All of it. I want to know and I think that deep down beneath that tough hide of yours that you know it's time to share it."

He set the bottle down, took another couple of puffs of his cigarette and turned his face toward her. When he did, she saw that he was looking at her in a completely different way, the penetrating gaze of an old mariner navigating through uncharted waters. He studied her face as if he were reading a nautical chart, making certain that his sailing was clear before forging ahead. She saw in those cautious eyes the moment that the old captain reckoned his course clear, his sailing smooth.

"All right. The judge brought me a thick dossier on Doug not long after he came to me. It brought me to my knees when I read it. I don't think you could even begin to imagine what this boy has suffered. I'll tell you, but if you've got the goodness in you that I think you do, it'll tear you apart. It did me. You sure you want to do this?"

"Yes. I feel a kinship with him now, you know?"

"Yeah. I reckon I do."

He stubbed out the cigarette and told her the story, from the beginning until its murderous denouement in the roar of a gun.

"The abuse started when Doug and his sister, Elizabeth, were still babies," he said. "Raymond Douglas Eleazer Sr., Ray, they called him, got kicked out of the Army and did some time at Leavenworth. After he got out, he met and married Angela, Doug's mom. She was just nineteen. There's a photo of her and the kids in the file. She's slight built with black hair and dark eyes, exotic looking. Doug's sister favors her a lot."

He reached for the familiar crutch of his cigarettes, tapped one from the pack, put it between his lips and was about to light it, then took it out of his mouth and returned it to the pack. A bull alligator bellowed near one end of the marsh where a shallow creek cut into it.

"At first it was slaps and shaking. Then it got worse. By the time Elizabeth was six, the beatings started. By then, Doug was three. Elizabeth's three years older."

He got up and walked over to the edge of the deck and leaned forward with his hands on the railing. Even in the dim light, Margie could see him struggling with it. He remained there for a few moments and then abruptly turned around. His fists were clenched at his sides and the fury on his face seemed carved there by a knife.

"That's when the sorry bastard started burning his little boy with cigarettes and molesting his little girl. Touching and fondling at first, making her touch him. By the time she was fourteen, he was raping her."

Margie got up and took a step toward him.

"Jesus Christ! Those little round scars I saw all over his back and shoulders when you guys had your shirts off working one day—"

Jack spat out the words like venom he needed to be rid of. "Scars from cigarette burns. Burning a toddler with cigarettes. Now you see why I'm trying to quit smoking? I think about it every time I light one around him."

She went to him and put a hand on his shoulder. Tears dripped off her chin. Merkel reached into his pocket and handed her his neckerchief. She covered her mouth in horror.

"Where was mama when all this was going on?"

"Getting the shit beat out of her every time she got up off the floor and tried to help. He made her watch him hurt those children and then he'd beat her down when she tried to stop him."

"My God! She saw him rape their daughter?"

"No, she didn't know about the rape 'til Elizabeth was seventeen. Ray staggered in drunk one night. Elizabeth was watching television. Her mom was cooking supper. Doug, who was fourteen by then, was at baseball practice. Big Ray sat down on the sofa beside his daughter and started grabbing her breasts, putting his hand between her legs. She screamed. Angela came running from the kitchen and demanded to know what was wrong. Elizabeth jumped up off the sofa, ran to her and blurted it out. Ray pulled his pistol from his pocket, pointed it at her and pulled the trigger. He missed and she ran out into the dark. While he was distracted, Angela jumped him. The second shot hit her in the hand when she grabbed at the gun.

The next one hit her in the chest. Then he put the gun to his own head and pulled the trigger."

They stood there in the darkness a long time saying nothing. The bridge tender sounded his horn and the drawbridge creaked up and allowed a large boat to pass.

"How did this all come out?" Margie said. "I mean, with both witnesses dead and the girl run off into the night before it happened?"

"I need to go sit back down," Jack said. "Come on."

When they were settled he continued. "Doug came home and found them. His mama wasn't dead yet. She was so weak by then that she could only whisper in his ear what happened. She didn't know the old man was already dead and she told Doug to go find Elizabeth and run away. Doug held her and cried and begged her not to die. She told him she loved him and died in his arms."

The big boat growled by in the darkness. Jack waited until it was gone.

"Doug thought maybe Elizabeth had run to an old friend's house in the next county and thumbed a ride there looking for her. But when he got there, the family didn't live there anymore. The cops found him the next morning and handed him over to the child welfare folks while they sorted things out. While he was at the shelter, Doug spilled the whole story to another kid. Told him his old man had been raping his sister. He'd heard her crying one night after a baseball game and his mama was still at work at the convenience store. The bastard was on top of her, drunk, and Doug took his baseball bat to him. Got some good licks in, too, but ol' Ray managed to take the bat away from him and broke his arm with it. Told him that if he told anyone what he saw him doing to his sister that he'd kill her and make him watch and then he'd kill him."

Margie reached for his wrist and squeezed it.

"And the girl? What happened to her?"

"Doug never saw her again. He's been looking for her ever since. There were no living kin by then and no close friends because the old man wouldn't allow it, and because they moved around so much. Doug ended up a ward of the state. But every time he got sent somewhere, be it a juvenile jail for a petty crime, a halfway house, an orphanage or a foster home, he ran. He's run eleven times, always looking for Elizabeth. He'd hear a rumor here or there and no matter where he was, he'd escape and go looking for her. It's been going on four years. He's pretty much been living on the streets."

"I'm gonna slip in and check on him," she said, getting up. "I hope he hasn't heard us out here talking."

She came back out a few moments later and sat back down, scooting her chair against his so that their arms were touching. "Not to worry," she said. "I can hear him snoring back there. So, how'd he end up here with you?"

Jack told her about the break-in, the vandalism of the boat, the boy's arrest and eventual release into his custody and the arrangement with the court. Margie listened intently and didn't say anything until he finished the story, fishing trip and all.

"I like this judge," she said. "And I think the sheriff has a heart of gold under that gold badge, too. So, how does this story end?"

He considered the question for a moment and smiled. "I'm gonna treat him like my son. Give him the home he needs. I love this kid, Margie."

She leaned over, buried her face against his shoulder and wept. He slid an arm around her and held her. After a while, she pulled away and wiped her eyes with his neckerchief.

"You okay?" he said.

"Yeah, but I need to be near my boys now. I think I'd better be going."

When they got up, she stood on her tiptoes and kissed his cheek, then turned and ran down the stairs. He watched her until she climbed aboard her boat and disappeared inside. He stood there for a long time gazing out into the darkness. Just before going in, he reached up and touched the place where she'd kissed him.

CHAPTER 19

MARGIE HELD OUT HER hand for Jack to steady her as she stepped off the dock onto Rafe's twenty-three-foot Boston Whaler, the storm damage freshly repaired.

"So, where are we going this fine evening, Cap'n? Is this a date?"

He laughed and started the boat as Margie sat down beside him. He pulled away from the dock, the engine purring kitten soft.

"Oh, I don't know that anyone would consider fried food served on tabletops covered with newspaper at O'Brien's Seafood Shak a proper date. Just the looks of the place are enough to scare most people away."

She laughed and bumped her shoulder against his. "Oh. So you're taking me to a greasy spoon dive where I might catch some sort of creepy stomach bug that'll make me so sick I barf all the way back kind of first date, huh?"

The sun, sinking low, trickled peach-colored rays between them and mirrored itself on the burnished gun metal gray water. As the light dimmed, Margie watched the marsh grass go from the color of emeralds to the dark green of an overripe avocado. She glanced sidelong at Jack and took note of the serene smile on his face, the way he never seemed to miss anything, whether it was the tiniest ripple on the water, the subtle shifting of the breeze or the smell of the air just before it rained. She reached into the pocket of her jeans, pulled out her cell phone and took his picture in profile. She had meant to be discreet, but he turned his head and looked at her, still smiling.

"Why'd you take my picture?"

She put her cell phone back in her pocket and smiled back. "That's a face I want to remember."

"Just an ordinary face. A few wrinkles, a scar or two. Just a beat-up old sailor's face, nothing special about it."

He returned his gaze to the river, eased the throttle forward, increasing the speed until the boat skimmed along the surface of the water like a sea bird. A large dolphin rolled in the boat's white wake and disappeared.

"Bullshit, Merkel. Your face is anything but ordinary. Yeah, the sun's played a few games with it like everyone else's, mine included. But you have the most handsome face of any man I've ever known."

He laughed loud and hard.

"What's so funny?"

"Now it's my turn to call bullshit. I'm already buying you supper. You angling for dessert, too?"

He eased the wheel to starboard and pointed the bow at the distant lights of downtown Morgan's Island. When he looked back at her she was leaning off to one side, arms folded beneath her breasts, eyebrows cocked and a coquettish smile on her face.

"Are you sure you want to ask me that question, sailor?"

"Well, sure. You ain't had dessert 'til you've had one of Jackie's pies. Coconut cream and pecan is great. But the Key lime? I could sit there and eat it 'til I bust. Thought I was gonna have to drag Doug outta there. Good lord, does that boy like him some Key lime pie."

Margie clapped her hands to her forehead. *"Aghhhhh!"*

"What's the matter? Love bug hit you in the eye? There's some eyewash in the glove box. Here."

He reached inside and pulled out a small plastic bottle and handed it to her. She brushed it away and laughed. "No, a love bug didn't hit me in the *eye*. God, you're hopeless. Anyway, I was talking about your face."

"What about it?"

"It's a face full of geography and sailor's stories shared around a table in a little tavern where the beer's cold and cheap and the grub's warm and fills the belly. You could be old Santiago sailing his little boat out into the Gulf Stream to test his mettle against a marlin bigger than his boat."

"I could be Ahab, too."

"No, you could never be Ahab. He was wicked and cruel."

"No he wasn't. He was a whaler. He was just doing his job and got a little too carried away by it."

"No, no, no. Listen to me. He was obsessed with the idea of killing that whale. He put himself and his whole crew in peril. He was seeking revenge."

"Well, of course he was seeking revenge. Damn thing bit off his leg."

"But the whale was just minding his own business 'til Ahab tried to kill him," she said. "He was just being true to his nature. Ahab was consumed by hatred of something that hurt him and all he could think about, to his demise, was getting even. No, you can't be Ahab. You're his exact opposite."

"How so?

"Because you're not a vengeful man. You could've demanded Doug's hide for what he did to that beautiful boat and I've no doubt that the sheriff and the judge would've been only too happy to oblige.

Instead of knocking him down, wild thing that he was, you reached out your hand to him."

"And he didn't bite it off. I guess I couldn't be Ahab after all."

She laughed and bumped shoulders with him again.

"But I was talking about your face. I've never seen such a kind one, Jack. And you're gonna be a great father to Doug. He's so lucky. I envy him."

"Why do you envy him?"

She sat quietly for a moment watching the river flow by, choosing her words as carefully as if she were selecting just the right fruit off a tree. "Because you love him. Because he'll always be close to your heart. Because you make a great father, the kind of father my boys never had and I wish they did. Boys need a solid father. A good, wholesome man who teaches them to respect everyone, especially women. Mine never had one like that."

When he didn't reply, she looked away and quickly changed the subject. "So, what's your suggestion for the menu at your friend's restaurant?"

"You're a Baltimore girl so my suggestion is to go for the crab cakes. He'll fill your plate and you'll eat every one and order some to go. One other suggestion, though."

"What's that?"

"Don't call his seafood shack a restaurant. He's worked hard to build and preserve its image as a belly-busting alternative to all the *frou-frou* eating establishments in town, he calls them. You won't find a thing in it other than the beer, the Key limes and the cornmeal that didn't come out of the water around here or from somebody's farm across the bridge out in the country, right on down to the potatoes he makes his French fries with. And don't even think about asking for wine."

They were still laughing when Jack edged the boat alongside the dilapidated docks where O'Brien's Seafood Shak leaned askew like a drunk. The smell of batter frying in grease filled the air like a cloud of incense. Inside, a group laughed and talked loudly, occasionally erupting into cheers and boos over the baseball game on the television screen. A voice roared above the din.

"Quiet, goddamnit! Jaysus, Mary and Joey, I can't heah myself bloody think above all the racket!"

Margie opened her mouth and looked at Jack who just shrugged as the noise came to an abrupt halt and then immediately resumed. She cast a suspicious glance at the building.

"Oh, God! What was that?"

He laughed as he climbed onto the rickety dock and held out his hand to help her out of the boat, assisting her up an equally rickety ladder.

"That would be the proprietor, Jackie O'Brien. Welcome to his tasty little shop of horrors."

"Is he crazy? And that accent. Good Lord."

"No, he's not crazy. He's not the same person outside the restaurant. It's all part of his gimmick. The locals and his regulars love him, although he does tend to scare the dickens out of anyone who's never been here before. He grew up a poor Irish American kid on the south side of Boston in the neighborhood they call Southie. He's proud to call himself shanty Irish, too. He'll probably say something insulting to you, so be prepared. And if you really want to impress him, give it right back to him. Let's go eat."

The place was crowded and the only table was near the counter, where the red-faced owner leaned on the palms of his hands while an inebriated customer fumbled with money to pay his bill. Shabby crabbers and fishermen and mill workers mixed in among preppy-looking couples in expensive clothes, every one of them laughing and talking at once. Signs on the raw cypress wood walls proclaimed cranky admonitions like *Shut your pie hole and eat! Customers who complain will be charged double. No there's no restroom, piss off the dock. Wine is for sissies, drink beer.*

The proprietor snapped his fingers at his slowpoke customer.

"C'mon, c'mon, c'mon, ya drunken bastihd; you're holding up the show. Here, gimme the damn money. I'll count it."

He looked across the man's shoulders at another man standing behind him waiting to pay.

"Spike, take this souse home, will ya? He's shitfaced. He won't get a block before he runs over somebody or gets his license yanked."

And then in a quieter, gentler tone to the drunk man, "Billy, you're short a coupla bucks here, boyo. Pay me next week when your check comes, okay? Now get outta heah. Spike's gonna drive you home. You can get your car tomorrow. Gimme the keys."

The drunk surrendered his keys and waited for the tall, pock-faced man called Spike to pay his bill and then the two of them left together. O'Brien shook his head before turning his attention to Jack and Margie as they picked their way among the crowded tables to their own.

He hailed them so loudly that the noise died and everyone stopped what they were doing and watched as the proprietor limped over to their table.

"Oho! Where'ja find this tasty little piece of jailbait, ya horny old bastihd?"

Jack looked sideways at Margie, who fixed O'Brien with a hot glare that looked real enough to scorch the varnished tabletop. At the same time, she fanned one hand in front of her face and took a step back, meeting his eyes and staring him down.

"Ugh, this place smells like a friggin' grease trap. And so do you."

He drew himself up and puffed out his chest, jabbed a fat finger at her and hooted. "I like this one, Merkel. Sit down, kids. What'll ya have?"

A busboy rushed over, wiped off the table with a stained wet rag and laid some fresh newspaper down. Jack helped Margie to her seat.

"Let's start with a cold one for both of us, Jackie. I'm gonna have the fried shrimp platter. I'll let the lady order hers."

O'Brien leered comically at Margie. "What's the lady's name, pray tell?"

"Margie. And since I'm jailbait from Baltimore, I'm gonna have your crab cakes. And if they're too greasy, I'm gonna puke on your floor, not that it'll matter to all the cockroaches."

O'Brien roared laughter and hobbled off to the kitchen, berating the young busboy who insolently gave him the finger. O'Brien laughed again and cuffed him playfully on the side of the head before pouring two frosty mugs of beer and returning to the table. Margie and Jack lifted their mugs and clinked them together.

"To friends," he said.

"Here's looking at you," she replied.

Jack waited until Margie sat in the boat before starting the engine. It was dark and the waning moon hung over the river and polished the black water to an oily sheen. He started the boat and nosed it into the current. The sounds of laughter and noise faded behind them and within minutes, the only sound was the muted droning of the engine as he headed up the river. He'd gone pensive again and she watched him peering ahead into the darkness. She decided to leave him to his thoughts and leaned back on the head rest and close her eyes. The drone of the engine and the rush of water made her drowsy. She was just beginning to dream, a sensation of being kissed, when he spoke to her in his quiet, even way.

"Not conking out on me over there, are you? We can turn around and go back home if you're sleepy."

She sat up, rubbed at her eyes and scooted over until she was touching his side. When he didn't move away, her heart quickened.

"No, just got a little cozy there for a moment. You know how you start to dream sometimes when you're just starting to drift off but aren't really asleep yet?"

"Yeah. It must've been a nice dream."

"Whys that?" she said, wanting to tell him.

"The smile on your face. I watched you for a little bit before I said anything. What were your dreaming?"

She laughed and elbowed him. "Is it bad luck to tell?"

"Maybe it actually helps one to come true if you share it with someone."

"Okay. I dreamed someone was kissing me."

"The cad. Did you get a name?"

"I saw his face. I didn't need to ask his name."

He quickly pointed into the darkness.

"There's Cumberland Island just ahead. Something there I want to show you."

He throttled back on the engine and they idled along, leaving barely a wake. Moving closer to the shoreline, he eased the boat around a curve. She saw silhouettes in the moonlight. There were eight that she could count along the shoreline. She sucked in a breath and stood up so that she could see them better.

"Oh my God! Horses. Are they wild?"

"Yeah. They're all over Cumberland. They're so used to people that you can walk right up to most of them."

He turned off the engine and the boat drifted along in the current drawing near the shoreline and the horses.

"I've never seen a herd of wild horses before," she said. "They're so regal looking. And that little one nursing its mama, how precious."

He reached into the boat's glove box and took out a camera and handed it to her. "Don't use the flash; it'll spook them. There's enough moonlight and this camera's lens will self-adjust for night photography."

She took the camera out of its case and began taking pictures, focusing the lens on the foal.

"How'd they get here?"

"Well, the rumor locals tell the tourists is that they're the descendants of horses the Spaniards brought here in the sixteenth century, but it's not true. Wealthy families like the Carnegies brought them here. In 1921, a bunch of free-range horses from Arizona were brought here and turned loose."

She zoomed in the lens as much as she could and took one more picture of the mare nursing her foal.

"Who looks after them?"

"Federal park regulations say no one looks after them. They don't want them to get too numerous because they damage the environment when there are too many. They don't live long, seven, eight years on average. Parasites, diseases and poor diet high in salt keeps the herd pretty thin."

She handed the camera back to him. "That's so sad."

"Nature's a cruel mistress. Ready to go? Something else I wanna show you."

He started the engine and headed north into the darkness. A few minutes later, they came to the entrance of a small channel. Once again, Merkel slowed the boat to near idle speed.

"Brickhill River. Lots of deer back here. You should be able to see them pretty good in the moonlight once we get to where we're going."

The river snaked its way through a jungle of spartina. Around the river bend there was marsh on one side and a bluff and forest on the other side. It was so dark that the only light came from the moon. Jack turned off the engine and let the boat drift. There were no other sounds. It was like being in the depths of a cavern, an almost holy silence.

"Look up at the sky," Jack said.

The Milky Way Galaxy sprawled above them and down to the horizon ahead of them, a river of purest silver flowing across the stygian altar of the gods. The sound of their breathing seemed as loud as rushing water when a choked-off shriek pierced the night. Margie felt her skin break into gooseflesh and the shriek came again, but louder and longer, a fever-pitched scream like a terrified woman.

Once, twice, three times, louder and longer each time. She pressed herself to the safety of Jack's side. "Oh God, what is that?"

He put an arm around her and held her tight. "*Shhhh.* It's okay. Just a bobcat."

He put his hand under her chin and they kissed. The boat drifted and turned lazy circles in the languid current and the timid moon painted them with its pale light, but neither of them noticed at all.

CHAPTER 20

RAFE SPOOLED THE HEAVY diesel fuel hose onto its rack and shut down the pump. "Fuel tank's topped off and the water tank'll be full in a jiff."

In the cockpit, Seth nodded and started the engine. "Thanks, Rafe."

Margie and John stood on the dock with Jack and Doug. *Starshine* rode her dock lines beside them. The morning sky was overcast and already it was hot and muggy.

"Why don't you wait for the incoming tide and see if this cloud cover breaks?" Jack said to Margie. "Probably be a little more wind by then, too."

"Thanks, hon, but I need to get underway. It's going on mid-August. Classes at the University of Virginia start in a couple of weeks. I gotta get Seth to Charlottesville and help him get ready for school after we drop *Starshine* off in Baltimore."

Jack started to say something and instead moved a short distance away, turning to look out at the marsh and the river.

Margie reached into the pocket of her baggy shorts and pulled out a small gift-wrapped box.

"Hey, Doug, come here. I've got something for you."

He shuffled over, looking sad. She put her arms around him, kissed him on the cheek and then stepped back and handed him the package.

"What is it?"

"Open it up and see, silly."

He fumbled with the paper for a few moments and finally got the little box open. He stood there for a moment staring into it and then looked up at her and grinned. He took the big, gold hoop earring out of its bed of cotton and admired it. "It's awesome! Where'd you get it?"

"Remember when I borrowed Jack's car and said I needed to run into town the other day? Well, there's a nice lady with a little shop right downtown who sells gold jewelry. I saw this in the store and knew it was made just for you. It's fourteen karat gold, and it's not hollow either. Here, let me put it on for you."

He stepped closer to her and tilted his head to the side. She untied his red bandana and then put it back on his head, fussing with it until she'd tied a smart knot on the side above his left ear so that the bandana tails dangled down the side of his neck. She then slipped the earring on his earlobe, and secured it.

"My, what a fiercely handsome pirate you make," she said, standing back and admiring her work.

Jack went over to join them.

"Mighty fine-looking pirate. But you know what they say, every pirate's gotta have a nickname."

They tossed one nickname and then another one around, laughing at the sillier ones until John joined in the fun. "I've got a good one. Since you got your skull busted, I think your pirate name should be Skully."

Everyone broke into applause at that.

"All right, Skully," Jack said. "Now get down there on the dock and let's get *Starshine* sailing. Captain's orders."

The boys walked away laughing and chatting. Margie noticed Jack's smile had a wistful quality that hadn't been there a moment earlier. She reached out and ran her fingertips along one cheek, feeling the stubble of his whiskers. He smelled like seasoned wood and varnish, the pluff mud in the marsh, and the deep river running down to the ocean. He closed his eyes while she traced the long line of his jaw and she closed hers to mark it well and remember it. He put his arms around her saying nothing, but in his silence she heard all the words he would've spoken to her but for his reticence. She pressed her face to his chest and took in a deep breath and let it out slowly.

"Me, too," she said. "Me, too."

When the moment ended, his smile returned and he held out his arm to her and laughed quietly. "Well, c'mon, Captain. I'll escort you to your ship so the pirates and bobcats won't get you."

She laughed and put her arm through his, and they walked arm-in-arm to the idling boat. Doug, Rafe and both of Margie's sons waited beside it. She let Merkel help her step aboard.

"Crew, you may board," she said at last.

While her sons scrambled to their assigned stations, Margie stepped over to the starboard side of the boat. Without a word, she beckoned Doug, Rafe and Jack to her. She leaned over the rail and hugged Rafe's thick neck and kissed his cheek. Then she embraced Doug and kissed him on both cheeks, evoking tears. Jack stepped forward, looking directly into her eyes until finally a thin smile emerged. She put her hands on his cheeks and kissed him lightly on both sides of his mouth and hopped behind the helm. She was about to put her hands on the wheel, then stopped and frowned. "Shit. I forgot to pay my bill."

Jack grinned and pointed toward the boat's cabin.

"It's on the table in the salon. You didn't think I'd let you sneak off without paying, did you?"

She laughed again and then beckoned to her sons.

"C'mon lads. Let's go sailing."

Jack, Doug and Rafe untied the dock lines and handed them over to Margie's sons, and then the three of them gave the big boat a shove. Sounding a loud blast on the horn, Margie navigated the boat down the channel and slid out of sight down the Intracoastal. Both of her sons were pensive. John kept looking back over his shoulder as the marina faded. Seth took a seat beside her and stared away into the distance. The night before, both boys told her they wished they could stay. For once, Seth didn't seem excited about starting college. When the boat was safely in the deep waterway, she asked Seth to take the helm so she could go below and use the bathroom. As she walked back through the salon, she spotted a large manila envelope with her name on atop the mahogany table. She stopped and opened it. It was a note in Jack's meticulous penmanship and a photo.

"Dear Margie, It's been a long time since I felt this way. I don't have the words to say how I feel. Doug and me will miss you and we'll always remember what you did, for both of us."

The photograph was one she'd taken the day they put on the new rudder and they'd all gone sailing for the afternoon. Doug was at the helm and Jack stood beside him. Both of them were laughing. She looked on the back of the photo and saw a note there, too.

Don't be a stranger. We'll hold a slip open for you.

Fondly, Jack and Doug

She wiped her eyes with the back of her hand, tucked the photo into the envelope and returned to the cockpit.

Jack and Doug stood on the dock awhile after *Starshine* left, neither of them saying anything. Doug glanced over at Merkel and saw the faraway look. "You gonna be okay?"

"Yeah, how 'bout you?"

Doug laughed and gave him an affectionate hug. "I'm good, Pop."

Jack tugged playfully on the tails of the boy's bandana. "C'mon, Skully. We've got a marina to run and a sailboat to finish."

Pogy saw them coming and ran to greet them, dancing and cavorting. In that moment, Doug knew he'd found his forever home.

Later that evening, Jack went downstairs to the office to get a Coke out of the machine. Doug had already gone to bed and Pogy had plopped down on the floor beside him. Both of them were snoring. He opened the bottle and walked over to his desk and picked up his cigarettes. He put one in his mouth and was just about to light it, but then tossed it and the rest of the pack into the trash can. Reaching across the desk, he picked up the framed photograph of Penny and Teddy, their bright smiles captured forever in an eight-by-ten photograph, studied it for a few moments and then held it to his heart. He kissed the picture and then set it on a nearby shelf. He was about to walk away when he noticed a package on the counter beside the coffee pot. He took his knife out of his pocket and cut the hemp string that bound the box in its plain brown wrapping paper. Inside was a bronze statue of an old sea captain standing at the helm, pipe in one corner of his mouth as he squinted into the wind. He turned it in his hands and then noticed the engraving on its base.

Captain Jack Merkel. A sailor's sailor. I know you don't have the words so I'll say them for you.
I love you.
Margie.

He looked at the statue for a long time, reading again and again the inscription on its base. He set it on his desk and climbed up the stairs to bed.

CHAPTER 21

THE CALL FROM JUDGE Kicklighter came a week later while Merkel was cooking breakfast.

"How's the boy, Jack?"

"Better every day," Jack answered. "He's taking a shower right now and I'm fixing breakfast for us. What's going on that you're bothering me at such an early hour? I beat you fair and square at poker last night. Are you still going on about that?"

The judge rumbled his laughter and cursed Jack for a cheat before saying what he had to say.

"Listen, I want to see both of you in my courtroom this morning at nine sharp. Any problem with that?"

Jack was suddenly wary. "Not unless you're fixing to give me some bad news. What's going on, Harley? What am I walking this poor kid into? Damn it. I don't think it's a good time for this."

"You're wrong about that, Jack. No, trust me, this is a good time. I want to get this resolved today."

"Damn it, Harley. It's only been a month. Can't this wait a little longer?"

"Sure, Jack, it could but I don't want to wait, and I have my reasons. I'll see you in court. Don't be late."

Jack waited until they'd finished their breakfast before telling Doug about the telephone call.

"Am I in trouble?" he said, looking uneasy and sounding nervous.

"No reason to think so. Judge Kicklighter gets a bee in his bonnet from time to time about one thing or another and nothing to do but hear him out. Probably just something procedural he wants to talk about."

They drove to the courthouse in silence. Doug got out of the car and froze on the courthouse steps.

"I'm scared."

Jack put his arm around him and hugged him.

"Don't be. I ain't gonna let anything happen to you. I promise."

The prosecutor and Doug's lawyer were already at their tables when Doug and Jack walked into the courtroom. They sat in the front row, and Mason Bryce came over to talk to them. Brad Reynolds ignored them.

"What's going on, Mr. Bryce?" Doug said. "Am I in trouble for something?"

The attorney shook his head and looked at both of them. "No, you're not in trouble. I can tell you that much."

"Well, what's going on then, Mason?" Jack asked.

The lawyer straightened his tie and wiped the lenses of his glasses. "I'm not supposed to say. The judge will tell you when he comes in. Come on to the table with me, Doug, and sit down."

Doug and Jack exchanged puzzled glances and then the boy followed his lawyer to his table where the two of them engaged in a whispered conversation. Just before nine, Sheriff Patterson strolled in, sat down beside Jack, clapped him on the shoulder and winked. Moments later, at nine o'clock sharp, the judge strode into the courtroom. After taking his place on the bench, Kicklighter wasted no time.

"I've met with Counselor Bryce, Assistant State Attorney Reynolds and Sheriff Patterson this morning after a conference call with them yesterday. I told them I want to resolve this case today. The honorable sheriff, counsel for the defense and the state have all agreed. Mr. Bryce, would you kindly take Mr. Eleazer here to the side and explain the terms we've discussed with him?"

The boy turned around and shot Jack a glance overflowing with apprehension. Jack stood and looked at the judge, who scowled. "Sit down, Mr. Merkel. I'll hear from you directly."

Jack sat and listened to the attorney's whispers and the swoosh of the ceiling fan and the sound of traffic on the street below as his mind flashed back to the first day he'd been in the courtroom after Doug's arrest. He saw Doug's head nodding as his lawyer spoke with him, and after a few moments they returned to their seats. Doug looked back at him and tried to smile. Kicklighter cleared his throat. "Are we ready to proceed, gentlemen?"

The prosecutor stood and nodded. "Yes, Your Honor."

"Yes, Your Honor," Doug's lawyer said, standing.

"Very well, then. Mr. Eleazer, has your attorney advised you of the reason you're here today and of the terms discussed between the three of us? I want to hear it from you, son."

Doug stood and looked at the judge with an unwavering gaze. "Yes, Your Honor. He says you're willing to take a plea today and you'll decide what to do after hearing what I have to say and what Mr. Merkel has to say about it."

The judge looked at the boy and raised his eyebrows.

"And what are your choices, Mr. Eleazer?"

"I can plead innocent and you'll set the case for trial or I can plead no contest or guilty and you'll decide right now what you're going to do."

Kicklighter smiled. "Good. I'm sure you know the difference between guilty and innocent, but did he explain a no-contest plea to you?"

Doug continued to look right into the judge's eyes. "Yes, Your Honor. No contest means I'm not saying I didn't do it and I'm not admitting I did do it. He said that would be his recommendation, Your Honor."

The judge tilted his big chair back. Jack held his breath and prayed. Doug stood in front of the bench like a soldier, tall and erect, shoulders back, head held high.

"Well, then, Mr. Eleazer. Do you wish to enter a plea at this time?"

"Yes, Your Honor. I plead guilty."

His words drew a gasp from Jack, from his attorney, as well as the prosecutor. Kicklighter peered at him intently. "Are you sure you want to do that, son, against the advice of counsel?"

"Yes, Your Honor. I can't stand here in front of you and Mr. Merkel and not admit wrongdoing. I did what I'm accused of doin'." He turned around and locked eyes with Jack, who looked at him pleadingly and then turned back around to face the judge.

"I busted into his boatyard and damaged something near and dear to him. Since then, he ain't shown me anything but compassion and kindness. It'd be dishonest of me not to own up to it, even though I know he's forgiven me."

He stopped to take a breath. "I plead guilty as charged, Your Honor. You do what you have to do."

Kicklighter's eyes went from Doug to Mason Bryce, who blanched, to Brad Reynolds, who looked confused, and then to Jack, whose mouth was open in astonishment. The judge, leaned forward on his bench, put his face in his hands and sighed.

"Mr. Eleazer, you do understand that if you enter a plea of guilty I can sentence you right now to a term in prison. So, I'm asking you one more time. Is that what you want to do?"

"Yes, sir."

Jack felt his face getting hot as his heart began to pound in his chest. Chilly sweat dribbled down the back of his neck and made him shiver. He scrambled to his feet. "Your Honor—"

"Calm down, Mr. Merkel. I was just about to ask you if you have something you want to say as the victim in this case before I proceed. Now, if you can compose yourself, I'll allow you to say whatever's on your mind. But keep it brief. I'm not in the mood for long-winded speeches."

Jack looked over at Doug who looked back at him and smiled weakly.

"Your Honor, I'm willing to forgive and forget. Already done both. Doug has been a joy to me. He works hard. He's made amends to me. He's honest and he deserves a good life. You know how sorry it's been until recently and you're the only one here who can change it. He's paid his dues and then some. Let him go, judge."

Kicklighter held his hand up. "That'll be enough, Mr. Merkel. Please sit down."

The judge leaned forward and addressed Doug. "I could sentence you to time served and let you go right now. Of course, if I opted not to withhold judgment, you'd have another red mark on your record." And then he shot the startled prosecutor a withering stare. "Or, if Mr. Reynolds here has a shred of decency in him, he can just dismiss the charges altogether, seeing how strongly the victim in this case feels about it. If it were me, Mr. Reynolds, I think I'd be inclined to do just that."

The prosecutor stood and looked at Doug and then back at the judge. "Your Honor, the State agrees with the court's assessment and, in keeping with the victim's wishes, I will withdraw all charges against Mr. Eleazer."

The judged stared him down. "I want it done before I adjourn this hearing so this boy can walk out of my courtroom with clean hands."

"Yes, Your Honor. Consider it done."

Kicklighter looked at Doug and crooked his finger for him to come forward.

"You've had a wretched life, son," Kicklighter said. "Lord knows you have. But now you've got a new one. This man who just spoke so eloquently and passionately in your defense has deeply moved this court. I remember saying one day, early on when this case first came before me, that you can't fix every broken thing. I also recall Mr. Bryce here telling me about breaking that treasured gold pocket watch that his father inherited from his own father and how sure he was that it couldn't be fixed until an old watch repairman proved otherwise. I believe Mr. Bryce's sage words to this court that day were that sometimes even those things that appear to be broken beyond repair can be repaired by the hands of the right craftsman."

He stopped and pointed at Jack.

"And that man sitting right out there who got on his feet and challenged me to show you the same mercy and forgiveness that he has shown you is about the finest craftsman you'll ever find. Don't you ever forget that, son, and don't you ever let him down. What you've always lacked in your life is a father. Let this man be one to you."

He cast an admonishing look at Jack, held it for a few moments and then grinned.

"And maybe one of these days the stubborn, tight-lipped son of a gun can find you a mother, too. Case dismissed."

"All rise," the bailiff cried. "This court is now in recess."

Before he left the courtroom, Kicklighter jabbed his finger at Jack. "You owe me another fishing trip, buddy."

CHAPTER 22

DOUG TOOK POGY FOR a walk one evening three weeks later and stopped to check the mailbox on the way back. He returned a few minutes later with a stack of envelopes and magazines and gave them to Jack who was cleaning up from supper. Jack leafed through them and held up an envelope for Doug to see, then tore it open.

"Letter from Margie."

Doug plopped down on the sofa beside him and leaned over, gazing at Margie's loopy handwriting. "What does she say? Is she coming back?"

Jack read the letter, hearing Margie's rapid-fire manner of speaking, and then handed it to Doug.

"Says she got Seth off to college and John enrolled in junior high school in Baltimore," Doug said. "They're living aboard *Starshine* in a nice marina, but she liked it here better. Doesn't say anything about coming back." He paused and looked at Jack. "She says she misses us a lot."

Jack got up and went to the kitchen for coffee.

"Want some iced tea?"

"Sure. Why do you always do that, Pop?"

"Do what?"

The boy frowned and shook his head. "You know what I mean. Change the subject when someone asks you a question sometimes."

"Do I?"

The boy rolled his eyes. "See? You're doing it again. I miss them, Margie especially. Don't you?

"Yeah, I do, son."

"Then why'd you let her go? She would've stayed. She was waiting for you to ask."

Jack sipped his tea and smiled. "Well now, did she tell you that or are you just guessing?"

"I just got the feeling, you know? I really wanted her to stay and I thought she might."

Jack set down his glass and picked at a fingernail as the awkward moment passed.

"It's a little more complicated than that," he said. "It's a big step to take and I'm not sure either one of us is ready for it. I'm still sorting some things out. Some days I think I'm there. Others I don't feel like I've made any progress at all. Do you understand?"

Doug gnawed his bottom lip and seemed to be lost in thought for a moment. The brass ship's clock on the shelf chimed nine p.m. "Pop, what happened to your wife and son?"

Jack waited for clock to stop chiming while collecting his thoughts. Doug thought that he'd overstepped his bounds.

"I'm sorry. I shouldn't have asked you that."

"No offense taken and no apology necessary. I reckon it's been kind of hanging out there just waiting for one of us to bump into, anyway. It's a fair question. They died. Tragically."

Doug put his fist to his mouth and bit down on his knuckle. "Jesus. Jesus. I'm so sorry."

Jack realized that for the first time he'd said those two words without losing his composure. Instead of feeling like crying, all he wanted to do was comfort the stricken boy sitting next to him.

He got up from the sofa and extended his hand to Doug, pulling him to his feet. "C'mon. Let's take a walk and I'll tell you about some things and then we can move on together."

With Pogy trailing they went outside into the dark vastness of the night and walked across the yard.

"Where we headed?" Doug said.

"You'll see. I want to show you something and tell you a story."

There was no moon that night, only the stars to cast their dim, flickering light as the two men made their way amongst the silhouettes of boats resting in cradles and on metal jacks. A raccoon waddled across the yard in front of them, paused to study them for a moment through its burglar's mask and then went on about its business. They walked on, neither speaking until they stood before the last boat in the yard and then stopped. Jack stepped over to it, ran the palm of his hand over the smooth fiberglass.

"She's gonna be a beauty when we're done with her," he said. "I want you to do something."

"Sure, what's that?"

"I want you to step right here where I am, close your eyes and put your hand right where mine is."

Doug gave him a puzzled glance, shrugged, and stepped over, putting his hand on the boat just as Jack had asked him to do. Jack looked up at the stars.

"Their names were Penny and Teddy. They died ten years ago on the same day. He drowned in a surfing accident and she was fatally injured rushing to the hospital. I got there too late to tell either one goodbye. I've been alone ever since, working and doing the things a person's gotta do to get along, but not getting much enjoyment out of any of it. I think you know what I mean."

"Yes, sir."

Jack put his other hand on Doug's shoulder and gave him a gentle nudge. He closed his eyes. "Hold my hand and walk with me. This unfinished boat's got a story to tell.

"We laid up the hull, right here in the yard nearly eleven years ago. Teddy was eighteen, same as you. It was a family project. I'd talked about sailing and the sea for so many years that I got both of them addicted to my stories, my recollections, my dreams. One evening, while we were sitting on the deck after supper, Penny pipes up and says, 'Why don't we build our own boat, honey, just the three of us?'"

Jack felt his heart stir at the memory.

"'Yeah, Dad! let's do it.' Teddy said. 'Let's build our very own boat and go sailing off together. Just the three of us.'"

Jack became pensive for a moment.

"And just like that, I decided, hell yeah, let's do it. I've done a lot of work on boats, but I've never done something like lay up a hull. There's a lot to it. I bought every book on boatbuilding I could find. The three of us studied like college students every night for months, reading and making drawings and quizzing one another until we were sure we were up to the task. We went out and bought the material—the fiberglass cloth and the resin, the wood, the tools and all the other things we needed. I thought I'd break the bank account before we were ready to take the first swipe at it."

Jack kept walking, eyes still shut, one small step at a time.

"You still with me?"

"Yes sir."

"We hit some rough spots here and there. And I don't think I've ever heard Penny cuss so much, but once we got going, our confidence grew and things sailed right along. Before we knew it, we had the hull done. We sanded the raw fiberglass 'til it was smooth like it is now and then painted on primer to keep it clean and protect it from the weather. We painted all the exposed fiberglass surfaces inside—I hate unfinished fiberglass—and then we started on the woodwork. We'd just gotten some of the teak on the bulkheads and overhead, and the doors and some of the cabinetry installed when Penny and Teddy got killed—just shy of Teddy's nineteenth birthday."

He stopped walking for a moment and in the silence, Doug's breathing and Pogy's panting sounded enormous, like the tidal wave of grief that threatened sweep over him. But rather than give in to the hurt, for the first time he pushed it away.

"I never went near it again. After their funeral, it sat out there in the yard like the bad memory it was 'til Rafe came along with the lift one day, picked it up and put it in that barn out yonder. And there it stayed 'til about a month before you—"

"I'm sorry, Pop."

"Hush. That ain't important now. That was another Doug, another Jack Merkel. What happened was, I can't abide unfinished business, never have. Used to drive Penny crazy with my doggedness. One afternoon, after chewing on it for pretty near a week, I got Rafe to help me haul it back out and I started working on it again. But it was grim work. I made myself do it every day but there wasn't any joy in it . . . not like before. I was just goin' through the motions. I kept thinking I'd warm to it but never did. It was a family project from its birth and my family was gone."

He stopped again and thought for a moment. "Truth of the matter is, I'd pretty much had a belly full of it 'til you came along. Before the night you came in here, I hadn't worked on it much in days. I told Rafe one morning that I was about ready to just give the damn thing away to somebody who'd love it the way I once had and finish it. You showed up the next night."

Doug bit his lip. "And I smashed something you and your wife and son created together."

"No. Listen to me. Do you believe in God? It's okay if you don't."

"Sure I do. He sent me here to be redeemed."

"Yes, I think he did. But he also sent you here to redeem me."

Doug stood still and ran the palm of his hand back and forth over the fiberglass, feeling its unblemished smoothness.

"But I took a hammer to it," he said, bitterly.

"Yeah, you did. And I'm not generally a man to leave my tools out when I'm done with them. But if I hadn't and you hadn't, we wouldn't be working on this boat right now. It would've been gone. The sheriff hauled you out here a few days later and here we are."

"I don't get it, Pop."

"I felt sorry for you, but I was pissed off, too. I meant to have my pound of flesh out of you. I figured to just let you help me fix what you messed up and then I'd go to court and ask Harley to go easy on you. But in the meantime, something happened. Having somebody to help me work on this boat again made me want to keep working on it. It wasn't just some lonesome, depressing task anymore. I wanted to do it. Everything worked out the way it was meant, for both of us, I think."

They came to the bow of the boat and Jack stepped around it, never taking his hands off it. Doug followed close on his heels.

"It was a family project and I feel like I have a family again. I just wanted to help a kid in trouble, punish him a little in my own way, but it never occurred to me that one day he'd feel like family."

He paused again and stood waiting for Doug to walk away from him. Instead, the boy put a hand on his shoulder. "I don't think I could've said it the way you did but . . . me, too, Pop"

"So, where do we go from here?"

Doug's smile was bright in the darkness. "We build us a sailboat. No unfinished business. We're family."

Jack pivoted and looked into Doug's eyes. "Now, put one hand back on her and do what I tell you to do."

"Okay, I'm ready."

"Close your eyes and walk all the way around her. Never take your hand off her. Think about the sun and the sea. Lose yourself in moonlit nights, and the rise and fall of the swells, the waves and the sudden flash of lightning, the scare-the-shit-out-of-you crack of thunder. Walk around this boat and feel her heartbeat. Smell the sanded fiberglass. Taste the salt air. Listen to her voice. Look into her soul. Go on. Do it and then come back to me and tell me something. You'll know what it is."

Jack stepped back in the darkness and watched Doug shuffle around the boat with one hand on it, pausing from time to time and then moving onward again, slow like the changing of the tide, like the waxing and the waning of the moon. His hand went high and it went low along the boat's long, sleek, curved surface as he put one foot in front of the other. He disappeared behind the stern and when he came into view again, Jack could see, even in the pale starlight, that his face had changed. There was a confidence and steadiness to it that hadn't been there before, as if he'd changed faces in the brief interval before he cleared the stern and emerged on the other side. What did emerge on the other side, it occurred to Merkel, was no longer just a scared kid, but the beginnings of a man, still in need of some fine sanding and preparation, but not far from being complete. He also wore a smile that Jack couldn't think of a better word to describe than *joy*—joy as pure as the wind in the sails and as deep as the sea.

When Doug was within arm's reach of him, Jack put both hands on his shoulders and told him to stop and open his eyes. When he did, Jack looked into them again and smiled. "Tell me who you are."

Doug stood tall and returned his smile. "I'm a mariner. I'm the son of a mariner and this is our ship."

Jack held him away at arm's length and gazed at his face. "You'll be a captain one day. This'll be *your* ship."

With pride welling up like a spring from his core, Doug fixed his eyes on the boat.

"I've got a name for her already."

Jack put a finger to his lips. "Hush. Bad luck to tell right now. Wait 'til we christen her. Now come on, let's get some sleep. Big day tomorrow, skipper." They put their arms around one another and headed back, with Pogy trailing.

CHAPTER 23

IT WAS AN APPLE-CRISP, golden Saturday afternoon in late September. Jack and Doug were applying varnish to the interior woodwork of their boat. The summer crunch was over at Merkel's Marina, and he was finally able to let his crew have some badly needed time off. Eddie had passed his captain's license test a week earlier and was excited about starting his own charter fishing business. Jack was thrilled for the hard working and ambitious young man with the perpetual smile, but his soon departure was going to leave him short a forklift operator. He consulted with Rafe and Neal and decided to start training Doug for the job.

The boy was eager and willing to learn any task in the yard. He caught on quick and did a good job no matter the task, and never complained. Neal grumbled about having to help train him but relented, and Jack noticed to his surprise one day that the marina's resident grouch and pessimist seemed to have taken a grudging liking to his charge, not that he'd ever admit it to anyone, especially Doug.

Doug and Jack had been working on the boat since sunrise. Because the slow schedule allowed for it, they'd been putting in a lot of hours on the boat over the preceding few weeks. The spartina grass had shed most of its summer raiment of emerald green and was turning a pale greenish-yellow. In a few more weeks, it would wear the honey golden tint of a Midwestern wheat field, by winter, the grayish-brown of a pelican. Doug set his paintbrush to the side and leaned over to smell the aroma of teak and spar varnish. Jack applied the amber-colored varnish on the other end of the wall they were painting in long, even strokes. He watched Doug and saw the boy close his eyes, inhale deeply and smile. "Smells better than biscuits baking, don't it?" Jack said.

Doug picked up his brush again and resumed applying the varnish. "I can't get enough of it. It has a sort of exotic tropical smell to it."

"I reckon that's about how I'd describe it, too. But you might be tired of it by the time we're done varnishing all this teak. We've only got two coats on and we've got five more to go."

He paused to dip his beaver bristle brush back into the cup of varnish beside him and saw Doug frown and make as if to try and pinch something on the wet varnish. He stopped him. "Uh-uh. Leave that gnat alone. It ain't gonna hurt nothing. When this coat cures out, we'll be shed of him when we fine sand for our next coat. Come on, let's finish up here and take a break."

After they finished they walked out onto the docks to get some fresh air and stretch for a while. Both had been working in the same confined space most of the day. But even though he was getting tired and sore, Doug marveled at how good he felt on the inside. He loved the smell of the wood and the varnish and the feel of the paintbrushes and sandpaper and other tools in his hands. The boat was like an unfinished house on the inside. But day by day, he could see it becoming not just a house, but a home. He loved working alongside Jack. Pop was a patient teacher, quick with praise and liberal in his encouragement. He didn't get angry or frustrated about mistakes. He always gave his instructions and corrections speaking in his low, easy cadence. He rarely raised his voice except to laugh, which Doug noticed that he did more and more lately. And the stories he told were endlessly fascinating. His eyes glowed as he described, in almost poetic terms, Doug thought, every port in every country he'd ever been to.

"After I retired from the Merchant Marine, I had a pile of money saved," he said as they walked down a nearby dock. "What does a retired sailor do with his time when he ain't ready to just go fishing 'til he's toes up in the bone yard? Well, this old mariner decided to take up shrimping and that's what I did, 'til Penny came along. I was head-over-heels in love with her and couldn't stand being away from her for days at a time. So I sold the shrimp boat, added another chunk from my retirement money and bought this marina."

He stopped walking and looked around. "I got it on the cheap and fixed it up, adding to it when I could. Penny got pregnant, but she threw herself into the project anyway. Rafe came to us not long after. The three of us lived on a big old abandoned sailboat while we finished building the place.

Jack was animated, and by the time their break ended, Doug felt as if he'd known his friend and mentor all his life. There was no hint of pain or grief in his memories about the loss of Penny and Teddy.

"Penny was just a girl when we met and I was already a crusty old timer," Jack recounted with a laugh. "She was only twenty and just barely at that. I was thirty-eight. Can you believe that?"

Doug pantomimed reeling in a fish. "Well, she must've realized right away that you were a good catch. I can almost see her the way you describe her."

Jack laughed. "Good catch? What am I, a flounder?" He went on with his story.

"Well, she got her hook in me all right. I asked her what in thunder she saw in an old squid like me after the first time she showed up at the docks to ask me out. Must've been a week after I met her picking flowers down by the cemetery. God, she was so beautiful. The sun seemed to shine out of her and never stopped shining 'til the day her and Teddy died. She wrote me a letter she gave to my first mate that said I had character and color and that she'd had her eye on me around town for a while. Didn't cotton much to any of the young guys around here, she said, because most of 'em didn't have the sense God gave a gopher tortoise."

"So when was the first time y'all went out together?"

Jack's laughter rang as clear as a ship's bell. "The same day. Soon as I got to the boat that morning, my first mate handed me the envelope. I went off to the side and opened it. She said she wanted me to call her soon as I read it. Bossy little thing. Come to think of it, Margie reminds me a bit of her sometimes."

Doug noticed that he mentioned Margie in the present tense, and inwardly rejoiced.

"Anyway," Jack went on, "I went across the street to a phone booth and called her and she told me to pick her up at six that evening. I told her I didn't have any proper clothes to go out courting. She just laughed and said that where we were going, a pair of shorts and a T-shirt would do fine, but to bring some bug repellant."

Doug laughed. "Sounds like my kinda girl. Where'd y'all go?"

"There's a sand dune on the south end of the island. NaNa, they call it. I think it means Queen in one of the African languages. Way back when, the Sea Islands from South Carolina down this way were settlements of Gullah people, descendants of African slaves who held to the old ways of their ancestors and still spoke a sort of dialect that's a mix of West African languages and English. They're mostly all gone now except a place or two along the coast of South Carolina and Georgia."

He bent over to tie one of his boot laces. "Anyway, it's the highest sand dune in the state, pretty near tall as a six-story building.

That's where Penny wanted me to go with her that evening. I didn't understand why 'til the full moon began to rise. I'd never seen anything like it before, not even at sea; it was a rusty reddish color and so big it seemed to fill the sky. We sat there an hour without either of us saying a word. When we finally got up and shook the sand off and walked back to the car, I knew I'd found my soul mate, or, more accurately I suppose, she'd found hers."

They stopped again to watch a sea turtle eating a jellyfish. A freshening breeze that bore the first kiss of the cool autumn weather rippled the water. A snowy egret eating a shrimp farther along the dock watched their approach with bright yellow eyes. Having had no luck finding rabbits to chase, Pogy came charging down the dock barking as the bird flew away, and both of them laughed at the dog's antics.

"Penny sounds a lot like Mama," Doug said. "She always said she should've been at Woodstock but was born too late. She really was a hippie at heart. Elizabeth and me used to tease her all the time about it."

"Penny was a flower child, all right," Jack said. "In love with nature and in awe of it as a kid. I watched her stalk a dragonfly for nearly a half hour one day after it flew into the office and couldn't find its way out. 'Penny,' I said to her. 'Get a minnow net and trap the dang thing.' Oh, no, she wouldn't hear of it. She was afraid she'd damage its delicate wings and it wouldn't be able to fly. She persisted 'til the poor wild thing was exhausted and then she snuck up on it, cupped her hands around it, took it to the front door and turned it loose. I swear to God, I coulda swore I heard it say 'thank you' as it flew away."

"So, Teddy was a surfer, huh?" Doug said.

"Yeah, he was quite the surfer, all right. It's all he wanted to do from the day I bought him his first board when he was six. Lord knows how many times he cut classes and I'd get a call from the school and have to go to the beach and fetch him. But it kept him out of trouble otherwise."

Jack looked at the fading spartina and watched an osprey stalking a mullet.

"Yep, Teddy was a hard-core surfer by the time he was twelve. And you know what? As bad as it hurt to lose him, and as much as I still miss him—both of them—Teddy died doing something he loved. He was never happier than when he was surfing. That's a comfort to me."

Doug wasn't sure how to respond or even if he should. Jack saved him from having to decide.

"Come on. Something I want to show you."

They stood beside an older model sailboat near the back of the yard. It was perched in a V-shaped metal cradle looking forlorn. Jack ran his hand over the fiberglass and frowned at the dirt on his palm. Doug walked around it and inspected it.

"This is the boat you said the old guy from New Jersey left here when he died, ain't it?"

Jack picked up a ladder and propped it against the side of the little boat.

"Yep. *Island Time* is a Catalina 25, built in '84. The old gent took a lot of pride in it and made a lot of improvements to it, too. Come on up and I'll show you."

Jack climbed up the ladder, lithe for a man his age. Doug followed him and when he reached the top, Jack gave him his hand and helped him step over the rail.

"This little jewel's an ideal boat for you to learn how to sail on," Jack said, as they climbed back to the cockpit. "She's just twenty-five feet, light, easy to handle, very forgiving of mistakes." He paused, then looked at Doug and smiled. "Your first lesson will be tomorrow."

"Yes!" Doug said, pumping both fists in the air.

Jack grinned and put a hand on Doug's shoulder.

"I knew you'd be excited. I've been scheming about this for a while."

"I won't sleep a wink tonight."

"Well, you'd better try," Jack said. "Sailing can be physically taxing and mentally draining while you're learning. But you'll be fine."

Doug looked around in amazement and then back at Jack.

"I heard you tell Margie that you sailed this boat to Charleston last spring? How long did that take?"

Jack thought for a moment.

"Well, I wasn't in a hurry so it took me pretty near a week. A boat this size isn't as fast as the one we're building, which is nowhere near as fast as Margie's. I decided to split the trip into bites and enjoy the scenery."

"Could you do it faster in this boat if you wanted to?"

"Sure you could. I made it back in four days, but that was hustling. But if you knew how and had a good wind and were willing to sail nonstop, catching catnaps in the cockpit, which I don't recommend 'til you have some open sea experience behind you, it's possible to do it in about three days."

"God, that sounds like fun," Doug said. "How long will it take me to learn how to sail like that?"

Jack looked at him and grinned.

"Depends on you, how quick you learn, how much grit you've got, which I figure is plenty. It comes natural to some people. A fourteen-year-old girl from Amsterdam sailed solo around the world. As you can see, this is a tiller boat. It doesn't have a wheel like Margie's. It's best to learn to sail on a tiller boat. Your arm becomes an extension of the rudder. You feel every little movement and change in the boat's attitude. Master a tiller 'til you can navigate with your eyes closed, and then a helm-steered boat's a piece of cake. Now come on, let's call it a day and run down to Jackie O'Brien's and get us some supper."

CHAPTER 24

NEAR SUNSET ON HALLOWEEN evening, Jack and Doug were making final adjustments on the diesel engine they'd installed in the boat they were building when Merkel's radio crackled with a familiar, cheery voice.

"Merkel's Marina, Merkel's Marina. This is *Starshine.* Trick or treat, fellas."

Before Jack could get to his radio, Doug was off the boat and running across the yard and onto the docks. Pogy abandoned his rabbit tracking and ran after him. Jack's grease-stained hands shook and his heart raced as he picked up his radio and responded.

"Lord ha' mercy, Margie. This is a treat indeed. Where the dickens are you?"

"Just now passing green buoy eleven. Should be there in about ten. Got a place for me?"

He thought about how to answer. "I'll always have a place for you."

"I was hoping that'd be your answer. I might be here awhile this time, if that's okay."

He climbed out of the boat and wiped a spill of grease off it. "Who's with you?"

There were excited voices in the background.

"The boys," she said, and then, "Pipe down guys! I can't hear a thing. Agghhh! They're about to drive me crazy to hurry up and get there."

"I thought Seth was in college and John was going to stay with his dad awhile," Jack said.

"Well, there's a bit of story on both accounts. I'll tell you later. Say, where's Skully?"

"Standing out there with Pogy at the end of the dock waiting for you. But listen, you need to get off the radio now. You've got a couple of nasty sandbars coming up, so you be on the lookout."

Margie signed off and Jack headed toward the cleanup station to wash up. He washed his hands and face, combed his hair, pulled back his ponytail and went to join Doug on the dock, his eyes on the river. Jack quick-stepped down the dock.

"How far out is she?" Doug asked. "Is she gonna stay awhile or is she just passing through going back to the islands?"

Jack stepped beside him and peered out at the river.

"Looks like ol' Pogy here is as excited as me and you."

"There you go again, dodging the question."

Jack grinned. "We'll see."

The sun began its descent beneath the western horizon, still cluttered with puffy, blue-gray clouds left by a passing shower earlier. A smear of orange delighted the late autumn sky. Moments later, Jack's tugboat captain friend plowed by on his way home and sounded a long note on his horn. And as he always did, Jack raised his arm in silent greeting, wondering whether his friend could see him or if he, too, sometimes just did things out of comforting habit. *Some things never change,* he thought. The river moved steadily on. The spartina lived and died and lived again. The North Star was always fixed in its place, a guide to mariners leading them home. Jack treasured things that were immutable. They brought him peace.

The wild creature that a man wearing a badge and a gun had laid at Jack's feet one similar evening not four months prior had vanished like a sprite at daybreak. It'd been replaced by a steady, clear-eyed young man, gentle of spirit, profound of thought, easy in laughter and single-minded in his determination to expunge the brutality of a bloodstained past. When Jack set his adoring eyes on Doug, the shadow of his past was no longer visible, only what he'd become, and the dauntless promise of future things, as if the teen had shed his old and ragged skin like a snake, left it crumpled in a thicket and gone forth with its new scales gleaming in the sun.

Now the two of them stood side by side, taking in the beauty that charmed and captivated them both. Neither spoke, for nothing they could say would equal what their eyes beheld.

Moments later, Margie's big yacht hove into view and headed up the channel toward them. Doug turned to Jack, held out his arms and embraced him.

Jack returned the embrace and smiled. A few minutes later, just as darkness was settling, the two of them tied Margie's sailboat to the dock cleats, binding her to home.

While Jack cooked two steaks on the grill, Margie took the baked potatoes out of the oven, tossed a salad, poured two glasses of red wine and then joined him on the deck. Her sons were antsy from having been cooped up on a boat for days with no company but their mother, and they were anxious for the company of other males. Doug was overjoyed to see them and announced that he wanted to introduce them to supper at Jackie's and then take them flounder gigging and camping overnight. After some discussion, Jack and Margie agreed it'd be good for the three of them. Jack gave Doug permission to use his flats boat and warned him to be careful and to call him right away if he needed assistance. The boys then loaded their flounder gigging gear in the boat and took off, leaving Margie and Merkel.

"I have a feeling the boys plotted to give us some time to be alone," Jack said, watching them motor away.

Waving goodbye to the boys she said, "Golly, Merkel. Ya think?"

He seemed to be lost in thought when she came outside to join him while he finished cooking the steaks. She wore a pastel green cotton skirt, a white, lightweight cotton sweater and sandals that matched her skirt. When she got closer, she noticed that his eyes were closed and he was smiling. She stopped and stood a short distance away. She studied his face like a map. She let her eyes roam the long length of his jaw, the slight tilt of his head, and then her gaze was drawn back to the smile that she could never drink her fill of. He'd showered and put on a comfortably well-worn pair of khaki pants, a long-sleeved, pale orange fisherman's shirt and tan canvas shoes. She inhaled the masculine scent of the body soap he'd used and found herself yearning to be held by him. Then, as if sensing that she was there, he turned his smile on her.

"Well, hey. Kinda snuck up on me."

She handed him a glass of wine. Then she took his other hand, held it to her lips and kissed it lightly, sliding her other arm around his waist.

"What were you thinking about just now?"

"You, I guess."

She bumped her hip against his. "You guess? My, how romantic of you. So typical Merkel. I've missed you. I really have. And look at you, all dressed up for me?"

"Well, after all, this is a steak dinner, not greasy fish and chips at Jackie's. I haven't had a reason to get spiffed up in a while."

He turned the steaks. "I've missed you, too. A lot. And so has Doug."

They chatted and sipped their wine until the steaks were done. He followed her inside and noticed her meticulous preparations—dimmed lights, a tall, white candle casting a steady glow in the middle of the table, a freshly poured glass of wine beside each place setting. Soft music played in the living room and he realized that she'd discovered his ancient turntable and the collection of vinyl albums he rarely played anymore. She took the platter of steaks from him, set it on the table, turned back to him, put her arms around his neck and kissed him full on the lips. He put his arms around her and returned her kiss. After a few moments, she pulled away, her face flushed.

"Whew! Let's eat supper. I'm famished."

He pulled her chair out for her and sat down across from her.

"So, this a formal date?"

"I think it's about time. Don't you?"

She gave him her brightest smile. "Yes. I do."

A brief thunderstorm passed through while they ate and talked. She told him enigmatically she'd saved the dessert for later and helped him wash the dishes. When she excused herself to go to the bathroom, he went outside and toweled the rainwater off the deck chairs. She came out a few minutes later with the rest of the wine and their glasses. He pushed their chairs together and they sat down and watched the horizon flicker with whitish-blue light from the storm too far away to hear the thunder. The clouds slipped away and the deck was awash in moonlight.

"The storm's a long way off now," he said. "I reckon it's safely past. What do you think?"

She looked at him and smiled, her teeth gleaming. "I don't think we need to worry about any more storms. I think they're all gone."

Without a word, she got up and sat in his lap, casually swinging her legs over the arm of his chair. He put his arms around her and held her tight against his chest. She buried her face in his neck, then reached behind his head and removed the clip that held his ponytail in place. When his hair spilled down his shoulders, she ran her fingers through it. She closed her eyes and kissed his neck over and over and felt his shiver of delight. He closed his eyes and let the moment take him away.

"I love you," she whispered. "I do. And I love this beautiful, magical place. I never want to leave your side again."

He cradled her head in his hands, running his fingers along her cheeks and through her hair, breathing in her shampoo that smelled of heather and reminded him of an Irish mountain meadow in late July. Then he said the words that he'd long thought he'd never say again, drawing a quiver from her.

"I love you, too. And if you really think you can put up with me, I want you to stay here forever."

The turntable needle moved to the next song, one that Jack hadn't heard since he was a young man. It was slow and sweet and without even thinking about it, he lifted her off his lap, took her by her hands and drew her to the middle of the deck. She put her arms around him and lay her head against his chest. His hands went to her waist and then they began moving together in languid steps, barely moving their feet. Their kiss lingered. Then she stepped away from him, took his hands in hers and gave him a gentle, but urgent tug.

"Make love to me."

His voice was hoarse with emotion when he answered. "I'm a little out of practice . . . I'm afraid."

She kissed his hands and led him to the door. "Come on. We'll practice together. Time for that dessert."

He opened the door and, lifted her as effortlessly as if she was a basket of sweet-smelling heather blossoms, and carried her inside.

CHAPTER 25

MARGIE RUBBED HER FOOT up and down Jack's leg under the breakfast table and giggled.

"Out of practice, my ass. You sure hit a couple of home runs last night, slugger."

He had his coffee cup halfway to his mouth and it froze there.

"Why, Jack Merkel, I do believe you're blushing. And so prettily, too. Get used to it, sweetheart. I intend to thoroughly corrupt your morals."

"Is that a promise?"

She puckered and made a kissing sound. "Bet your ass. Want some more eggs and bacon? There's still some left. Better eat up before the boys get here or you'll have to wait 'til I make more."

"Speaking of the boys, what's the deal with yours? What happened with Seth's college plans and John going back to your ex?"

"Well," she said, leaning on her elbows and grinning. "Thanks to all your exotic stories about seeing the world as a professional mariner, Seth has decided to apply to the US Merchant Marine Academy. He wants to hang out here for a while and then apply for an appointment. He understands that part can be tricky because a congressman or senator has to nominate you."

Jack clapped his hands and grinned. "Margie, that's great! He's brilliant and has a great attitude. He'll go far with it. Maybe even a career. Don't worry about the political thing. Judge Kicklighter's a political animal. He's got connections galore."

"Well," Margie said. "Prepare to get barraged with questions. He's filled a small notebook with them."

She poured herself another cup of coffee, added milk and a dollop of tupelo honey. "John's gone from being his asshole of a father's carbon copy to not sure if he ever wants to see him again since spending time here."

"Maybe he should give it a sort of a sea trial," Jack said. "He might always question himself if he doesn't try."

"We really are on the same page. That's almost word for word what I told him. He's willing to give it a try. He wants to hang out here with us for a week and then I'll fly him over. I told him to give it 'til Christmas unless he decides that he just can't do it."

Jack sopped up the remainder of his fried egg with a biscuit. "That's a good plan. It's not all that long. And, like you say, he can break it off any time he wants to but this time, it'll be his decision."

"Okay, my turn now. Tell me what all's going on with Doug. He seems so much more mature, so focused."

"It's been like a complete transformation. He's really taken off since I taught him to sail. I can't believe how fast he caught on, way faster than I did. He can't get enough. He's taking that little sailboat, *Island Time*, out by himself all the time, now."

"Do you think that's a good idea?"

"Yeah, he doesn't go far and it's rigged for single-handed sailing anyway. He's got it in his blood. I've never seen anyone excel so fast. He asks me questions sometimes I can't even answer. Oh, and he's working on his GED."

Margie went to the kitchen and put more bacon in the frying pan for the boys. "My daddy always told me that everyone's born for something special," she said from the kitchen. "Some people pick up a fiddle or sit down at a piano, practice a few times and get it just right. Maybe this is Doug's calling."

The boys tromped in a few minutes later. Jack stopped them at the door with a warning.

"Leave those muddy boots outside. I swept and swabbed this deck yesterday. I find a speck of pluff mud on it, you three swabbies are going to be doing some serious field day. Copy that?"

John glanced from Jack to Doug. "Huh?"

Doug rolled his eyes and laughed. "It's one of his sailor sayings. It means cleaning a ship top to bottom, fore and aft and all points in between. You work like a field hand all day and then he does a Marine Corps drill sergeant white glove inspection and makes you start over. Hang out here long enough, you'll hear 'em all."

"That's mean. Do you really do that?" Margie asked Jack as they boys trudged back inside after removing their shoes.

"No, shipmate here's exaggerating. Truth is, he's a bigger neatnik than I am by a lot," Jack said.

Doug winked at Seth. "He just rinses the dishes off with hot water after meals and doesn't use soap. Sometimes he even lets Pogy lick them and get them all slobbery. He's been living by himself too long. If I hadn't come along to teach him how to wash dishes properly, he'd eventually get some gross dog disease. I'm surprised he ain't already."

Jack leaned back in his chair and grinned. "Well, you know what they say about dogs' mouths."

Doug fired back. "Yeah, they lick their butts with them."

Margie went to the kitchen and got the bacon out of the frying pan and brought it to the dining room.

"Eat up boys," she said. "We've got a mess of fish to clean."

Later she helped Jack clear the table and take the dishes to the kitchen. Just before following her sons out the door, she stopped and tipped Jack a lascivious wink. "See you later, slugger," she sang.

Jack cleared his throat and looked away. Doug raised his eyebrows "Huh? Slugger? What?"

Jack ignored him and began filling the sink with soapy water, Doug pointed at the dishwasher. "Why don't you use that?"

"Well, it's been just me for so long that it never made sense. But now that you mention it, I guess now's good since Margie and the boys are going to be staying."

"They're staying? Really?"

"Uh-huh. Happy now?"

Doug set down the skillet he'd been drying and wrapped Jack in a bear hug. "Yes!"

"I thought you would be," Jack said. "I'm happy, too. I didn't realize how much she'd come to mean to me 'til she was gone."

"You love her, don't you, Pop? You can tell me. I'll keep your secret."

"Well, it really ain't a secret anymore."

Doug's jaw dropped. "You didn't? No, wait. I know that look. You did, didn't you? You actually told her." Doug backed away and gave him a sly grin. "So, when's the wedding?"

Jack scooped a handful of sudsy water and flicked it on him.

CHAPTER 26

MARGIE AND DOUG SET sail from Merkel's Marina on the first of December en route to Port Lucaya, Grand Bahama, to bring John home. The boy had called his mother the day before and pleaded with her to come get him. During a tearful and angry thirty-minute telephone call, the boy told Margie that he'd grown to hate his father who, when he wasn't ignoring him, belittled him constantly because he "wasn't as smart as his older brother." The latter wasn't true at all but Howard Waller, unable to accept that his elder son wanted nothing to do with him, took his frustration out on his younger boy, the nearest target.

John, like Seth, had grown up around boats and sailing. But the man punished his son by refusing to take him along when he went sailing with friends. Nor would he make extra time for just the two of them to go sailing. The final straw was the day the John rolled his eyes at his father's latest girlfriend, and she screamed at him and called him an asshole. Howard snatched the phone away from his furious, crying son and yelled at Margie.

"He called Antoinette a bitch, an empty-headed, leg-spreading piece of arm candy! I'm not going to have it. He's as low class as you. If he wants to come back and waste his life with you and the other brat in some low-rent marina with a washed-up old sailor, that's fine with me. Come get his ass or else I'll put him on the next flight."

As badly as she wanted to lash out and excoriate her former husband, Margie held her fire for fear of the backlash against her son. Howard had always been a superficial and aloof husband and father. But Margie sensed a growing meanness in him and reckoned that it was part and parcel of his losing her. He hated losing and had begun to drink too much. The few friends he had were as one-dimensional as he was. The naïve young girls he partied with slipped away during the night after he passed out drunk. But Margie's better angels prevailed and, biting back her fury and her desire to unman him, she parried his thrusts impassively.

"Fine, Howard. Take him to Port Lucaya Marina and drop him off with Susie and Bill and I'll be there in a few days to pick him up. In the meantime, you will execute an agreement surrendering his sole custody to me. If this is what you want to do, it's going to be a clean break. Understood?"

"That's not fair, Margie. I didn't say I didn't want to see him again."

"Well, old boy. He clearly wants nothing else to do with you. I could force the issue in court because he's of age to make up his own mind. So these are your choices. Play nice or we'll go back to court."

"Why can't I just put him on a flight back to the states to you? Why do I have to wait for you to sail over and get him?"

She took a deep breath and counted to ten, intentionally drawing out the silence. "Because I won't have my son dumped at the goddamn airport like a suitcase. He admires Susie and Bill, and it'll do him good to spend some time with them 'til I get there. Plus, he'll love sailing back home with us."

His voice tightened and went up several octaves. "Us? Who's us?"

"None of your business. I'll call Susie and Bill and let them know you're bringing him. And Howard?"

"Yes?"

"Have him there by the end of the day today."

Margie stuck her cell phone in her pocket. Doug and Seth were below in the yard working with Rafe and Neal.

"Will he comply?" Jack said. "He won't take this out on John, will he?"

"No, he wouldn't dare. He'd have to misbehave in front of his— what did John call her? An empty-headed, leg-spreading piece of arm candy? I can't say I would've encouraged him to use that sort of language but I certainly don't disagree with the sentiment. No, he'll be fine. Susie and Bill will spoil him rotten 'til we get there."

"So, when do we leave?"

She thought about the question for a moment. "What do you think about Doug going with me? Seth enjoys being here so he can stay. The sailing will be good for Doug. I can teach him some things. He wants to learn celestial navigation, you know, and he needs to learn how to stand watches and nap at the helm. There'll come a day when he'll really need those skills."

"I think that's a great idea. Y'all can hop down to Fort Lauderdale. That's only two days and then if the winds aren't out of the north, you can pop over to West End and Port Lucaya in a day's time, easy. If the weather's favorable, you can be there and back in a week. With you to guide him, Doug knows enough about sailing right now that he'll be a good hand to have onboard. He'll love it."

She put her arms around him, pressed her body against his, kissed him on the mouth and nibbled his lip. "Sorry, slugger," she whispered in his ear when she felt him responding. "You're gonna have to wait a few days."

When the moment ended, both were flushed, but Margie continued their conversation. "Yes, it'll be an adventure for Doug. Do you have enough help here while we're gone, though?"

"Yeah. It'll be slow around here until spring. Eddie will help out too, because he's not chartering every day right now. We'll be fine. I'm really going to do a lot of work on the boat since it's almost done."

"How much longer do you think that'll take?"

"Oh, before Christmas, for sure. I have a Christmas surprise in mind for him."

She pulled away and smiled at him. "Oh? Do tell."

"Nope, it's my secret for now. I'll let you in on it later. Promise."

"Okay, but I'm going to nag you in the meantime. Now, let's go talk with Doug. I'd like to go ahead and leave today while the weather's nice and unseasonably warm. It looks like it's going to hold for the rest of the week, too."

They got underway just after lunch. With favorable winds and a light sea, they made excellent time. Wearing a light-yellow windbreaker, Doug stood at the helm of *Starshine* while Margie stood beside him sipping a cup of tea. As they neared the last sea buoy and prepared to head south into the open ocean, a flock of pelicans glided by them, inches above the water. Doug pointed them out and told Margie how Jack had explained to him that the phenomenon was known as the ground effect, that the pelicans literally navigated upon a cushion of compressed air between themselves and the water, amazing her yet again with his depth of knowledge. But for surrendering the helm to her while he grabbed a quick late-afternoon snack that Margie had prepared, he'd been navigating since they'd left Morgan's Island, and she was impressed by his calm seamanship and steady hand. He'd been reading up on the ancient practice of celestial navigation, he'd told her that afternoon, one of the oldest forms of direction-finding at sea, and she marveled at his understanding of a process that proved daunting to many sailors and even impossible to others.

"Pop bought me a book that really breaks it down into nice, bite-sized pieces," he said. "It's mostly just angles and time. Piece of cake, really. I can read a sextant already."

Margie raised her cup in a salute. "Wow! Where'd you learn how to do that?"

He made a slight course adjustment. "Rafe loaned me his. It belonged to his grandfather who passed it down to Rafe's father, who gave it to Rafe. He comes from a long family tradition of fisherman and mariners."

"Did you bring it with you? I've got one, too, if you didn't."

He nodded and pointed toward the companionway. "It's below in my bag."

"I'll get it for you." she said.

She went below and came back a few moments later carrying an exquisite cherry wood box with gleaming brass fittings. The old sextant owned by three generations of Mexican fishermen and sailors lay recessed in a bed of soft, dark blue velvet. Margie reached in and pulled the instrument out of its box. The brass was polished to a spit shine and the instrument's mirror and glass were flawlessly clean.

"My God, Doug. This is a work of art. I've never seen one so beautiful. This must be worth a fortune."

"*Mmm-hmm.* That's what Rafe said, so I have to take real good care of it. I can't believe he let me borrow it."

"Oh, I can. He's quite fond of you and believes that you have the ability to be a great sailor. I'll bet it was a point of pride for him to let you borrow it. Have you been practicing using it?"

"Yeah, a lot. It was a little tricky at first but now I can read it pretty good."

She ran her fingers over the smooth mahogany. "These are going the way of the dinosaur, sadly. GPS has more or less rendered them obsolete. You can get close to a location with a sextant, but a satellite GPS fix will put you right on top of it. But, if you lose power or your GPS just craps out on you, it pays to have one of these and know how to use it."

During the remainder of the day, Doug showed his prowess with the instrument, relying upon his electronics only to be certain he was taking correct readings. They ate a light supper as they sailed down the peninsula and just as the sun began to set, he asked her if she'd ever seen the elusive natural phenomenon known as the "green flash."

"Never," she said. "Have you?"

"Pop and me saw it at sunset one evening coming back from sailing. Beautiful. Something to do with the color spectrum during the final moments of sunlight. The green is the last to go and it sometimes appears to be a cap on the sun, but it only lasts a couple of seconds. He told me about a Jules Verne book called *The Green Ray*. Supposedly an ancient Scottish myth that anyone who sees it will always be able to see into the hearts of others and never be deceived. But there's a line in it that I loved so much when Merkel told me about it that I wrote it down and memorized it."

He cleared his throat and recited:

"A green that no painter is able to obtain on his palette, a green the like of which nature has never produced, not in the many varied shades of plants, or in the color of the clearest seas! If the color green exists in Paradise, it can only be of this shade, which is, without a doubt, the true green of Hope."

He paused for a few moments and then said, almost in a whisper, "That's what I have now, Margie, the true green of hope."

A few minutes later, Margie took the helm. Doug settled down on a cushion and fell asleep. They'd agreed to stand three-hour watches and Doug awoke for his next one without Margie's assistance. He sat in the cockpit sipping coffee from a thermos and watching her sail for a few minutes before she ever knew he'd awakened. She rested her fingertips gingerly on the helm, occasionally turning her head to admire the stars and moon and their reflection on the smooth sea surface. She seemed lost in her thoughts and gave a little start of surprise when he spoke to her.

"My goodness," she answered. "How long have you been awake?"

"Maybe five minutes or so. Just watching you navigate. You're really in your element, aren't you?"

"Yes, I think we both are. I believe you could do this on your own. You're a natural, kid."

He pointed at the scar on her wrist. "What really happened?"

She stepped away from the helm and motioned for him to take it while she sat down on a cockpit cushion and tucked her feet underneath.

"No fooling you, is there? I sliced my wrist with a kitchen knife one night."

"Why?"

"Howard was cheating on me. I got pissed off, then drunk and then I got stupid. Oh, I didn't try to kill myself; I was just lashing out at Howard. And then I realized I was only hurting myself and the boys. John was just ten. So I left the boys with the folks on the boat next to us and went to the emergency room and got it stitched. I told Howard I slipped cutting up a pineapple. Now you know."

He smiled at her and repeated the words she'd said to him the day in the marina after he'd fallen and gashed his chin. "We've all got scars of one kind or another."

She then recalled the rest of what she'd said to him that day. "Character references. They just make us more rugged looking."

And then they both were laughing under the stars.

Three days later, they arrived in Port Lucaya. John was waiting eagerly for them when they got there. Margie thanked her friends for looking out for him. The next morning, just after sunrise, Doug, under Margie's supervision, took *Starshine* out to sea while she spent some time comforting her son and assuring him that he wouldn't ever have to return to his father if he didn't want to.

CHAPTER 27

JACK'S PREDICTIONS ABOUT THE completion date on the boat proved correct. The last of the work began almost two weeks before Christmas. Doug, who'd chosen the paint scheme of hunter green with sand-colored and maroon accents, took note of Neal's every move as he carefully mixed and prepared the paint and laid out the foam rollers and fine badger-bristle brushes.

They'd gone to the marine supply store to buy their material. While they shopped, Neal told Doug that early to mid-winter in North Florida was usually a good time to paint. "Just what we need, mild temperatures and fairly low humidity. Hot, humid weather and glaring sunshine is your worst enemy when you're paintin' a boat, especially when you do it outside, like we'll be doing. Summer sun gets so friggin' hot the paint dries too fast, so you have to keep adding brushing liquid to thin in out. At some point, you get it so thin it wants to run on you. December weather's way more predictable."

When Neal turned around and looked at him, Doug was holding one of the brushes, running his fingers through the lush bristles.

"Pay attention, pissant. Them ain't some girl's tits."

Shifting his ever-present wad of chewing tobacco to the other side of his mouth, Neal scowled at him, removed his grubby ball cap and slapped him with it. "Come on, we're burning daylight here."

The next morning, Doug watched as the other man began pouring paint into a pan. "I thought we were gonna spray the paint on. Ain't that how it's usually done?"

Neal soaked a foam roller in the pan and rolled out the excess paint. "Yep, but it ain't the best way. What I'm fixin' to do is show you how they painted boats before anybody ever heard of a spray gun and a compressed air tank. It's the old way, the best way. It's called rolling and tipping. Simple two-step process. To dumb it down for you, the first step is to roll the paint onto the boat like this. Watch me and pay close attention, damn it."

He dipped the tips of the bristles on a brush into the paint and handed it to Doug, then stepped close to the stern of the boat, reached up with the roller and began applying the paint up and down in a smooth, nonstop motion, pausing momentarily to check his work as he progressed.

"You wanna roll vertically and tip horizontally. See? Hardly any bubbles or roller marks at all. Gimme that brush and watch me real close. This is the most important part."

He took the brush from Doug and stared at him to make sure he had his attention. "Watch me now."

He held the brush delicately with his fingertips, tilted just the tips of the bristles at a forty-five-degree angle, lightly touched them to the freshly painted surface and then swept them horizontally across the area he'd just rolled, starting at the top and working his way down to the bottom of the boat, which was taped off at the waterline to keep the new paint off the black bottom paint they'd applied the day before.

"See what I'm doing here? Roll the paint on 'til you've got enough to completely cover the primer underneath it, doing small sections at a time. Then you wanna use the very tip of your brush, which is why it's called tipping, and make a series of long, even strokes back to where you stopped rolling. On your next roll, you barely overlap the first one. That way, you'll always keep a wet edge. If you do it right, it'll lay down nice and purty, like it's been spray painted, only better. See here?"

He stepped back from the boat and motioned for Doug to stand where'd he just been standing. The wet, dark green paint glistened like a jewel, so glossy that Doug could see his reflection. He didn't see a blemish or a brush mark anywhere.

"Wow! It looks like a sheet of green glass," he said. "There's not even a stray bristle in it."

"That's why I took the time to slap those dry bristles on my fingers when I took the brush out of the package, to knock any loose ones off the brush."

He wet the roller again. "If you do happen to get one on there, don't fuck with it. You can get it after the paint dries when you're light sanding for the next coat. I'm sure Merkel already learned you that trick while y'all was varnishing inside."

Satisfied with the roller, he stepped back alongside the boat and repeated the process.

"See? And when you're tipping it's always one long stroke to where you left off. When you tip, do it once and once only, and proceed down to the next section. If you tip an area you already tipped, I guaran-goddamn-tee you that you'll leave brush marks."

After he'd made a few more passes, he stopped and handed the roller to Doug.

"You want me to do it?"

"How'd you learn to swim, pissant? Someone showed you and then threw your ass in the water, right?"

"Well, yeah but—"

Neal waved him off before he could finish. "You won't fuck this up because I ain't gonna let you."

Neal reached into his pocket, pulled out his chewing tobacco and crammed some more in his cheek. "All right. Let's get moving. Merkel wants this done before Christmas."

"Why?" Doug asked.

"Beats me, pissant."

Within three hours, they painted both sides of the boat. Neal stepped back, looked at it and nodded. "Take a goddamn gander at that baby."

They were cleaning their brushes with solvent when Jack, Margie and Rafe came out to inspect. Margie clapped her hands, Rafe nodded his approval and Jack grinned and shook hands with Doug and Neal.

"Fine work, men. Damn fine work. She's gonna be a jewel when y'all are finished. I think we'll let her sit in the yard 'til Christmas and let the paint cure out real good before we splash her."

He tipped Margie a wink. She smiled and returned it.

On Christmas morning, Jack, Doug, Rafe, Margie and her sons gathered in the living room to exchange gifts. The room was dominated by a fragrant and imposing spruce tree surrounded by mounds of brightly wrapped packages. Jack, who usually celebrated a low-key Christmas with Rafe, wasn't accustomed to so much celebration. Doug, Margie and her sons had strung lights and tinsel from one end of the house to the other. For the finishing touches, the boys shinnied up the palm trees around the deck and yard and wrapped the trunks from top to bottom with strings of tiny white and red lights. At night they glowed like candy canes. Between all the talking, laughter and Christmas music playing on the stereo, Jack's house was clamorous with celebration.

After a few minutes of waiting for everyone to get settled in, Merkel got up from his big rocking chair and whistled. The room fell silent and all eyes focused on him.

"As y'all know, it's been a long time since a family Christmas was celebrated in this house."

"Home, Pop," Doug corrected. "Home."

Jack looked at him and smiled. "Home. Yes, this old house is a home again. I ain't gonna go on all morning with a speech, but I will say this."

He paused to make sure he had their attention. "With the exception of mine and Rafe's yearly custom of swapping bottles of liquor, drinking beer, farting and fishing all day, there ain't been a family Christmas celebration in this home for ten years. And before we get started here, I just want to take a moment for all of us to bow our heads in silence and be grateful for us having one another."

Doug got up and walked over to Jack and put his arms around him and hugged him. "Merry Christmas, Pop," he whispered in his ear. And then for the first time ever, "I love you."

Jack's heartbeat quickened. "I love you, too, son," he whispered back to Doug. "Merry Christmas."

After all the gifts had been exchanged and everyone was sipping eggnog, Jack stood and tapped the side of his glass with a spoon. "Rafe and me have a little custom we've been following every year."

Rafe groaned. "Oh, no. That again?"

Jack grinned. "As I was saying before I was so rudely interrupted, we have this custom of exchanging one special gift each year. Rafe gave it to me last year. This year, it's his turn to receive it. Rafe? Step up here."

Rafe looked around the room and rolled his eyes before going up to stand in front of Jack. The two men looked at each other and laughed and then Jack handed him an old, crumpled brown paper bag he'd been hiding behind his chair.

"I thought maybe you'd forget this silly damn thing with everything else going on this year," Rafe said. "All right. Guess I might as well get it over with."

He sighed in resignation, reached into the bag and pulled out a hideous-looking red crocheted hat made with beer can labels. The room erupted with laughter. Rafe donned the tacky hat and mugged while Margie laughed and took pictures.

"Oh, my God!" she said. "That's the ugliest thing I've ever seen in my life. Where in the dickens did y'all get that?"

"Rafe here picked it up in a flea market, what was it, seven, eight years back? Thought he was being a smartass wrapping it up and giving it to me. Come the next year, I decided to return the damn thing. It's so ugly I didn't think it deserved wrapping paper, so I gave it to him in this bag. We've been swapping it back and forth every year since."

"The worst part's the recipient has to wear it every day until New Year's Eve, when we get roaring drunk and throw it in the garbage can," Rafe said. "But before the night's over, one of us has to rescue it for the next year."

After the laughter died down, Jack reached behind the tree, retrieved a bright red envelope and handed it to Doug. "Merry Christmas, son."

Doug looked at the expressions on Jack and Margie's faces and knew something was up. He opened the envelope, which Jack had left unsealed so that its contents wouldn't get ruined. Everyone in the room gazed at Doug as he pulled out a folded white piece of paper, opened it and began to read to himself. Margie walked over to Jack, put her arms around him and kissed his cheek. Doug scanned the page and looked at him, puzzled. "It's a contract with a private investigator."

He continued reading until he got to the end, at which point he looked up and beamed. "To find my sister! To find Elizabeth! Oh, my God! I can't believe this. It's the best Christmas present ever!"

He strode over to Jack, threw his arms around him and lifted him off the floor in a bear hug. Then he did the same to Margie.

"Now understand, son, there are no guarantees," Jack said. "But Judge Kicklighter has known this fellow for years. He's a retired FBI agent and has all kinds of connections. Harley says that if Mr. Tradd can't find her, no one can. He'll start his search tomorrow."

Everyone in the room jumped up and went over to embrace Doug, who clutched the document like a life preserver.

"One last thing here before we end today's festivities," Jack said. "Margie, the blindfold, please."

She wrapped it around Doug's head and tied it in the back. Then they led him out of the house, across the yard and onto the docks. Doug had to wear the black mask until everyone was standing beside him and then Margie turned him in a circle and took the blindfold off. Before his eyes, which blazed with amazement, was the sailboat he'd helped Jack build. Margie had hoisted a huge, red bow to the top of the mast. Another red envelope, this one bulkier than the first, lay on the deck. At Jack's encouraging, Doug picked it up, tore it open and took out the envelope and pulled out a Christmas card. He read it and then put his fingers back in the envelope and pulled out a shiny brass key on a maroon-colored lanyard. Holding the key and lanyard over his head like a trophy, he whooped in delight and read the card aloud. "Merry Christmas, Captain. Fair winds and following seas. Love, Pop."

Everyone applauded and congratulated him. He hugged Jack for so long that Margie thought he'd never let him go. Then he hopped into the cockpit. "Well, come on, everybody. Let's take 'er for a spin."

Pogy leapt into the cockpit with him. Jack folded his arms and shook his head. "Sorry, skipper. Can't put her to sea 'til she's been properly blessed and christened with her new name."

"I'm gonna name her—"

Jack threw up his palm and cut him off. "Uh-uh-uh. Remember, bad luck to reveal the name 'til she's christened."

"So, when can we christen her?"

Jack elbowed Margie and smiled. "What do you think, Captain?"

She smiled back at him and then at Doug. "Let's do it New Year's Eve at the stroke of midnight. We'll have fireworks and champagne and when the clock strikes twelve, we'll pop the bubbly, spray her bow and you can uncover her name and welcome her into the family."

CHAPTER 28

THE DAY AFTER CHRISTMAS, Doug asked Neal to pull the boat out of the water and put it on blocks in the rear of the boatyard where he could work in private. A cold drizzle fell from flat gray skies and the rain beaded and glistened like tiny sapphires on the boat's fresh paint. Not particularly happy about having to work in a chilly rain, Neal grumbled as he set grimly to his task.

"God, she's beautiful," Doug said to Jack while Neal maneuvered the boat from the water. "I never dreamed I'd ever have anything like this. And I don't mean just the boat. I mean a family, a home, a good job, things to call my own . . . the whole nine yards."

Jack raised his hand to get Neal's attention and signaled to him that the boat was clear and to start moving it back into the yard.

"Things sure have changed a lot since Hal Patterson showed up here with you that evening last summer, huh?" he said.

"Judge Kicklighter called me into his chambers that first morning after court and told me I was fighting a lost cause. Still remember what he said that day: 'You can't fix every broken thing in this world.' We sure showed him, didn't we?"

"We sure did," Doug beamed. "But what made you decide to want to even try? I've never been able to figure that out, especially after all the terrible things I said to you that evening."

"Oh, hell. I'm a stubborn sumbitch, as you know, and I don't cotton much to people telling me I can't do things. Only person in this world who knows how to push my buttons is Harley. He challenged me and I think he meant to. Somebody tells me I can't fix something, I'm by God gonna do my dead level best to prove 'em wrong."

The lift's diesel engine growled as Neal began setting the boat down. Jack watched with Rafe.

Doug looked at Jack as they stood where they could make sure the boat set squarely on the blocks.

"So, you didn't think I was a lost cause?"

"I don't believe in lost causes, only challenges—and I've never shied away from one," Jack said. "I knew you'd be a hard case. Oh, I was mighty pissed off at first but I didn't think sending you off to prison would solve anything. I figured letting you work off your punishment would teach you some things."

Jack took a quick look at the boat's position and gave Hernandez the OK signal.

"When did you realize that things were gonna work out between us?" Doug asked.

"The afternoon you fell down and cut your chin and bolted."

"Really? That soon?"

"Yep. Something about the way you looked at me in the emergency room parking lot that afternoon. I still didn't know what to call you because you wouldn't talk to me. And then out of the blue, you said, 'Doug. My name's Doug. That's what I prefer to be called.' Something told me right then and there we were gonna be okay."

"But how'd you know I wouldn't run again first chance I got? I ain't ever done anything but run."

"Because you said you wouldn't and I trusted you. And it wasn't too long after that you started to trust me, little by little, but more and more every day."

"What made you think that?"

Jack let the question hang for a moment.

"Because I was runnin' from something, too. It'd been going on ten years and I was worn out. Just like you were."

Doug cocked his head to one side and gave him a questioning look.

"What were *you* running from?"

"Ghosts," he said, after a pause. "I was running from ghosts. Do you know how to get rid of ghosts, Doug?"

"No, sir. How?"

"You just have to let them go. Once you turn loose of them, they'll leave you alone from then on. It seems impossible at first but you can. Trust me. It took me ten years and you and Margie coming along for me to figure that out. Nobody should be haunted that long for any reason, nobody. I want you to do yourself a favor and think on that, okay?"

Doug nodded. "I will, Pop." Tears began spilling from Doug's eyes. "I miss Elizabeth so bad, Pop. Every day. It hurts. What if Mr. Tradd can't find her?"

"He will, son. You gotta have hope. That true green of hope, remember?"

Jack changed the subject and pointed at the boat. "So, have you figured out how you want to go about the process of lettering your boat to get her ready for the big day?"

Doug wiped his nose on his sleeve. "I have. I know exactly what I want to do but I don't know how to go about it."

"Why not?"

"Well, I'm not an artist."

Neal climbed down from the travel lift and headed for the shop. Rafe joined Jack and Doug. "You fellas gonna stand out here like a couple of wet ducks and gab or what? I'm heading off to the shop and get in out of the rain."

Doug pointed across the yard toward the sailboat slips.

"Who owns the cream-colored boat with the red accents and the cute little cartoon surfer girl on the sides? In fact, I think that's her name, *Surfer Girl.*"

Jack peered through the drizzle and looked in the direction Doug was pointing.

"Oh," Jack said. "The old Cal 28? It's an antique, a 1969. You'd never guess to look at her she's that old, though. Guy that owns her found her abandoned, brought up here and set about totally restoring her. Took him two years but she looks brand new. What's the fellow's name, Rafe? Kind of an eccentric type."

Rafe laughed. "Eccentric? Well, that's being polite. Gary Cunningham. God, that old hippie would make nutty seem normal. What do you wanna know about it, Doug?"

"I like the looks of the graphics and lettering. Did he do it himself or did he pay somebody?"

"I don't have a clue," Jack said. "He pretty much kept to himself. All I know is he showed up in the shop one evening and said he was ready to put her in the water. Ain't seen him lately, but we've got his contact information. Come on, it's in the office."

A nor'easter had begun to blow. The rain slanted across the yard in pale gray sheets. Margie sat at the desk reading the newspaper.

"Don't come in here dripping water and tracking mud all over the place. It took me nearly two weeks to clean and organize this place. I don't know how you managed to get any work done in here, Merkel. God, what a mess."

He went to her and kissed her on the cheek. "Well, I won't get anything done in here now, for sure. The place looks like a library."

She picked up a piece of paper, wadded it and threw it at him. He ducked and it sailed across the room and bounced off Seth who was sitting on the sofa reading and listening to music. He looked around the room and then pulled his headphones off, throwing his mother a quizzical look.

"What?" he said.

"Nothing, Einstein. Put your nose back in that book."

He put his headphones back on and resumed reading.

"Do me a favor, Marge," Jack said. "Look up Gary Cunningham's number, give him a ring and ask him who did the lettering and graphics on *Surfer Girl*."

Seth pulled off his headphones and looked at them. "What do y'all want to know about graphics? Graphics is easy stuff. You can do most of it on a good computer."

Pogy scratched at the door from outside and whined. Doug opened the front door and the big Dane barged in and shook, spraying water everywhere. Margie waved her arms, exasperated, grabbed an old towel off the wall rack and blotted up the water. She took Pogy by the collar and shoved him out into the shop.

Seth got off the sofa and came over. "Who needs graphics work?"

"I do," Doug said. "Before I can christen the boat, I need to get the lettering and graphics worked out, get it all made and put on the boat by New Year's Eve."

"No problem," Seth said. "You already know what you want. That'll help a lot since the design work itself is the bulk of it. A good print shop that does lettering and graphics can print something like that in a day. We can design it ourselves on the computer. Easy peasey. What do you have in mind?"

Doug started to reply then stopped and pulled Seth to the other side of the room. The two boys went into the corner together. Doug picked up a magazine and held it up while he whispered in Seth's ear. After a few moments, he dropped the magazine on the sofa. Seth looked at him and grinned.

"Sweet! Piece of cake, dude!" Seth replied.

Margie, Rafe, Jack and John went to supper at Jackie's while Doug and Seth huddled together over the laptop. When everyone else came back from supper, the two teens were in the living room watching a movie, bottles of soft drink in their hands and a big bowl of chips on the table in front of them. Pogy, dozing on the rug in front of them, glanced up when they all came in, then promptly went back to sleep. Margie stopped and hung her coat on the rack.

"How are y'all coming along on the graphics project, guys?"

Doug and Seth gave each other high fives.

"Guess you're gonna have to wait 'til New Year's Eve and find out," Doug said.

CHAPTER 29

NEW YEAR'S EVE ARRIVED with intermittent showers. But by midmorning, they'd moved on and good weather was predicted for the next few days. The day before, Jack had gone into town to Rufus Tuten's seafood house and bought two bushels of fresh Apalachicola oysters to roast. He'd invited the crew, Sheriff Patterson and his wife, Judge Kicklighter and his wife, Jackie O'Brien, Father Keith O'Connell and even the grubby bait fisherman, Bucky Howard, over for New Year's Eve.

"Why the priest" Doug asked.

"Gotta bless the boat, son and ain't no one around here does a boat blessing like Father Keith."

Rafe, who had just put two cases of Red Stripe beer on ice, hooted. "Got that right. Especially after Padre's had a drop or two of

Irish whiskey. I hope you didn't buy cheap stuff for an occasion like this, my friend."

Jack opened his liquor cabinet and took out a bottle of honey-colored whiskey.

"Oh, I think Father Keith will be satisfied with this vintage. *Midelton Dair Ghaelich.* I had to look up how to pronounce it. It cost a bundle, and the only place in Florida I could find any was a liquor store in Miami. Thank God they ship."

He handed the bottle to Rafe who held it to the light and studied it. "That's some fine-looking whiskey. Even the name sounds expensive. What'd it cost?"

Jack leaned over and whispered. "Two hundred and ninety-nine bucks. It's twenty-two years old. They age it in virgin Irish oak barrels. If Father Keith doesn't like this stuff, I'm gonna shove his ass off the dock."

The guests began trickling in and by eleven that evening all the oysters had been eaten. A chunk had been knocked out of the beer supply. Father Keith tasted the whiskey, blessed the bottle, and requested a half glass of it. When Jack poured the whiskey glass half full, the priest squinted and teased Jack.

"That's half empty, not half full. But since I've a boat to bless it'll have to do."

After the libations had been poured and drank all the way around, everyone but Neal, Jack, Rafe and Doug went down to the slip that would be the boat's new home to prepare to welcome in the New Year and christen the newest addition to the marina family. The flawless black sky with a sliver of moonlight gracing it was so still that the universe seemed to be holding its breath, as if in anticipation of something momentous. There was not so much as a ripple on the water, which lay below the sky like a black mirror.

Jack, Doug, Neal and Rafe walked almost reverently to the back of the boat yard. Even Neal seemed more mellow than usual. Doug had taken the time to conceal the boat's new name with towels draped over the aft gunnels and taped loosely to hold them in place for instant removal at the climax of the christening ceremony. Neal looked around to see if everyone was in their places, then climbed up onto the high seat of the lift and started the engine. At the first growl of it, those gathered below on the docks erupted into wild cheers. When the boat was in the slings and ready to make her short journey to the water, Jack saluted Doug and gave him his handheld marine radio. "You've got the helm, Captain. The vessel is yours."

A chill of excitement ran through the boy. He held the radio tight in his hand and looked up at the sky. He filled his lungs with the cool dry air as he stood there, tall, proud and straight as a mast, for a long moment contemplating an event that in another life, he couldn't have even begun to imagine. He thought back to what Merkel said about ridding oneself of ghosts. Then he parted his lips and let his breath out in a rush, as if releasing his own ghosts. He put the radio to his lips.

"Okay, Neal, let's splash my lady."

Through the radio they heard, above the low rumble of the idling diesel engine and a soft chuckle, "Aye, aye, Skipper. All hands stand by."

At that, the lift began moving toward the water. Under Doug's calm guidance and with the assistance of Jack and Rafe, Neal carried the boat to the water as gently as if he was cradling a baby. He set it down so tenderly that no one heard the watery kiss. As soon as Neal cleared the lift from the boat and moved it back into the yard, Doug climbed down the ladder on the dock and stepped into the cockpit. Jack wouldn't allow Doug to start the engine and move the boat until it had been properly blessed and named, so they waited for Rafe to tow Doug's boat to its slip with his boat. It was ten minutes before midnight when everything was finally set to go.

Father Keith O'Connell, dressed in fine robes and carrying a holy water dispenser, walked slowly down the dock toward the boat, singing a hymn in Latin. When everyone was at last standing alongside, Doug looked at the priest and signaled him to bless the boat. The priest began the ritual in a dialect still strong after years in America and fortified by the high-priced whiskey he'd consumed.

"Father in heaven. We ask you to look down upon this gathering, this family, these friends we love, and upon this new vessel which, like a newborn child, lies waiting before you to be christened with her name. Protect her from foul winds and angry seas—from storms, lightning, pirates and others who would do her or her captain, crew and passengers harm. Fill her sails with the sweetness of your breath. Gentle her on her way and, when her journeys are done, guide her home with the lights in your heavens. The sea is so big and our ships are so small."

He said a prayer in Latin as he sprinkled holy water from bow to stern. When he was done, he checked his watch and nodded at Doug.

"We've only a little over a minute left, lad. Are you ready to proceed?"

"Yes, sir."

Doug stepped forward holding an open bottle of wine. Turning to face north, south, east and west, he poured it into the water, offering his responses. "May it please the gods of sea, sky and wind, I present to you my vessel and ask your blessings. Guide me always as a sailor and captain. May Saint Brendan the Navigator, patron saint of mariners, be always present when I stand at the helm. Hold my hands in yours upon the wheel and set my course true. The sea is so big and our ships are so small."

Doug stepped off the dock and into the cockpit and waited for the last seconds of the old year to peel away, taking with them a life of pain and loneliness. He closed the door upon the ghosts of a past, feeling upon his skin the cold breath of the last one when it departed. On the dock, Rafe began counting backwards from ten. Jack caught Doug's eye, smiled at him and mouthed the words "I love you," and gave him a thumbs up. Doug returned the smile, pulled the lanyard from his shirt pocket and inserted the key into the ignition. Margie stepped up to the bow of the boat and, at the exact moment that the New Year was born, she popped the cork on a bottle of expensive champagne she'd bought for the occasion and sprayed it across the bow. Then Doug cried out in the stalwart voice of a captain to his crew, "I christen thee *Vagabond Wind!*"

There was a long inhalation of breath from the gathering, and a collective *AHHH* from all when Margie's younger son yanked the thin cord tied to the towel covering the boat's name. The name stood out in swept-back maroon letters outlined in white. Beneath them, a cartoon-face cloud blew a mighty gust from puckered lips. The boat's engine rumbled to life. Doug sounded a long note on the horn and its low bass call carried in the still night air across the sleeping river and marshes like the voice of Neptune himself, as the sky filled up with fireworks.

A piper appeared like an apparition on the dock and played a merry seafaring tune that flowed over the marina like honeyed whiskey.

When the tune ended, Doug thanked the musician and shook his hand and tipped him. Jack handed Doug a flute of champagne and raised his own in a toast. "To the New Year, a new captain and a new boat. God bless *Vagabond Wind.*"

When the last of the champagne was gone, Margie took Doug's hands in his and danced in a circle with him. "Okay, Captain," she said, finally releasing him. "That's about the coolest name for a sailboat I ever heard. How'd you come up with it?"

Doug took her hand, led her to Jack and held his hand so that the three of them stood linked like a chain.

"Remember when we were waiting for Hurricane Brenda to come and that weather guy commented on how it kept roaming this way and that? He called it a vagabond wind. From the moment I heard those words, I knew they were important to me. And I finally figured out why. It was that wind that blew all of us here together.

When you think about it, how many people ain't sort of wandering from one place to another sometime during their lives, not really knowing where to go?"

He squeezed both their hands and continued. "We're all vagabonds, Pop— you, Margie, Seth, John. Even Rafe. Every one of us has been blown around by a wind that didn't seem to have any true bearing, one that tossed us this way and that, a gypsy wind, a vagabond wind. But it was that vagabond wind that brought us all here, to our safe harbor. Where would we have ended up without it? I can't think of a better way to commemorate that than by giving that name to the boat you were working on, Pop, the first time we met."

The piper began playing *Auld Lang Syne.*

CHAPTER 30

DÚN LAOGHAIRE/ DUBLIN IRELAND

DOUG HAD SETTLED INTO his new routine at the marina in Dún Laoghaire, a tiny coastal town that was formerly a fishing village, on the outskirts of Dublin. The compelling story Jack had told two years earlier about Ireland made him yearn to go there. It was the trip of his dreams. It sang to him in the clean, trembling notes of a harp until he could no longer resist its music. Upon his arrival, he was awed by the quaint beauty of the little town and its large harbor, famous for its two granite piers, which reached out like arms into the cold, blue-green waters of Dublin Bay. He gazed at the beauty surrounding him and recalled the night of his twentieth birthday on April fifteenth. After the fabulous party Margie and Jack had thrown him, and after all the guests had departed, he broke the news to them about the gift that he wanted to give himself: a voyage to Ireland on *Vagabond Wind*. And then he thought about the best birthday present he'd received that evening, the official document from Judge Kicklighter stating that his past misdeeds had been expunged. Many times during the six-week journey across the broad Atlantic, he reflected upon the night when he, Jack and Margie planned every detail of his long-awaited excursion. His only regret was that he hadn't been able to share it with his sister.

Despite his exhaustive efforts and doggedness, Tradd had not been able to find her. Every trail proved a dead end, although the investigator vowed to keep trying. Even so, Doug reasoned, he'd never find his sister.

By the time he embarked upon his voyage, he was an experienced, confident sailor who'd recorded the particulars of every trip he'd made, near and far, in the ornate captain's log Rafe had given him. He painstakingly noted every detail of everything he saw, smelled, heard, felt and tasted, including the raw tuna he caught and ate one day while sailing to Bimini.

His preparations complete, he set sail on a warm, sunny morning the last week in April. Just before he pushed away from the dock, Eddie gave him a fine woolen sea captain's hat, but it was the silver medal of St. Brendan the Navigator that Neal gave him that made him laugh when he recalled his crude friend's presentation. *"Don't you lose this, pissant. It cost me a bundle."*

What Neal did next had surprised everyone. He grasped Doug's shoulder, drew him close, put the medal around his neck and gave him an awkward hug. "God go with you, buddy," he'd said. "Fair winds and following seas." And then, embarrassed by his public display of affection, he pulled off his greasy ball cap, slapped Doug with it and snarled, "Beat it, pissant, before you lose the tide."

Everyone cheered and whistled and waved goodbye when Doug sounded the horn and made for the channel. Pogy chased after him on the dock as far as he could and then sat, lifted his muzzle to the sky and bayed mournfully.

The transatlantic crossing had been serene and inspiring, but for a couple of bone-jarring, gut-clenching, stormy nights when he'd wondered if his decision to go alone had been unwise. But the nights were so black that sea and sky seemed of a piece, with nothing but the brilliance of the moon and stars to mark their boundaries, and they held him spellbound. Near the Azores one morning, just before first light, he sat in the cockpit sipping coffee, waiting for the sunrise as he did each day. Little by little, he became aware of what sounded like moans that had a cadenced quality about them. The moans soon became interspersed squeals and almost human-like cries. He sat raptly, trying to decipher what he was hearing when it dawned on him that it was the vocalizations of whales in the vicinity. Just as the sun's orange ball cleared the horizon, several humpback whales, some longer than buses, and two nursing babies, appeared close by to starboard. He watched in astonishment as one exceptionally large whale rolled several times in the water fifty yards away, and finally slapped its tail upon the surface with a sound as loud as a gunshot. He watched the whales cavort as they continued on toward their feeding grounds far to the north. After they were gone, he sat in silent wonder for several minutes, reflecting on what seemed to him a sacred experience. That evening he wrote in his log, *At sunrise, the sea sang to me a sailor's song, a mariner's tale, in the voices of migrating humpback whales. I took it as a sign that, no matter where we are on this blue planet, with its endless seas, we're never truly alone. God sends angels, great and small, to watch over us.*

He sailed into Dún Laoghaire the first week in June and offered his services tending boats and working as a marina crewmember in exchange for free dockage during the duration of his stay. The marina manager, Kevin Cooley, a garrulous, white-haired old Dubliner with ruddy cheeks and crinkly, hazel eyes, promptly accepted the offer after checking with the marina's owners.

"Y'can stay for as long as you like," Cooley said, shaking his hand. "I'll help arrange a temporary work permit, as well. Sure, and it'll be good to have a qualified seaman such as yourself about the place."

Afterwards, Cooley showed him around the marina, where hundreds of sailboats crowded into slips around the cold, murky-green harbor. He took Doug for a stroll on the piers and pointed across Dublin Bay, where scenic Howth, with its dun-colored and green hills and fields of buttery-yellow gorse, lifted its broad shoulders. A row of cabbage palm trees growing in front of the marina office building caught Doug's eye and he wondered if they were fake.

Noting Doug's attention, Cooley said, "They're able to survive here because of the warm water of the Gulf Stream. If you find yourself missin' Florida, well, here you are."

Doug, with his easy smile and seemingly innate skill at "slagging" his new friends, an Irish custom involving good-natured, high-speed taunts and teasing, fit right in with the other marina employees. His wind-burnished, sea-chiseled, handsome face and neat, close-cropped whiskers soon caught the admiring eye of a young marina office secretary named Bridget Sullivan, a petite, nineteen-year-old with freckles, thick, ginger-colored hair, rust-brown eyes and a daring smile. She took every opportunity to be near him and was smitten by his languid Southern drawl. Her attentions kindled stirrings in him he'd never felt before. He considered asking her out for an evening on the town, but he worried that she might reject him.

Toward the end of his second week there, Bridget strolled over one evening after work on the pretense of admiring *Vagabond Wind*, and promptly invited him to walk with her to Teddy's for an ice cream. The evening was cool. She wore a dove-gray summer dress, her favorite jeans jacket and purple Doc Martens. Doug dressed in faded blue jeans, a hunter-green Galway sweater he'd gotten from Kevin Cooley and canvas deck shoes. Bridget talked animatedly in rapid-fire Dublin slang along the way, evincing howls of laughter from Doug as she shared steamy gossip with him about all the marina employees, especially her girlfriends, all of whom, she boasted, were already green with envy. Doug bought a vanilla cone for himself and one with chocolate cookie crumbles for Bridget. They walked back holding hands, eating their ice creams and laughing about the wizened little pensioner who came into the famous ice cream shop every evening at seven and sang for his ice cream. They ambled along the pier under the pale light of a full moon and sat on a bench at the end of it, still holding hands. Doug, his heart fluttering, wondered what it'd be like to kiss her. As if reading his mind, the corners of her full lips lifted in a mischievous smile. Without a word, she cupped his cheeks in her hands, put her lips to his and kissed him shamelessly. His breath taken away by her overture, he closed his eyes and returned her kiss. After a few moments, she pulled away and snuggled under his arm.

"Will you stay?" she asked, hopefully.

He stroked her thick hair while staring across the bay, with its scrim of moonlight. He'd seen the green ray and sensed no deceit in Bridget's young heart. He leaned down and put his lips to her ear.

"You make it hard to say no. I need to think about it. Will maybe do for now?"

"Will you love me as long as you're here," she whispered to him.

"I will. I think I already do." Then he kissed her again.

Peter Tradd called Doug late in the afternoon on June twenty-eighth. Kevin Cooley came to the docks and told him he had a call from the states. Doug excused himself and ran to the office.

"I've got a possible line on your sister," Tradd said, without preamble. "After she ran away, she ended up working in an Irish pub in Brooklyn. She became close friends with an elderly Irish couple who ate there most nights—Padraig and Emma O'Toole. She eventually moved in with them and became their housekeeper. The old man died and when the old lady went back to Ireland to bury him, Elizabeth went with her. I spoke with Mrs. O'Toole just a few minutes ago. She lives in Terenure Village on the south side of

Dublin. Dublin 6, they call it there. She wants you to come see her right away."

"Did she say anything about Elizabeth?" Doug asked.

Tradd's reply was guarded.

"That's why she wants you to come see her. She heard a lot about you from Elizabeth and is anxious to meet you. She wouldn't tell me anything else. Here's her number. She's expecting your call."

Doug jotted down the number.

"Doug, I think you should prepare yourself for the possibility of unpleasant news. I can't imagine why she wouldn't share anything about Elizabeth, but is so insistent that you come at once. Call me after you speak with her."

Doug's insides went as cold as Dublin Bay. The bright hope that'd taken flight in him had plummeted like an anchor to the sea bottom. He called the number Tradd gave him and spoke to the woman who insisted that he come see her straightaway. She wouldn't tell him anything else. Trembling, he put the phone down and went outside to look for Kevin Cooley. He was sitting on a bench smoking his pipe and watching a regatta. When he saw Doug's face, he patted the bench.

"Not good news, eh? I'm sorry. I wish I could offer words of comfort, but I know none will do."

Doug told him the news. "I'm sorry, Mr. Cooley, but I need to leave now if you can manage."

The old man relit his pipe and nodded. "Off y'go, then. I'll have Sean relieve you. If y'hurry, y'can catch the next train to Booterstown Station. It leaves in ten minutes. A taxi'll have you in Terenure in about twenty minutes. Here." He took out his wallet and handed Doug some money. When Doug protested, the old man pushed his hand away.

"Hurry, now. I'll say a rosary. Maybe this'll come to good."

Minutes later, Doug boarded the train and it rattled off to Booterstown Station a few miles away.

Emma O'Toole greeted him at the door. She was of medium height and slender but regal in her bearing, with silver hair and eyes the color of sapphires. She smelled of rose petals and had features as delicate as a China doll. She'd dressed as if going out for an evening in a pale blue dress in a floral print with two-inch pumps that matched the blue in her dress. She wore a strand of small, antique natural pearls around her neck, and matching earrings. Tradd had told him that she was eighty, and Doug thought she'd probably been beautiful when she was young. He wished he'd dressed better, feeling shabby in his marina uniform.

The house she shared with her family was a tidy red Victorian with a slate roof on a quiet street lined with lush yew trees. Moss-covered stone walls, smartly trimmed hedges, holly trees and black, wrought iron fences lined the narrow sidewalks like sentries. Every yard of every home was aflame with colorful flowers. The house was around the corner from the 200-year-old St. Joseph's Church with its stained-glass windows created by Harry Clarke, the country's famous glassmaker. At a nearby school, uniformed schoolboys played a boisterous game of rugby.

She kissed Doug's cheek, took his hand and led him to an expansive library with overstuffed leather chairs and sofas. She'd set a plate of scones, still warm from the oven, a teapot, two cups and saucers, milk and sugar on a dainty mahogany tea table. They sat across from one another in antique armchairs. Doug felt awkward in the elegant setting and imitated her motions preparing his tea and eating the sweet scone. Her son and daughter-in-law, both doctors, had gone into the city and wouldn't be home until late. Doug was anxious to hear about his sister but the woman didn't seem inclined to talk about it right away, so they talked about Ireland and his trip across the Atlantic, which she found riveting.

"Will you have another cuppa?" she asked, noticing his empty cup.

"No, ma'am."

"Then I'll tell you about your sister. It's a long story and I tend to draw things out."

She smiled brightly at him and the intensity of it and her charming humor made him smile back at her. Her voice was melodious.

"Padraig, Paddy I called him, and I had been living in New York for fifteen years after he was transferred there by his company. Like many men who work too much, his health failed after he retired. I tried to convince him to come home but he was having none of it. He loved being a New Yorker. We had Irish friends in Brooklyn, so we stayed."

She folded her hands in her lap and leaned forward. "That's where we met Elizabeth, or Liz as Paddy and I called her. We took our supper most nights at Flannigan's. They have the most delightful fish and chips. Liz waited tables there. She always got ours and Paddy and I became quite fond of her. 'Twas plain she was struggling financially. She shared a flat with some other girls but they quarreled frequently. People came and went all hours of the night and it was difficult to read or sleep."

She paused and indicated the remaining scones and tea. He put another scone on his plate and poured more tea.

"We were dining there one evening and Liz seemed cross," the old woman continued "When I inquired, she whispered to me that the bartender was becoming fresh with her. I suggested that she just slap his face and tell him to mind himself. 'Twasn't until much later that I learned why his advances upset her so. Anyway, she said she was going to quit. When she came back with our pints, we'd already decided to ask her to come live with us and be our housekeeper. Oh, I hope that doesn't offend you."

"That she worked for you in your home? No ma'am. I'm sure you treated her very well."

"We did. She had free room and board and Paddy paid her quite handsomely. We even took her on trips with us because Paddy was getting frail. He was also quite smitten with her. He'd always wanted a little girl to spoil. We have six sons and Liz became the daughter I couldn't give him."

Doug thought about how Jack had officially adopted him as his son, after marrying Margie nearly two years earlier, and how proud he was to share his father's name.

"I don't know what we would've done without her," Emma O'Toole continued, "especially after Paddy got dementia. She had such a soothing way with him."

She excused herself and left the room. Doug got up and walked over to a wall lined with books. He didn't hear her when she returned.

"Liz is quite an avid reader," she said, stepping beside him. "One of our sons, Liam, is a professor at Trinity College. They used to sit up all night discussing literature. Where was I? Oh, yes. When Paddy died and I decided to come home to bury him, I knew I'd stay and I asked Liz if she'd come stay with me awhile. She agreed and decided to remain in Ireland. Our youngest son, Brian, is a solicitor and handled her immigration papers. He eventually hired her to work in his office."

She took his hand and led him to a big, leather sofa. "Sit down and I'll finish telling you about your sister." They talked about Elizabeth and her new life in Ireland and how happy she was. Eventually, Liz confided in her elderly friend and benefactor the horror her family endured at the hands of their father, including being raped.

"She could barely speak of it without crying. She'd be thrilled to know that you've found a home and happiness of your own. She wanted that more than anything."

Emma's eyes welled with tears when she recounted the horrifying tale Elizabeth told her about going back home the morning after their father had killed their mother and then himself—the house surrounded by yellow crime scene tape; the drunken, sour-looking woman next door storming out of her ramshackle house glaring at Elizabeth as if she were an accomplice to the crime. "Murderer!" she screamed. "Bitch!" She told Elizabeth the police were looking for her and ran back inside her house yelling that she was going to call them. Not knowing what else to do or where to look for her brother, Elizabeth ran away, flitting gypsy-like from one place to another, never staying anywhere long for fear of being found and arrested. She finally threw in with two other girls on the run and made her way north, living a desperate hand-to-mouth existence. The other two girls sank into prostitution to survive. One was murdered by a deranged john and the other simply disappeared one night in Philadelphia after getting in a car with a man.

Elizabeth never yielded to the sordid lure of selling her body for sustenance, and finally made her way to New York City a week before her eighteenth birthday. She walked into Flannigan's one rainy afternoon and applied for a dishwasher position. The owner was impressed and promoted her to busing tables and then to waitress. Her first night busing tables, she met Padraig and Emma O'Toole.

"And there we are," the old woman told Doug. "As happy as she was, she couldn't stop thinking about you. She prayed every day that the two of you would somehow be reunited." The woman took his hand in hers and smiled at him. "And now, after all these years, here you are."

Doug gave her hand a delicate squeeze and then looked around the room hoping that Elizabeth was standing nearby just waiting for the moment to come to him. The old woman took note of it and got up, tugging on his hand.

"I know you'd love nothing more than for her to pop into the room, embrace you and smother you with kisses, but she isn't here. She fell in love with a young man who owns a pub and moved away not long ago. But I have something I want to give you."

She walked over to a writing desk, opened a drawer and took out a white envelope, then came back and handed it to him.

"Open it," she urged him. "It's a special gift just for you."

His hands trembled as he opened the envelope and took out

a photograph of a beautiful young woman with milky-white skin, flashing, coal-black eyes and a thick braid of black hair draped across one shoulder. He recognized her puckish, lopsided grin at once. His tears flowed hot down his cheeks as he cried unabashedly, the long-held sobs coming from deep inside. Emma took him into her arms and cuddled him like the loving mother she was, murmuring words of comfort. When he stopped crying, she took both of his hands in hers and smiled at him.

"Come with me," she said, playfully. "It's getting late and I have the most wonderful secret to tell you before you go."

She led him to the door and opened it. The late afternoon sky crept cat-like toward its finale with a stunning evening. The air was filled with the scent of lavender blossoms in the flower beds. A trio of thrushes warbled in the shrubbery. The pleasantly cool air felt like silk pajamas on his skin. They stepped into the golden sunlight filtering through the yew trees. Emma had told him *Terenure* meant *Land of the yew trees* in the native Irish tongue. They walked hand-in-hand toward the street and a car and driver she'd discreetly summoned. Puzzled, he was about to ask her why she was sending him away without telling him the secret. When they reached the end of the walk, she smiled at him and inclined her cheek. When he leaned to kiss it, she drew him close and whispered the secret in his ear.

"Hurry now," she said. "And come see me again."

He climbed into the back seat of the car. The driver greeted him and pulled away from the walkway, where Emma O'Toole stood smiling and waving until they turned the corner and were out of sight.

Doug stood beside the window of Eamon Nolan's pub in Grafton Street and peered inside. The sun anointed the evening sky with one last splash and made its exit, stage west, leaving the Dublin skyline smeared with the colors of marmalade and plums. A boyish-looking

busker on the street corner fingered a melody on a Pan flute. A
diminutive teenage girl with a trilling, honey-sweet voice, taking
her first steps toward superstardom, accompanied him on guitar
and sang, a tune Doug recognized as a song his mother sometimes
sang to him and Elizabeth.

The bright green, heavy wooden pub door with its stained-glass
window swept open, and the smell of Guinness pie trailed behind a
young couple who ran away down the sidewalk, holding hands and
laughing. Doug watched them leave and pressed his face to the glass
again, scanning the faces in the crowd, his heart pounding. When
he couldn't find the face he sought, the old trepidation he'd thought
that he'd rid himself of whispered bitterly in his ear that it was all
for naught. He found himself again on the cold ledge of despair, the
true green of hope that he'd clung to so hard threatening to evaporate
like an apparition.

Pushing it away, he reached into his coat pocket for the
photograph Emma had given him, halfway expecting it not to be
there, beginning to think that it'd all been just a dream. But then
his fingers found it and he pulled it out and studied it. As he did, he
realized that a scrawny, scared little boy who no longer existed was
seeking a skinny, hollow-eyed girl who no longer existed either. He
tucked the photo back in his pocket, looked in the window again
and smiled. His story, a mariner's tale, had come almost full circle.
Almost, but not quite. The only thing needed to complete that circle
lay behind the green door before him. Green for hope. Green for go.
He put his hand on it and opened it.

ACKNOWLEDGMENTS

SO MANY PEOPLE HELPED me tend the sails on this voyage. They are: Martha Monroe Veon and Monica Tidwell, both with me from the first page; fairy godmother and friend Marly Rusoff, Mihail Radulescu, Cassandra King Conroy, Steve Berry, Tim Conroy, Kathleen Harvey, Mary Greene, Lynn Smith, Connie Green, Judy Kurtz Goldman, Stephanie Austin Edwards, Jill Bosie Dillingham, Cindy Gass Fetch, dear friend Jocelyn Woods Griffo, Dickie Anderson, Donna Paz Kaufman, Denton and Gail Kurtz, Rebecca Alexander, Karen Ellis, Gayle Q. Rybicki, Mandy Haynes, Nancy Siegel, Sheila Cocchi, Bren McClain, Susan Cushman, Nicole Seitz and Janis Owens. To my Irish friends both here and there who helped me keep it real: Sarah Burnley, Mary Callaghan Clarke, Jacqueline Kane McManus, Elaine McCourt, Paddy Ó Conghaile, Iulian and Anastasia Pusca who showed me lovely Terenure Village, Yvonne

O'Keeffe and William, Fionn, Gillian and everyone at the Castle Hotel in Dublin, Rob Rankin, Driftwood/Vagabond Tours in Dublin, The Rick O'Shea Book Club, Madge O'Callaghan, Connie Ryan and Aer Lingus and the town of Dún Laoghaire. To my brother-in-law Richard R. Stimer, Jr., Col. USAF (Ret). To Captains Phillip Thrift, Gene Hartmann, Bob Canon, Robert Warner and Graeme Nichol. To my sons Trey and Richard, my sisters Michele and Mary and Elaine Stehens, née Thomas, my high school creative writing teacher. To Jonathan Haupt and the Pat Conroy Literary Center and Festival. To Shari Stauch and to John, Joe, Skyler and Marshall at Koehler Books. I hope I didn't forget anyone. I'll be so damn mortified if I did.